Allen, T.D.
   Doctor in buckskin.

DATE DUE

JAN 3 1 79			
OCT J 0 79			
Renewed OCT 24 79			

Roberta Stone

Doctor in Buckskin

Doctor in Buckskin

by

T. D. ALLEN

✳✳✳✳✳✳✳✳✳✳✳✳✳✳✳✳✳✳✳✳✳✳✳✳

Harper & Brothers Publishers

New York

Stamped on his brow is a great deal of what David Crockett would call "God Almighty's Common Sense."

Civis, *New York Spectator*,
April 5, 1843

Doctor in Buckskin

PART I

*

CHAPTER

1

FOUR o'clock would never come at this minute-by-sluggish-minute pace. Marcus raked his fingers through his hair and, shivering, hunched the feather bed back over his arm. No use trying to sleep. "And no use seeing Narcissa Prentiss again, either," he told himself.

Might as well get up now. Mount old Sulphur and start on West. Why give that girl a chance to hang a doctor's scalp on her eighteen-inch belt along with the others she'd taken, if the talk were true? The handsome farmer who owned half the county. Or especially that persistent young preacher. If she wouldn't marry a minister, nobody could suit her. And if she intended to say "Yes" she'd have said it when Marcus first asked her and not put him off until the last minute this way.

But his sane thirty-three-year-old reasoning did little to quench his boyish excitement. After all, it had been Narcissa's idea to get up and see him off, in spite of his having to start before dawn. And, as long as she hadn't said "No"—

When the slow hands of his brass watch showed three-thirty, at last, Marcus flung off the quilts and feather bed. His bare chest tightened as he drew in the cold air and swung his red-drawered legs off the bunk.

Taking care not to waken his host and go through all those good-bys again, he screwed himself into woolen socks, two linsey shirts, tight nankeen pantaloons, and the knee-high boots that his brother,

Augustus, had made especially heavy for his ride across the continent. Dressed, he coaxed from the banked fire a light for the candle in his lantern. Then, catching up his coat, he unlatched the door and slid out into the morning.

Cold as it was, he strode to the barn without putting on his coat. His fur cap, along with his pistol and bowie knife, he'd stuck in the top of his saddlebag the night before. Just now his fluster at the thought of seeing Narcissa kept him warm. Plenty warm.

"By the eternal, any grown man ought to have more sense. Getting all shivery inside over a girl!"

And a fofarraw white gal at that, as Joe Meek would say.

When Marcus had told Joe Meek the Board's policy—that men they sent West to work among the Indians should be married—Joe had scoffed.

"Store clothes stuffed with Bostons! Whata them thar cold codfish know about the West? This old hoss'll tell you true, Doc. Aren't a man in the mountains as'll marry up with no fofarraw white gal. You come West and find you a likely-lookin' Injun woman. With a few yard of woven cloth you kin bug her soft eyes half outen her head. Then you dicker with her menfolks and they'll toss a blanket over the two of you. And, you got you a gal that's some now. What airthly good's a white gal out thar? Cain't make moccasins. Nor tan hides. Nor chop wood. Nor raise a skin lodge. And no white gal's goin' to stand for you lodge-polin' her when she needs it, neither, and that's a fact."

Marcus opened the barn door. Sulphur whinnied. "Quiet, boy, you'll wake them." With a pat he eased the horse over so he could side-step along the stall to his head. Warming the bit in his hands before giving it to Sulphur, he said, "Hope you slept better than I did. Here now, boy, try this."

The quarter-mile ride across the village left Marcus' throat dry, his palms damp. Still, at the Prentiss gate, he did not hesitate. He dropped Sulphur's reins over his head and then the frost in the porch was cracking under his boots. The door backed away before he could knock. And Narcissa stood before him—a blue and gold design in curved lines against a panel of light.

She said nothing but her opening hand and a tilt of her head invited him in. Marcus' knees melted. He had to know, at once.

Afraid to give himself time to consider, he blurted, "Miss Prentiss,

(2)

I can't leave like this. Got to know. Couldn't blame you, if you said 'No.' Must be dozens of men can offer you a better life than I can."

Narcissa's eyes widened. "Possibly," she admitted.

"Pratt, for instance," Marcus plunged on. "Why don't you marry him? You'd have a fine house with French wallpaper and a new-fangled carriage and—"

"Doctor Whitman . . ." Head high, her eyes unreadable, Narcissa backed toward the fireplace. "Are you asking in behalf of Mr. Pratt or Miles Standish?"

"I mean it." He made it sound offhand. She mustn't know how desperate he felt about it. "You're beautiful and talented and you could have any man in the county. But since you applied to go teach Indians and since I need a wife—" Now it sounded like barter—so many pounds of beef for such-and-such length of muslin. Marcus forced a swallow down his throat and kept talking. "Or that young Spalding— I can't hope you'd take me in preference to him. As a minister's wife you'd be looked up to and—"

Narcissa's fingers on his lips stopped him. "I'd better say 'Yes' quickly before you talk me out of it. I shall be honored and . . ." her shining head bowed before him, "and excited to be your wife, Doctor Whitman."

She seemed so untouched that, for a long moment, Marcus could not believe her words. Then, she was in his arms.

"I can't believe it." His voice no longer sounded like his.

Then, almost at once, his leaving was upon them. Narcissa clung to his arm, pressed it against her ribs. He could feel her quick breathing but she said nothing. Marcus hoped that she, too, was discarding words too small for the wonder in her and too trivial for saying in the face of months they must be apart.

Then she flung herself on him. "Marcus, take me with you. I want to go now." Her head burrowed into his chest. "Marcus, you're so strong. I wouldn't be afraid. Take me now, and then you won't have to come back for me."

Having just found her, how could a man ride away from such a girl? Marcus held her a moment and then cupped her face in his hands. Another day, her eyes would puzzle him again, he was sure. But for now, they held nothing back. Impossible. Still, by some miracle, she loved him. And that was how he could leave her for a time.

She whispered, "Your hands are so strong and so gentle, Marcus."
She closed her eyes. Then, with a shudder, she drew back. "My
darling, a thousand deaths could overtake you." She slipped the gray
shawl from her shoulders. "Here. Take this to keep you warm. I wove
it myself and it's light enough to fold into your pocket. You must
have something from me."

"From me, remember I love you."

"Oh Marcus."

"God bless you, Narcissa."

"God keep you, my love."

In that moment, Marcus could have given up the whole idea of
exploring the Oregon Country—, almost but not quite. From his
boyhood, he had been accustomed to a tug of war within him. The
drive of his mother's busy sternness against his father's time for
laughter. His own desire to be a doctor, after his father's death,
against his adopted uncle's insisting on the ministry. His concern
for his fellow man against his friend, Joe Meek's, "You gotta be
your own man, Doc, and the mountains are the place to be it!" And
now, Narcissa against the West. Then and now he fought to reconcile
these perverse mistresses. Failing that, he must find a way to serve
them all.

CHAPTER

2

RIDING, nooning, camping, days linked themselves together by the light of Marcus' campfires—banked after a late supper, fanned up for breakfast and an early start.

He loved his saddle. Nothing fancy about it, just plain cowhide, not even dyed. But each day now it was taking on polish from the buffing of his body while Sulphur's hoofs drummed across the frozen Genesee . . . the Allegheny . . . the Conewango. While they slushed through the Little Miami . . . the Ohio . . . and the Wabash. By April first—six weeks, nine hundred miles from Narcissa—that saddle fit Marcus like a Windsor rocker.

Mr. Parker was not difficult to locate even in the metropolis of St. Louis. Marcus squeezed in on Sulphur's reins before the tavern pillars bracing up the largest number of men. There, the immaculate Parson Parker held forth. His hair shone like sewing silk in the Missouri sunshine. Seen against the grizzled hides of his listeners, his shaved skin looked pink as an infant's. But nothing could make those square jaws, that horseman's frame look childlike. And Parker's voice boomed out until the leaners at the tavern across the street and those a city square away could also fill their ears with exhortations.

Marcus swung off Sulphur onto the tobacco-splattered steps. Parker's head nodded in recognition, but he finished his point on the evils of illicit women before coming over to shake hands.

"Doctor Whitman! What kept you? I've been waiting a week."

Marcus gave the older man's hand a grip that ignored all the reproof in his words and accepted, instead, the welcome in his eyes. "I kicked in the puddles. But you'll probably be ahead of me all the way."

Parker's full lips stretched into a quick smile. "We're all ready to go." His big hand dug inside his coat and came out with two letters. "See. I have our appointments. This one, from the American Board of Commissioners for Foreign Missions, authorizing us to explore the Oregon Country with a view to establishing mission stations among the western Indians. And this—" Not merely to Marcus but to his congregation, he displayed the folded paper weighted with sealing wax and War Department inkings— "this is from Washington. Our permit for crossing Indian lands."

While they wrangled for a cheap pack mule and arranged steamer passage up the Missouri for themselves and their animals, Marcus watched Parker and marveled at his drive. At fifty-six Mr. Parker had the enthusiasm of a schoolboy plus the fixed purpose of a swarm of yellow jackets.

Just how they would get on together, traveling horseback across the continent, Marcus wanted and needed to know. So, while the river steamer, *Siam*, chugged them on west toward Liberty, he made the most of every opportunity to get really acquainted with Mr. Parker. Bunking with him, whiling away the days on deck in conversation, Marcus came to like his travel companion and to respect his stiff-spined expectations of life and of his fellow human beings. Also, he came to entertain some needling doubts about the trip that lay ahead.

Mrs. Parker had said before they started, "Think of him as your father, Doctor. He's used to me taking care of him." And apparently, Parker intended to stay used to someone taking care of him. Marcus prepared their meals and made up their bunks every day on the steamer. But, to give him his due, Mr. Parker did make copious entries in his journal and he took full responsibility for lecturing the crew on their sins. So, perhaps they were even.

It was no more than right, Marcus told himself when they scraped alongside the dock at Liberty, that the older man should leave their luggage and animals to him. Mr. Parker should go directly to the tavern. Unless he might be willing to join the caravan camp at once.

"Not tonight!" Mr. Parker answered Marcus' wordless gaze toward

(6)

the spangle of campfires beyond the town. "Let's get one more night's rest in a bed. Plenty of time to join the caravan tomorrow."

Mr. Parker on his way, Marcus took time to stand on the dock and locate himself. So this was Liberty—jumping-off place, outer brink of civilization.

He hardly saw the weather-grayed shacks with their square cutouts of light. He barely heard the raucous calls and clatter that went with unloading the steamer. The feel of this one-street settlement was that of a line drawn. And, as if this were a game of prisoner's base, he couldn't wait to step across the line. He was ready, this night, to mount old Sulphur and plunge into the West. The smell and sizzle of those hundred campfires, upriver to the west, nagged and wheedled at him. Still, as Mr. Parker had insisted, there'd be time to join the caravan tomorrow.

Long before light the next morning, Marcus eased himself from the tavern bed. Mr. Parker would not relish being wakened this early. Nor did the boy at the livery stable.

Marcus could see through an inch-wide crack in the door on which he banged. The kid's red hair flapped off the end of his cot. Trying to shut off Marcus' racket, he yanked at his blanket and uncovered his feet. Finally giving up, he straggled to the door.

Marcus teased, "You'll lose out on the fattest worms, sleeping till all hours this way."

But the kid was still too groggy for jokes. "Aren't no need of goin' out to camp this airly, Mister. They tell me it might be weeks yet, afore they start."

"Weeks?" Marcus' dismay roused Sulphur into an eager whinny.

The boy yawned and stretched his shirt free of his pantaloons. "Thar's your bridle and saddle, if you just got to go but without it rains, thar aren't goin' to be grass for your yaller hoss and sway-back mule, let alone them two-three hundred hosses and mules Cap'n Fontenelle's got rounded up."

Weeks! Weeks that he might have spent with Narcissa. If only something had held him in New York State! But he'd ride out and see for himself. This boy could be talking in his sleep.

The caravan's falling-in camp, a mile or so beyond Liberty, had trampled itself a road that Sulphur could have followed blindfolded. And campfires, dotting the plain, beckoned now with cottonwood smoke and the smell of searing meat.

(7)

"Won't rain till that wind gets around to the east," Marcus told Sulphur. Hearing the first slam of sledges on loosened tent stakes, the first hawks and curses of waking men, the first slap of hatchets on breakfast firewood, Sulphur answered Marcus' mood by breaking from his sedate walk into a gallop.

One more recruit made about as much difference to the fur company caravan as another blooming sunflower. Marcus rode about, skirting stacks of new pine boxes, staked-out oxen, men still snoring on the ground, hobbled horses, canvas tents, Conestoga wagons, men crouched over breakfast fires, men toting water from the river. He caused no more ripple in the caravan's morning than an occasional "Howdy."

Marcus moved through this assorted welter until all the breakfasts were downed. He didn't want to start off beholden to these men. Besides, the dust that hung above these cluttered twenty acres stuffed his nostrils. The sudden feel of standing on the brink of the West swelled tight in his throat. He couldn't have swallowed food had someone insisted.

Too eager to wait longer, he looked up the captain.

Lucien Fontenelle stood several inches shorter than Marcus but he gave a tall impression. One big boot perched on the tongue of a Conestoga, the dark-haired Frenchman looked every bit as swashbuckling as the romantic stories Marcus had heard about him in St. Louis. His dark eyes waited, noncommittal, while Marcus introduced himself, told him about Mr. Parker, and explained their mission. "We'll pack our own victuals and equipment. We've a War Department permit to cross—"

"Got a permit from the American Fur Company?" A trace of cunning narrowed Fontenelle's eyes.

"No, but I thought you could—"

"And so I can. But don't you forget this here's the Fur Company outfit. And don't make no trouble 'mongst my men or, by gor, back you go and the cussed Injuns can dance over your scalp," Fontenelle warned. "Got troubles nuff without addin' two greenhorns and one a preacher too old to set a hoss."

Marcus picked up Sulphur's reins and moved away as Fontenelle called, "Shunar!" to a young giant in fringed buckskin. By the captain's tone, Shunar, for all his size, was about to learn that Fontenelle was in charge.

Near a cluster of red-and-black-checked backs hunched above an assortment of jobs laid on the ground, Marcus stopped. Tall, young, tough as rawhide, these men. From the way they stared when he wandered up, then resettled their black fur caps and went on with their jobs, these teamsters held themselves proud and set apart. But Marcus watched anyway. He needed to learn all he could about caravan travel. Next year, it might be, he'd bring a wagon himself. A lady would, no doubt, find a wagon seat a restful change from a sidesaddle.

He picked out a man paddling thick grease into a hungry wagon hub. "Takes lots of grease, doesn't it?" Marcus asked, just making conversation.

The fellow looked up without unbending, squinted in distaste at what he saw, and went on with his work.

Marcus gave him another chance to be civil. "You headed for Oregon?"

Like a woman testing jelly, the teamster poised his grease paddle in the air long enough for one black blob to separate and fall into the bucket. "Headin' Santa Fe way," he drawled, "and hopin' thar won't be no greenhorns along."

Santa Fe! Marcus shucked off the insult and considered the useful grain of intelligence in the teamster's words. So some of these men were putting out for ports other than Oregon. He gazed into the West. He was indeed, as folks put it, on the shore of a great harbor. Funny how a man could stand on one spot at one particular time and the place not be just a grassy plain, the time not merely a hot Tuesday in April, 1835. This place, this time, for instance—all this felt like waiting at the edge of something big happening.

Sulphur stamped his impatience with this staring and pulled toward a rangy teamster who was using his teeth as well as his hands, splicing harness. Marcus watched in silence awhile. Then, really wanting to know, he asked, "What's the best weight harness for an outfit like this?"

The fellow tongued his cud of tobacco from his right jaw to his left. Without looking up he muttered, "I got no time fer idjucatin' greenhorns."

Marcus swung into his saddle. "Thanks." He pulled Sulphur around and headed for the river. No sullen teamster could spoil this day for him. And he wouldn't stay green for long, either. He turned

Sulphur into the path that led downstream to the loading docks. This waiting must be made to pay for itself in information gathered, in polishing off his greenhorn look. He urged Sulphur along with a soft-spoken heel.

At the docks he found a dozen traders, strutting about in store coats, trousers, and beaver hats. They called out orders with an air tailored to their natty broadcloths and fustians. Leaving Sulphur on the bank to graze, Marcus tramped down a swaying dock.

The crack of a fist to a jaw stopped him. To his astonishment, he saw one spruce trader sit down hard on the end of the dock. Toward Marcus slouched a stringy-haired mountain man, wearing no expression of anger nor of pleasure. He met Marcus without a glance and shuffled on by.

Marcus hurried to pick up the trader. But assistance seemed to surprise him far more than the mountain man's attack. "What are you doing there?" he objected as Marcus caught him under the arms and pulled him to his shiny feet.

"You hurt?" Marcus asked.

"Hurt? Who? . . . Oh, me." The little fellow flapped his knees from side to side to lengthen his broadcloth pantaloons. He screwed his chin up from his linen collar. "Naw. Nobody's hurt. You new, Mister?"

"But what happened?" Marcus persisted.

"What happened? What do you mean? Oh, you mean that trapper." He shrugged. "Same old thing. He don't like my clothes." The dapper merchant leaned over the end of the dock and called down, "Hurry it up there!" He turned back to Marcus. "Mountain men!" The right corner of his mouth pulled out of shape to emit a disgusted rattle from his throat. "They got no use for civilized doin's. Whatever they don't like, they hits or shoots. You're new, ain't you, Mister?"

Marcus admitted it. "How far can all these goods travel by water?"

"Bellevue, Mister. Yep, Bellevue by water. That's I reckon two hundred miles up the old Mizzou," the trader volunteered. He excused himself with a wag of his beaver hat and stepped again to the edge of the dock. "Spread them rifle boxes. Take care with them kegs." Then, as if glad for an audience, he came back to Marcus. "Fontenelle loads it all onto them big Conestogas at Bellevue and

(10)

wheels it far as Laramie. There on, he'll pack it. You sure don't know much of what goes on, do you, Mister?"

Marcus laughed. "Just got in." Below him, packers were spreading heavy crates of rifles to cover a barge floor. Kegs shaped to fit the sides and backs of mules leaked out trader whisky. Black ropes of tobacco softened in the sun and gave off a tarlike odor. Bolts of bright calico seemed oddly out of place with all these men's trappings. Reading SCALPING KNIVES on a flank of boxes, Marcus drew back. "That cloth—"

The trader guffawed. "You are new, Mister! That's how you get your wood chopped. How you get your tent raised. Best of all," he confided, "you can dazzle a squaw into anything, just anything, with woven cloth. You'll soon find out, a likely-looking fellow like you."

The trader stayed with Marcus, answering questions, volunteering information that would save him from being an out-and-out greenhorn ever again. The only item of intelligence on which this man proved totally ignorant was the date the caravan would roll. He didn't know. Nobody knew. Not till grass conditions looked up to the west. They couldn't travel without grass as even a greenhorn must know.

Feeling a little guilty, Marcus climbed to the tavern piazza just at sunset. He found Mr. Parker dozing and not inclined to be critical of being left to himself all day.

"When does the caravan start?" he inquired.

"How did you pick out first the only question I don't know the answer to?" Marcus objected.

"Well, we've got to know that."

"So we have, but we don't. Nobody knows. We're waiting for grass."

"Grass. That's ridiculous."

"Not quite. The stock has to graze its way."

"Ridiculous," Mr. Parker snorted. "What's wrong with carrying feed?"

"Plenty. When you see what-all they're carrying now. I watched them load enough rifles today to outfit the army."

"Why rifles?"

Marcus explained. The Fur Company's trappers had been out there in the Far West in little bands or by themselves, storing up buffalo robes and beaver skins since this time last year. The Fur

Company had to go out and buy up their catches. And, as they went, they took out the fixings and gewgaws that trappers would buy with their money, if they could come on a spree to the States. "It's a regular store, half a dozen stores, really. You never saw the like. Whisky and tobacco—enough to corrupt the very Rocky Mountains themselves. Beaver traps, beads and awls, axes and tomahawks, vermilion paint, powder and flints, bolts of calico—"

Mr. Parker stopped him with an upraised hand. "You mean the Company goes out with money to buy up the trappers' furs. Then the trappers take that money and give it all back to the Company for things like whisky and tobacco. So the Company men come back with the furs and the money they started out with. Is that it?"

Marcus squirmed under Parker's gaze. "I didn't set up the system." Parker persisted. "But that's it, isn't it?"

"That's most of it," Marcus had to agree.

Parker stood up. "Then I must ride out there tonight and have a talk with the captain—that Fontenelle. From what I hear, this is not the first escapade of which he needs to repent."

Having learned not to appear too concerned, Marcus kept his voice low. "We can talk it over while we have something to eat, Mr. Parker. Missed most of my meals today, somehow."

"Well, I'll eat with you," Mr. Parker agreed. "But the whole business is wrong and I'll tell them so."

Marcus suggested, "There'll be plenty of time, from the looks of things."

Marcus persuaded Mr. Parker to move out to camp the next day. They had their tent and all their equipment. What was the use of spending the Board's money to stay at the tavern? But, he reminded himself while pitching their tent, he'd have to keep an eye on Mr. Parker out here. Mustn't let anything make an occasion for Fontenelle to decide that the caravan had no room for two greenhorn hangers-on.

About the Fur Company system, Mr. Parker had argued far into the night. The system was wrong and he would tell them so. Marcus reminded him that civilization had often followed exploitation and that, without the fur caravan, Parker and he could not get West.

"But it's wrong to keep still in the face of sin," Parker insisted.

"And right for us to get West," Marcus came back.

Late on the day after they joined the camp, Marcus decided to try out their mule for size. Beside that sway-backed animal, their trappings appeared to be load enough for a Conestoga. If Marcus had been able to win his point, they'd have bought two mules, both bigger and stronger than this one. But Mr. Parker insisted that one was enough and since this one was cheap, he would do.

However, he wouldn't do. When Marcus got him packed, their tent and large cooking pot simply could not be added to the load.

"Well, come on," he said to Parker. "Now's as good a time as any for you to meet Captain Fontenelle."

They found the captain at his headquarters Conestoga. Marcus introduced Mr. Parker and, before Parker might start his harangue, presented their problem.

Coming to a slow decision, the captain grunted. "Reckon we can stow your leftovers in a company wagon." But he squinted toward Parker and, slopping a puddle of tobacco juice at the preacher's feet, wheeled and strode off.

"Got to keep those two apart," Marcus told himself again.

Days stacked into weeks, and weeks of waiting wore on. Marcus grew more restless. All this time, he might have been with Narcissa. If only they'd start riding so he could get back for his wife!

Never having made much headway with the teamsters and finding a visit with one of the traders pretty apt to be interrupted by a fight, Marcus looked for other company. Their clothes first attracted his attention to the mountain men. The giant, Shunar, in his fringed buckskin tunic and Indian-made moccasins caught Marcus' imagination. In fact, one look at those clothes and he felt a little prick of envy. Comfortable, they looked, like they'd never need to come off.

Later Marcus noticed these mountain men—a dozen or so had got caught in the States for the winter—around the saloons in Liberty. These shrewd-eyed, openhanded "old hosses" hung around town and spent their waiting time in flinging away their dollars. As long as they could stand, they drank to "heaps a beaver," treating all comers. When standing became precarious, they wriggled up onto their horses and jogged out to camp. There each sat before his private campfire, long hair matted over grimy face, and stared into the flames until he could stand again and ride into Liberty.

Finally one afternoon when the wind had pulled around to the east and a solid gray covered the parching sun, Marcus found one

(13)

of the mountain men at his campfire but looking sober enough to talk. "Know Joe Meek?" he asked as an opener.

"Old Joe Meek?"

"Yes, old Joe Meek," Marcus agreed, thinking Joe must be as old as twenty-four or -five, at least.

"Sartin sure. Ever white man and Injun and Spaniard and Frenchman and half-breed in the mountains knows old Joe Meek." Having caught his own attention with this outburst, the grisly young man grabbed a handful of hair in each hand and looked out at Marcus through the parted curtain. "Man, if you don't know old Joe Meek, yer aren't no gentleman."

Marcus grinned. "But I do know him. Met up with him last fall in New York State."

The fellow's face broke open like a ripe watermelon. "So yer a friend of old Joe Meek. Well, don't that beat all! Set, you old hoss."

Marcus sat. "Joe Meek was heading West without a caravan when he left me," he said. "Reckon he made it?"

"Sartin sure. Nothin' could stop old Joe Meek and that's a fact." The mountain man picked up a stick of wood but its weight, small as it was, pulled him off balance.

He grunted approval when Marcus built up his fire.

"You goin' West to trap in Jim Bridger's brigade?"

"I aim to doctor," Marcus told him. "Indians."

"Not Injuns!" Pushing himself up now without apparent effort, the mountain man stood sober above Marcus. "Yer no friend of old Joe Meek. He'd a told you 'bout Injun medicine men. Aren't no doc as aren't had too much trader whisky a goin' to head into them Injun tomahaws. You ought not try drinkin' it 'thout no water, Doc. You looks to be man enough but thar's some as can keep ther head and others as gits idees like doctorin' the cussed Injuns."

Grinning, Marcus gave himself a boost and hopped to his feet. "You're wrong there, friend. Joe Meek told me, all right. How Indian medicine men either cure their patients or get killed by the dead one's next-of-kin. Joe Meek and his big talk are half responsible for my going West. Somebody's got to teach Indians better manners toward their doctors."

"Jest like old Joe Meek said," the mountain man muttered. "Short on gumption. 'Keep yer eye skinned for him,' he says." Jabbing out his hand, the fellow grinned. "Name's Gunther, Doc. You'll be

(14)

seein' me around when you need me and, sartin sure, you'll be needin' me like old Joe Meek says, and long afore Rendezvous."

Ignoring the splatter of rain about him, Marcus sauntered to the river. These white trappers knew the western Indians and yet did not know what they could become, given half a chance. The Nez Percé tribe, for instance. Joe Meek had known these Indians well. Had lived among them, off and on. And yet he'd heard nothing about the four braves sent by their tribe as far east as St. Louis to get the white man's Book of Heaven, to learn the white man's way of worshiping the Great Spirit. Everyone in the East had read about this Nez Percé delegation and knew that only one young warrior returned to his tribe. Returned with a white man's disease. Without the Book. And Marcus knew that Indians who were searching for help could be helped. Knew it before he saw them. Joe Meek and now this Gunther yapping about a doctor being in danger among such Indians was all nonsense and he'd prove it. Just let him at the West!

When the caravan finally tightened its last hitches and tossed down its last civilized drinks, Marcus had taken all the waiting he could stomach. This May morning had been made for moving on and, given his way, he'd have started long before light. Now he fidgeted and watched the sun climb over the cottonwoods beyond the river while fifty or sixty company men—teamsters, traders, and packers—the six big wagons, three yoke of oxen, the dozen mountain men, and two hundred horses and mules snaked into a ragged line of march. He wondered how Mr. Parker could sit his mount at the rear of the line, waiting unmoved for the order, "Travel!"

The primitive reds and blacks of the procession drummed at Marcus with a prodding rhythm. A bouquet blended of rawhide and sweat and fresh-cropped grass drifted back along the line and he gulped it down like a tonic.

Spurring up his black stallion, Fontenelle shouted, "Let 'em roll. Let 'em roll!"

The caravan nosed into the lawnlike prairie.

CHAPTER

3

DURING their five-weeks' packing-up stay in Liberty, men of the fur caravan had observed enough of the proprieties to cover up their improprieties. Beyond Liberty, strength and numbers wrote the only code.

Company traders soon joined the teamsters to sneer at the caravan's missionary hangers-on. Reasons for sneering could be of any caliber. Because the greenhorns were only two. Because they wore store clothes. Or because fifty-six was old by their standards and "Old Parson Parker" couldn't even pack a mule so's to carry fifty feet.

Actually, Parker seldom packed the mule. Marcus saw to all their personal chores and then wore calluses on his shoulder from heaving it against wagon wheels bogged in mud. He thonged rafts together for river crossings. Built bridges. Carried trade goods on his aching back to lighten loads for the pack mules. He did considerably more than his share while he waited for a showdown. He knew for certain fact that it would, in time, be up to him to keep the unstable peace or fight the war that was brewing.

So, when their overloaded mule slipped her pack, Marcus took the blame and redistributed the load. When Fontenelle decided that it was too much trouble to carry the missionaries' tent and utensils, Marcus used rope he had salvaged and spliced to tie more onto their mule. All of this life seemed so good to him compared with his easy village doctoring back home that no abuse touched him. The caravan considered itself put upon, but not Marcus.

(16)

One morning from his old life back in Wheeler, New York, he kept near at hand like an outgrown coat to slip into frequently as he rode. He loved to flex his muscles and feel the seams rip. For this Marcus was no longer the same man as the one who had answered the knock at his office door that cold day, only a matter of weeks ago.

Easing into his memory, drawing it on slowly so he could feel all its confining tightness, Marcus closed his eyes to see again that fellow on his doorstep. Of medium build, the man's drooping stance made him look small. His linsey coloring faded him into the gray winter morning. He stared and forgot to speak when Marcus opened the door.

"You looking for a doctor?" Marcus had asked.

"Nope."

Marcus had pills to roll and a new supply of calomel to pulverize. "Well then," he began, "I've got work to—"

"Woman's 'bout to have a baby," the man said. "Ain't no reason why she needs a doctor, as I can see. Had four kids already with Tom Brackett's woman midwifin' her. But doctors are gettin' to be a fad."

Quickly Marcus packed what he would need. "Where do you live?"

"Eight mile due east. What'll the trip cost, if you go?"

Marcus buckled his saddlebag and reached for his coat. "Come on, man. We may be too late." He shouldered the stranger out the door. "Charge is fifty cents for five miles. Six and a quarter cents a mile over that. Babies come higher, usually, but let it go." He tightened Sulphur's cinch. "Comes to sixty-nine cents on eight miles."

Working their boots into their stirrups, they swung up.

"Sixty-eight, I make it."

"All right. Sixty-eight."

"It's a sight of money to fling away on a fad. Tom Brackett's woman don't cost nothin' but her dinner and she don't eat so hearty. Still," the man sighed from the toes of his muddy boots, "I learned you gotta go along with a woman's notions sometimes. Even when it costs money." Having given birth to this philosophy, the fellow slumped in his saddle and rode the cold eight miles in silence.

And, sure enough, a doctor turned out to be about as necessary as five legs on a horse. The new father's words, "Doctors are gettin' to be a fad," pestered Marcus all the way home. Had pestered him, actually, until he'd ridden out of the States and into the West.

Thinking of it now, riding through grass tall enough to sweep

Sulphur's belly, the only time he could remember feeling of real use back home was during the cholera epidemic of '32. Then he had kept Steuben County considerably healthier than other doctors' territories but he'd been lucky. He'd just happened to get the Edinburgh pamphlet on cholera and had known about fever because of writing his thesis on "Caloric" at Fairfield Medical College. For the most part, people in the States were sick because they ate too much and Marcus did not relish prescribing pills when all a patient needed was to go to bed without his supper. Now that he was on his way to serve both the souls and bodies of human beings in real need, he rode tall and breathed deep. He was his own man, as Joe Meek put it. And no matter how loud or how obscene became the curses spit out at the two missionaries. No matter that the teamsters ran out of words and started threatening with heavier ammunition.

Sixteen days northwest of Liberty well up the Missouri, the caravan pitched camp in the valley just to the south of the handful of shacks —saloon, trading post, saloon, government fort, and saloon—that made up Bellevue. Marcus led his mule back to the north toward the bluffs. He unpacked as usual and, as usual, started their evening meal. Then he noticed the men of the caravan pour toward a nucleus already assembled among their cluster of half-pitched tents.

Curious, he raked his fire in to hold, left the water on for tea, and set his pan of ham inside the tent. He was not surprised, as he neared the crowd, to find Mr. Parker preaching. But what, by the eternal, would ever induce all the drivers and traders and some of the mountain men to be on hand for a sermon? Skirting the edge of the circle, Marcus approached the rock on which Parker stood, pouring out his denouncement of the waterfront saloons.

"You're a little late, my friend," Marcus thought. Most of the men had patronized the saloons to near the limit of their capacity. This, no doubt, added fire both to the message and to the listeners. Still, it did not explain the large attendance.

Trying to figure it out, Marcus heard Parker proclaim, "Demon rum has you in his grip. You're servants of the devil. You commit crimes against the Indians. You loot, rape, and murder."

Still the men listened.

Parker's voice swelled. "You talk of scalping the Otoes who killed the white men before we came. I tell you that I will send to President Jackson the names and descriptions of every man who comes into camp with the blood of an Indian on his hands. And I will carry on the fight until each man is punished according to the law of the land."

Marcus saw the men stiffen, smelled their sour breath. Then his eye caught a streak of light as the first missile sailed through the air. He thought, "A stone," and remembered Mrs. Parker's, "Think of him as your father, Doctor." He ran in and threw up his arms.

The stone turned out to be an egg, well seasoned by warm weather. And the first one served merely as a signal. Every ruffian in the crowd let fly. Anger boiled up in Marcus. It would have eased his outrage to take on any half-dozen of the mob and wallop their living daylights. But the hoodlums wanted exactly that, he knew. A fight would give them cover for an accident to both Parker and himself.

Marcus stood his ground. On came the eggs. Cracking and raining down, exploding and splattering, they dripped from his hair, his clothes. His nose rebelled at taking any part in breathing. But, relieved, he saw Parker's head disappear beyond a swell in the ground, off toward their tent. "Now hurry up and get rid of those eggs." He turned his back and set his teeth.

Eggs hailed at him from every side. They squashed into his linsey shirts with muted thuds and came through warm and slimy on his shoulders. "This can't go on forever," he told himself and waited for the supply to be exhausted. At last, the bombardment slowed . . . and stopped. As Marcus turned, his boots crunching shells and forcing the vomitous odor into his nostrils, his assailants had begun to scuff away.

"This hyar hoss is agoin' to hunt Injuns, Old Parson Parker or not." This from one of the mountain men.

Shunar waved the others in behind him. "By gar, I'm de beeg buck of dees lick, *moi!* And aren't no hell-fire preacher goin' to stop me from doin' my duty. Let's go!"

A gang of eight or ten cutthroats mounted their worn horses and spurred out across the prairie. The rest of the crowd made off for the saloons. Looked as if Parker had turned most of the ruffians from the Indians and driven them to drink.

Marcus stood in the reeking puddle and watched bright checkered backs, fringed buckskin backs, store clothes backs move away. For a long moment, washing seemed hardly worth the effort. Then, he went at it.

Dragging himself to the river, he sank onto the muddy bank. He yanked off his boots and looked them over. The smell would never leave the leather. He must remember to have Augustus make a pair of heavy boots for Narcissa next year.

He waded into the liver-colored water. He'd get off some of this perfume before he went for the one change of clothes he had along. He scrubbed his hair, his ears, his shirts. Then he ducked his head again. Another try at the clothes he wore and he gave up. Instead, he peeled himself and flung the whole putrid mess onto the bank. His shirts would have to be beat into holes to get out that smell.

Trying not to breathe, shuddering when he did, he climbed out and rubbed down his arms, down his long bare legs. Then, picking up his boots in one hand, his clothes in the other and holding them as far as possible from his nose, he began the weary drag up the hill. A hundred yards from his half-pitched camp he could see Parker in the closing dusk, head in his hands, beside the dying fire. And, coming up behind him, a man in buckskin. The stalker carried his right hand in his belt at the hilt of his knife.

Marcus forgot the shale that gashed his feet, forgot his aching exhaustion. Dropping everything, stooping low, he ran.

The mountain man had his knife out when Marcus cut him off. As the two faced each other, however, the fellow slid the knife into his belt.

"It's you," he said.

"In the flesh," Marcus answered. "You're Gunther." He wasn't sure whether Gunther had been with the egging mob. He couldn't tell from his face what he intended.

"Come up on the sly so's the others wouldn't take no notice," Gunther explained and stuck out a calloused hand. "Remember Joe Meek said for me to look out for you, anyhow I could. Warn't a heap of help down thar. You hurt some?"

Marcus shook Gunther's hand. The trapper's muscles bulged his buckskin in the right places and his angular clean-shaven face had a kid-brother look about it. "Forgot we had a friend of Joe Meek's along," he said. "Our victuals will be slim tonight, but you're welcome."

"This hoss'll be more use to you afore any others lay their sights on us together. Reason you aren't been seein' me along the trail. Joe Meek told me a doc such as you be might turn out worth keepin' with his hair on."

Marcus grinned. "Joe Meek didn't know how my hair would smell about now."

Gunther didn't laugh. "Mind you keep your eyes skinned. A pretty smart lot of boys are fixin' for you and that preacher feller to lay wolf's meat afore they put out across prairie."

"You're joking. They don't like us much, I admit. But they wouldn't actually—"

"You're the one are jokin', Doc." Gunther's voice dropped to a sandy whisper. "They aren't aimin' for you to leave Bellevue, goin' neither direction. They aren't hankerin' to let your old Parson Parker dry up their trip and they don't like havin' their consciouses riled up by his talk. 'Cain't let down yer pantaloons,' they say, 'without Old Parson Parker tellin' ye it are a sin to dirty up the peraira.' They sartin sure aren't aimin' to ride into Rendezvous with him holy-swearin' at 'em all the way and you kin lay to that."

Marcus blinked. "You mean they'd actually kill us? I don't believe it."

"Not tonight. It'll be our last night hyar so's they'll be leavin' afore word gets round." Gunther held out his hand. "Take 'er easy two-three day and then, come dark, look out. This beaver'll stand fust guard that night." And he moved off into the gloom.

Forgetting his nakedness, Marcus stood staring down into camp. So the egg attack was merely the prelude, a cocking of guns. Suddenly he knew it was true. Thinking with the mind of the West, it could be so easily true. He had seen a dozen brutal fights picked for no better reason than that one man didn't like another's clothes. He'd seen a mountain man push and yank on his favorite mule to get her to move ten feet from the place where she'd stopped to the place where he wanted to camp. When she refused to budge, he'd whipped out his pistol and blown a hole through her head.

"This is eye-for-an-eye country," Marcus reminded himself. "These men don't draw fine lines of distinction." Life, being cheap, would seem to them none too generous a swap for their sensual liberty which was dear, and with which Parker interfered. Death, by the law of the "peraira," would be fitting fate for a kill-joy.

Marcus went back for his clothes and trudged on up the hill to his tent. What should he do? To be fair, Parker was not too much to blame. Who could tell just where silence, in the presence of sin, became approval? For himself, he had faced the problem and he faced it again. It still seemed to him that bucking this burly caravan wouldn't pay. That getting to their destination was a greater good than could come of reprimanding these devils. That, if he could doctor the Indians and take them the Book, his conscience would not disturb him about these white men. They'd all had a civilized upbringing and had deliberately chosen their ways.

Still, Parker disagreed. They'd been over it a dozen times and always Mr. Parker wound up with: "I will not sanction wickedness under my very nose by keeping quiet."

"So, it's up to me to get us out of this trap we're in," Marcus admitted and hurried into the tent to find dry pantaloons and a shirt. Parker and he, divided on policy, were one to the mob.

CHAPTER

4

FONTENELLE let the horses and mules graze two days and two nights at Bellevue. During that time, the sun did not shine but threatening clouds released no rain. Dreary games of euchre went on and on, twenty hours at a stretch. Fontenelle's temper grew short as loggy packers fumbled boxes and packs of trade goods from river barge to Conestoga. Men swore louder, were sullen and silent longer than they had been on the trail. The third day, the greasy dishwater gray of the sky turned to slate. But still, no rain.

The hotheads of the camp, instruments of justice, had lost the trail of the Otoes in two directions. Now they spoiled for blood. Whisky-soaked mountain men and teamsters roared around camp, looking for trouble. They eyed Marcus and Parker with a promissory gleam and passed by, licking their chops.

Then came the caravan's last evening before putting out. Firing their guns into the air, the Injun hunters could not wait for dark. They thundered past the saloons as the sun broke through for a moment, bleary-eyed, the height of a man in the sky. They splashed into the river and up the incline on the other side. A flourlike dust kilned by the many fires of the camp the last three days, powdered the air. Sitting cross-legged before his tent, Marcus licked at the dust on his lips and found it bitter. He drew Narcissa's shawl close around his shoulders.

When the quiet got too heavy, he built up a crackling fire. Better cook supper for Mr. Parker. He had no appetite himself. Ominous silence lay on the camp. Even Parker, coming out when Marcus called him, ate his ham and corn bread without talking. Marcus gulped a tin cup of tea. A rumble of laughter from one of the saloons punctuated, now and then, the anxious quiet. Mr. Parker went in to bed.

Marcus had barely seen Gunther these three days since the eggs but he saw him now, sitting cross-legged before a fire some fifty yards away. A pipe sagged cold from his mouth. Long hair hung limp to cover his face. Marcus sprawled in the tent for an hour and tried to sleep. But no use. He stepped outside and kicked at the embers of his fire, a signal to Gunther for changing the guard.

The mountain man unfolded himself and ambled off without a glance. Second guard. Marcus fingered the frayed end of a length of rope in his pocket.

He propped back the tent flap and consciously practiced the way a mountain man folded down to the earth. Wide awake, he waited. He tried to think what he'd do when the attack came. He did not decide except that he must divert it from Parker.

Mr. Parker, in these brief weeks on the way, had proved himself without fear. He'd been willing—too willing—to stand up to any ruffian in the company. Parker believed in truth, as the rough men of the caravan believed in guns and fists. And he was a speaker of real force. If he got through to Oregon and back to the East, Mr. Parker, with his accurate notes on country and people, could stir up more interest in the western Indians and more support for work among them than any other six men. Yes, Parker must get through to Oregon.

Marcus felt sure that the caravan captain, in spite of his fuss over their supplies, would not actively consent to their death at the hands of his men. He might go to Fontenelle. But he found something arresting in his sure knowledge that, once they were dead, Fontenelle would raise no objection nor even report the event to the States. No, he would not ask Fontenelle for help. Somehow, he had to work this out alone.

He'd been watching a couple of hours when galloping hoofs made the ground tremble. Marcus stood up.

The stage was set. The caravan would snake out at dawn, the criminals be gone from the scene of the crime. No questions asked.

Marcus' thumb polished the butt of the pistol stuck in his belt.

His stomach tightened and pulled away from its barrel. He moved to the shadowed side of his tent to wait.

Shooting and shouting, the gang of Indian hunters roared into camp. From half their long guns trailed reeking scalps. Someone stirred up a sleeping fire for light. They would not be quieted until the camp had turned out to admire their prowess and exclaim in turn over each gory scalp.

Marcus pushed Parker back onto his robes and blankets, and kept to his post in the shadow of their tent, waiting.

A roar of laughter greeted Shunar's account of the half-scalped Injun who got away. The men all feared Shunar. When he told a joke, they laughed.

Marcus waited.

Talk slowed at last, and the ruffians scattered to their tents. Fires died. Stooping to his tent flap, Marcus noted Parker's even breathing. He straightened at the whisper of a sound, listened, heard nothing. "Getting as bad as trappers, feeling Injun sign in their bones," he scolded. But there, he heard it again. Nothing definite but something. He waited. Not afraid but not knowing, either, what he would do.

Then, he saw across the compound a lone bulky figure. Dead black against the black beyond the tents, it moved. Now, it disappeared. Marcus waited. It showed again for an instant, closer now, black on black. Closer again and Marcus was sure. Shunar, the mighty man himself. No other stood such a hulking mass. And, since Liberty, Shunar had been spoiling for a fight with Marcus.

A fight? Marcus' fists knotted. This was not intended as a fight. Nothing short of murder would save Shunar's face after all his sneers and threats. Nothing short of murder required this panther-like stalking of the prey. Closer now. Twenty yards away. Ten. Marcus turned, keeping his eyes fixed on the moving black figure.

He could give an alarm. Open his dry mouth and yell to wake the whole camp. He ground his teeth together.

Suppose he gave an alarm. All the brutes in camp would slam through their tent flaps and come roaring out to help. To help Shunar.

He watched Shunar bend low and come on. His moccasins on the dry grass made a rhythmic whish-whish. The vinegar smell of sweat and buckskin came to Marcus in a wave. His hand slid up the seam of his denim pantaloons and curved around the cold hilt of his

(25)

bowie. His jaws tightened. He pressed himself deep into the shadow of his tent and stopped breathing.

Shunar stood not three feet away from him now at the tent flap. His top-heavy bulk showed clearly between Marcus and the wash of hot light from his banked fire. Shunar crouched, off balance, fumbling for the tent flap.

Marcus braced his feet, sending up into his own face the stench of rotten eggs as his leg muscles bulged in his boots.

Finding the tent flap, Shunar eased it back. His head bent low, level with Marcus' hand on the hilt of his knife. The giant's right hand swung back to his shoulder. From his fist curved out and down a gleaming blade. Two silent thrusts and that would be that.

Not figuring it out, Marcus clamped on Shunar's knife arm, snapped it backward and up. At the same instant he caught Shunar's slack knees with a mighty swing of his boot.

The big cutthroat shook the ground as he fell. The back of his head smacked the shale. He relaxed like a sleeping child, unconscious.

Working against time, Marcus swung Narcissa's shawl from his shoulders and down over his victim's face. He pulled the ends tight around his neck. Sawed the cloth into a bit that cut across the corners of Shunar's mouth and would keep him quiet awhile. Clinched it at the base of his skull, crossed it over his eyes and tied it hard at the back of his head. Shunar groaned.

Marcus caught one hairy arm and heaved Shunar onto his face. Securely he lashed his hands together. Shunar would wear rope burns on his wrists all the way to Rendezvous.

Marcus straightened and tried breathing once more. Clean air washed into him. The sweat and grease of the Frenchman, the rotten smell of his own boots were gone. Grinning, he stepped over Shunar to build up his fire. Why waste such a wonderful night on sleep?

Soon Parker's head emerged from the tent. "The one able to sit up would be you, I presume, Doctor Whitman."

Parker's fire-shadow loomed grotesque against the tent's dark cone. "Us boys are playing blindman's buff," Marcus said. "You'd better get your sleep."

Parker nodded toward the now writhing, swearing mass at his feet. "You've saved me from a long, long sleep, I see."

"Maybe."

(26)

Emphatically Parker's head moved up and down and he ducked back inside. Marcus wanted no further thanks.

When, at last, Shunar got to his uncertain feet and went feeling his way across camp, Marcus noticed that the sun was beginning to fade the sky like a linsey shirt left out too long. A coyote yelped twice and another answered. A field mouse advanced to the edge of the firelight. But, seeing Marcus, he hoisted his sharp tail in the air and pattered fine gravel on Marcus' boot sole with the rush of his departure.

Marcus laid his head back on his neck and laughed aloud. He guessed he had the whole world scared of him. And he was the fellow who was going to show the Indians how to live in civilized peace with God and their neighbors.

Before the rest of the camp had stirred up its fires, Gunther sidled up to Marcus and strung Narcissa's gray shawl from the pocket of his buckskin tunic. "It waar hours," he reported with an admiring sock on Marcus' shoulder, "afore anybody quit laughin' long enough to ontie old Shunar."

Marcus uncramped his legs and stood up. Following the way Narcissa had creased it, he folded the shawl.

Gunther eyed it with a grin. "Might nigh as good as a two-shoot gun," he said. "I doubt that you'll be needin' me from hyar on." And he moved toward the river.

Marcus felt good. He poked down his fire and went in to waken Parker, to get his frying pan and ham for breakfast.

But outside again, the feel of the camp bore down upon him all wrong. The sky hung low. The sounds of breaking camp to move on—the slap of thrown-down tent poles, the stamping, rearing objections of horses to their saddles, the swearing of teamsters—these came slowed and muted. All wrong.

CHAPTER

5

EYES frightened, manner guarded, a young company man ran up to Marcus. "Doctor?"

Marcus nodded.

"Doc, the captain wants you to come with me. He don't want it known."

A trap! Or else Fontenelle was taking a hand in the job Shunar had failed to finish.

Marcus considered for one moment only. The boy hadn't asked for Parker. Perhaps the plot had been changed. Do away with Marcus only—the one who'd made a laughingstock of big Shunar. They might even take "Old Parson Parker" on through since he'd not been a party to the night before. Parker would make them a rib-splitting scapegoat, they might figure.

Marcus set his frying pan on the ground inside the tent. "Let's go," he told the boy.

They shifted around the west edge of the encampment, passed the horse guard, and entered a tent pitched on the very bank of the river. A pair of candles did little to light the blackness. A sickbed stench hit Marcus' nose. If this were a trap, its filth seemed more to be dreaded than its spring.

Looking to find the mouth of a pistol sighted on him, Marcus bored his eyes into the heaped-up trappings and trade goods cramming the eaves of the tent. Then, as he could make out faces, Fontenelle stood before him.

Marcus forgot his suspicions. He asked, "What is it?"

Fontenelle turned and pointed. On the ground behind him, a teamster writhed and pulled his knees to his chest. Fontenelle said, "Doc Whitman, see what you make of him."

Marcus squatted. "Hold that candle over," he ordered.

The wagging tongue of light washed the blue of the poor fellow's face and turned it green. A young man, Marcus knew, but not by his appearance now. His skin wrinkled around pinched features. His eyes lay deep in withered sockets. He groaned and clamped his arms across his stomach, drew up his legs. "Water," he begged.

His ridged forehead felt cold. His pulse was too weak to exert any pressure on the vein. Marcus twisted around to Fontenelle. "How long?"

"Sometime in the night. I knew a half hour ago. No more."

"Urine?"

Fontenelle shook his head. "None."

On his heels, Marcus waited. It wouldn't be long. Soon the doomed man's wretchings would slow and lose their violence. Marcus waited and, helpless, watched it happen. Now the purple fingers ceased to grope. The forehead changed from cold to warm. And Marcus arranged the teamster's hand on his red-and-black checked chest. Straightening, he said to Fontenelle, "Cholera."

Fontenelle stiffened.

A heaviness bore down on Marcus. He grieved for the man at his feet. And for the others who must inevitably, also, die within the next few days. But his shoulders lifted. Here was his chance to prove to himself, to prove before God, his fitness for the West. The caravan might be wiped out here on the festering bank of the Missouri, but not without a fight.

With a jerk of his head, he motioned Fontenelle outside.

The captain's voice came too small. "What'll we do?"

"Send for a half-dozen men who'll take orders," Marcus answered. "Gunther for one. Line up the others for questioning. First we'll move camp. High on the bluff. Keep everybody out of the saloons and back from the river. Set a big tent for patients out yonder to the west, beyond that cut, away from the others. And hurry. Get me six men. I'll do the rest."

Fontenelle rounded up the men. Marcus gave orders, moved along the protesting line of men, asking questions, keeping records.

"Had any diarrhea?"

He heard his question translated into one syllable and hawked ahead of him down the line. But he pulled out three first-stage cases, stayed with them through the day, gave orders through the tent flap to his aides. He administered salt when his patients begged for water, filled them with quinine when they became exhausted from vomiting, poured down them anticholera mixture.

One man died just as rain began to splatter on the hide tent at noon the next day. Marcus gave Gunther minute directions for deep burial, for burning his clothes, for burying even the fellow's pistol and knife. "And get Mr. Parker for the funeral," he added, "but make him keep away from the body."

Shunar was carried in at dusk. More cases developed. Marcus got Gunther to set up another sick tent. And then, in the middle of the night, the boy who had come for the doctor at dawn the day before, came again. The horror in his eyes led Marcus away from his patients for the first time and to Fontenelle's tent.

Fontenelle!

They dared not lose their captain. Without him the whole camp would be demoralized, would run amuck and scatter, carrying this scourge far and wide. Without Fontenelle, the caravan had no earthly chance of getting through to Rendezvous.

"Bring him to sick tent," Marcus ordered and stopped for one precious moment on his way back to raise his eyes to the stars and pray.

Fontenelle must not die.

Days and nights now came to Marcus as matched links in an iron chain. Sleep he took in quarter-hour snatches. Gunther brought, now and then, meat crusty-brown and smelling of a campfire. Each time, Marcus thought he was hungry. But, in his hand, the meat took on the odor of the three tents in which he tended his patients. He drank coffee from a tin cup as strong as a cob pipe, gagged down enough food to keep going. He made the rounds of sick tents—emptying buckets, holding clammy foreheads, doling out salt, anticholera mixture, quinine, and prayer. Any moments of rest, he took on a three-legged stool at Fontenelle's side.

Fontenelle must not die. But he was not responding.

Marcus watched the captain's skin, cold to the touch, dry and wither in one day. Saw his eyes become the black holes in a bleaching skull. Heard the voice that had shouted, "Let 'em roll!" weaken to a croupy, pleading, "Water."

Desperate, Marcus remixed his treatment. Now to one part cleaning up and medication he stirred in nine parts prayer. An epidemic must not sweep the caravan. Disorder must not become an epidemic.

One sign alone gave Marcus hope. The captain had not died the first day. Nor the second. Nor the third, although another patient did. If Fontenelle could only hold on a little longer . . .

Carrying out orders to the letter, Gunther buried the dead especially deep to avoid wolves digging them up and spreading the disease. He burned clothes and belongings and could not be bribed out of beaver traps, pistols, long rifles, bowie knives, or the keepsake odds and ends that mountain men called "possibles."

Marcus saw to disposal of his patients' body wastes himself, carrying them to a shaly cave-in away from the river. Gunther kept a man on guard at this pit whose duty it was to herd all others back. Before the caravan left—if it left—they'd dump all refuse from the camp into this hole and set it on fire.

Returning from the pit at dawn, the eighth day of the siege, Marcus found Fontenelle too weak to ask for water. His mouth fell open and his tongue, swollen and white, moved from side to side. His arm rolled toward Marcus like a log loosened on a hillside.

Praying, Marcus felt for the captain's pulse. His finger tips sank into an unmoving furrow between the bones. Reaching for quinine, he thought, "Stock's running low. But soon it won't make any difference."

He knocked a generous dose of the white crystals into a spoon and sifted it onto Fontenelle's tongue. Then, lifting him as a mother would a child, he poured in a little coffee from his own tin cup. Gently he laid the captain back onto his blankets. "Must remember not to use that cup again," he said and sat on his stool to wait.

Time to dose the other tents. Marcus gathered up his bottles but stopped to try, once more, to find the captain's pulse. The next few minutes would decide it. Decide about the captain's death and about the lives of others in the caravan. About all the lives these others might or might not shape, depending on Fontenelle.

The mountain men who'd wait at Rendezvous for the caravan to come buy their furs. A winter's work tossed away and another winter before them with no powder and balls, no coffee, and no traps. Or the Indians in Oregon who would or wouldn't hear of medicine and Christianity, depending on whether he and Parker got across the mountains.

Marcus shook his head above Fontenelle. One man's life, with so many other lives bet on it. And the doctor had done all he could. He hurried on his rounds.

He dreaded returning to examine Fontenelle. Shunar was going to recover, from the look of things now. Why should Shunar live and Fontenelle die? What purpose, except that of the devil's, could be manifested by such a lottery?

Fontenelle lay sprawled on his blankets, one leg off the side in a grotesque twist that made Marcus gasp. He had seen many cases of cholera but he never got accustomed to the strange muscular adjustments that occurred after death. Squatting, he laid his hand on Fontenelle's forehead and pulled back with a start. Then, breathing a deep stubborn breath, he felt again. The skin was warm to his touch now. The rise in body temperature after death by cholera was another thing that never ceased to surprise him. But, as he felt the second time, Fontenelle's skin lay warm but not, actually, too warm under his hand.

He caught up the wrist that lolled toward him and felt for a pulse. None. Then, a faint quiver. Or was he wanting it too hard? His finger tips dug into the furrow. Yes, a weak pulse.

At dawn Fontenelle wakened from a night-long sleep and asked for food. Not out of danger, Marcus knew, still— He'd seen cases appear completely cured and then had them relapse and die within an hour. But, with care, the captain had a chance.

Three days and no new cases developed. Marcus began to hope. Men of the caravan swore they'd rather have the disease than go on being shut out of the saloons. But, underneath their bluster, Marcus heard a note of relief. They'd all been thoroughly frightened. And now, whenever any of them saw Marcus within hailing distance, they'd call out. Complaint or greeting, it was always man to man.

When Marcus finally pronounced Fontenelle out of danger and released his other patients to return to the main camp, a gun-banging, stunt-riding celebration broke loose. And just as Marcus had been included in the teamsters' and mountain men's opposition to the pious "Old Parson Parker" so now, Mr. Parker was included in their new respect for Marcus. The two caravan passengers had paid their way.

CHAPTER

6

WHEN, the last week in June, the caravan could travel again, Marcus still rode in the dust at the rear of the line but only from choice. Mr. Parker rode up front and often changed, as a rest from his saddle, to the springless driver's seat of a Conestoga. They were both welcome company now. Their own men. They could do as they pleased.

It pleased Marcus to jog along on old Sulphur far enough back for the dust to rise like a veil between him and the caravan. Sometimes he could almost see Narcissa beside the driver of the end wagon. Yes, next time, he must bring a wagon.

Days of riding trail, crossing rivers, stopping, all reminded him of Narcissa. Next time, he'd need a wagon bed to plaster with skins so Narcissa could ride in a boat across the Elkhorn. Next time, Narcissa would charm the Pawnees with her songs. Next time, she'd ford the Platte, erect on her horse, without a wetting. And at Fort Laramie, perhaps Narcissa could sleep a night or two in an honest-to-goodness room. He even went so far as to mention that possibility to Fontenelle.

Since Fort Laramie needed a factor and since Fontenelle—even in the five weeks since Bellevue—had grown none too strong for travel, he had decided to stop and take the job.

"So you're countin' on bringin' a woman out next time!" Fontenelle's bellow gathered in an audience from the bar to add to the sport. "By gor, Doc, seems you're dead set on civilizin' the fur caravan."

"With you settling down, next year's caravan might not be so much in need of civilizing," Marcus bantered. "Just thought I'd mention the room now and give you time to wash your sheets."

"Sheets! By gor, if you're aimin' to bring a woman here, I'm goin' to put window glass in the walls and sell tickets."

"Good idea," Marcus agreed. "I figure I'll be entitled to about ninety per cent of what you take in."

"You win, Doc."

For himself, Marcus stuck with his tent and the caravan camp on the plain east of the fort. No sleep ever did him as much good as that he got on his bed of bear and buffalo robes with his saddle under his head. No food ever relished so well as the fat hump-ribs of buffalo, their outsides crusty-black from the campfire. No table and white linen would ever suit him as well as eating cross-legged before a fire too lazy to give off heat, with men sprawled about, telling tall tales of the West.

"Think Joe Meek will be at Rendezvous this year?" Marcus asked Gunther their last night at Laramie.

"Sure as shootin'." Gunther speared another slab of ribs from the fire and swore pleasantly when hot fat dripped on his hand. "Couldn't be no Rendezvous 'thout old Joe Meek and old Jim Bridger. Old Gabe! Now thar's the dangedest liar in the mountains though it's a sight that coon's gone over and some say a heap of the tales tumblin' outen his mouth started out true. Old Gabe are the child as trapped hisself into Yaller Stone. Fust one thar, they tell."

"Be good to meet up with Joe Meek again," Marcus said. "He's a man with gumption."

Gunther tore the meat from a rib with his smoky teeth. "Waal, in the West, gumption's the thing. 'Thout it a man goes under afore he kin make out which way his stick floats."

To finish his meal, Marcus sliced a tidbit from the buffalo tongue at the side of the fire, and speared it into his mouth. He looked forward to meeting Jim Bridger and to seeing old Joe Meek again. The two short times he'd talked with Meek in the States had whetted his appetite for more. He was a man to take for friend. Grinning at this, Marcus went to bed. Nobody in his right mind would deliberately pick Joe Meek for an enemy.

When the caravan sighted the smokes of Rendezvous like banners staking out the bend in Green River, talk and laughter broke out along the line. Men forgot the heat of mid-August and their month-old dry. When they could make out lodges pointing toward the noonday sun, they spurred their horses to a gallop. Rifles barked into the air and men shouted to split their throats.

Marcus laid his hundred and eighty pounds on his reins. "Whoa, Sulphur." He yanked off his tired-brimmed hat and let the wind bristle his hair. Then, settling his leather pantaloons into his saddle, he thrust his neck forward and galloped and shouted with the others. For a moment, he wondered whether early arrivals at Rendezvous might take this greeting for attack and start returning fire. But soon a whirlwind of horsemen thundered out to meet the caravan and these, too, banged their guns into the air. A wild introduction to Rendezvous, an appropriate one.

Rendezvous was wild. It was noisy. A concentrated social season and going-to-market. Trappers who had spent the year in small bands, cut off from all contacts, deprived of heathen squaws and civilized liquor, renewed old friendships in a hurry.

Marcus had just looped off his horse when he felt a slap on the back like a kick from a mule. "Doc, you old hoss! Knowed you'd make it. Wagh! Have a drink."

He whipped around. "Joe Meek!" The man seemed taller in the West than he had in the East. A handsome devil in his buckskin pantaloons and tunic and soft leather moccasins. His face was the color of molasses gingerbread, his eyes laughing black raisins.

"Doc, so you seed the light and are givin' up that fofarraw doctorin' to trap. Knowed in my bones the fust time I seed you, you were a mountain man."

Marcus let go and laughed. Suddenly it felt wonderful to laugh.

"Hush up that thar bellerin', Doc. You'll tickle the hindsights offen the pistol in your belt. Let's find Jim Bridger right off. He'll want you in his band. This old beaver'll tell him he wants you."

"Not so fast, Meek. I'm here to doctor."

Joe Meek's face sobered, all but his eyes. He poked Marcus with his thumb. "Doc, you must be full of guts in thar. Else you're for-gittin' what this child told you 'bout them Injun *te-wats* gittin' their-selves sent under fast as their patients git put outen the way. It's a rule strict as hell."

"Remember every word," Marcus said. "But I'm sick of doing jobs any midwife can handle."

(35)

"Guts," Joe Meek muttered. "Let's save 'em." He turned and hauled Marcus through the mob. They pulled up before a pair of gray eyes. "Bridger, hyar's the young medic I told you 'bout meetin' up with in the States. Winter afore last, it were. Make a straight-shootin' trapper. You'd not go wrong to put him in your brigade."

Bridger's grip was a bear trap. "Doc, this yere Joe Meek says yer some now. And ef yer all this yere old coon claims, ye got a job. Dang blasted Blackfoot sunk a arrow in me nigh three y'ar back. Doggone thing keeps workin' me. Allays figgered ef I ever met up with a real good doc, I'd get him to go in thar after the cussed thing."

Joe Meek elbowed Marcus back. "Cain't be done, Bridger. He aren't doctorin' no more. After three year, that Blackfoot souvenir of yours aren't goin' to come out easy and you know which way the stick floats. Anythin' happen to you and the doc are goin' to have Injuns and trappers both layin' for him. His life'd be worth 'bout one buffler chip."

"Sure I'll operate, Bridger," Marcus assured the trapper. "Anytime you say."

"Sculp my old head ef 'twouldn't be easy 'thout that durned iron in thar. 'Course, Joe Meek's right. They are some danger should anythin' slip."

"Nothin's slippin'. He aren't slicin' into you and you can go your pile on it. If you don't want him for trappin', I know a old hoss as'll use him scoutin'. Come 'long over hyar, Doc." Joe Meek tilted his head toward the river.

When Joe latched onto his arm, Marcus wagged his head to let Bridger know he'd see him later and went along.

But before they reached their target, Meek stopped. "See that big devil?" He fired a black look toward Shunar's back. "Meanest cussed Frenchman in the West. Nary a old hoss as knows him'll ride ahead of him. Shunar, by name, and it's best to spit after you say it." He took his own advice.

"I know," Marcus answered. "Came out with us. A kind of enemy of mine, too, Shunar is."

Meek asked, "And you're still hyar to tell it?"

"Let Shunar tell you sometime."

Joe Meek shook his head. "Doc, you're a puzzler, and that's a fact." He made directly for a buckskin figure, smaller than most, who stood slack on the bank of the river, gazing toward the cluster of Indian lodges on the other side. When they came up, Meek socked the fellow's shoulder with the heel of his hand.

"Hyar, you old beaver! Meet up with a born mountain man and a medic. This hyar's Doc Whitman come out to stay." He turned to Marcus. "And this old coon's Kit Carson. Aren't a man in the West as can shine with Carson, hyar, when it comes to Injun sign and raisin' hair. Wagh!"

Kit Carson extended his hand and Marcus looked into a pair of eyes as sharp as blue steel tacks. The man was whetted down, his features neatly chiseled as a girl's. Yet everything about him suggested strength. Everything except his voice. His voice came soft and slow. "Pleased to meet you, Doc."

Marcus thought, "That voice could disarm a man, while this nice freckle-faced youngster drew a bead on him." He said, "Good to know you, Carson."

"Kit, to a friend of Joe Meek's," Carson drawled. Then as he looked beyond Marcus, his eyes closed down to a blade edge. His back stiffened.

Following his gaze up the river, Marcus saw Shunar. The big Frenchman now had by the arm a shapely dark-haired girl dressed in calico.

Kit said, "See you later, Doc. Excuse me, please."

Joe Meek nodded. "That's how it are. And last year the same. Seems Shunar just always are wantin' Kit's gal. Only this time, Kit are gone beaver over that punkin."

"But is Carson big enough to handle Shunar?" Marcus had some notion of following to help.

"No, he sure aren't big enough." Joe Meek stood his ground. "But he are man enough and that's a fact. Thar's a difference, Doc."

Together they turned back toward the color, the laughter, the push of whites and Indians that made up Rendezvous.

Marcus could not resist the excitement in the air. Trade that first day seemed to be all in liquor. The mountain men's pleasure seemed all to be in squaws. A bawdy riotous gathering. But, to Marcus, the many tribes of Indians blanketed in scarlet and dirty white were a warming surprise. He hadn't expected to find western Indians in any number until he and Mr. Parker had crossed the mountains. But here they were. Hundreds of lodges, thousands of Indians.

High on the shaly plain that circled back from the river, Marcus spotted Parker surrounded by a crowd.

Before he asked, Joe Meek answered. "Injuns are linin' up for a handshakin'. You'll be wanted, Doc."

Pushing into the circle to join Parker, Marcus heard whispered from mouth to mouth, "White *te-wat*." Then, each syllable accented but all one word, "Man-close-to-God." And, as he and Mr. Parker moved along the line, clearly arranged by a protocol of age and influence from first chiefs down to suckling babes, he heard over and over, "Black-robes."

Shaking hands, Marcus examined faces and blanketed bodies. He saw muscular men and women, for the most part, but they were crusted and scaly with dirt. Their hair hung in grease-caked, ragged tendrils around their brawny shoulders. Their faces, neither friendly nor hostile, were curious only. To learn anything more about these Indians they had come to study, they'd have to wait for an interpreter to sober up. In the meantime, they could shake hands.

That evening Joe Meek and Jim Bridger sat by Marcus' campfire while Marcus and Parker asked them a hundred questions. The big tribe off to the right across the river. Who were they?

"Shoshone," Jim Bridger answered, "and doggone fine Injuns. Must be two thousand on 'em hyar this y'ar." He took his red clay pipe from the beaded case that hung on a thong around his neck. "Been thinkin' some 'bout a Shoshone squaw."

Marcus felt Mr. Parker's horrified eyes on the back of his neck.

Jim tamped tobacco into his pipe and pulled a lighting stick from the fire. "Either Shoshone or Nez Percé. Nez Percé squaws raise a doggone tight tent and don't whine none."

"Nez Percé squaws are some now," Joe Meek agreed. "Got your hindsights laid on one in perticlar?"

Marcus flicked a silencing glance toward Parker. He wanted to hear this.

Jim leaned back and blew a cloud of smoke toward the sky. "Thinkin' some 'bout Big Star, granddaughter of old Chief Twisted Hair."

Marcus saw Joe Meek's eyes widen. "Big Star's some now, that is a fact. The biggest kind of punkin. But warn't that her this child seed with that Cayuse second chief name of Feathercap?" His head worried from side to side. "You aren't hankerin' for no run-in with that cussed Cayuse, Gabe, and that's a fact."

Jim knocked out his pipe on his moccasin. "Ner this yere child aren't aimin' to let no cussed Injun shine whar a mountain man cain't." He tightened his crossed feet to his rump and pushed himself up in one long piece. "Waal, mought amble down to gratify my dry and set a game," he said and wandered off toward the river.

Frowning after him, Joe Meek heaved himself up, too. "Old Gabe aren't hisself," he moaned. "He aren't knowin' whether his rifle's got hindsights or not. Likely it are that thar squaw that are ailin' him and, sure as shootin' thar'll be fightin' to clawin' with that cussed Injun."

"Meek, you think we could get a council with the chiefs of these Indians?" Marcus asked. "Want to find out what they'd do to help me set up a home and learn their language—build up a civilized settlement among them."

Before Joe Meek could answer, Jim Bridger wheeled and came back. "Doc, could ye go in thar after that arrow 'bout nigh noon tomorrow?"

"Sure. Glad to."

"Maybeso I mought get ahead with my tradin' meantime, then," he said.

"Sot as a mule." Joe Meek's shrug gave up bucking the operation. "Tell you one thing, Doc, and you can go your pile on it. Aren't no chiefs goin' to set in no talk with you ever, if anythin' slips."

The two mountain men paddled off together.

Marcus turned to Parker. "Think I'll walk down to the river. Like to go along?"

Mr. Parker got his coat. "About those men," he began. "Are you going to keep quiet while they take Indian squaws? And about the drinking going on around here! Somebody's got to speak out. These evils must be stopped."

They circled to the left to avoid the trader's tents, each with its pushing crowd of customers.

Marcus asked, "Just who's to stop what goes on?"

"The government ought to stop it."

"But the government has no real authority," Marcus pointed out.

"And authority or not, it's got no men here to enforce any regulations."

Parker stopped in his tracks and looked out over the carousing, fly-by-night town. Finally he said, "Then I'll at least do what I can to stop it. I will not sanction wickedness by keeping quiet."

"You're right in one way, Mr. Parker," Marcus said. They walked on toward the river. "But in another way, we're going to have to deal with these traders and with the mountain men, too. The way I see it, we can roil them now and never get beyond here. Or, we can keep our eyes open and our mouths shut now. Then do what we can to buck these evils after we're settled and working among the Indians in Oregon Country."

Parker protested, his voice droning on, but Marcus heard countless Indian dogs yapping at good-natured games of tag. He heard the blended sounds of courting laughter, of barter, of "Down in the Valley" passed from one campfire to another, of lazy haggling over games. Blended, these sounds did not add up to evil and degradation. They had a rhythm, gay and sure-footed. They were their own excuse for being.

"Are you ready to turn in?" Parker asked. "It's getting dark and we have a busy day ahead of us. I've engaged an interpreter."

Starting back to their tent, they came upon a game of euchre. In the circle sat several familiar figures. Marcus spoke to Carson and Bridger, nodded toward Shunar, touched Joe Meek's pantaloons with the toe of his boot, and would have passed on. But not Mr. Parker.

The men drank liquor from half-pint tin cups and swore long and loud at a bad run of cards. They played using the dusty ground for a table. And Mr. Parker stopped with his heel on a nine-spot, reproach in the very way he sank his boot into the card.

"What a scene of degradation!"

Shunar, first on the left in the circle, bared sooty teeth to emit an oath.

Mr. Parker pointed. "You ought to be ashamed."

Marcus stepped up and took Parker's arm. They could still go on, but only if they went at once. Shunar, he knew, would not take that tone of voice without striking back.

But Parker's ire was up. He shook off Marcus and stood his ground.

Several loud guffaws popped like corks from the throats of the gamblers.

Attention, even the attention of ridicule, was all that Parker needed. "Men, I plead with you. Throw away your cups and cards. This is the road to eternal damnation."

Marcus waited. Too late now to stop Mr. Parker.

"Hear me, all of you. These cups and cards are dragging you straight to perdition."

Someone sneered, "Sounds like old Bill Williams come back. This'n will get over it, too."

Drunk, Shunar managed to get to his feet. "*Oui.* Good idea," he said, his tongue thick. He'd been sitting next to Jim Bridger who now fumbled for his pipe and paid the Frenchman no mind. Shunar kicked over Jim's cup. "Preacher got idee," Shunar blabbed. "Trow away ze cup-and-card. Get squaw. Damnation!" He stomped through the campfire and toward his horse. "Damnation!" he repeated. "Eternal damnation!"

Marcus watched him make three attempts to mount and assumed that he'd give up and wander away. Parker, no doubt, figured the same and took up his lecture at the point where he'd been interrupted.

But Shunar succeeded in getting into his saddle. His horse, stabbed by Shunar's spurs, leaped into the air and came down not more than ten feet from Mr. Parker. The horse bellowed in pain as the bit tore his mouth. Shunar's fist beat the air. "Damnation preacher! Scalp dees old head if any damnation squaw preacher's goin' to dry up dees spree like at Bellevue." He leaned down and jabbed his fist at Parker's face. "Might as well heem go under. *Oui.*"

Marcus jerked Parker back as Joe Meek struck Shunar's horse on the flank with a rope of tobacco. The horse side-stepped Marcus and plunged away before Shunar could control him.

The men in the circle laughed and picked up their cards. Then Shunar was back in a swaggering rage. "*Enfant de garce!* I'm de beeg buck of dees lick, *moi!* By gar, I can lick any Frenchman or *sacres* American or Spaniard or Injun in camp, onct I rub out dees eternal damnation preacher." And he drove his horse straight for Parker.

Marcus stepped in fast and caught the horse's bridle. The leather sliced into his hand. Tendons pulled with stabbing pain in his shoulder. He scrambled for footing as the horse jerked him backward. His feet scraped and left the ground. He dangled. He tried again to find footing. Shunar's fist struck at his face. Then the horse found Marcus' weight too much to carry on his neck. He slowed and stopped.

"Come down off that horse," Marcus told Shunar. "I've taken all I'll stand from you."

"No, you don't." Joe Meek's voice came slow. "Git out of hyar, Shunar, and keep your filthy mouth shut." Joe turned on Marcus and elbowed him back while he kept one eye on Shunar. "You git out, too, Doc. You gotta be in one piece tomorrow so's you can go in after Old Gabe's arrow."

Marcus' saved-up anger overflowed. "I'm sick of this bully. He's hounded me all the way from Liberty."

Kit Carson said, "Excuse me, please," slid from the circle, and mounted his buffalo horse. "What's that you say about fightin' any American?" he called, his voice soft as gunpowder. "Hyar's an American, Shunar. I'll rip your guts out! Savvy?"

By this time Shunar's fury had stiffened his spine. He snapped back his head and yelled, "Owgh! Owgh! Owgh-h-h-h!"

Carson rode in a circle like a cock before closing in for a fight. Then he whirled and drove his horse toward Shunar.

Blood shone on the flank of the Frenchman's mount as he lunged forward. "Owgh! Owgh-h-h-h!"

Two pistols barked. Shunar rose high in his saddle, twisted, and fell with a howl to the ground. But he was not dead.

Carson dropped to his feet. Shunar, dragging his mangled gun arm, got to his knees. Taking his time, Kit pulled from his saddlebag another pistol.

Shunar's one good arm shielded his face. The flesh of his other arm, all mixed with shredded hide and beads from his tunic, dangled from the bone.

Marcus' throat burned. He stepped in but Joe Meek blocked his way. "Don't, Kit," Marcus called out. "You've taught him a lesson. That's enough. Let me take a look at that arm."

Kit had time, as usual. "Every man to his own fight," he said as if he were reading poetry in a parlor.

Mr. Parker's arm came out of the dark and into the campfire's glow. "Mr. Carson, thou shalt not kill."

At this, Shunar yanked his bowie from his belt. "Shut up, you damnation devil. *Vous savez?* Vamos! Dees beaver's not a goin' to listen to dat old damnation skonk preacher."

As Marcus cried, "No!" and made a grab for Shunar's knife, Carson took two long steps backward, swung his pistol up from his thigh, and fired.

Shunar's head lifted. His good arm wavered . . . relaxed. Then, like a tired man going to bed, he lurched to the right, heaved once, and went over.

Kit Carson had kept his eyes coolly on Shunar's. Now, he stooped and gave the smoking mouth of his pistol two swipes on the bulge of the Frenchman's pantaloons and eased it into his belt. Without a word, he sat back in his place and picked up his cards.

"Your play, Bridger," someone said.

"Devil of a hand this coon's got," Bridger answered.

Someone filled the cups from an earthen jug.

Marcus stood and watched. Parker hurried away. No one commented on what had happened. No one glanced toward Shunar's body.

"Set in, Doc?"

Marcus opened his mouth. But something had happened to his vocal cords. He shook his head.

The game went on.

After a while Joe Meek stood up and gave Jim Bridger a friendly kick. "Time you were beddin', you old beaver. So's you won't whine like a squaw while the doc's cuttin' on you tomorrow."

Jim tossed in his cards. He drained his cup and hung it on his belt. The circle broke up.

Wanting time to digest this day, Marcus wandered down to the river. He needed to set himself straight, needed to rethink his stand against Parker. Right or wrong, Shunar's death surely bolstered the case for keeping quiet awhile.

At the soft slip of moccasins behind him, Marcus started.

Kit Carson, pipe sagging in his mouth, dropped down at his side on the river bank. For a long minute and then another, he said nothing.

Marcus wondered whether Kit's conscience might be working him and he'd come to talk it out.

But when he finally spoke, Kit's was the voice of a man at peace with himself and his God. It was Marcus he was worried about.

"Doc, I been thinkin'. You sartin sure you can cut that arrow out of Old Gabe and him not go under?"

Marcus sighed instead of laughing. These men! You never knew what to expect. But Kit sounded so sober he'd want a sober answer. "Bad business, letting a foreign body stay as long as three years," he said. "Might have nosed in quite a way."

Carson fretted, "I been thinkin' the same."

Marcus went on. "I can try, that's all. A doctor can't always promise in advance."

"That's why I'm comin' out with it, Doc. You're a man with guts and I'm for you. But I'm tellin' you," Kit's voice softened to strike harder, "you better be a heap sure afore you cut into Bridger. That band of his sets store a-plenty by old Jim Bridger. They'd get riled up 'bout like Sioux Injuns if anything was to go askew with their captain. And Gabe's a friend of lots of tribes, to boot. Best to leave him be, if you aren't sartin. Savvy?"

Marcus protested. "But he asked me himself and I promised. Of course I'll perform the operation."

Kit remembered his pipe and gave it a pull. "Doc, you're new to these parts. I'm wonderin' did you ever see a white man that's been set upon by Injuns." He paused but not long enough for Marcus to answer. "Ears hacked off. Scalp peeled and oozin'. Arm meat jerked out by the roots and et. Fingers hangin', some gone. His groin beat to mush with stones—the squaws do that afore they'll let their menfolk rub him out. And other dealin' as might turn your belly if I was to tell you." Kit stood up. "Well, I reckon you savvy. Long sight best to leave him be, seein' you're not sartin sure. Come 'long over to 'Rapaho camp and get in the soup dance."

"Looks like I'm in soup enough," Marcus answered. "See you tomorrow. I'll need you to help build up an operating table, if you're not too busy."

CHAPTER

7

"OLD GABE never laid on such a fofarraw bed in all his days."
Joe Meek piled more beaver skins on the table concocted from
liquor kegs and lodge poles. They'd set up for Jim Bridger's surgery
under a wide-spreading cottonwood, near the river but—wanting
some privacy—off a way from the Rendezvous camp. "By gor, Jim
won't never want to get up, unless to see what kind of trade he can
make with these hyar beaver plews. Best to kiver up my plews
afore Gabe gits hyar, this coon's thinkin'. Toss me that thar white
blanket, Doc."

"You call this white?" Marcus got the blanket from a crotch in
the cottonwood. "I've seen whiter pigsties."

"Aw, Doc, this are a right civilized blanket for the West."
Meek gave it a flick and spread it out to finish off their operating
table. "You're prehaps thinkin' of blankets for a fofarraw white
gal, Doc."

"Prehaps," Marcus agreed. He turned back the purple velvet flaps
of his instrument roll and slipped his largest scalpel from its leather
loop.

"What'll you use to get in thar with, Doc?" Kit Carson pulled another scalpel from the roll and tested its edge on his thumb. "Your
grapplin' irons look to be some poor doin's."

Carson was right, in a way. All the tools that Marcus had with
him were small. "I could use my set of amputating knives," he said,
"but they're back in the States." The three-inch blade of his longest

scalpel did look a mite delicate. Still— "I reckon this will have to do the trick."

"Better use your bowie."

Marcus grinned. "Might have to use them all before I'm through." He unwrapped his whetstone.

"You're sartin sure you want to try it, Doc?" Carson asked once more.

A rumble came from a slate-blue wall that backed Rendezvous to the west.

Marcus turned to Meek. "Where is Bridger, anyway? Should have been here by now. We'd better get this over before that storm breaks."

Joe Meek hitched up his buckskins. "I'll fotch him." He leap-frogged onto his gray mule's back.

"Bridger was swappin' beaver plews for bacca and knives this mornin'," Carson said. "He won't come till he's out of plews."

"He'd better come soon or our table may blow away." Marcus frowned into the sky. The wall of cloud had developed green eddies. "There's wind in that."

"And hail, this beaver's thinkin'."

Marcus circled the longest scalpel on his whetstone. Carson watched in easy silence.

The preparations under the cottonwood had attracted several Indians by now.

"All Injuns got souls the shape of a question," Joe Meek had told Marcus. And he'd learned for himself that two or three in a huddle were bait enough to catch a tribe. Soon Indians in once-white blankets filled the grassy gallery. Then teamsters and traders joined the crowd. Still, the doctor had no patient. Someone started a game of "seven-up." Carson sat in. A mountain man hurried toward the river, his arm around the waist of a giggling Indian girl.

Marcus stooped to his saddlebag under the table and pulled out a white shirt. He felt for another but this seemed to be the last one. Well, no matter. The women of his church had said, "Here are six shirts to help you on your trip." And they had helped. The others he'd traded for his buckskin pantaloons and his moccasins. And now he needed swabs for operating. Tearing the cloth into handy strips, he reminded himself to tell the ladies, when he got back, what a help the shirts had been. Not what kind of help, perhaps, but how much.

The cloud that towered above Rendezvous now cracked open like a china plate to show up the fiery hell behind it. Against the green that closed in then, Marcus saw Joe Meek and Bridger, nodding up on their mules.

He studied the sky and, not sure himself, interrupted Carson's game. "What do you think? How long before that storm breaks?"

Kit Carson barely glanced up. Marcus had noticed that these mountain men told weather the same as Indian sign—by feel. "Half-hour, I reckon." Kit went on with his deal.

Bridger dropped off his mule beside the table. He gave Marcus a sheepish grin and peeled up his tunic.

Marcus heard a gasp run through his spectators like a change of wind in a grove of aspen. Then came the faint tinkle of metal bells. Turning to follow the stares fixed beyond him he, too, drew in a quick breath.

Erect on a black and white pony, an Indian girl pulled every eye in her direction. Her antelope skirt and waist-length cape, bleached milk-white, swayed more than was caused by her light-stepping mount. Into the black braids that curved with her breasts, she'd woven porcupine quills dyed vermilion and blue. Thin vermilion lines fanned out on her cheeks. Worked into her pony's halter and the trappings about his chest and loins were feathers and beads and many small brass bells.

Not until she reined in at a vantage point back from the table could Marcus get on with his business. Annoyed with himself for being distracted, he glanced at the broiling cloud and scolded Bridger. "You almost missed this party. Storm's about on us."

"Waal, yere's the way it waar, Doc. This old hoss got to figgerin' thar's no time like the prissint." Jim gave his attention to hitching his belt up a notch as if his talk were just to kill time. "Got my day's tradin' done airly so I rode acrosst river and talked her pappy 'round to tossin' the blanket over Big Star and me."

Joe Meek tittered.

"You mean you married that Nez Percé girl? The one that rode up just now? That beauty?"

"Glad ye like 'er, Doc." Jim answered. "Figgered a purty squaw mought be a comfort to a man after a ugly medic quit slicin' him."

(47)

Twisting his arm behind him, he touched with a grimy thumb a spot below his shoulder blade and to the right. "She's right thar, Doc."

Joe Meek stepped into the crowd and back with a jug. "He'll need somethin' for his dry." But, before handing the jug on to Bridger, he waited for Marcus' nod.

"Got a piece of rawhide in your possibles?" Marcus asked Kit Carson. "Might help for him to bite on."

Kit sliced a finger length from the end of his bootlace and handed it up.

"Thanks."

Jim got onto the table while Joe Meek held it down. Marcus turned Bridger's head to the side and slipped the rawhide into his mouth. Spectators closed in. Thunder cracked near at hand.

Holding aloft a beaded leather bag, an Indian medicine man writhed and danced his way to the head of the table. Smears of vermilion on black masked his face. Around his neck a thong strung with bones and teeth, all black, supported a blackened drum. Black streaked his body and, twisting himself this way and that, he raked long scratches across his chest, up his thighs.

Just behind the *te-wat* in Marcus' vision whenever he raised his eyes from Jim's back, Feathercap stood. His hair, unlike that of all the other Indians at Rendezvous, scraggled off at neck length. And, instead of flapping in greasy locks on his shoulders, Feathercap's hair ruffed out from his face like a war bonnet.

Joe Meek leaned in. "Feathercap's fixin' a spell on you, Doc, with his cussed eyes. It's him brung the *te-wat*. Don't let nothin' slip." Joe slapped Jim Bridger's leather pantaloons. "Thar'll be fightin' to clawin' like I say."

Marcus said, "Out of my way, Meek. It's getting dark."

The thin light still left in the day was green and opaque. Thunder grumbled and rolled without letting up.

Marcus stooped low over Jim Bridger's back, exploring with his finger tips until they felt iron in the flesh. He said, "Bite, man. Here goes," and, avoiding the tough scar tissue where the thing had entered, he made a clean slice in the muscle. Bridger's arms tensed. Marcus deepened the cut and came to the neck where the shaft had pulled off. He mopped out blood with a strip from his shirt. Lightning flashed. The *te-wat* wailed.

The arrowhead lay buried deep. Much deeper than Marcus had

thought from his first look at the shadow beneath the skin. He slipped the scalpel down along the arrow's curved side and felt the end touch bone. If the arrow's point should be hooked in the bone, this would take some doing.

Bridger's back heaved.

Marcus mopped blood. He sliced the scalpel down the other side of the iron. That arrowhead must be at least three inches long. His tweezers and probe were far too delicate for this job. He lengthened the incision and grasped the neck of the arrow with his thumb and finger. He gave it a turn and a pull.

The muscles in Bridger's back corded.

The Indian *te-wat* leaped into the air with a shriek.

Feathercap stalked closer. His eyes gloated and greeded toward Big Star.

Thunder rumbled in Marcus' ears. Mopping blood once more, he could see into the incision. Cartilage had grown around the barbed tip of the arrow. This he'd have to cut, if his scalpel would take the strain. Maybe he should have used his bowie. Slow delicate work. He needed more light.

Joe Meek came around to the end of the table and held Bridger's heels.

Painstakingly, giving it all the pressure the scalpel would bear, Marcus cut away at the cartilage on the upper side. At last, it appeared to be loose. But the other side held. He worked in green darkness now and a spatter of rain nettled the cottonwood leaves. The air filled with the dusty spice of wet sagebrush.

The Indian *te-wat* groveled in the dirt and increased the volume of his incantations.

Marcus took a firm grip on the arrow, slipping his thumb and index finger deep into the gap in the flesh, and pulled. His hand skidded on blood. He pushed in deeper and tried again.

The remaining cartilage broke loose. Marcus held in his gory hand the iron missile.

But before he could enjoy a moment of triumph, the storm broke. He had to clean the incision, apply packing, and bind a rawhide band around Bridger's body in a shower of hailstones and rain. Finished, he turned to Joe Meek.

"Can some of you carry him up to my tent? I'll be able to see after him there and he's got to have care."

Meek answered, "Sure as shootin'."

But Bridger came up on his knees and slid off the table onto his feet. He reeled a bit but his voice came steady. "By gor, no old coon's goin' to fotch this beaver nowhar. What kind a fofarraw doin's do ye think this are?"

The wind had caught up with the storm. The branches of the cottonwood whipped in a fury. The few remaining spectators scurried away. When Marcus remembered Feathercap and the *te-wat,* they were gone, too. He wondered what had happened to Big Star.

"Thar's a shelter tother side a that knoll," Jim told Marcus. "Heap sight better'n a lodge."

They took him there, Jim protesting with every step that they had no call to give him their shoulders since he warn't no bellerin' squaw.

All well soaked before they'd gone the hundred yards, they ducked into the red shale cave.

And Big Star welcomed them. The antelope cape she held in both hands, now, at her back. Her firm young breasts curved high, supporting a spray necklace of blue and yellow beads. Her eyes were the color of a rifle barrel.

Marcus thought of Narcissa.

With Jim settled on a bear robe pallet, Marcus told him, "Well, Gabe, you're more of a man than I knew." The arrowhead covered his palm. "Quite a hunk of iron. Don't see why you didn't die of gangrene years ago."

"Aw Doc, meat don't spoil in the mountains." Bridger reached for his souvenir. He held up the trophy for Big Star to admire. *"Ainees penamina,"* he said and Marcus saw a warm flare light her eyes.

Big Star touched the arrow. She whispered one word.

Without understanding the language, Marcus felt an intruder. He said, "Be glad to stay with you tonight, Gabe. See that everything's all right."

Jim raised up on his elbow. "By gor, Doc, ef ye don't git outen hyar, I'll know sartin sure ye are layin' fer my squaw."

Joe Meek laughed fit to pull the cave down on them.

Marcus asked Jim, "Can you tell her you've got to be kept warm?"

"Maybeso I mought say a few words to her. Previdin' I kin git her to myself a minute."

(50)

"And you're to have meat. Plenty of meat. Tell her that."

Jim flapped his hand in dismissal. "Will ye jest kindly git!"

Marcus caught his wrist and felt his pulse. Slow and firm. Jim would soon sleep.

Marcus followed Joe Meek. They stooped to clear the ledge at the mouth of the cave and straightened into the storm. Marcus felt good. The wind drove cold rain against his face, through his clothes. Yes sir, he felt fine. No midwife could have cut out that arrow.

"I'm afraid you did it all wrong." Mr. Parker sat his saddle, straddling a stream of water that sliced across their tent floor. "Letting those Indians carry on that tomfoolery was a tactical error. If the man lives, they'll say they did it."

Marcus slapped water from the sleeves of his coat. He stepped to the back of the tent and kicked dirt into the gully, diverting the water. "I'll hear that painted fellow's chant till the day I die," he said. "Thank heaven, nothing slipped."

"But already the chiefs have postponed our council from today until tomorrow," Parker reproved. "They say they want to see who has the biggest medicine before they join in talk with us."

"They'll see." Marcus pulled off his coat. "Think I'll bed down awhile then, if there's to be no talk today. Seem to feel like sleeping."

But next morning when he rode old Sulphur down to the cave to examine his patient, a white line bordered Jim's tight-drawn mouth. Talk poured out of him in a scramble. His pulse raced.

Ripping off the rawhide band, Marcus stared in disbelief into what had been a clean incision. Now, like a circle around the moon, an angry ridge of flesh surrounded a black sore.

"By the eternal!" Marcus bent closer. He got a probe from his instrument roll.

Bridger groaned.

Far back in the cave, Big Star cowered. She clutched a scarlet blanket around her.

"If you can talk English, you'd better start talking," Marcus called. "Come out here."

Big Star cringed against the wall.

Grabbing her by the wrist, Marcus pulled her into the light.

(51)

"Listen to me. What happened? What have you done to him?" He pointed to Bridger, tried to put the questions into signs.

Uncomprehending, her eyes told him nothing except that she was frightened.

Marcus let her go and, from the mouth of the cave, fired his pistol into the air. Then he pulled Jim's pallet out where he could see. In the light, he found thrust deep into the wound, a wad of black fur. Horrified, he tweezed it out and cleaned the incision. He soaked a strip of his shirt in spirits of turpentine and made a pad for the wound.

Joe Meek dove in. "What's ailin' you, Doc? That your shot?"

"Needin' help?" Here was Kit Carson.

The two of them—neither one very good at Nez Percé, they admitted—finally got through enough signs to badger the trembling squaw into confessing. Feathercap had come with the *te-wat* in the night. Feathercap had promised, "Make evil spirit go fast." They'd put *te-wat* medicine on Jim Bridger's back.

Dully Marcus listened. He did what he could. And then he could do no more except to sit on the damp ground beside Bridger and wait.

Joe Meek crossed his feet and folded himself down. It was the first time that Marcus had seen his eyes with no laugh in them. "Beaver fur's good for a slice, Doc. But that Feathercap aren't above addin' a pinch of berry poison that *te-wat* might previde him."

Kit Carson gave up trying to question Big Star and came over. "Doc, you'd best cache awhile. This are bad. There just are no accountin' for what Bridger's men and these Injuns'll do, with things in this fix."

Mr. Parker's head poked into the cave. "What's this I hear? There's talk all over camp that Mr. Bridger is dyin'. Is it true?"

Marcus frowned. Surely nobody, outside that cave, knew anything about old Gabe's condition. He turned his frown on Kit Carson.

Kit drawled, "You're new in the West, Whitman. News travels same as wind through the sagebrush. They're talkin' all right."

"But tell me what has happened," Mr. Parker insisted.

Kit Carson answered. "Poison, we're thinkin'."

Joe Meek went into implications. "It are like this, Parson. The doc hyar are a *te-wat*, a medicine man, far as Injuns figger. And *te-wats* aren't dyin' from old age. *Te-wats* aren't gittin' far as this child can spit when one of their patients goes under. It are a rule strict as hell."

Parker's eyes blazed. "Man, do you know what you're saying? Is this true?"

"Sure as shootin' and that's a fact."

Marcus heard all this without feeling it. Let them talk. He had his hands full and would have for the next day or two. Unless Bridger didn't pull through. In that case, it wouldn't be long. He kept his fingers on Jim's pulse, willing it to slow down, praying in time to its thudding against his grip.

Real concern in his touch, Parker pressed Marcus' shoulder. "Doctor Whitman, you must take Mr. Carson's advice. You can get away, if you start before Bridger dies. We can arrange to meet later on, someplace along the trail. Go on, son. There's no time to lose."

Marcus tested Bridger's cheek with the back of his hand. Did he imagine it, or did it feel cooler? No. Too soon to tell.

"Doctor Whitman," Parker cried. "Hurry!"

"I've got plenty of time," Marcus answered. "I'm not hiding out and I'm not leaving right here till I pull old Gabe through, if there's any way. Go get the Indians together for that council about our work among them. Joe Meek or Carson can guard Bridger long enough for me to come meet with the chiefs."

Joe Meek's black eyes snapped. "Doc, just like I been sayin'. You got your hide plumb full of guts. But you got a short measure of gumption. And thar aren't no Injuns in these parts as'll join any talk with you this day. Not afore they sees how this hyar varmint fares from your slicin' him. Injuns is mutterin' ahind their blankets all over this mornin'. A-mutterin' and a-waitin'."

CHAPTER

8

MARCUS sent the others away. This was his job.

But the comfortable rush time of cleaning Jim's incision, changing bandages, checking pulse and temperature soon ran out. Now he could only stay on guard at Bridger's side and wait. Nothing to do but sit here, cross-legged, with the red shale slicing into his pantaloons, the stiff fibers of the rope he was splicing pricking his hands.

He should be out with Parker, collecting information about the Indians. Or with the mountain men, pumping them for intelligence concerning the country to the west.

Could be he'd been wrong to operate on Bridger. Perhaps his job on this trip was exploring with no room for doctoring. Maybe this setback had come to put him in his place.

Still, in spite of other demands of duty, Marcus knew that his place was here. A great man, Jim Bridger. A man to keep alive against all odds. Because of his skill as an explorer and guide, because he was one white man the Indians trusted. But Marcus' best reason for taking extra precautions was that he liked Jim Bridger—his gray eyes, his humor, his straight-line way of thinking. Fear could never make Marcus run away from a patient who might be saved. But, in this case, his personal feeling for old Gabe held him on guard through the noisy morning, through the lazy afternoon, and into the rowdy evening.

Toward nightfall he built a fire near the mouth of the cave.

After the day's trading, feasting, and gambling slumped Joe Meek and Kit Carson rambled in.

"Go git you some food and a mite of fun," Joe Meek ordered. "We'll take over hyar."

Marcus had no appetite for food nor fun. "Think I'm going to leave the first company I've had all day?" he said. "Nap off that stuff you've been drinking and you two might take a couple of turns watching tonight."

Both men were too much at peace with the world to resist.

"Keep an eye skinned for slitherin' varmints then," Kit Carson drawled. "Feathercap's on the prowl. Remember this, Doc, a good Injun's one that's noisy as all hell broke loose."

Marcus squatted on his heels and studied his friends as they bedded down. Blankets and buffalo robes they threw on the ground, spoking out from the fire to their saddle pillows. Kicking off moccasins, they stretched bare feet toward the warmth.

Half asleep as they were, they skipped none of their routine. Kit drew the pistol from his belt and laid it on his saddle. He unsheathed his bowie and stabbed it into the ground. Bedding his long rifle beside him, he folded the blanket over them both. "Big Star been around?" he asked.

Marcus shook his head.

"Thought so," Joe Meek murmured. "Keep an eye skinned, Doc." And he was asleep.

Kit Carson screwed his hips into the shale. "Next watch'll be mine, Doc. Mind you don't hit Lulu Belle's trigger when you kick me awake."

Marcus kept guard and didn't have the heart to wake Kit and Joe for their watches. No need anyway. He meant to keep an eye on Bridger himself. He wouldn't sleep till old Gabe pulled out of danger.

The blanket cocoons by the fire gave birth to legs and heads soon after dawn came over the Wind River Mountains.

And just then they heard a growl in the cave at their backs. "Ye mangy coyotes, tryin' to wet nurse this old beaver! Git on about yer business afore I sic my dogs on ye."

Meek exposed handy artillery as his blanket fell away. "Gabe, you old hoss thief!"

Rushing into the cave, they found Bridger trying out his operation, flexing every muscle in its vicinity. Marcus got him to sit by the fire long enough for a new dressing. But Jim considered this mighty fofarraw. He had to get on with his trading. And his doctor could hardly object since he found no inflammation, almost no swelling, nothing but a healing incision.

Marcus felt fine. He'd won another battle.

Later that day he felt less sure about his victory. Looked more as if he'd started a war.

Old Gabe, strutting about camp, wore his iron arrowhead tied around his neck on a buckskin thong. Men of Bridger's Brigade drained many a tip cup of fotched-in liquor to the health of the trapper and to the honor of Doc Whitman. Nez Percés, Flatheads, and Shoshones reverenced the Blackfoot arrow as "big medicine." None of their te-wats had ever performed such magic with all their dancing and juggling.

Mountain men and Indians besieged the doctor to put them on his table. They begged him to cut out arrowheads, treat running sores, patch up fight wounds. Marcus needed to get on with his observations for the Board. But at the request of "Broken Hand" Fitzpatrick who was in charge of things now, he laid out his surgical kit and medicine bottles under the cottonwood. Word spread for Indians and whites to bring on their ailments. Somehow he'd have to serve Hippocrates and the Board.

As he worked, he asked questions and listened and watched. He drew out tales of exploration from the Spanish trail to the Yellowstone country. He learned to tune his ear to the winds bearing news through the wilderness. He taught himself to stay on guard, without seeming on guard, against Feathercap and his te-wats.

Late on the afternoon that the cottonwood clinic was a full week old, Parker came striding into its grassy reception room. "At last," he said with a sigh, "the first and second chiefs of the Nez Percés and Flatheads and Cayuses have agreed to hold a council. They're preparing a feast and ceremonial demonstration for us Bostons. You'll have to come right away."

Marcus finished splinting a broken arm and beckoned to a Nez Percé girl whose eyes were inflamed.

"Doctor Whitman," Mr. Parker objected. "You'll have to come now. Surely, after I've spent a week getting those chiefs to agree to a council, the least you can do is—"

"Got an interpreter?" Marcus rolled a strip of linen around a cottonwood twig for a swab.

"Right here—as you could see, if you'd take the time to be civil." Marcus stepped over and extended his hand.

"Charles Compo," Parker said. "French-Canadian and perfectly sober."

"Fine." Marcus smiled into a pair of childlike blue eyes.

He got a snaggle-toothed, quarter-moon grin in return. Compo took his offered hand. *"Bon soir,"* he said and shook his head. Then he changed his greeting to, *"Tois tax,"* and finally blurted, "How do?"

Marcus wondered who they'd get to translate Compo's interpretation but he merely sent Parker and Compo back to delay the council until he could get there.

When waning light closed the clinic for the day, Marcus wiped his instruments and fitted pill bottles back into their case. He slung his saddlebags across his arm and walked to Joe Meek's lodge in time to snatch a slab of venison from the rack over the meat-fragrant fire. Joe agreed to ride to the council to help interpret. But Kit Carson hustled down to Arapaho camp, hoping that the spirited Waa-nibe would choose him in the soup dance.

Across the river, Joe and Marcus ducked through the flap of the tallest skin lodge. Parker fumed. "At last, Doctor Whitman. You made it embarrassing to excuse your absence from the feast and the riding exhibition."

"Sorry," Marcus apologized, "but let's get on with the business."

He glanced around the circle. Three elder and six young second chiefs in full council regalia—eagle feathers, paint, and animal claws—stood to shake hands. Then the oldest chief of the Flatheads dropped his blanket to the ground and sat down cross-legged. The other chiefs followed and the white men filled in the circle. The oldest chief reached toward the fire for a taper and lighted the long-stemmed pipe that had rested on his arm. He drew deep and blew out smoke—to the heavens and to the earth. Then he passed the pipe to the next in age and on around the circle's descending order of protocol to the young chiefs.

Joe Meek whispered names as chiefs took the pipe. Hol-lol-sote-tote. Tack-en-su-a-tis. Tiloukaikt. Feathercap and, next, Tamahas of the Cayuse.

Cringing, Marcus watched cankered lips suck on the pipe. But in his turn, Mr. Parker closed his eyes, drew long, and puffed pleasantly.

Marcus, too, smoked and, relieved, passed the pipe on.

"Ask whether they want teachers to come among them to instruct them in the knowledge of God," Parker prompted Compo.

Marcus added, "Ask whether they want white *te-wats* to live near their tribes, to make their sick ones well. What will they do to help teachers and doctors, if they come?"

Compo put the questions into French-accented Nez Percé.

The oldest chief of the Flatheads strained up to his uncertain feet and hugged his red Mackinaw blanket around him. "I am old," he said, according to Compo. "I walk like tired buffalo. I am deaf and sit all day in silence. But my heart is young and runs to meet what I never saw before—man-near-to-God. He must teach my people."

Another elder chief spoke. "I hear man-near-to-God ride to visit my people. I lead my village out three days' journey but not find caravan. War party of Crows come upon us in night. Short battle. Not count coup. But take horses. Take horse I greatly love. But now I forget all since my heart is made glad to see man-near-to-God." He turned to the bronze-cast Tack-en-su-a-tis before he sat down. "Let our young men speak."

Tack-en-su-a-tis' coarse bang covered his forehead, giving him a scowling expression. But he pulled his blanket around his shoulders and clasped his hands, the back of his left hand down in the sign for peace.

Joe Meek commented in an undertone on Compo's official translation. "Nez Percé tribe. Some punkins," he whispered. "Better'n most. Name means Rotten Belly. Maybeso he needs a good doc like you."

"My people clasp hand in peace to Bostons," Tack-en-su-a-tis said. "My people hear from white men some little about God which go only in ears. My people wish know more to go down in heart." He crossed his moccasins and lowered himself to the ground.

Marcus tried to read meanings on the faces in the circle. Most showed neither approval nor opposition but he noted two exceptions. Chief Hol-lol-sote-tote approved. He sat gazing into the council fire with the expression of a benign young Buddha. Not so,

(58)

second chief Feathercap. His slitted eyes were of the devil. His head swayed like the head of a coiled snake. He spat into the fire.

"Feathercap's about to strike," Joe Meek muttered when Tack-en-su-a-tis finished.

But Chief Hol-lol-sote-tote spoke next. "Blood brothers, we have seen brave man-near-to-God," his hand swept toward Parker, "rebuke those who do wrong. We have seen strong white *te-wat* cut big medicine from many who have hurt in flesh. We have seen white *te-wat* make not-sick with medicine-in-the-mouth. Now my heart comes together with Bostons. My people desire them live with us. My people cut lodge poles, soften animal skins, make great feasts for white men. My people raise strong bows to keep them from harm. They come to us now."

Chief Tamahas sprang to his feet. He spoke with such fury that Marcus supposed he meant to put the Bostons in their place. But when Compo could get in a few words he said that Tamahas spoke with pride of the Cayuses' many horses. And then Tilou-kaikt rose tall and square to promise that the Cayuse would outdo all other tribes in welcoming the Black-robes. Compo, hard pressed to translate their outpourings finally gave up, saying, "Zey contest wiz ze beeg promise. Mean not a damn."

Distant thunder rolled an obbligato to Feathercap's words. "Blood brothers make talk like squaws. Brothers forget First Chief Um-tippe's words to keep Cayuse heads tall, Cayuse hearts hot against white-livered Bostons. When Umtippe sick in belly, can't ride Rendezvous, blood brothers forget their chief. Forget spirits of ancestors. Forget Indian *te-wats* drive out evil spirits. *Te-wats* make people strong for hunt. Brave for war to take scalps and horses. Let Bostons keep evil white *te-wat*. Let braves cut out loose tongue of man-called-near-to-God. Let blood brothers act like braves with heads tall—not like squaws!"

Marcus listened to grunts he could not translate, saw the young chiefs turn their ears to Feathercap's hissing. He waited.

Tack-en-su-a-tis got up once more. His words came slow, each one weighted. "Our people beyond the mountains open hearts to teachers, to Boston *te-wat*. Come now to valley where we winter. Come teach my people good hearts before they die. Come work big medicine, make not-sick. Nez Percés treat like brothers."

Tiloukaikt's small eyes flicked Tack-en-su-a-tis. He squared his shoulders under his dirt-caked blanket. "Chiefs of Nez Percé and Flathead brothers not steal Bostons away from Cayuse. Cayuse great people. Cayuse will have man-near-to-God and white *te-wat*. Cayuse not squaws to let blood brothers make them small. Cayuse take these Bostons. Make great dog feast. Cayuse squaws raise tall tipi. Bostons ride fast Cayuse horses."

Feathercap growled deep in his throat. "Umtippe he hear this!" he shouted in English and raised a choking dust in the lodge with his exit.

Marcus leaned over Joe Meek to speak to Parker. "What can we do?"

"You can ride back to the States at once with the returning traders and bring enough helpers to Oregon next spring to go to all these tribes. I'll get on with the exploration."

"But, Mr. Parker, I can't leave you. I'm responsible for your safety."

"Doctor Whitman, we could not safely go on together without divine protection. With it, I can go on alone. Tell the Indians we accept their invitation." Teasing, Parker added, "Here's your chance to bring Miss Narcissa to Indian country at once."

"Tell them we accept," Marcus said to Compo. "I return at once to bring out enough helpers to live among all their tribes and teach them. And say this, next summer a beautiful singing-white-squaw comes, also. She'll make music such as they have never heard."

Marcus loaded a scrawny pack horse early the next morning. He asked Mr. Parker to see that the animal didn't collapse while he splashed Sulphur across to the Nez Percé lodges for a quick good-by. When he returned, two Indian boys on sleek buffalo ponies rode behind him.

"Mr. Parker," Marcus apologized, "the two chiefs who spoke to you—well, they talked me into taking their sons. Want them to see the land of the white men, learn their ways. Then ride back with me next summer. Wouldn't take 'No' for an answer. So, meet Tackitonitis—I'm calling him Richard for short—and John Ais."

"This is a good idea, Doctor. Fact of the matter is, I suggested it," Mr. Parker admitted. "Leave John Ais with my wife in Ithaca. She'll see that he gets good schooling."

"Your idea! You do pull strings, don't you, Parson? But maybe

they'll help us interpret when we get to Oregon. Come on, boys."
He pulled Sulphur's head around to the east. He hoped he wasn't
doing wrong to leave Mr. Parker—one lone man in a savage land
—while he rode back to civilization. If anything should happen,
the whole United States would blame him. And these Indian boys
—John Ais, son of a chief, Richard-Tackitonitis, favorite of his
father. A thousand deaths might overtake them. Repercussions
could stir up a thousand Indian forays.

Still Marcus touched Sulphur's flank with his heel. "Narcissa,
here we come," he whispered and settled into his saddle.

CHAPTER

9

ERECT and uncomfortable in his broadcloth suit and stiff shoes, Marcus' palm polished the arm of the pew. Now and then he turned to smile down at the Nez Percé boy beside him. Richard had changed in these six months since they left Rendezvous on the Green. And not changed, too, Marcus admitted. Richard-Tackitonitis still looked plenty odd, sitting here in the plain little church of Angelica, New York. He was still a Nez Percé even in his American haircut and clothes of woven cloth. But then, as far as that went, Marcus felt out of place himself now that the time for the ceremony had stalked up so close to his heels.

Strange to marry a woman he'd seen for only four short visits. That memorable week end before he went West with Mr. Parker. The two days in the fall as soon as he got back to the States. The snowy night only a week ago when he'd asked her to push forward the date for their wedding since the westbound caravan would leave the frontier early this spring. And this afternoon when Narcissa's father had raised so many questions about the wisdom of his daughter making the five or six months' ride and winding up in a heathen land with "that man Spalding." "That young upstart actually had the gall to come courting Narcissa a while back," her father had finally said, straight out. And he hadn't seemed to like Marcus' answering, "That merely proves he's got good eyes."

The church was filling rapidly now. The back of Marcus' neck, shaved for this occasion, prickled as whispers and pokings ran through the congregation.

"There he is," he heard distinctly and then Narcissa's name in tones that said, "Really? I wonder what she sees in him."

Marcus rubbed his neck and grinned down at Richard who stared back, solemn-eyed, and scratched his wool-encased leg.

"Got to?" Richard had asked when they were dressing for the wedding at the Prentiss house. They'd been assigned the gable bedroom usually shared by Narcissa and her sister, Jane. And suddenly the sight of Richard standing naked, his body copper in the linen-filtered light of that sedate and civilized room, had struck Marcus as side-splitting funny.

"I suppose you want to go to my wedding in a breechcloth," he teased when he could stop laughing.

The boy had actually reached for his scrap of beaded leather.

"You're forgetting this is February in New York State," Marcus reminded him and pointed through the window to fence-high snow drifts. Now, even with a church full of wedding guests looking on, he didn't have the heart to shake his head against Richard's un-bridled scratching. Instead he bent and whispered, "Not much longer." Then, with a quick rush of sympathy, he put the same meaning into the homesick boy's native tongue.

For answer, Richard reached down the back of his coat and scratched his shoulder blade.

The Reverend Mr. Hull announced the first hymn and the Prentiss women filed into the pew across the aisle. Marcus kept his eyes straight ahead. Judge Prentiss stepped to the front of the church and blew a reedy note on his pitchpipe.

"Do, do . . . me." He raised his hands and everyone sang.

The hymn finished, the minister said, "Friends, we are gathered for the holy sacrament that will unite Sister Narcissa Prentiss to the explorer and doctor, Brother Marcus Whitman. Sister Prentiss, Brother Whitman, you stand right here." His index finger pointed out a spot on the bare pine floor in front of the pulpit.

Narcissa stood tall in the aisle, her black bombazine rustling as she smoothed its three wide tucks around her hips. She squared her shoulders under the puffs in her sleeves and took a deep breath that rounded her bosom and made the small tucks in her bodice stand out alive. Marcus pressed Richard's knee to keep him from following and stepped to Narcissa's side. Together they stood before the minister.

Impatient until now with the delays that had slowed his preparations for returning West, Marcus felt that this ceremony rushed pell-mell.

"Do you?" "I do."—"Will you?" "I will."

A man needed time for traveling from one world into another. One short step like this allowed no interval for a difference to be born. No time for learning what a man needed to know about a woman before he plunged from his solitary moving about the earth and into her waking and sleeping, her working and eating, her tears and her laughter. These words were not enough. They were over too quickly. A minister pronouncing "Man and wife" still left two people—each set in independent ways of doing and thinking—who must work out the difference or suffer the aloneness of union "until death us do part."

But following their vows Dr. and Mrs. Whitman were expected to stand before the minister for the sermon of the evening. This was not so short with a hundred eyes on Marcus' neck and his bride's hand firm in his that took spells of trembling.

"My text," the minister began, "is found in Luke 9:62. 'No man, having put his hand to the plough, and looking back, is fit. . . .' "

He referred to the four Nez Percé Indians who had visited St. Louis four and a half years before, in the fall of 1831, in search of the white man's Book of Heaven. "Have no doubt," he said, "that their visit to the States was of God. . . . These two who stand before us tonight have received a divine call that will claim them both until death releases them from its demands. . . . As they have become one in holy matrimony, so they are one with the will of God and so they shall remain through life. . . ."

When the sermon was lastly, finally, and in conclusion ended, the minister raised his hand in blessing. "Our Heavenly Father, go with thy servants into the savage lands beyond the States, fulfilling thy promise, 'Lo, I am with you alway, even unto the end of the world.' Amen. . . . And now, let us stand and sing hymn number three hundred and ninety-seven—'Yes, My Native Land! I Love Thee.' All five stanzas, please. Brother Prentiss, the pitch."

Starched petticoats rustled. Boots creaked as the congregation rose.

Marcus shifted his weight and smiled at Narcissa without turning his head. Judge Prentiss sounded his pitchpipe.

No doubt relieved that the long service was ending, everyone burst into song. "Yes, my native land! I love thee; All thy scenes I love them well. . . . Can I leave you, Far in heathen lands to dwell?"

Marcus, no singer himself, followed the words and watched Narcissa's father. The judge had to stop to blow his nose before he could join in the second stanza, even brokenly, for it spoke of "Home!—thy joys are passing lovely. Joys no stranger-heart can tell. . . . Happy home!—'tis sure I love thee. . . ."

Marcus heard muffled sobs behind him. Voices broke and trailed. Only the Reverend Mr. Hull and a few in the back of the church could sing with Narcissa, "In the deserts let me labor, On the mountains let me tell. . . . Let me hasten, Far in heathen lands to dwell."

The minister stopped to swallow and could not go on. Voices at the rear of the church clogged and stopped.

Without a pause, without a tremor, Narcissa finished the hymn alone—head high, her clear soprano voice steady.

A little awed, Marcus listened.

> Yes! I hasten gladly,
> From the scenes I love so well;
> Far away, ye billows! bear me;
> Lovely native land!—farewell:
>   Pleased I leave thee,
> Far in heathen lands to dwell.

Hours later Marcus and Narcissa escaped from her friends and family to the Prentiss girls' room. A plain room with bare floor except for one small braided rug beside the bed and one in front of the burned-down fire. A plain room but warm and homelike. Marcus looked at the square-posted bed, bulging with feather ticks, and could not help seeing filthy Indian blankets at Rendezvous. Narcissa's leather-covered trunk beneath the gable window waited open for its final trinkets. A red scarf lay, a neat triangle, on the trunk's raised top. Narcissa's walnut writing desk, bias edges closed, brass lock fastened, stood upright on a marble-topped commode.

Staring at these civilized trappings, Marcus saw Indian squaws in a hair-pulling fight over one colored bead necklace.

He walked to the hearth and stared into the fire. He heard Narcissa move about the room but he was in the western wilderness. Narcissa belonged with niceties of living, belonged among people who could appreciate her beauty, who could stimulate her to witty talk. She belonged where she could wear red scarfs, dress at a marble-topped commode. And no doubt Judge Prentiss could be right. Difficulties might arise between Narcissa and Henry Spalding. After all, Marcus had chosen Spalding because he'd been the only minister he could round up for Oregon on such short notice. But, minister or not and even married, Spalding was human and a three-thousand-mile trip lay before them. Three thousand miles and a lifetime of working with a man who'd asked your wife to be his. Still, the Spaldings were willing and, without a minister, the Board would not send Marcus back to the West.

Perhaps his first wonderings about Narcissa deserved more notice than he'd given them. Narcissa was different from other women. She set goals and moved toward them, dogged as a mountain man. It could be that she'd been willing to marry him because "unattached females" were not wanted for Oregon. The Board had written her that when she first applied to go teach Indians. Marcus knew that he'd never, as long as he lived, forget the look on her face and the sound of her voice as she sang, alone, the last stanza of that hymn. Such complete abandoning of home and friends without reserve could be love. . . . But, too, it might be devotion.

And yet, she had married him. She was his. He covered his face with his hands to quiet the thumping of his heart. She was his but he must still win her. The wedding ceremony allowed no time for getting acquainted. He'd have to give her time.

"Husband." Marcus realized that she'd been humming as she moved about the room. Deliberately he waited, making her speak again so he could hear once more the emotion in her tone. So he could be sure.

"Husband." Narcissa touched his arm. A fold of her blue dressing gown fell on his hand.

He turned. Her golden hair fell loose to her waist. Blue flames blazed in her eyes. He'd been wrong about Narcissa. No need to give her time.

Marcus held her close. Miraculously she was small in his arms, no longer the erect determined woman who could sing on after her friends had choked with heartbreak. Gloriously she was warm and human and her arms circled his neck. "My darling," he whispered.

Her fingers touched his lips, caressed his cheek. "My husband." She stood on tiptoe, eager.

And then, almost but not quite silently, the door slitted open and Richard oozed through. Narcissa stirred and pulled away.

Transfixed, Richard stared at the golden fall of Narcissa's hair. He meant no harm and he was not embarrassed. But Narcissa—

Marcus grinned at his wife to explain about Richard.

Her body went rigid. She drew back, not from the Indian boy alone but from Marcus as well. Her hands made fists.

Torn between tenderness for her and his need to help the Indian, Marcus spoke to Narcissa. "He doesn't understand. He means no wrong."

Her eyes shut him out. "Neither do I understand!" she flung back and turned away from the two of them.

Marcus tried to explain. "Their lodges don't have doors and no one insists on being to himself for anything. They just don't understand. You'll see how it is when you get there."

Narcissa's chin lifted. "Suppose you make him see how it is. Now. He's been under my feet all day and I suppose he'll be under my feet all the way across the continent. Well, then, surely you can make him understand that I must have some privacy."

"Wedding-day nerves," Marcus diagnosed to himself. He said, "You're tired, my darling."

He understood Narcissa's distress over the Indian boy's intrusion just at that moment. But he also knew something of the boy's inner disturbance at being imprisoned among people who spoke and acted and made rules of privacy as no one had ever done before.

"*Penemeek?*" Richard asked quietly.

That was it. No one had told him where to sleep and he'd been used to tagging Marcus through every hour of the day.

But, before Marcus could move, Narcissa swept across the room. "Richard," she said and took his hand, "you didn't have a piece of our wedding cake. Come with me."

Marcus sank down on the edge of the bed to wait. Narcissa's kisses warmed his lips. This was his wife. Her anger chilled his heart. This, too, was the spirited woman he had married.

Narcissa rapped on the door when she returned with Richard. "Come in."

Richard clutched a slice of wedding cake in each hand. Marcus grinned. Narcissa's eyes danced with mischief.

Then she spread a blanket on the rug before the hearth and, patting a pillow smooth, tossed it down. "Richard will sleep here by the fire tonight, Doctor Whitman."

Marcus stood up. "Beautiful and wonderful, to boot," he told himself. This pride he felt in her was almost as good as having her alone. And her kindness to the Indian lad would make Richard her friend for life. Through him, she'd win his tribe and others.

Marcus opened his arms.

Gently her hand stopped his embrace. Her light kiss mothered him. She caught up her embroidered gown from the foot of the bed. "I'd like to sleep with Jane this last night," she said sweetly and was gone.

This, too, was his wife.

Marcus stared at the closed door and heard no footsteps. He could have stopped her. Perhaps she wanted to be stopped. But his own independence bristled a little. By the eternal, she had made her cherished privacy. Let her lie in it—tonight.

CHAPTER

10

MARCUS had hardly quieted himself to sleep before he heard the chatter of the cookstove shaken down for breakfast. In the bustle of getting off before dawn, he was barely aware of eating, hitching up, and finally of roping Narcissa's trunk to the back of their borrowed buckboard. When Narcissa's big family gathered round with their smoking lanterns, of them all, he saw only Jane as separate from the others. A bright-spirited young lady, Jane, even if his bride had slept with her on their wedding night.

Muffled, lantern-swinging neighbors hustled up through the black morning with last-minute warnings to be on guard and tearful predictions that they'd never see Narcissa again.

Marcus gave Richard a boost that landed him high on the load in the buckboard. "All right?"

"Sure as shootin'," the Indian boy came back. No perch would seem too knobby to Richard as long as it carried him West.

"Better have this blanket."

Marcus turned to lift his wife to the scat. But Mrs. Prentiss held open before Narcissa a ledger-like book. "You're to write in it every day," she was saying, "starting today. See, I've put in the date myself—February 19, 1835. And I don't want you to miss a day." Narcissa's mother turned to Marcus. "Doctor, you see that she writes in this journal every day, beginning when you stop tonight."

Marcus promised and had to blow his nose after he'd tucked the

(69)

ledger into a findable place in the load. But Narcissa, as he swung her to the seat and arranged hot stones where her feet could reach them, did not wipe her eyes nor sniffle. "Good-by!" she called gaily across the sobbing group of family and neighbors. "Now don't forget us the moment we're out of sight. Write to us."

Marcus hoisted himself to the seat beside her and flapped the reins. "On to Oregon," he said, more to himself than to the others.

No time for getting to know Narcissa in private. Rolling west-ward—in borrowed buckboards, hired sleighs, crowded river boats—they gathered their travel companions. Marcus came to know Narcissa, not as his wife, but as sister-mother to Richard and to John Ais when they picked up John from Mr. Parker's home at Ithaca. He saw her as a lovely stranger who elicited second and third looks from the river boat crews and from her fellow travelers. He watched her make friends, nurse the ailing, charm one and all with witty talk or with her singing.

Always she moved at a distance from him. But, to be fair, it was a distance not made by her but by their situation. They shared their quarters at night with the two Indian boys or with other couples. During the days, she sat beside him, looking like a wife but cluck-ing over her Indian charges, singing an impersonal folk song, talking politics or geography. They skimmed across the icy days of February and blew into March without coming upon one hour they could really call their own.

Marcus watched Narcissa's color heighten, her flame-touched hair loosen and curl about her face. And then, before he could convince himself that patience was a virtue in a man, they landed at Cin-cinnati. He'd been dreading this a little.

Still, he hurried Narcissa to the inn where he'd arranged to meet the Spaldings. Beside the gray frame hostelry, he spied a light Dearborn wagon. He'd seen it before—when he met and persuaded the Spaldings that they were needed for Oregon—but now the wagon gleamed with new meaning. These wheels would roll across prairies and mountains all the way to the Pacific.

Marcus caught Narcissa's hand and hurried her past the inn to the wagon. They'd just reached out to touch it when an atten-tion demanding "Har-r-rump" pulled them back.

Henry Spalding, pushing his wife's elbow ahead of her, strode

(70)

toward them. "How do you do, Doctor Whitman," he called. Coming up, he gave Narcissa a stiff nod. "And Mrs. Whitman, I presume. Meet Mrs. Spalding."

Narcissa side-stepped the tall, black-bearded Henry to extend both her hands to his wife. "I'm so pleased, Mrs. Spalding." Then, having put Henry in his proper order, she turned. "And Brother Spalding, how nice to see you—married."

Marcus saw the long-coated parson flush above his whiskers as he gave her hand one curt downward yank. Whatever had possessed Narcissa?

But instantly she stepped back to embrace the plain Eliza Spalding and kiss her cheek. Marcus forgot her moment of almost rudeness. The contrast between these two women would, he knew, call forth comment all the way across the continent. Narcissa—smart, head high, shoulders square under her caped broadcloth coat. Eliza —homespun, unadorned, retiring. A song bird beside a molting sparrow. And yet he felt no apprehension about their working together. Narcissa was spectacular; Eliza human. They'd get along.

One feature alone stood out to reveal Eliza's youth—her hands. Marcus had noticed them when he first met the Spaldings. All at once now he knew that Eliza was proud of her hands and he even liked that in her. "Eliza Spalding needs pride as most women need humility," he thought. He liked, too, Eliza's firm grip. In time they'd get used to her coarse voice. Yes, Eliza would do. She and Narcissa complemented each other like brown and gold.

Spalding said, "My wife and I—" With visible effort he kept his eyes off Narcissa. "We didn't hear your boat whistle."

"Quite all right," Marcus told him. "You said you'd be at the Inn and here you are. We spied your wagon and had to look it over. A welcome sight, Mr. Spalding. Most encouraging." He stroked a blue and yellow wheel. "Heard from the Board yet? Your appointment, I mean?"

Henry cleared his throat. "Har-r-rump." Maddeningly deliberate, he poked a searching party of two fingers into a dozen pockets before he finally drew out a folded sheet. Then smoothing it open, bending back each crease, Marcus saw his nostrils flare, heard his breathing quicken.

"Har-r-rump. Yes, the Prudential Committee of the Board approves the transfer, changing us from the Osage to the Oregon Indians. But . . ."

Marcus gripped Henry's arm. "Fine. Takes a load off my mind. Now then, provided the War Department comes through with our permit to cross Indian country, we're all set." He vaulted into the wagon and sat on the driver's seat, seeing down a sagebrush trail.

Narcissa left Eliza and came over. Standing by the front wheel, she turned up a troubled face. "Marcus, what do you mean—'War Department'? Another 'if'? And after all our haste?"

Marcus sucked in as much breath as he'd need to explain in a hurry. "Didn't want to worry you. Bound to come through, or reasonably so. That wheel you hold will roll clear to Oregon, Mrs. Whitman."

Eliza sat down on the wagon tongue and Henry stood behind her as if she were a pulpit. "Har-r-rump. Doctor Whitman, I would be agreeable, God willing, but . . ." He glanced down. "Well, problems have arisen since I talked with you back in New York State about going West."

Marcus swung to the wheel hub and down. Perhaps the moody prophet had brooded too long over his old antagonism toward Narcissa and her father. "What is it, Mr. Spalding?"

Henry toyed with the square-linked chain that sagged across his waistcoat. "Well, my wife and I drove through Pittsburgh a couple of weeks ago. We met up with an artist, name of Catlin. Seems he's been all over the country. Paints the Rockies and sketches Indians."

Narcissa's voice froze as it fell. "Just what has this to do with your appointment, Mr. Spalding?" Marcus had not heard this voice of his wife's.

"I'm getting to that," Henry snapped and turned his shoulder so as to cut off Narcissa. He spoke to Marcus only. "This man, Catlin, he says he wouldn't attempt to take a white female into that wild country. Not west of the Missouri, he wouldn't."

"Catlin's a good painter," Marcus said, forcing a calm tone, talking down his flare of anger. "Sketched Rabbit-Skin-Leggins and No-Horns-on-His-Head of the Nez Percé delegation. But what, exactly, does he know about taking white women to Oregon? Must be only theory with him."

Henry jabbed the air with an emphatic middle finger. "Catlin says for me not to dare take a white woman."

Narcissa stamped her foot. "Catlin!"

Marcus said, "Always got to be a first to venture. Mrs. Whitman's willing to go."

Narcissa's eyes hurled defiance at Henry. "Not merely willing. I can hardly wait."

Spalding widened his stance like a man taking aim. "It's a matter of judgment! Catlin knows Indians. He fears the desire of the savages, on seeing a white woman, might easily lead to their unrestrained passion. He claims the degenerate heathen can't be trusted."

"Neither could the redskins around Plymouth or Boston or New Amsterdam—at first. Now they're different. That's why we're being sent to Oregon."

"Furthermore, Catlin believes the fatigues of the desert journey would destroy a white woman. Mrs. Spalding's none too strong."

Marshaling an adequate answer, Marcus stood tense. The party had reached a crisis. Without Spalding, they'd be forced to turn back. Those were the Board's terms—they must take a minister. Marcus remembered his promises to the chiefs at Rendezvous, the rush of patients to his cottonwood clinic. Everything he'd hoped for and promised was at stake.

Then Eliza's coarse voice shaped auspicious words. "As for me, I'll trust God and go forward without fear. I like the command just as it stands, 'Go ye into all the world,' and no exceptions for poor health."

Narcissa swept over and dropped to one knee. Her arm curved around Eliza's shoulders for a quick squeeze. "I love you for that, Mrs. Spalding! We'll get along."

"Of course," Henry said, stepping back from Narcissa. "I don't say it's impossible. But I don't like responsibility for the risk, the dangers."

"Full responsibility rests on me," Marcus blurted. "These wheels will get the women through to Rendezvous under caravan protection. The Nez Percés and Flatheads have promised a safe journey the rest of the way. You'll be proud to have the first wagon to cross the continent."

"But in that undeveloped land on the Pacific, what good is one wagon? We'll need farmers and carpenters. The Board should—"

"At the outset," Marcus broke in, "we'll doctor their sick, set up schools and a church, and there you are. Medicine, education, religion—three great civilizing forces. We've both had experience farming and folks tell me you're good at building. The Board wanted to send a carpenter but, when I left, they hadn't found one who'd go. You and I can make a start. Other things later."

Spalding hesitated and fixed a frown on the top of Narcissa's wool bonnet. "I don't know. Maybe you've been unduly influenced to take a light-minded view of this whole affair."

Marcus drew in a quick breath the way he'd seen other men do as they reached for their guns. If Spalding meant to hedge like this all the way and blame it on Narcissa, they'd better have it out now, once and for all.

But before he could speak, Narcissa, head erect, began to hum an old air. They all knew the words. "Yes, I hasten gladly, from the scenes I love so well. . . . Far in heathen lands to dwell."

A change came over the little group. Eyes straight ahead, young hands clasped on her breast, Eliza got to her feet. Even Henry came down off his rostrum manner and became a sober but human young man, his gaze fixed on a pillar of cloud.

Narcissa had worked magic with her voice. "Good medicine and a good omen for the years ahead," Marcus thought.

Henry asked, "But what about roads?"

Marcus ran his hand along the iron rim of a wheel. "Clear a road. Another first, Mr. Spalding. Think of it—a wagon road from the States to the Pacific."

Henry Spalding subsided with one last "Harrump" that settled his lips in a straight pink buttonhole worked through his black plush beard.

But Marcus had no time to bask in the warmth from his second winning of Spalding for Oregon. Before he could start clearing a road, he must load the wagon and his passengers onto river boats to float them down the Ohio and up the Mississippi to St. Louis. He must spend more travel weeks beside Narcissa but apart from her. And now he had her old beau on his hands, to boot.

During the winter when he'd been searching so desperately for a minister to go to Oregon, he'd heard but discounted bits of gossip. Now he wasn't sure. Folks had told him that Henry Spalding was ranting up and down the state of New York: "That woman. I don't trust her judgment. I'll never go to Oregon, if Narcissa Prentiss goes. Just wait. Time will bring out her character."

From the looks of things now, there may have been truth in the whispered reports. Truth or not, Marcus could see that Henry, even though he'd been married to Eliza for more than a year, had not managed to settle his feelings for Narcissa.

Just what this would mean for their life in Oregon, Marcus could not predict. But he had a feeling something akin to the mixed recoil and challenge he'd experienced that night at Bellevue, examining their first cholera patient and knowing they were in for an epidemic. Just how their little party would survive an epidemic of unsettled emotions, only time could tell.

CHAPTER

11

AN AMERICAN FUR COMPANY official whose tobacco juice ran more freely from the corners of his mouth at mention of women scratched through the hedge of hair on his face while Marcus sat in his St. Louis office and begged for help.

"Waal, you'll have to git 'em to Liberty," the big man answered finally. "But I reckon our company boat, *The Diana,* kin stow aboard your females and baggage there and hawl 'em fer as Bellevue. *The Diana*'ll hit Liberty come three-four weeks."

His hope pinned on the War Department still getting a permit to them, Marcus herded his party to the St. Louis dock once more. The Dearborn wagon and their animals on board, the Spaldings and Whitmans and the two Indian boys slithered stiff-legged up the wet gangplank of a rickety steamboat.

"How long to Liberty?" Marcus asked the mountain of hickory gray that turned out to be the captain.

"A week, barrin' leaks and too blasted many skirts on deck."

Marcus hurried Narcissa to the cabin that the whole party would share. "At least, another week ought to give the War Department time to send through our permit." He didn't add, Liberty's the end of the line for Uncle Sam—our last chance for mail. No need to make Narcissa face turning back before she had to.

"Sure, I'm sure," the Liberty postmaster stormed. "People always blames me. A body'd think I was supposed to write the letters."

"It can still come," Marcus told Narcissa. "We've got till *The Diana* docks."

He liked her decisive nod.

In the meantime, he shrank from the thought of not being ready to go, if the permit should come through. Narcissa's disappointment would be highly spiced with scorn. And he'd gambled this much. Might as well "go your pile on it," he told himself, thinking of Joe Meek somewhere in the West that very minute. Joe Meek out there, being his own man.

So he went his pile—the Board's pile, literally. They finished laying in the last keg and button necessary for the trip. There it all stood in an orderly heap in the tavern barn and still no Fur Company boat and no War Department permit. Time was running out. From all the intelligence he could gather, Marcus figured the caravan would be bound to put out from Bellevue by the middle of May, no later. And here it was, the last week in April and them just sitting, all ready to move but sitting, two hundred miles away.

Then, that night, the long rumbling toot of a river boat stabbed him wide awake. Forgetting how the tavern bed squawked with every movement, he came up fast. Narcissa stirred and, beyond the curtain partition in the room, Henry Spalding's "Har-r-rump" scolded. But Marcus gave his full attention to the boat's "Toot, to-o-ot."

He tore into his clothes and whispered to Narcissa he'd hurry back with word. He slithered his way to the boat landing as passengers began to creep down the wet gangplank. A man's high-pitched voice, raised above the babble of unloading, inquired for Dr. Whitman.

"Here," Marcus shouted. "My name's Whitman." He pushed through to the tall young man whose calculating eyes, even in the water-blurred lantern light, seemed cold enough for a Fur Company official's. "Can this be *The Diana*? We're all ready to go."

"I'm Gray. William S. Gray," the man intoned. His manner expected his name to be known. "I'm here, at last. I was sent by the American Board posthaste to overtake you. I'm needed in Oregon." He flicked water from his sleeve. "My appointment is as lay assistant in charge of building and et cetera." He paused, then went on importantly, "I happen to know that the Fur Company boat will be here in about ten days." He glanced around and struck out to lead the way toward town. "I've never been imposed on such an awful night."

Marcus told himself that not even Henry Spalding would demand perfection of speech in a carpenter to assist them in Oregon. "A wonderful night, Mr. Gray," he said and, reaching for the man's satchel, took the lead. What would Narcissa think of this addition to their party? "We're mighty glad to have you. Come along."

While the tavern proprietor took his time about an extra bunk, Marcus could not help studying Gray's back as he sauntered across the lobby, his black coat skirting brown streaked spittoons. Then, not wanting to pass judgment on the basis of mere uneasiness, he turned back to the proprietor.

But a lusty whoop came from the bar off the far end of the lobby. Marcus wheeled in time to see the surprised Mr. Gray lifted bodily into the next room by the scruff of his great coat collar.

Marcus ran to the still flapping door and looked over to see Gray dabbing out at the red-and-black-checked bellies that surrounded him. A dozen teamster barflies side-stepped around him, examining his eastern clothes. Curious about this new man of his, Marcus waited.

"By gar! If it ain't alive and crawlin'. *Sacre diablo.*"

"Can't be, Pablo. Reckon mebbe it's a long-legged doll. Mebbe ordered for some senorita down in Santy Fee."

"Let's see if'n it kin pull on a jug. Here, *amigo,* a little fire—"

Gray pushed at the jug. "I'll thank you to know with who you're meddling. I don't hold by intoxicated liquors. You're drunk."

"Ja hear, Pablo? Says yer drunk. Har!"

"*Si.* Mebbe tee-tote-ler talk too much. Mebbe greenhorn skunk want Pablo make meat of too much tongue. *Si?*"

Gray glared. He slapped spilled whisky off his coat. His small close-together eyes took on a green heat. He raised his hand to shove aside the one runt in the crowd. Then, as a husky raised a bottle to crash on Gray's skull, Marcus let out a loud, "Owgh! Owgh-h-h!" This and the rotgut liquor inside the bully combined to make his aim uncertain. The bottle glanced off Gray's hat but still he crumpled to the floor.

Bleary eyes looked around for the source of the battle cry. Marcus pulled back the swinging door and lounged against it. "River boat's in, *amigos.* River rats are spoilin' for a fight. Why waste time on a fofarraw greenhorn?"

Dulled eyes blinked. The pack, as if on signal, hitched up their belts, lumbered through the door, and on outside. When the cold rain hit them, they went howling toward the dock.

Marcus helped Gray to his feet. "Sorry. Rough way to introduce

(78)

you to the West. But don't you know enough not to antagonize these she-b'ars?"

"I intend to be respected, Whitman, in this or any other society."

"Have it your way, Gray. But I sorta hanker to land you in Oregon in one piece. We'll need you out there. I'd begun to think we'd have to go without a helper."

Meticulously Gray brushed himself off. "I, personal, don't think it was very ethical to send them to the river for a fight."

Marcus grinned. "Well, I'm responsible for your hide. Anyhow, their fire water will get pretty well diluted by the time they slosh through this rain to the dock."

Back in bed, Marcus whispered to Narcissa, "Darling, our little tinderbox is picking up more explosives."

From the Spalding bed beyond the curtain came a gravelly, "Har-rump!"

"Tell you in the morning," Marcus said against Narcissa's ear and did not go to sleep again that night.

Far too late to ship William Gray back to the Board with the request that they send a carpenter with a different personality. Silly, too, Marcus told himself. What difference did it make how much respect the man, "personal," demanded as long as he could wield a hammer to help them build homes and clinics and churches in the wilderness? And yet he knew that it did make a difference.

CHAPTER

12

WHEN *The Diana* saluted Liberty with an indifferent "Toot, toot" from mid-river and steamed ahead, it did not occur to Marcus to take this for excuse to disband his party and let Oregon wait another year. And when, from habit, he strode up the dock and across to the post office, he took for a good omen, instead of a slap in the face, the arrival on that very day of the War Department's letter, permitting his outfit to cross Indian lands.

Fortunately they had used their waiting time for *The Diana,* to get the last of their supplies together. Now Marcus rushed to the tavern carriage yard, calculating on the run the time they'd need to load their newly purchased heavy wagon, to get the Spaldings' wagon greased, the cattle and horses rounded up, and the whole kit and caboodle underway.

He pulled up in the barn before their stack of stores. Sliding his eyes over the items, he mentally checked them off and distributed them in the load. The barrels of flour and Narcissa's blue-rimmed dishes, their iron pots, their tents, the hoes and plowshares, Narcissa's trunk, that big wooden box of Mrs. Spalding's, Mr. Gray's chest of tools—they'd all go into the heavy wagon. If Spalding could pack in with his things the tea and sugar and the hams—

"Hey, there. Goodyear!"

"Sure, Doc. Coming."

Marcus had put him off the day before. It hadn't seemed quite right to be a party to this downy-cheeked youngster getting to the mountains to become a trapper. But now . . .

Miles Goodyear's dark eyes sparked with hope as he loped up.

"You still itching to go West?" Marcus asked.

"Sure as shootin'."

Marcus slowed his words to give him time between for telling his conscience that Miles Goodyear would get West, no matter what, and he'd better get there in civilized company. "Well, I reckon Narcissa can mother three boys on the trail as well as two. You're sure?"

"Sure? Of course I'm sure!" Excitement turned Miles to all arms and legs which he flung about like a doll too loosely stuffed. "That's great, Doc. When do we start?"

Marcus steadied Miles with a hand on his shoulder and told him they'd start at dawn the next day and it would take every last one of them from now till then to get the outfit packed and rolling.

Marcus wakened Narcissa with a kiss on the top of her head and a playful spank on the curve under her blanket. "Get up, sleepy head. I thought you were going to Oregon."

Narcissa came awake all in a piece. "The sun's not up yet, why should I be?" she asked. But her bare feet, pink beneath the embroidered ruffles of her nightgown, slid to the floor. She stood on tiptoe to touch her lips to his. "I'll hurry," she promised. "Be down before you can say Richard-Tackitonitis."

Thank heaven, she hadn't asked whether he knew for sure that they could catch the caravan before it left Bellevue and headed into hostile Indian territory. Marcus could admit to himself that their chances were slim. About a hundred to one, he reckoned. Still, they'd spent so much, outfitting and coming this far. It wouldn't be much worse, turning back from Bellevue than from here.

Breakfast over, he rounded up a mule and a horse for Narcissa to pick a mount. She looked small and delicate in her green pongee habit and he half hoped she'd choose the sane, steady mule. While she patted each nose in turn, her head tilted in decision, Richard broke one of his devoted silences.

"That very bad mule. Can't catch buffalo."

Narcissa swung around. "That settles it, Doctor. I must catch buffalo, they tell me, or I'll starve."

Owl-eyed, Richard watched Marcus sidesaddle the horse. But not

(81)

until Narcissa was up, her knee crooked over the misplaced horn did the boy comment in woeful tone, "That very bad saddle."

Eliza, also, chose a horse to ride and Marcus saw to her trappings. This time, Richard only shook his head and scooted to the rear of the outfit where John Ais and Miles Goodyear rounded the cattle into moving formation.

"You take the lead," Marcus told the women. "Less dust. You can set the pace as long as it's fast." He swung onto his own new horse, Old Muddy, and called out, "Let's go!"

And now time became their master. It cracked a whip from the first smear of dawn till gritty famished dark, one muscle-weary day stacked heavy upon the day before and building into a mountain of fatigue. Still, on they drove—against time, against Gray's bickering, against a vague distress in Henry Spalding that Marcus had to doctor as indigestion.

Miles Goodyear, driving the heavy wagon after Gray decided that was "dirty work," grew tired in the manner of a child and slept at his reins until Marcus would ride back and give his horses a switching to remind them of the hurry. Eliza's weariness made her pale but she kept up with the others. Richard and John Ais, in the dusty rear of the race, crusted over with dirt and bacon grease as the days blew by, forgot to speak English in their at-homeness. They herded the stock in Nez Percé, ate in silence, and slept. Their cheeks filled out under the dirt and their hips thinned down beneath the jeans they begged every day to discard.

And Narcissa took to travel as if born on a sidesaddle. Often she forgot and let her bonnet fall back on her neck while the wind loosened her hair and the sun shaded her face from cream to tan. Her laughter rippled back along the line as frequently at the end of day, at the end of a week, as at its start. Narcissa did not complain at the end of two weeks. But Marcus watched the forward-looking grow in her eyes and knew what hurt and censure would replace it, if they got to Bellevue only to find that the caravan had left without them and they could go no farther. Turning back, the song would die in Narcissa. Marcus shrank from picturing the rest of their lives together, if he should fail Narcissa now.

Tortoiselike they crept on north, headed for the Platte. Delayed by a guide who circled and lost an invisible point of destination in the prairie sameness below Bellevue, stopped by sickness, resting over Sunday, Marcus read unlikely "sign" long before he could actually see the settlement. And then his fears came true.

Empty of travelers, Bellevue. "Broken Hand" Fitzpatrick, captaining the caravan, was four days on his way.

Inquiries, Indian warnings, repairs, and on the little outfit raced against all reason, against all sane advice. An hour to sort and cut down baggage and three days to swim and boat the rest across the Platte. From dark to dark, one day of dust, and then the Elkhorn River. Forty miles, another day till almost midnight. And now their camp lay only a short ride below Loup Fork, well within Pawnee striking distance. Marcus calculated through the miseried hours before he could wake the others. An outfit the size of his dared not attempt to pass the Pawnee villages without protection. Morning must mark the end of their race or the beginning of another in reverse, Pawnees on their heels.

Perhaps the dread of what he would see in his wife's eyes kept Marcus from giving up. At three, he touched Narcissa's hair, a glow of light in the morning blackness, and found her cheek with his lips. "Hate to do this but it's the last time, my sweet," he promised. "We catch them today or run for our lives back out of here." Might as well give her an inkling.

Narcissa tossed off her blankets. "If you'd arrange to have a moon on these occasions, I could see who's kissing me."

Scouting up toward the Loup a ways in front of the others, Marcus found by the first smear of gray light fresh sign of travelers in the hoof-deep dust. Hard to estimate exactly how long since their passing. If the wind had failed to blow, the tracks could be days old. Still, no animal trails appeared to cross the line. Almost allowing himself to hope, he spurred up the wagons.

"I think it's going to rain." Narcissa pointed to the north as he rode by.

"Looks like it. You able to pick it up a little, Mrs. Spalding?"

"Of course," Eliza answered and tapped her stirrup against her horse's side.

Gray's head sagged over his saddle horn. "Lend the boys a hand with the cattle, Mr. Gray," Marcus called.

Gray jogged straight ahead.

"Gray!" Marcus reined in.

"I heard you, Doc. It's too dusty for I back there. That's the kids' job, nohow."

Marcus glared but kept his voice soft the way he'd heard Kit Carson's in emergencies. "Mr. Gray, your scalp is hanging to your skull by about one hair this minute. If you want to wear it through the day, you'd better get back there and hurry up those cattle."

Eyes scared, Gray pulled his horse around. "I'll go, this time. But don't get no ideas about orderin' me to do the dirty work whenever it don't suit you to do it."

Marcus galloped up ahead to set the pace. Gray was just tired, he told himself. He'd be all right as soon as they could take time to sleep enough and ride along at a decent gait.

"Well, my little weather prophet," Marcus greeted Narcissa, coming up behind her. "Here's your rain. And here's your coat," he added, unbuckling her saddlebag and trailing out her India-rubber coat. "Need help with yours, Mrs. Spalding?"

"I have it," Eliza called back. "Thank you."

Marcus watched her struggle into her sleeves. Strange how awkward one woman could be, and another be Narcissa. "Have to go a little faster," he called above the quickening splatter and bounce of raindrops in the chalky dust.

The dust doughed and thinned to gravy. Gray sky squeezed low and blurred its rigid line of meeting with the prairie. Water dumped down on the racing outfit. Rubber coats gave little protection and the wagon wheels turned mud that thickened and wadded up in the spokes to make the going heavy.

But they were nearing the Loup ford, if Marcus remembered rightly that clump of tall cottonwoods ahead. "Come on, Old Muddy. Let's take a look." They galloped on into the stream. Marcus rode across and back to the middle, beckoning the others in with a sweep of his arm. He backed Muddy off to the side to wait and help the boys with the cattle.

His outfit through, he turned midstream to check the trail behind them. He blinked and stood high in his stirrups. Peering through the gray rain screen, on the opposite side of the Platte but little more than a mile to the rear of his party, he saw a moving herd of something. Riders? Indians? The blurred image came and went like a dream he'd been having of late. Maybe he'd brooded too much on the

(84)

possibility of just this. Maybe— He froze until he was sure. Then he laid a risky plan as he splashed to the far bank of Loup Fork.

Kit Carson had told him once, "An Injun'll stop any doin's to get a horse. It's somethin' to remember."

Marcus had never needed to test the theory till now. He prayed that Carson was right.

"John Ais," he called. "Cut out that spotted mare."

The Nez Percé boy nodded. He waved the mare out from the herd, dropped a lariat around her neck, and reined in to hand her over to Marcus. His head tipped backward and his voice barely brushed one word, "Pawnee."

"Get along with you," Marcus answered. "We need those cattle."

"Need you like . . . like . . . likewise," John Ais left behind him.

"Hurry," Marcus yelled. "Drive the others. Hurry." He cupped his hands around his mouth. "Run for it," he shouted. "Run for your lives."

Old Muddy got the idea and reared and snorted against tight reins. Holding him, Marcus prayed for Narcissa. No lustful Pawnee must catch sight of her. He glanced behind. The rain had slowed now and the Indians were gaining fast. He could see them plainly, their wet backs low along their ponies' necks glowed like hardwood rifle butts in the returning light. Their ponies stretched in long shallow scallops, coming on. Only Indian ponies, intent on buffalo or raising hair, covered ground in just this manner.

Marcus stole another glance to see that his party was racing ahead. Then he pawed deep in his saddlebag for ropes of strong tobacco and gratefully drew out a string of colored trade beads he'd forgot about having. The Pawnee scouts splashed into the Platte. The spotted mare yanked at her lead rope and reared. Old Muddy, snorting at the smell of Indians, tried to pull away. All the Indians were in the water now, coming fast. Marcus turned in his saddle, measured the distance between his outfit and the charging Indians. Once those savages got across the river, his party had little chance of outrunning them.

Gauging the time, he still held Muddy with a tight rein and clung to the mare's rope. He picked a scrawny willow less than a hundred yards away as his marker. When the first Pawnee came up even with that willow, he'd have to run for it. Until then every second he stayed gave the others a few feet of leeway.

(85)

Perhaps it was fear but as he sat his rearing horse, measuring the distance between him and the enemy, his nostrils filled with the sweet stench of rotting human flesh. Marcus' hand passed over his eyes. He should never have brought Narcissa. Catlin had been right. The risk was too great.

Then a Pawnee scout plunged his pony past the willow marker.

Marcus gave the spotted mare a whack with her rope and waved her downstream into the Loup. He broke the string of red and purple beads and sowed them out in plain sight on the bank. Knifing off hand lengths, he tossed a dozen baits of tobacco on the rain flattened grass.

An arrow sang past his ear.

He pulled his rifle from its saddle sling, cocked it, then tore off to join his outfit, if he could.

He squeezed Old Muddy's sides and stretched along his neck. The delay had given the others perhaps a half-mile lead. He talked to his horse, urging him on, each word a prayer. As he prayed, he tried to figure. Suppose the Indians did interrupt their chase to get the horse. If so, how much time would they take before they came on? Time enough to fort up for an attack? Two wagons made a mighty poor barricade but any buffer was better than none in this level land. Still, would his outfit have time to get into any kind of position?

"Come on, Old Muddy."

The sun rayed out from under the lifting gray and shone down on the mouth of a ravine not more than a mile ahead. If they could make that ravine and if it narrowed down enough, they might be able to fort up there.

"Come on, Muddy!" Spaces on the prairie pulled in so slowly. Might still be a mile or two miles to that ravine. "Come on, Mud!"

Marcus stole a look over his shoulder and his muscles slackened. Carson had been right. The Indians had stopped for the horse. Perhaps the tobacco and beads would hold them long enough for— Now suddenly the ravine opened out in a **V**. Too wide unless it narrowed fast. Unless—

Marcus raked at his hair and found his hat gone. But ahead, a dozen fingers of smoke raised from the ground and bent off to the left. He hauled up on his reins. He closed his eyes and opened them again to be sure. And before him in an inverted funnel of yellow light lay, unmistakably, a camp.

The fur caravan!

CHAPTER

13

THE caravan was a town on horseshoes. Four hundred animals. A dozen covered wagons. Almost a hundred men. Two women. All headed west. It moved, it jawed, it swapped tales around a campfire. It moved on west. It cursed, it moved, it stopped to eat. It moved, it laughed, it slept. Always it moved, always west. Fifteen, sometimes twenty miles a day on tea and meat for breakfast. Meat and tea at noon. One day, ten days, twenty days—all matched. And then a square brown box set off one green prairie billow from the others. The box reared taller . . . wider, and became Fort Laramie.

Marcus went directly to the factor. "Got two white women in my party, just like I said last fall, Fontenelle. You're holding my reservations, I presume."

Fontenelle flung himself at Marcus across the counter. "Doc! You old hoss thief! By gor, man, reservations! For one sight of a white female critter on two legs, I'd move out to a prairie dog hole myself and give you the blasted fort. But you ain't meanin' it."

Hanging on while Fontenelle pumped, Marcus remembered this same man's first chilly reluctance to take along the store-dressed parson and young medic little more than a year before. "Mean it, all right. Come see. And, if you can put us in a room for our stay, you may never get shed of us."

One look at Narcissa in her swishing habit, her hair loose around her face, and Marcus saw Fontenelle succumb. He escorted them past the stares of blanketed Indian men, of squaws in calico and trinkets, of trappers arrested in their pawing—their eyes discarding squaws their arms still held. Up the splintered steps, off a narrow balcony, Fontenelle kicked open the heavy door to a room in Fort Laramie's northeast bastion. "Your room, my lady," he said with a bow and then whacked Marcus on the shoulder. "You lucky devil!"

Narcissa held out her arms to the room and sighed, "Heaven." She flew to the slit of window and peeked out. She even caressed the light cannon that stood guard behind it. A step and she touched the bed—a crude platform nailed to the wall. Then she flung her arms around Marcus and kissed him while the others watched.

Henry snorted and turned away.

"We can never thank you enough, Mr. Fontenelle," Narcissa cried and more than did it with her eyes.

Fontenelle grinned and gave Marcus a shove on into the room. "You old hoss thief!" he said and led the Spaldings along the balcony to adjoining quarters.

Marcus kicked shut the door and held Narcissa close for one promissory moment. Then he skimmed down the steps and saw to their unpacking and looked after the stock and took the Indian boys and Goodyear a fresh supply of meat and saw that Gray was bunked inside to keep him from complaining. Before his chores were finished and he could climb the stairs again, he was sure he'd find his wife in an exhausted ball of sleep.

Testing, he knocked on the door.

Narcissa sang out at once, "Come in, Richard," and stood beside the threshold, bursting with her joke. Her hair fell to her waist and she wore the blue dressing gown that Marcus had seen only on their wedding night.

"Got a good notion to lead you out and feed you cake," he said and took her in his arms.

"Ummmm," she hummed. "Good frosting."

In the compound below, a guitar twanged and throbbed. Raucous laughter of a trapper who had traded the lonely silence of his woodland stalking for fotched-in whisky sliced through a squaw's high giggle. In the distance a prairie wolf yapped. A dog beneath the bastion window whined and dug long quivering scratches down the barred and buttressed compound gate.

"Narcissa. My darling."

"My husband."

Her eyes, her lips, her arms denied all Marcus' wonderings about her feeling for him. If this were true—this four-walled room, this night, and this woman with the waiting in her body—then he was a man whose questions were unfounded. The tag-end pieces of puzzle about Narcissa's reasons for marrying him instead of Pratt, instead of Henry Spalding, he'd put away forever. The enigma of just why she was going to Oregon he'd stop dissecting.

For the first time in four months, light wakened Marcus the next morning. The arm on which Narcissa lay was numb but he did not move. Instead, he breathed more lightly so as not to disturb her while he drank in her loveliness, remembered the exquisite delight of her poured-out love.

And then Narcissa stirred and it was she, this time, who pressed her lips to his for their first morning kiss. He felt a difference in him. A difference in her.

She purred and stretched her arms above her head. "I'm starved."

"You're not. You're beautiful." He pulled her to him.

Through the thin wall of the adjoining room a loud, "Har-r-rump," broke in upon them but it had lost its power to perturb.

Giggling, they climbed into their clothes and rushed out to greet the morning.

From that day on, the whole trip changed for Marcus. Instead of going away from the States, away from civilization, now he was going west toward home. He and his woman, together.

Now he could ignore Henry Spalding's "Har-r-rump," registering disapproval throughout the summer. Also, the trouble that William Gray habitually brewed in his cast-iron ego. He could wait before judging these helpers of his. Perhaps in Oregon— Well, give them time.

Under Narcissa's pointing-out, Marcus did give notice to Eliza. Eliza, too weak to sit her horse, unable to digest their diet of buffalo. Eliza who might have found a thousand reasons for being jealous of Narcissa. Eliza kept calm and sweet day after day, week after week, month after month. Even at Rendezvous when the traders and trappers showed marked preference for Narcissa's company, Eliza's earthy plainness attracted the Indians to her. No question about Eliza. She, too, was moving forward, headed home. She'd fit in Oregon. Her eyes, steady on the future, clearly said, "If God be for us, who can be against us?"

It wasn't until early September, as they neared Vancouver only a whoop and a holler from the Pacific, that Marcus allowed questions to upend themselves. In order to settle and work in the Oregon Country, his party must have "for them" both God and Dr. John McLoughlin.

McLoughlin, White Eagle to all the West, chief factor of Hudson's Bay Company, ruled his vast fur trapping empire as virtual king. Shrewd businessman, McLoughlin. Settlers had to be written down as liabilities in wild fur country. And McLoughlin was a judge of men—Joe Meek had said it a dozen times. Perhaps he would not approve the American Board's selections. With one shake of his great white head he could refuse permission for them to settle in his domain. An ill-timed "Don't try to shove the dirty work off on I" of Mr. Gray's could write the end to this long trip.

Their two-thousand-mile horseback ride finished, Marcus' party floated with the current of the mighty Columbia in a six-oared bateau that belonged to Pierre Pambrun, Hudson's Bay factor at Fort Walla Walla. The oarsmen were Pambrun's employees. The sleekly handsome Frenchman, Pambrun himself, sat in the stern directing their rapid scud toward Fort Vancouver. In a way they all seemed to Marcus so many guileless beaver, drifting toward the cunning steel jaws of Hudson's Bay Company. And then Narcissa laid her hand on his.

Through her cool finger tips, he could feel a pulse. Not hers alone, nor his, but added to theirs the pulse of their child who would be born in Oregon, at home.

PART II

*

CHAPTER

1

MARCUS leaned back in the crowded bateau and watched the near bank of the Columbia. Already patches of leaves, here and there, were yellowing into autumn. "Getting late," he told himself, "No time to dally about getting located and throwing up a shelter against winter." He squeezed Narcissa's hand as a kind of knocking-on-wood. "Make friends with Doctor McLoughlin the way you did with the trappers at Rendezvous and the hard part will be over."

She touched her cheek to his. "Or the hard part can begin, don't you mean?" She pointed to the shoreline above them. "Looks like quite an establishment."

"You know what depends on this?"

"You've been jumpy as an antelope all the way down river," Narcissa said.

"I have?"

"Another 'if,' I told myself. 'Ifs' bother you, don't they, Doctor?" Marcus slid his arm around her.

Spalding harrumped and scraped his heavy boots. Turning to look past him at the dock they were approaching, Marcus saw veins bulge in Henry's temple. Was he never to caress his wife, he wondered, except under Henry's burning gaze?

Then he forgot everything in the flurry of docking. And, as they climbed over the side and up to the pier, a wedge of men strode through the compound gate and toward them. They jarred the heavy planks as they came.

"Must be McLoughlin—" Marcus whispered to Narcissa, "the one in the lead. Just like Joe Meek said he looked." He stepped forward.

The White Eagle towered a good deal over six solid feet. Shoulder-length white hair fanned in the breeze when he swept off his black hat and bowed low before the party. "Welcome to Fort Vancouver."

He captured Marcus' hand. "You're Doctor Whitman. Every mountain man in the country's been telling me you're a better medic than I am. I've heard about Jim Bridger's operation a hundred times."

His eyes were the blue of campfire smoke at noon and his gaze, in spite of his great height, as level as a prairie skyline. McLoughlin's chest was the only one Marcus had ever seen spacious enough to support the wide satin lapels of the latest mode. Brushed white sideburns framed McLoughlin's square jaws and tasseled out at his collar. This man would require some figuring and, possibly, some maneuvering.

Marcus turned to Narcissa. "Mrs. Whitman, this is Doctor McLoughlin." He had to look around Henry to find Eliza. "And Mrs. Spalding."

McLoughlin's manners were perfect. He took each lady's hand in turn and complimented them on making the overland journey from the States. But his eyes, not quite so proper, returned to Narcissa even while he met Spalding and Gray and greeted Factor Pambrun. McLoughlin was susceptible to charm and beauty then. Good. So much the better for their cause.

McLoughlin presented his associates and, offering his arm to Narcissa, led the procession to the compound gate, inside past store and bar and clanging blacksmith shop, along a zinnia bordered path to his house.

Very little, from the outside, set this building apart from others in the compound. It wore a second story but so did the granary and fur storage barns and several other units. But inside McLoughlin's house, Narcissa's hand covered her enchanted up-scale, "Oh-h-h!"

Stepping to her side, Marcus understood. After the dust and heat and meager living along the trail, this seemed a house imagined. Narcissa stooped to touch the thick gray carpet. She caressed a rosewood table. She exclaimed over the porcelain figurines that filled one cabinet. Then she sat down, at the factor's invitation, on a patterned haircloth sofa and polished its walnut arm with her hand.

Everyone talked at once. The men of the fort wanted to know about the trip. The visitors asked about the fort. And then the talk cut off. In the doorway stood a half-breed woman, richly dressed in gray silk. She wore a pearl and diamond brooch at her throat and rings on her fingers. Behind her hovered a child of ten or twelve, Marcus guessed. A skinny child with intent eyes and ash-blond curls.

Dr. McLoughlin introduced his wife.

All Marcus' training and background prompted him to recoil. But the half-breed Mrs. McLoughlin's manner—her modest carriage, the warm glow of contentment in her dark eyes, the poise of her greeting in spite of lack of English words—all these told him that here was an exception to his accepted rules. And Narcissa's smile, as she shook the sturdy hand of this quiet woman, held no censure. Only Gray saw fit to to take that moment to turn and leave the house.

"And this—" McLoughlin's tone was proud— "is my daughter, Maria."

The child ducked her head. "I had to see the white ladies."

McLoughlin led her to Narcissa.

"Maria. What a pretty name," Narcissa said. "And how nice of you to come and make us welcome."

Both hands extended, Eliza stepped forward. Maria threw her arms around her. Then she backed off and curtsied. "I get to show you to your rooms."

McLoughlin laughed. "That's right. Go along with Maria and freshen up. Dinner's at seven."

The dining room, across the hall from the parlor, wore party dress that night. A hundred candles twinkled in a crystal chandelier. Irish crystal goblets winked down on parchment-thin plates set out for ten. The mirror at the foot of the table doubled the party mood of the room.

And Dr. McLoughlin spoke in a party voice. "Mrs. Whitman, I'd be honored, if you'd sit up here by me."

"The honor is mine, Doctor McLoughlin," Narcissa answered and gave Marcus' hand a squeeze, leading him with her to the head of the table.

"That's right, Whitman," McLoughlin approved. "You next. Then, the rest along."

Marcus couldn't help wondering about the why of all this fuss. But this dinner, he knew, would sparkle in Narcissa's eyes for years to come. Perhaps it had been prepared for just that purpose. To impress Narcissa and make her want to stay. Or to remind Narcissa of all she'd miss in the undeveloped wilderness and make her want to head back for the States at once.

Marcus ate his way through steaming thick vegetable soup, duck roasted fork-tender, boiled pork, and charcoal-broiled fresh salmon while he watched the color rise in Narcissa's cheeks. Around the margin of his attention, he observed and weighed.

He weighed Henry Spalding's soberness against their chances of bargaining with the chief factor for the supplies they had to have in order to establish bases. Weighed Narcissa's open delight with all these niceties against his chances of keeping her happy in a wilderness home hand-hewn from whatever Providence and Hudson's Bay might see fit to supply. Since their hands were, irrevocably, on the plow, how could Henry Spalding eat this man's food, accept the hospitality of his roof, and still blare out:

"Doctor McLoughlin, I'm deeply grieved by your open flouting of the laws of temperance. Do you know that this wine, of which you and your associates partake so freely, is an instrument of the devil? I dare say that, if you had been with us at Rendezvous and had seen the immorality induced by the white man's drink, you would cease this very day to allow a drop of this vile poison in your home."

A hush clapped its hand over the festive room for a moment only.

"But Mr. Spalding," Dr. McLoughlin answered, "you're a student of the Bible. We live by it here. Remember, 'take a little wine for thy stomach's sake'? And speaking of toasts," he went on, "I have one for Mrs. Whitman and Mrs. Spalding." He bowed to each in turn. "I wish to express my honor and respect for the feat of hardihood and tenacity you have just accomplished in crossing the continent overland. And, because you are the first white ladies ever to complete this significant journey, I hereby dub you First Ladies of the Sidesaddle. I bestow upon you all the rights and privileges of honor citizens of Oregon, and the protection of his Majesty, King William IV and of our illustrious Princess Victoria."

From beneath the table at his feet he lifted two baskets filled with fruit. He presented each of his honorary "Ladies" with a basket.

"And now, Mrs. Whitman, I've heard all the way from Rendezvous that you can sing 'Annie Laurie' to wring tears from the toughest trapper in the mountains. Would you be kind enough to come into the parlor and sing a wee bit for this Scotsman's hungry ears?"

Days of lavish entertainment wound up as a week of noncommitments on McLoughlin's part. Marcus had his hands full, keeping Mr. Spalding's criticisms muted. But plainly, McLoughlin loved Narcissa's company and reveled in her singing. He begged her to teach the children of the fort all the songs she knew and he always sat in himself on singing sessions. Marcus did all he could do to give McLoughlin plenty of Narcissa and little of William Gray in his effort to win the factor's support for their work.

But something of the Indians' leisure ruled McLoughlin. He would discuss with Marcus, hours on end, medicine, farming, government, or Indian character. But when the subject of getting located for their work came up, McLoughlin was needed to attend to business someplace else about the fort. Had the factor sized up the party and decided they could do no good in Oregon? Perhaps he planned to stall them off until winter so they'd give up going inland and be willing to settle in the Willamette Valley. After all, McLoughlin, a Hudson's Bay man, must keep the Company's interests foremost. Day after day, nothing happened.

Then, as they were leaving the festive dining room one night, McLoughlin grasped Marcus' hand. "Just a minute, Doctor. I want you and Mrs. Whitman to know that you can count on the Company and on me for anything you want or need as long as you stay in Oregon. I'll back you with supplies and food and friendship. You can have a boat to go exploring for your station whenever you say."

Marcus could not answer.

"Doctor McLoughlin," Narcissa cried. "How wonderful! You'll never know how grateful we are."

"Mrs. Whitman, I hope you and Mrs. Spalding will stay here with us until your new home is completed. We need your singing. And Mrs. Spalding's serenity is catching. She does us all good."

Narcissa laughed. "I love Vancouver, Dr. McLoughlin, and would like to stay awhile. But not too long. I left my two boys at Walla

Walla and they need me. Besides, my doctor prescribes that I be with my husband for a very special event in our family early next spring."

"Well," McLoughlin told her, "he's the doctor and a good one. We want you here as long as you'll stay. After that, I couldn't put you in better hands. Goodnight, fair lady." Still smiling, he swung to Marcus. "Whitman, come into my office. We'll take a look at the big map there. See what we can work out."

"Fine." Marcus spied Henry at the foot of the stairs. "Mr. Spalding, Doctor McLoughlin is going to help us pick out our stations. Come along."

McLoughlin, following Marcus' glance over his shoulder, said, "Your wife is charming. A lovely lady. I dread the hardships of frontier life for her. Especially, just now."

"Yes, I dread that part of it, too. But she's stronger now than when we left the States. Cheerful, too. Hardships become her."

"A remarkable woman," Dr. McLoughlin mused.

Henry snapped, "Let's get on with our work. We've wasted enough time. What have you got to suggest about locations?"

McLoughlin drew three chairs to the fire in his office off the dining room. He motioned Marcus and Spalding to seats. "There you go saying, 'locations' again," he accused. He stood with his back to the fire. "You gentlemen don't seem to realize that you're in a savage land among Indians whose only morality is based on strength and fear."

"Har-r-rump."

McLoughlin's square palm stopped this attempt at interrupting. "Yes, I know all about their promises at Rendezvous. Well, add promises to strength and fear and what do you get? Treachery. Every Indian, particularly every Cayuse, Doctor Whitman, is out for himself. It's been bred in him through his father and his grandfather and he knows nothing else."

"But several Cayuse chiefs showed real interest in our work when we talked to them about it at Rendezvous."

"I can't say exactly what they hope to get from you," the factor answered, "but I can guess. They want magic—power over nature and over their foes. They think you have it. When they learn that your medicine is calomel and sulphur instead of magic spells and incantations, don't trust their promises. And you, Mr. Spalding, when they learn that you come preaching 'Love your enemies' instead of rob and cheat and scalp your enemies and drive them from the land, then you're going to need the protection that comes from other men on your side and guns to stress your sermons." McLoughlin tossed his head and sat down between them. "I'm sorry. I didn't intend to make a speech. You're both of age. Now, that much is free. What else do you want to know?"

"We need your advice about locations."

McLoughlin chuckled. "Advice on everything except about two stations. Right?"

Marcus would have let it go at that. Apparently Narcissa had so charmed McLoughlin that he was ready to humor them.

But Spalding had to clinch it. "Doctor McLoughlin, you may as well know, since you have shown such favoritism, that we insist on two stations because I refuse to go to a location with that Mrs.—"

"There are several reasons, from our point of view, Doctor," Marcus put in. "No need to go into them."

"All right. I'll do what I can the same as I did for Mr. Lee and his party of Methodists on the Willamette. For one thing, I can let you have enough hogs for a start. Also seed corn, fruit tree cuttings, and such."

Marcus said, "That's fine. A big help."

Henry Spalding asked, "For how much?"

McLoughlin turned to Spalding and studied him intently. "For your promise to do as much for others as you have the opportunity."

Spalding fidgeted and cleared his throat.

"Here's my hand on it." Marcus and McLoughlin sealed the bargain.

"Mr. Parker was supposed to explore the country for locations and stay long enough to guide us. Instead, we had a letter from him at Rendezvous. He suggested Grande Ronde and the Clearwater. The Indians almost decided us against Grande Ronde."

"Too bad Mr. Parker didn't stay to help you locate but he thought he ought to get on back to the States. Sailed from here the middle of June. Still, you can manage all right." McLoughlin spread a crackling parchment before them. "Now right in here," his finger rested on a spot well beyond the northward bend in the Columbia, "is where the Cayuses winter mostly. There's a creek that doesn't show on this map but it enters the Walla Walla just about here. That triangle of land, bordered on the south by the Walla Walla and on the northwest by

(97)

the creek will provide as fine a place as you'll find outside the Willamette Valley for a settlement. It's called Waiilatpu. Means 'the place of the rye grass.' The soil's deep and fertile. There's always water. And, if you're willing to take your chances with the Cayuses, there's where they'll be."

"Waiilatpu. Sounds like the place," Marcus agreed and bent to locate it exactly in his mind. "How far do you call that above Fort Walla Walla?"

"Twenty . . . twenty-five miles. Near enough we can give you a little protection, if need be, and remember I'm not guaranteeing you won't need it. The Cayuse are a tricky, haughty people. They're quick-witted. Some say treacherous. I don't want to harp but I'm going to say just once more, it's dangerous for one white man and one white woman to build a home in the midst of the Cayuse. They can't be trusted." McLoughlin turned to Spalding. "As for Nez Percés, you can find them without much trouble. The Clearwater here," he pointed on the map, "would be a good location. I'm inclined to think Lapwai Creek might be even better."

Marcus nodded. "Isn't that the place Chief Rotten Belly mentioned?"

"Sounds something like it," Spalding agreed.

McLoughlin nodded. "That's his country. The trouble is, it's too far away from the other site. Three days' ride at best. Don't think I'm trying to alarm you. I'm not. But I know that country and I know those Indians. And I say you shouldn't settle that far apart."

Spalding bristled. "Ten days' ride from Mrs. Whitman and it would suit me better," he exploded. "But my wishes don't count for much. If that's as far away as it can be, I'll take it."

"Provided the Nez Percés still want it that way when you arrive," McLoughlin added.

Spalding stood up and yawned. "They'll want it that way. Chief Rotten Belly is meeting me at Walla Walla with an escort."

It sounded as if the whole buffalo had been cut and dried before they came to Fort Vancouver and it hadn't. Marcus had been completely honest in asking for advice. But McLoughlin would lump him inevitably with Spalding and think the whole business a farce to curry favor. Marcus wouldn't have blamed the factor if he'd turned them all out that night to show them they couldn't get along without him. As it was, he would be fully justified, if he instructed his

(98)

traders that they could spare no food nor household goods nor farm equipment for this bullheaded party. Better pin the arrangement down at once, if possible.

"Think we could get started soon?" Marcus asked.

"Pambrun goes back to Walla Walla day after tomorrow. Tomorrow I'll let you have supplies from the Company store on credit. My men will help you pack them into one of my boats and you can go up with Pambrun. That soon enough to suit you?"

No Indian leisure in this man now. Tonight he was the White Eagle and Marcus had him on his side. But McLoughlin would accept no thanks.

"No, don't thank me," he said, backing away. "I'm doing this against my better judgment. You're my friend and I may very likely be sending you to your death. My only excuse is, I'm curious to see what men with your guts and your faith can do against savages with neither."

CHAPTER

2

THREE days, three portages, and three hundred miles up the Columbia from Vancouver, Whitman, Spalding, and Gray leaped ashore with the Factor Pambrun at his Walla Walla post. While they unloaded the food, plows, seed, and tools that McLoughlin had given them on note and credit, Richard and John Ais flung themselves around Marcus like hungry puppies. They begged to know when Mother would return.

When Marcus pointed out the motherly half-breed, Mrs. Pambrun, and Pambrun's pretty daughter, Richard pouted. "That very bad family. Need Mother."

And John Ais added, "Need you likewise."

Marcus promised he'd have a home for them soon and threw a staggering sack of wheat onto his shoulder and started for the warehouse. Maybe he'd done wrong to take the Indian boys East. From their first reunion at Rendezvous they'd seemed cut off from their own families. The boys' travels and schooling had set them apart. They were now at odds with their old surroundings and yet where could they find new ones? They made themselves of some use interpreting, but not enough. And Richard, particularly, had developed a philosophy half savage, half civilized—a belief in socialism with private property privileges for himself—that completely unfitted him for any society. Fact was, he just plain stole things. Still, if they could get settled in a home of their own, Narcissa would find a way to handle even Richard.

Marcus called the others out at dawn the next morning. Piloted by Pambrun, their small canoe pushed up the Walla Walla, winding in and out along the fringe of cottonwoods and birch till late afternoon. Then Marcus called to the Indian paddlers to land on the pebbly north bank at the bend McLoughlin had circled on his map.

Marcus pushed himself sideways through the shrub willows. Snapping through the stiff-armed cottonwoods, suddenly he stood knee-high in virgin grass. He stopped. He heard the chorded rhythm of the Walla Walla at his back join with the melody of the creek ahead to blend into a song of at-homeness. Here he belonged. Here he would bring Narcissa. Here their child would be born. From this spot, one Christian home would reach out industrious, healing fingers to touch the Oregon Country.

Without needing to stoop, he pulled off a broad blade of grass. It tasted spicy sweet. Almost good enough for human food, he told himself, thinking how quickly his trail-thin cattle would sleeken in this valley. He'd have Richard and John Ais drive them here from Walla Walla as soon as he got a house begun. The house must come first —a shelter for Narcissa.

Elation took hold of Marcus. Standing to his knees in moist grass, tasting its life-giving goodness, drinking down the peace of this snug valley, words fitted themselves to the bass of the Walla Walla and the treble of the creek. "If God be for us, who can be against us?"

He bounded through the grass, beckoning the others to follow. He stooped where a spot of earth lay exposed to run his fingers down into the soil and lift a handful to his nose. Its fragrance, its silky escape through his fingers told him the story of centuries of spring floods. On he went toward the knoll to the northeast. From that vantage point, he'd be able to see his valley in one piece. Impatient with his companions' deliberate progress through the grass, he climbed the knoll.

Panting a little, Marcus stood at the crest of the knoll and turned. His valley lay an emerald arrowhead at his feet. Amply watered and protected, some eighty rods of fence across its base would enclose two—maybe three—hundred acres of fertile land.

Across the Walla Walla, beyond the entrance of the creek, he could distinguish five or six villages of Indian lodges like clusters of a child's short-topped X's. The Cayuse villages. Estimating quickly as Joe Meek had taught him from "how many's the lodge?" he guessed that the Cayuse would number perhaps three hundred. All close enough to reach with teaching and doctoring. Far enough away for privacy.

As he turned on to his left, the comforting arm of the Blue Mountains curved along the southern horizon and lifted to a shoulder in the east. Here, perhaps a day's ride away, waited mast-straight pines to cut into building logs.

Gray's voice at his back startled Marcus. "I don't think it'll do. I, personal, wouldn't come so far from Walla Walla. I like it there."

Marcus turned to face Pambrun's frown. "But I understand ze chief factor to say—"

"Right," Marcus agreed. "McLoughlin stretched a point, suggesting a location this close to the Company's settlement."

Spalding cleared his throat. "Har-r-rump! I'm more interested in Mr. Parker's opinion than McLoughlin's. I think you made a mistake to pass up Grande Ronde. It's the Nez Percés he thought we ought to go to."

Pambrun said, "With Monsieur Parker I travel conseederable. He favor ze Nez Percé people. I not understand why you select to reesk your life here with ze Cayuse. But eef you must be so brave," his arm swept the valley at their feet, freely giving it to Marcus, *"aide-toi, le ciel t'aidera."*

But being able to help himself soon appeared questionable. And heaven's help began to look downright unlikely. For, as Pambrun spoke, a whirling cloud of dust swept in from the north. As the cloud skirted to the west, the men on the knoll looked down on a score of Indians, charging in low on their ponies, swerving, weaving, splitting their throats with animal howls. Guns and bows ready for action, the painted redmen circled the base of the knoll.

Pambrun stepped forward and extended his clasped hands in the sign of peace. Then, his open right hand went to his mouth and moved outward to request a council.

The leader of the Indians motioned the others to follow and their horses came snorting up the steep hillside. At the top, the leader reared his pony and raised a choking swirl of dust, coming to a standstill.

Pambrun signaled the chief to come forward and place his gun on the ground.

For answer, the Indian jerked on his rope bridle and his right hand gripped his rifle. Directly behind this Indian, Feathercap, sullen and giving no sign of recognition, sat his pony. The others were strangers to Marcus. They had not been at Rendezvous. His gaze returned to the old chief whose suspicious eyes ran up and down each of the white men.

Pambrun signed again for him to dismount.

Instead, the chief shook his head. And Marcus saw the jaws of each Indian set tight, saw each mouth become a hunting knife slash across a square of leather.

Pambrun turned to Marcus. "This Chief Umtippe. First chief of his village. He refuse to come down for talk."

Marcus grinned. "Well, then, let's talk to him on his horse."

Pambrun's nostrils flared in distaste at this humiliation but he signed for Umtippe to go ahead and talk.

Umtippe answered with a long flow of throat noises.

Marcus saw that these Cayuses wore scanty scraps of skin and woven cloth, tied and laced together to resemble no other clothing. Then he remembered that McLoughlin had told him the Cayuses counted their wealth in horses only. Themselves poor in food and clothes, their fine mounts pranced and strained against tight reins.

Pambrun interrupted the talkative chief to translate. "Umtippe weesh know why white man plant feet upon hees land? Why white man come to ze place of ze rye grass?"

"Tell Chief Umtippe," Marcus instructed, "we come to Waiilatpu to help Cayuse. Bring Book of Heaven. Come to teach hungry ones how to grow food. How make meat in Cayuse country so not go under in Blackfoot hunting grounds. Come to make sick ones live long, not suffer pain."

The bony, disheveled chief pricked up his ears even before Pambrun translated this into Nez Percé. He balanced his rifle across his pony's withers to spread his fingers and wave them in and out in front of his bloated stomach in the sign for sick. But his eyes narrowed again as Pambrun put into his tongue Marcus' suggestion of farming the river valley to grow food. At that, the chief waved a scrawny arm over a small area of the flat bottom land and lifted his upper lip to emit a mouthful of gutturals.

"Chief Umtippe weesh know, How much Bostons pay for land?"

Marcus countered, "White Eagle says build home here. Chief

(103)

Tiloukaikt and Chief Tamahas meet in council at Rendezvous. Smoke together. These Cayuse chiefs invite white *te-wat* make lodge here."

"Tell the lousy chief to mind his own business," Gray blurted, "and stay away from Waiilatpu."

Pambrun hesitated. "*Oui*, but not so easy. Umtippe and his people live here much long time. Thees words make trouble."

Impatient with the delay, Marcus reached deep into the pocket of his tunic. He drew out five lengths of tobacco and spread them on the ground between him and Umtippe. A heavy-browed young Indian slid from his pony, grabbed up the tobacco, and handed it to the chief.

It lay for one long moment across Umtippe's hand and suddenly disappeared inside his blanket. Then, wheeling his pony, the old chief lashed him down the hillside and across the valley. The young Cayuses howled off in his wake.

Marcus watched until Umtippe and his braves disappeared beyond the cottonwoods toward their village. Then he turned to Pambrun. "Bad start. Sorry to have this run-in with the old boy the first day. But we've no time to dicker. Have to get Mr. Spalding located and our houses up before cold weather."

Back at Walla Walla, Marcus arranged with Mr. Gray to take Compo to Waiilatpu and get his house underway. He stayed up far into the night, going over all plans with Gray, making sure that he understood exactly where the house was to set, how to cut out sod blocks for walls, what size timbers to fell for framework, and how much tobacco to pay Indian helpers to keep them happy and working.

Returning the three days' ride from Lapwai after getting Mr. Spalding located, Marcus found that Waiilatpu had changed very little during his week away.

Gray and Compo had managed to scythe the grass from a house site. But they'd cut no sod blocks. They'd dragged in no timbers for the frame. They hadn't tamped down the foundation. On the positive side, they'd somehow built up a wall of antagonism between them and the Cayuse that looked to Marcus almost unscalable.

Instead of helping with the work, the Indians were racing their ponies back and forth or playing catch from corner to corner of the house site. Watching over all this, Umtippe rode up and down on his spotted pony. Muttering, spewing tobacco juice, he stopped now and then to take rifle shots at whatever innocent target Mr. Gray happened to move near.

Questioned, Compo stalled and finally said, "Meester Gray, he make chief mad."

"Gray!" Marcus strode across the clearing. "What's been going on here?"

Gray dropped the hoe with which he'd been listlessly hacking at the foundation line. His hands went to his hips. "The dirty old chief ain't dependable. I ordered him to help. Told him you'd pay. I and Compo can't get a lick of work out of any lousy savage. Umtippe just rides and belches."

"But Tiloukaikt and Tamahas. None of the chiefs could outdo them in promises at Rendezvous."

"I ain't seen Tiloukaikt or Tamahas. Umtippe and Feathercap run things around here, far as I can make out, personal."

Marcus turned to Compo. "Call Umtippe. Ask him why no Cayuses help build our house."

In response to Compo's, "*Come*," Umtippe reined over as slowly as his horse could move. He only muttered and glared at Gray when Compo put Marcus' question to him. Then a long string of Nez Percé spun from him.

Compo's translation was: "Chief Umtippe no take orders. Umtippe geeve order. No take order from mouth of barking-dog-man."

Having crossed the country with Gray, Marcus could understand the implications in this. He grinned at Umtippe. "Compo," he said, "tell him white men friends of Cayuse. Want to help Umtippe. Do good for Umtippe's people. Make sick ones well."

Again came a long flow of Nez Percé.

"He say, Umtippe not now sick. Cayuse no need white *te-wat*."

"Tell chief white *te-wat* show him great wonder—if he quit acting like mad squaw. Say white *te-wat* bring white wife. She sings beautiful music, better than birds. When house is ready, she comes to the place of the rye grass. Umtippe help. Cayuse help. Then Umtippe hear white wife sing."

The old chief listened and forgot to leer. Plainly he was amazed and a bit suspicious.

Then Compo translated his noncommittal comment. "Umtippe no see singing-white-squaw."

(105)

"Tell him Cayuse must come tomorrow. Help build house."

Compo frowned as Umtippe spoke. "He say, Cayuse come."

But Umtippe had more to say. He spat and went on.

Compo nodded toward Gray when the chief finished. "Umtippe say barking-dog-man best hide tail between legs, run far from Cayuse land. Before trouble come with early rain."

Gray sat himself down as much as to say that no savage could tell him what to do. "I'd have the dirty scoundrel flogged."

Umtippe whirled his pony and raked his flanks. Gray ducked as the horse leaped over his head and plunged off toward the river.

Marcus could have enjoyed Gray's splutter more had he known exactly where he stood now with Umtippe. "Well, Compo, are they coming to work tomorrow or aren't they?"

Compo shrugged. "Maybe so, maybe not, I theenk. Some Cayuse good. Some bad. Umtippe no good. Always he make trouble."

Still, Indians did ride into the clearing early the next morning— Umtippe and two dozen of his blanketed young men. They dismounted, turned their horses loose to graze, and sat down. Crosslegged, cross-armed, they had come as Umtippe had agreed. They'd come to watch. They cluttered the house site through the day, looking on. They came again the next day—to watch. In the afternoon when a spatter of rain began, Umtippe reminded Compo that he'd predicted early rains.

"Rains stop white *te-wat*. Stop foolish talk of singing-white-squaw," Compo relayed.

Gray thrust his jaw at Umtippe. "Umtippe no make um rainum."

Disgusted, Marcus kept his voice low. "Mr. Gray! By the eternal, we've got enough languages around here without adding pidgeon Indian."

Umtippe bared irregular teeth to hiss the sounds that Compo interpreted: "Umtippe make rains come early. If *te-wat* smart, he go. Take barking-dog-man far off. Umtippe no see singing-white-squaw."

Marcus clung to his desire to surprise Umtippe with the coming of Narcissa. He worked on the house early and late, beyond his strength. He fought to hide his resentment of Gray's break with the chief and his people. He knew that the bullheaded tactics of his assistant had turned the Cayuse of Umtippe's village against the whole undertaking. But he still held to the hope that when Tiloukaikt and the other chiefs returned from fall hunt, all would be changed.

He clung to the belief that Narcissa could win over even the disgruntled Umtippe. Then he and Narcissa could keep the Cayuse entertained long enough to make them their friends. But he must finish the house before he could hope to bring Narcissa to Waiilatpu. Must race against the fast approaching winter with no time off duty for humoring Umtippe.

When they had placed, notched, and pegged the last rafter into place for the large house, Marcus could no longer ignore Pambrun's warning to expect snow any day. So he revised his plans and they constructed a log lean-to along the west side of the framework. They threw on a roof of poles and mud and straw, and nailed blankets at the door and window openings. They chinked the walls and fireplace with adobe, built in cranes for cooking, and pegged together two crude benches.

Then one afternoon early in December, as Marcus stood off to admire the one chair he'd just finished for Narcissa, the message came.

Trembling with excitement, he saddled Old Muddy and dashed off to Walla Walla to get his wife and bring her home.

When their two horses splashed into the Walla Walla, Marcus felt suddenly grateful for the dark that covered his efforts to provide Narcissa with a house. As they approached, tense silence wrapped itself around them. With a strange reluctance—he'd been in such a rush until now—Marcus helped Narcissa dismount.

A swirl of smoke and sparks rose from the flue. Feeble rays of light spilled out around the blankets at door and window. Marcus ushered Narcissa across the threshold of her Waiilatpu home.

He wanted to look away as his wife made a wide-eyed appraisal of the room and its crude furnishings. But her quick murmur of approval made him watch every movement. He followed her eyes as they took in the crude chair, the shelves and pegs he'd placed to hold dishes and medicines and, above the mantel, his long hunting rifle. Then, with an air of having lived here always, she dropped her bonnet back the length of its ribbons, seated herself on the low bench, and stretched her hands toward Compo's fire.

Flames puffed upward. Narcissa's head lifted and she reached for Marcus' hand. "My husband, who are we that we should be thus blessed of the Lord?"

Marcus breathed deep. He bent to kiss her waiting lips.

A flurry of moccasined feet at the doorway intruded upon them. They turned to see peering eyes at every slitted opening. Not waiting for an invitation, Umtippe and a crowd of men, squaws, and children filed in. The chief took charge. The Indians stalked past Marcus and Narcissa, shaking hands in solemn, single-file procession. "How do?" "How do?" each one intoned. Once past, squaws pointed back at Narcissa and began to giggle. Pantomiming comments on her face, her hair, her long full skirt, they murmured among themselves while the welcoming hosts smiled and repeated in endless monotony, "How do you do?"

When the line finally "how-do-ed" itself to an end, Narcissa's eyes asked Marcus, "What now?"

Just then a scrawny child burst into wails. His mother cuffed his face.

Instantly Narcissa knew what to do. She swept across the floor and caught up the child. The astonished squaw's hand opened as did her mouth, involuntarily. "Poor baby," Narcissa crooned, cuddling him in her full-sleeved arms. His eyes opened wide. His wails stopped short.

Marcus glanced at Umtippe and saw his bronze jaw set, his lips tighten. He wondered how he could explain his wife's amazing action to the stern-faced Indians. What would Umtippe do next to pay for this insult to their age-old tribal customs for disciplining the young? But Narcissa, still murmuring to the hypnotized child, walked to the chair beside the fireplace and sat down. Then, as naturally as if she were in her old home in Angelica with a neighbor's child in her arms, she began to sing.

> Rockaby, Baby
> In a tree top,
> Rockaby, Baby . . .

The leer drained from Umtippe's face and, for the first time, Marcus felt that there might be some good in the old chief. Black growls of protest died in the Indians' throats. They strained to catch each note of the song.

> And down will come baby, cradle, and all.

Marcus couldn't remember how many times she'd sung it. But her voice had never sounded sweeter. The faces of the affronted

Indians mellowed under her magic. The baby closed his eyes and slept but a pleased smile stayed awake, tweaking the corners of his mouth. Still humming, Narcissa handed him into his mother's arms.

As if the return of the sleeping child were a signal, the Indians began to file from the house. Umtippe lingered at the doorway. The others gone, he stood with the blanket door draped over his shoulder and his small eyes flinty on Narcissa. Slowly in guttural English he said, "Umtippe see singing-white-squaw."

Startled, Marcus did not allow himself to dwell on Umtippe's pretense, through all the weeks of building, that he spoke no English. Now his words were good. But their tone bristled with threat. And after Umtippe backed into the night his odor remained. The savage chief had seen the singing-white-squaw rebuke a Cayuse mother. He'd seen her defy a proud people's custom. He'd watched her wield magic greater than that of a *te-wat's* medicine bag over Umtippe's village.

Narcissa stared at the flimsy doorway as if she still saw Umtippe's image on the hanging blanket. Her lips moved. "He hates me." She turned to Marcus and covered her face with her hands. "Husband, husband," she sobbed. "He hates me. Whatever will become of us?"

CHAPTER

3

BUILDING up the fire the next morning, Marcus jumped when Narcissa called out, "Good morning, Doctor."

"Welcome to Waiilatpu," he said. "I was trying to be quiet and let you sleep." He went over to kneel beside her pallet. "You don't know how fofarraw a woman's voice sounds in this wild place."

Narcissa held up her arms to draw him down for a good-morning kiss. Then she looked around the rustic room. "What a beautiful house, Marcus! You're wonderful, and I'm proud of you."

"You look so elegant in these crude quarters."

"I love every board and peg you've built in."

"You'll give it a woman's touch, in time. But take it easy today."

"I can't wait another minute," she cried. "I'm getting up—with your help. I'm becoming pretty awkward. They fed me too well at Vancouver. Always hungry. Wait," she wailed, jerking up the blankets and pointing to the window. "What's that?"

Marcus laughed and stood up. "Callers. They want to know how a white woman puts on her fancy clothes. Wait a minute."

He went to the blanketed doorway. A dozen Indian women and children stood peering in around the edges there and at the window. Unabashed by his coming out, they continued to stare. He gestured for them to clear off and this, only, seemed to surprise them. So he stood guard until Narcissa, fully clothed and with her red shawl around her shoulders, joined him.

"Come, Marcus, show me everything," she ordered. "I couldn't see half enough last night."

"After breakfast," he suggested.

"Good. I could eat a horse."

"You're in luck. We're butchering one today."

Butchering. Clearing land. Fencing. Planting seed. Tending stock. Building beds and chairs. Partitioning off bedrooms at the ends of the lean-to. Learning enough Nez Percé words to start a school and church. Doctoring among the villages of Tiloukaikt and Tamahas. Guarding against the destructive tricks of Umtippe and Feathercap. Mediating between Mr. Gray and everybody, and finally, seeing Gray off to the Spaldings with a sigh of relief in spite of the work he'd left undone. Futilely trying to keep the Indians from spying on Narcissa. Supervising jobs laid out for Compo and their two Indian boys. These made up Marcus' first days of home life at Waiilatpu.

"This is just to get started," he kept telling himself. "Soon, we'll have the house and farm running themselves. Then we can spend our time teaching and doctoring the Indians."

Then after snows had covered Waiilatpu Valley half a month, a breeze sauntered in from the south. Soon after noon, Marcus looked up from the rail fence he was snaking across from the corral to the house and saw his wife come through the blanketed doorway. She wore his leather tunic over her yellow calico dress and a trail-frayed coat. Thinking that she was still graceful in spite of the baby, he watched while she climbed up on the stump outside the kitchen window. Then he knew that she intended to fit panes of glass into the new window casing that Mr. Pambrun had sent out from Walla Walla.

He called for Compo to take over with the split rails and strode to the house. "No can work like Umtippe's squaw," he said playfully, coming up behind Narcissa and lifting her down from the stump. "Doctor's orders."

She protested. "But Marcus, I've waited so long for windows. For privacy."

"That's my job—first chance I get. But not for you, young lady."

She sat down on the stump. She looked so disappointed that he decided to give her, at once, whatever privacy the window glass

(111)

might afford. He went to the side of the house and carried back the door that Pambrun had sent the day before along with the frames.

Narcissa beamed and jerked loose the old blanket. She stood by, humming, while he nailed on the iron hinges he'd bought at Vancouver.

She steadied the door in the opening when he was ready. "A very special kind of door," she said, laughing. "Same as the window frames. Made by a Frenchman with a crooked knife. By contrast I'm reminded of Father. How handy he was on jobs like this!"

"Does hanging a door make you homesick?"

Their eyes met for an instant of remembering but a shadow threw itself on the door between them.

Chief Umtippe rapped out in English, "What this?"

"This is a door, Chief," Marcus answered. For Narcissa's benefit he added with a wink, "A very handy emblem of civilized lodges—if it works."

"Take down," the chief ordered, threat in every undertone of his voice and in the whack of his fist on the wood.

Giving it no importance, Marcus laughed. "Not if I know what's good for my hide, Umtippe. Wife want door. Keep kitchen warm. Keep clean."

A rumble churned in Umtippe's throat and curdled.

Marcus swung the door on its hinges, testing. He closed it, opened it. "Wonderful," he said. "It works. Keep out lots of weather and . . . things."

He carried his tools to the window and Narcissa brought the panes of glass for him to set. He forgot Umtippe. Then the new door slammed and he felt the whole house quiver.

Narcissa jumped and dropped a precious pane of glass with a sickening shatter. Marcus saw angry color rise in her neck. She flew to the door and stamped her foot at the old chief. "Why did you do that?" she blurted. "You nearly frightened me to death. Now you get out and leave my door alone. Get out!" She stamped her foot again. Something in the way she swung her whole body into the gesture plainly said that she'd been wanting to stamp her foot at Umtippe since the first night they met.

And Marcus came close to understanding how she felt. But a chief rated a certain amount of respect. Deliberately Marcus laid on the stump the glass he was holding and stepped to Narcissa's side. When he slipped his arm around her, he felt her body stiffen. "Wife, wife," he said, keeping his voice low. Then he looked at Umtippe and knew this was wrong.

The chief took his words as reproof of Narcissa, defense of Umtippe. Fire died from the Indian's eyes. His head went up in defiance, his shoulders lifted. "That right," he gloated. "Make white squaw hold tongue."

Marcus would have loved to stamp his own foot now. Instead, he said, "Chief not understand. Wife not like big noise in ear. White man like to please wife."

Umtippe spat. "Umtippe squaw please Umtippe. Belong Umtippe, like Cayuse horse. White squaw not work hard like Umtippe squaw. No good. Why *te-wat* not whip white squaw, send far off?"

Marcus hooked his thumbs in his belt beside his pistol and bowie knife. He said, "Since you ask, listen to true words. White man love wife like love himself. Want wife happy. Try to keep wife well. Would die to keep her from hurt. Umtippe should love squaw same way and not make work too hard."

"Who tell chief this crazy talk?"

"You find it in the Book. Law of love say this."

"Umtippe is Cayuse book. Chief Umtippe make own law."

Impatient with arguing to no avail, Marcus gave up. "Listen, Umtippe. Very busy here today. You come back some other time."

Umtippe bristled. "Chief busy, too. Go see Feathercap. But come back."

Umtippe's moccasins hissed on the flattened grass and Marcus picked up his window pane to go to work. He did not look at Narcissa. He hadn't quite made up his mind. Should he scold her or tease her about the episode? He set one square of glass. Another, and another, beveling the putty with his thumb. And, still avoiding Narcissa's eyes, he stepped back to squint at the next frame and figure how to cut glass crooked enough to fit it.

Then he heard a bang, the house shuddered, and the last-set pane hit the edge of the stump with a tinkling shatter.

Marcus' head jerked around in time for him to see Umtippe's blanket disappear, with an insolent flip, beyond the corner. Next, he found himself standing, hand-in-hand with Narcissa, before the door that sagged, now, on one loosened hinge. It was a long moment before their eyes met. Then, together they exploded into laughter.

Narcissa laughed as Marcus hadn't heard her since they left the States—her lovely upward scale of mirth. They laughed until from weakness Marcus leaned against the door jamb and Narcissa leaned on him. He held her hard against him while their two bodies swayed as one with the tempest of their hilarity.

Precisely why they laughed, he didn't know. Perhaps they'd both been touched by his feeble lecture to Umtippe. Or maybe thoughts of home had bound them close. Or, was it more "what God hath joined together"? He wasn't sure.

But one fact he knew too well. The newly intertwined and fusing cord between him and Narcissa would, like a rope across an aisle, prove to be a barrier between the two of them and Chief Umtippe. They'd hung their door—of necessity and with every right. Somehow, by this ritual, their own union had been fortified. They had hung their door but Umtippe and his people were on the other side.

CHAPTER

4

AT DUSK the third day of March when Marcus returned from a stretch of stubbly plowing, he noticed Umtippe's earth-crusted blanket moving in a suspicious hurry away from the house and toward the river. Inside the kitchen door, he found Narcissa in a faint.

When he brought her back to consciousness, she soon calmed his anger. "No, Umtippe didn't exactly hit me. The door did. It could have been an accident. I was hanging curtains at the window. See." She frowned at the wad of blue-and-white-striped ticking on the floor. "They'll have to be ironed again."

"I ought to spank you," Marcus scolded. "You moved your trunk away from that window and climbed up on the milking stool."

"But darling, the curtains have to be up in time for the baby."

"Naturally."

Narcissa leaned back in the chair he'd made her, pulled her face into long Umtippe creases, and growled, "Umtippe no like ambush."

Narcissa's voice answered. "They're curtains, Chief Umtippe. To make the house look pretty."

"Umtippe no like curtains. No like pretty. Keep out Cayuse eyes. White *te-wat*, singing-white-squaw make magic. No let Cayuse see. This Cayuse *wai-tis*. Cayuse see all. Umtippe no like ambush-curtains-pretty."

Marcus carried her across the kitchen to their partitioned-off bedroom. Gently he placed her on the bed he'd just finished nailing to the wall the day before. He laid his fingers on her wrist. Making up his mind, he unhooked her calico dress, paying no attention to her protests, slipped off dress and petticoats, and slid her under blankets snowy white from her efficient wash barrel. "Now then, young lady. Here you stay till I get my daughter."

"Son," Narcissa corrected and held his hand to her cheek. "That's a funny joke, Doctor."

He sat on the edge of the bed. "You're more beautiful than ever."

"And more lazy, too. The idea of being in bed this time of afternoon! What would my mother say?"

"I've no idea."

Narcissa sobered. "I wish she'd say it in writing. Somehow, now —it seems so long. A year and a month since we left and not one letter from home."

Marcus kissed her. "You lie right here and think about it until we get you another little worry."

Narcissa pushed on his chest. "I've no time to listen to such nonsense. Out of my way, Doctor, so I can get those curtains ironed and up."

"Sorry, but I can't take the chance."

Narcissa's eyes opened wide in disbelief. "Darling, you're joking. I can't loll here doing nothing. It's ages yet before I need to go to bed."

"You're in bed," he reminded her, "and if you must have all the reasons, your heart is beating ninety strokes a minute. In bed, the baby may come slower but it's sure as shootin' you'll be safer. Now be a good girl and enjoy your rest."

She rebuttaled and begged but Marcus stood his ground and doubled up on his work.

He sent Richard to Walla Walla to bring back Mrs. Pambrun. She'd be little help because half-breed women caught on slowly to ways white people had of washing—their hands, their food, and their many possessions. But Narcissa would feel better with a woman in the house even though they could only converse in signs and smiles.

Marcus spent as much time as possible in the bedroom with Narcissa and, during visits with her, he began to carve out rockers for a cradle. Between household duties, he butchered another horse so there'd be fresh meat on hand. And, as he could, he cut seed potatoes and got them in the ground, plowed and planted peas, built up worm fence, and dug a few more feet along his irrigation line.

In the house, he cooked and cleaned, directed Compo in his chores, and tried to learn from Richard some necessary words of Nez Percé with which to say: "Drive those horses out of my field," or "Go back to your lodge, now, you've squatted in our kitchen long enough," or "No work, no food. This is a hoe. I'll show you how to raise plenty to eat."

But either the student had too much on his mind or Richard was a half-hearted teacher. The Indians continued to squat, their lice restless in Narcissa's clean kitchen. They did not understand or did not want to understand the uses of a hoe. And their horses suddenly developed a civilized affinity for cultivated fields.

Marcus was no stewer but he didn't like certain changes in Narcissa's condition. He felt sure that his precaution of keeping her in bed would forestall most of the trouble but he'd be glad, just the same, when it was over.

Plump Mrs. Pambrun arrived—to watch. Her greatest and almost only help was in keeping up the fire in the kitchen fireplace and the one in the stove that Mr. Pambrun had lent the Whitmans for their bedroom. All other activities of the household struck her as strange and wonderful, like a horse race or ceremonial dance. Something to observe but not to enter.

The morning of March 14, Marcus said, "Happy birthday, my sweet," and kissed Narcissa awake.

"Doctor Whitman," Narcissa said, "I'm never going to have this athletic baby unless I get some exercise. I'll just lie here until I'm cracked open like an egg shell. He all but kicked me out of bed last night."

"Never can surprise you, can I? That was to be your birthday treat—a rip-roaring walk from this bed, through that doorway over there, past the churn and wash bench in the kitchen, and on to the bench before the fire to have your morning coffee. Since you spoiled the surprise, I ought to keep you in bed."

But Narcissa sat up on the plank-and-blanket bed and swung her feet over the side. Marcus caught her as she swayed. "You're weak, darling. You'll have to lean on me. That's my part of the treat." He got her blue dressing gown from the peg at the foot of the bed.

"I hope he comes today," she said, "for my birthday."

"He?"

"Certainly."

"She!"

"Of course not. Any self-respecting female rides across the mountains to come to Oregon. She doesn't have to be born here."

Marcus bore Narcissa's weight and led her slowly through the door. "Imagine. First white American born beyond the Rocky Mountains. It's like being married to a statue."

"And I feel that heavy." Narcissa sighed and motioned for her favorite chair with the deerhide woven seat. "It's higher than the bench," she explained, "and I don't bend at the proper place."

Mrs. Pambrun poured a cup of coffee, muddy as the Platte, into Narcissa's blue-edged china cup, making this an occasion. Marcus handed it across and then caught it just in time. All color left Narcissa's face. Her fingers dug into her palms. Eyes swimming, she looked up at Marcus.

"First time that's happened?" he asked.

She nodded.

He handed back her coffee. "Drink this then. It'll be a while before the next."

"It's indecent for any man to know so much about a woman's business. Is this it?" she asked.

Before he could answer, the kitchen door burst open. Chief Feathercap, his tunic fringed and draped with medicine beads of wolf fangs, his ruff of hair bristling, followed the door and stood tall against it. His arm pointed past the fire to Marcus but his eyes examined Narcissa while he spoke. "White *te-wat* come. Make well, Chief Umtippe. Umtippe die."

Marcus didn't like the young buck's stares. He stepped in front of Narcissa. "Chief Umtippe not die," he promised. "But white *te-wat* busy here. Can't see chief now."

Narcissa tugged at his sleeve and he stooped to hear her. "Go, darling. It's your first medical call to Umtippe's village. The one you've waited for all these months. Go quickly. I'll be all right."

"No." Marcus turned to Feathercap. "Say white *te-wat* sorry. No come now. Come when sun drop in Columbia."

Feathercap glowered. His hand dropped to the knife in his belt. "Chief Umtippe strong. His people come when he say 'come.'

(118)

Chief Umtippe of Cayuse no like white *te-wat* 'no-come.'" He struck his bangled chest. "Feathercap no like!"

Narcissa gave Marcus a push. "I'll wait for you. I promise."

"You won't have to. I'll be here." To Feathercap he said, "Go now. Tell Umtippe my words."

Feathercap slammed the door.

"He's not as good at that as old Umtippe," Narcissa criticized. "Maybe that's why he's only a second chief. Umtippe can make my teeth rattle when he slams that door."

Her eyes told Marcus that she was whistling in the dark. He didn't want her frightened just now. "Ready to go back to your beloved bed?" he asked. Maybe they could ignore Feathercap's threats until after the baby came, at least.

"Could I have more coffee?" Narcissa asked.

Mrs. Pambrun smiled and took her extended cup. When Narcissa had emptied it again, the walk back to the bedroom turned the trick. Marcus tucked her in.

Narcissa painted, "I'm afraid for you. Feathercap's cruel. You—" Her face writhed and clenched and then relaxed. "You should have gone."

"Don't fret now, my sweet. I'll go. Umtippe won't die. He's a man with a cause. You don't think he'd die before he'd driven us from Oregon, do you? Not Umtippe. I've got plenty of time. You're the one who's going to have a baby—today."

"But he was trying to say that awful thing again. About the next of kin killing the *te-wat* when the patient dies. Feathercap is Umtippe's nearest relative. And he would stop at nothing. He'll be first chief when Umtippe's gone."

"Quiet now."

Color drained from Narcissa's face. She gripped Marcus' arm.

Suddenly in the lulls and quickening intensity, Marcus saw the little room in which Narcissa must bear her child. His mud chinking had softened with the spring rains after the winter's freezes and brown trickles now marred his split-log walls. Narcissa must give birth to her child upon a bed of hacked boards, nailed to the wall. Beneath the bed sprawled one meager buffalo robe for Narcissa's dainty feet, if—

Marcus stopped himself and consciously wiped out that "if." "When she gets up," he corrected and went to the kitchen for a kettle of water that he could set on Mr. Pambrun's iron stove, handy in the middle of the room.

Around the uncertain fit of the room's one window came the sound of the river. Marcus shook down the grate with a clatter.

"Marcus." Narcissa's golden head tossed. She gripped his hand while sweat beaded her brow and he could not stop the pain nor hurry it. "My darling husband," she whispered.

Marcus who had attended a hundred births, found only this one too much to bear. How could he have been so cruel—to bring this delicate, charming girl into the wilderness away from every comfort and security and let her suffer so? Nothing but insanity could make a man commit such treachery upon the woman he loved.

And then he was too busy to rebuke himself. So busy that he forgot to call Mrs. Pambrun. He made Narcissa safe and comfortable and held in his hands a plump baby girl with skin whiter than he had known was possible at birth and a fuzz of corn silk on her shapely head. His daughter.

Thinking Narcissa was asleep, he held the child at arm's length and gloried in her healthy squirming. The sacred moment of birth. And, as always, he was torn between a kind of holy kinship with the Lord of Creation and a sense of his own utter superfluity.

Narcissa's voice came from a long way off, through the voice of the river. "Could I have one tiny look?"

Marcus grinned and turned the child toward her mother. "Mrs. Whitman, may I present your daughter?"

Narcissa's limp smile faded slowly. She closed her eyes. "She'll do," she whispered, "so don't break her. You remember about her clothes in the . . ." She trailed off to sleep.

Then Marcus called Mrs. Pambrun. But he was the one who oiled the child with butter and selected her clothes from Narcissa's trunk beneath the kitchen window. And when Narcissa called, he wrapped his daughter in a small brown sheet and pulled a stool to the bed with his toe. There he sat and dressed the baby. Mrs. Pambrun hung over him, wide-eyed. And Narcissa offered a helping hand to pull down the flannel shirt and hold the diaper in place while he opened a blanket pin and worked it through the layers. Narcissa watched each move he made with solemn face in which her eyes were dancing.

The dressing finished, Alice Clarissa Whitman begged for food

(120)

and slept. Kneeling beside the crude bed, Marcus' arm cradled his wife and daughter. He swallowed and could not speak.

Narcissa turned her head and pressed her lips to his.

Solemn and majestic, the sound of the river now. But then the kitchen door slammed with a quake that rattled the bottles of medicine on the shelf in the corner. Marcus kissed his daughter on her sunny crown and went out to meet the raging Feathercap.

The young chief shook his fist and threatened. He slobbered and swore. He said he'd drive white *te-wat* from this land or spread him out upon it cut up in buzzard bites. "If chief die, next-of-kin," he hammered his chest, "kill white *te-wat* like evil spirit."

All the time, Marcus was getting into his coat and checking his saddlebags on the ready peg by the door. He felt wonderful. Nothing the blustering brave could do or say would make him feel bad this day. Even unmindful of fleas, for once, he gave Feathercap a friendly sock on the shoulder to help him out the door and toward his horse.

Umtippe was rolled in filthy blankets beyond the central fire of his lodge. Swearing rhythmically in English, he writhed in pain.

Marcus signed for Feathercap to clear out the relatives and dogs and moaning sympathizers. They all left except one squaw—Umtippe's favorite when sick—and a black-streaked *te-wat*.

This *te-wat*'s manner struck Marcus as theatric. He gave up his place at the patient's bedside, then backed away to a spot directly in Marcus' line of vision as he looked up from Umtippe—a spot that might have been rehearsed. Now, he went into a paroxysm of threatening fists, contorting legs, bared fangs. Feathercap stood at Umtippe's feet, arms folded, scowl fixed.

So, here was a trap set by the young warrior, next-of-kin to Umtippe. The *te-wat* had been more than willing to pass on his patient, his impending failure. Feathercap had recognized the chance he'd waited for since Rendezvous of '35 when Marcus had forestalled his plot to get Jim Bridger out of the way and take Big Star. Now, the old chief would die and the blood be on alien hands. As next-of-kin Feathercap would be bound by tradition to avenge Umtippe's death.

Umtippe's squaw stood with her back square against the lodge's only opening. Still, before making an examination or administering medicine, Marcus reminded himself that he could leave. The trap was not yet sprung.

(121)

Umtippe drew up his bony knees and wailed, "Chief Umtippe go under. White *te-wat* make big talk many moons. Now not reach out hand. Let Umtippe die."

"Umtippe wicked sinner, deserves to die." Marcus squatted beside the knotted mass of skins and blankets.

Umtippe let out a howl that proved he still had strength left in him. "Take white dog *te-wat* away. White *te-wat* kill Umtippe. Take away."

Trying to shut his nostrils against the smell that rose from the putrid chief, Marcus leaned close. He said, "Stick out your tongue."

Surprised, Umtippe obeyed.

"Camas?"

Umtippe rolled and swore and refused to answer.

Marcus thumped his chest, pressed his bloated belly. He turned to question Feathercap.

The surly chief spat out impatient answers. Yes, Umtippe and his village just returned from Hunt. Grande Ronde. Yes, dig camas, kill buffalo. Of course chief hold big feast. Big feast day past. Celebrate fine hunt. Why white *te-wat* not make fast well? White *te-wat* not know what to do, maybe. White *te-wat* no make strong medicine. Maybe send old chief under. Then Feathercap know what to do. "Feathercap follow trail many sleep. Make big fight. White *te-wat* go under."

Marcus dug into his saddlebag for calomel. But Feathercap's tirade made him wish for some strong medicine that would act at once. He'd give a lot to show that young buck a thing or two. Well, why not?

He bent over the chief's upturned face, spread his fingers and moved them before Umtippe's eyes in the kind of hypnotic gesture he'd seen Indian *te-wats* use to hold attention while they pretended to extract an evil spirit from a patient. Then, with Umtippe gaping, Marcus ran his index finger down the chief's gullet. He took his time, gave him two or three good prods, and hurriedly retreated.

Marcus stood up and then bent to support Umtippe's head while he vomited.

The Cayuse medicine man, waiting to point a death-sentence finger at the white *te-wat* when he failed, could not help recognizing the power of this exorcism.

When Umtippe finished and sank back on his robes, Marcus

stepped to the flap of the lodge. He breathed deep to force the stench from his nostrils. Then, for good measure, he gave the chief a dose of calomel and, without a glance toward Feathercap nor toward the Indian *te-wat*, stepped into the night.

He swung onto his mount. Narcissa would be worried. Still, a silver moon had ridden over the Blues and Old Muddy's hoofs, crossing the meadow to the house, raised a haying smell from the new rye grass. Hard to hurry on such a night. In the moonlight, Marcus saw Waiilatpu squared off and cultivated from river to creek and beyond as far as his eyes could gather in. The framework of his house took on a roof and walls. The Cayuse Indians were clean, upright, and moral. This was how it all must be and would be as a home for his wife and daughter.

In the house, Marcus had to elbow his way through the kitchen and to the bedroom doorway. There Chief Tiloukaikt—tall, sober, naked except for a beaded breechcloth—shook Narcissa's hand while he made a formal speech.

Marcus frowned in spite of himself. Tiloukaikt's two strapping sons and a daughter—Edward, David, and Jane, Narcissa had named them—had been sent to religious services and to hear Narcissa sing night after night. And Marcus liked Tiloukaikt. Still, the chief's close-set eyes had cunning in them even as he spoke kind-surfaced words above the baby.

". . . and Chief Tiloukaikt pleased. Cayuse on hunt, Cayuse at home, Cayuse at war all wait, their hands on heart, for borning of this small one. All our people now shake the hand. Our people pleased."

Marcus heard wrong beneath these words. He tried to think of reasons he could give these savages for shooing them out of his home. Liking Tiloukaikt, he still did not like his tiring Narcissa tonight with his endless handshake and the ragged ends of his hair, when he leaned over the baby, brushed her clean skin. But Marcus could not state such everydayness as a reason for the Indians' leaving. Their hurt would be past curing.

Tiloukaikt gave Narcissa's hand over to Tamahas who bent across the bed to touch the child's soft down with his knife-scarred fingers. Then, as Tiloukaikt talked on, Marcus heard an undertone like the deep push of water beneath a river's surface ripple.

"Now Tiloukaikt say call small one Cayuse *te-mi* for her borning come to pass on Cayuse *wai-tis*. She child of Cayuse land."

Through other speeches and more handshaking, Marcus told himself that the Cayuse's words were merely friendly and not possessive. But when the house was finally cleared, he dampened a cloth to wash Narcissa's face and hands, and searched his sleeping daughter for crawling souvenirs of her Cayuse welcome.

"How's Umtippe?" Narcissa asked him.

He washed a place on her cheek to kiss. "Weak and well. I doctored him with my finger in his throat."

Narcissa giggled. "Puke doctor," she teased. "Was their medicine man impressed?"

Marcus strutted. "He was. I'm a good doctor, I'll have you know. Just look what I've accomplished in this one day."

"Uh-huh," she murmured, accenting the second syllable. "You're some punkin."

"And that's a fact," Marcus agreed, picking up her mountain man lingo. "But if this old hoss are aimin' to get to bed this night, he's gotta get in thar to that bench and wash out that cache of diapers."

CHAPTER

5

MARCUS lay awake in the night, thinking, "June roses back in Wheeler. June brides and summer complaint." At Waiilatpu, the Indians were eating too much camas, salmon were fighting their way against the current.

The Whitmans, too, battled a current of chores and little time-consuming jobs that threatened always to sweep them backward away from the work they'd come to Oregon to do. Wide awake, Marcus nested his hands under his head and tried to practice his Nez Percé vocabulary. He'd attempted to explain the parable of the sower to the Cayuses who'd come to the house on Sunday. And a sorry job he'd made of it. He missed their Indian boys. John Ais, especially, since he'd gone to the Spaldings'. Richard— Well, missing him was mostly disappointment. It hurt to have his experiment with Richard end in having to send the boy back to his Indian village for discipline.

"You were studying your Nez Percé," he reminded himself. "Heaven—*accompenaka*. Grass—*pax*. Rain—*waikit*."

He must get his irrigation ditch finished. They were having rain enough now to keep the ground soft but not enough for cave-ins. And he ought to plant corn. If only he could get more of the Indians to help. But the wind had carried news that Mr. Gray was headed for Waiilatpu. Maybe this time he could figure out a way to keep Gray in better spirits, get more done.

"Worship—*tolla poosa*. God—*Hemàkis Tota*. Brother—*uskeep*. Wife—*waipna*."

(125)

If only he could make things easier for Narcissa! She needed time to regain her strength. No wonder she was cranky at times. He never came to the house without finding Narcissa up to her elbows, dipping candles or making vinegar or sewing or scrubbing or baking with her makeshift oven at the open fire. And always a row of Indians squatted around her kitchen, watching every move, forgetting to take their lice along when they left to make room for other squatters. Poor Narcissa. But soon things would be better.

"Good—*tois*. Bad—*kapseis*. Friend—*sextua*."

Old Muddy carried Marcus down river the next morning to Tiloukaikt's lodges. He played ball for a few precious minutes with Edward and David. Tiloukaikt, coming from his lodge in a clean tunic said, "Two fine sons. You let come back school after hunt time?"

"Sure as shootin'," Marcus answered. "Teach them singing, farming, praying."

"Good." The chief shook his hand. "Good to learn."

"Good to learn how to keep well, how to eat. Not eat too much like Umtippe."

"Umtippe eat like bear. Vomit like dog."

"Old chief need better stomach. Need better heart, like Chief Tiloukaikt and Chief Stickus."

"*Tois*. Chief of Umatillas very good. Evil spirit strike Stickus with cough in mouth but good spirit live in Stickus' heart. Chief Stickus friend of Bostons. *Tois*."

Marcus asked, "Why does Umtippe hate white doctor?"

"Tiloukaikt tell *te-wat* friend true." His flanked fingers moved downward over his heart. "Long time past, white man do to Umtippe bad. Steal most fond squâw." Tiloukaikt smiled, remembering that squaw. "She walk like fine horse. Much time laugh. Make sun much time shine in lodge. White man want." Tiloukaikt shrugged. "White man take. Now Umtippe wait long like panther—spring on white man. So."

Marcus intercepted the ball when Edward threw it to David. He feinted once to tickle the boys and under-handed the ball on to David. "Glad to know this thing about Umtippe," he told Tiloukaikt. "Helps me to know."

Tiloukaikt stepped close. "News come. *Te-wat*'s barking-dog-Gray want Flathead braves take horses far off to rising sun. Trade horses. Bring back cattle, knives, guns. Spokane Gary say 'No.' "

(126)

"Maybe Gray talk too many words," Marcus conceded. "Make big talk. Do not much. Gray stay here, I hope."

On the way home, that news about Gray galled Marcus. Chief Umtippe was old and couldn't be a nuisance for long. But Gray, young and cocksure, roiled the Indians at every turn. He might now be making an enemy of the influential chief, Spokane Gary. And Gray would never be able to lead a trading party East in safety. If he started through with horses and lost them on the way, the Indian owners would strike back. If he lost his Indian companions, their next-of-kin would avenge the wrong. He must block any such crazy scheme before Gray stirred up real trouble.

The drying winds of early June had speeded up the need for more irrigation ditches. So Marcus led a half-dozen reluctant helpers into the field to extend canals to his parching fields. They had barely worked up a sweat when Spalding and Gray rode in from the northeast.

"Just in time," Marcus called. "Draw up a shovel and dig in."

Spalding dismounted and grasped Marcus' extended hand.

"Glad to see you, Mr. Spalding. You're looking fine."

"I am fine," Spalding came back. Marcus noticed that he hadn't harrumped before speaking. Henry caught up a shovel.

Gray slumped on his horse. He said, "Can you have a talk—with I and Spalding?"

"No reason why not. Come on down and start talking. Might push a shovel as you go."

Gray dismounted and neglected to loosen his horse's cinch.

Marcus went to the panting animal, eased the girth, and stroked his muzzle. "What's up?" he inquired, going back and stepping on his shovel.

Spalding said, "Mr. Gray makes a proposition. About the setup here and up Spokane way."

Marcus waited, then said, "All right, out with it."

Gray toyed with a shovel of dirt from the ditch. "Well, it's thisaway, Doc. The American Board appointed me as clerical assistant here and—"

Marcus interposed, "Let's get it straight to start with. The appointment reads, 'carpenter and mechanic.' But go on."

Gray glanced at Spalding, digging ahead of him. "Now Mr. Spalding, he thinks different. I deserve a more higher position—

after all I've done. I clearly understood I'd be accorded my own station and equal rank."

Resting a moment on his shovel's long handle, Spalding explained, "Mr. Gray's been after me about how hard he worked here at Waiilatpu. Then he did lend a hand at Lapwai—part time, anyway. Maybe he's due a chance. A chance to do good on his own hook, as he puts it."

Still digging, Marcus asked, "How long did you help on my house, Mr. Gray?"

"I built practically your house and Mr. Spalding's."

"More like about six weeks here," Marcus continued, keeping his voice cool. "About the same at Lapwai, off and on, wouldn't you say, Spalding? The rest of the time you've been traveling—Vancouver, Walla Walla, and up Spokane way. Is that right?"

Gray raised his voice. The Indians slowed or stopped their digging to watch the white men. "Look here, Doc Whitman, if you think you own me, you got another think comin'."

Marcus saw the gaping Indians bend their ears toward the Bostons. Understanding few of the words, they could not fail to interpret the tones and glances. "Compo, try to keep things moving here," he said. "Going to the house for a while."

He walked Spalding and Gray across the field to the intake of the irrigation ditch. He pointed out, as they walked, strong plants of promising potatoes and small patches of melons and vegetables.

Spalding scratched under his black hat and commented, "Not bad for the first crops in this part of Oregon. Nothing better between Liberty and Vancouver." Then he examined the curving line of the irrigation ditches and said, "Doctor Whitman, you're way ahead of me in farming. A great valley, this."

"Only the beginning," Marcus answered. "Success depends on getting the Indians to plow and plant. We stand or fall on that."

"Quite true," Spalding agreed. "Success depends on the Bible and the hoe."

Gray put in, "I say our first responsibility is to hold the savages under our thumb. Learn 'em morals."

"Undernourished Indians will never make civilized Indians," Marcus replied.

Spalding said, "The trouble is, we spend too much of our time making a living for ourselves."

"We ain't got plenty of people to help us. The Board oughta send—"

Marcus broke in, "Of course. But those we have need to work about twice as hard." He steered the men toward the house.

"If you're referring to I," Gray flared, "you don't appreciate all I've done. I just been exploring up north. I found a needy field suits me to a T."

"So I hear."

"You mean Mr. Ermatinger tattled about my plans?"

"News travels on every breeze in this country, Mr. Gray."

Spalding wiped his brow with a red-bordered handkerchief. He stopped to pant in the heat and pointed his middle finger at Gray. "Mr. Gray, here, is dead set on starting a separate station—doing good on his own."

Marcus snorted. He waved his arm toward the bare framework of his house. Gray gave his attention to crunching clods of dirt with his boot. "Look, Mr. Gray, a half-finished house—and you dash off to do good on your own. Look at the fields. Ought to be twice as much growing. Look at the handful of Indian helpers. Could have had most of Umtippe's village working but you had to roil the old chief the first week. What good can you do on your own, Mr. Gray?"

"Well, I'll tell you this much, Doc," Gray countered. "I get either my own station or else—"

Narcissa banged on an iron skillet.

Marcus explained, "Mrs. Whitman's calling us for dinner. Mondays she has singing class in the afternoon so we eat early. If you don't mind taking your horses to the corral, I'll go ahead and have her set a couple of extra places. But hurry."

Marcus found dinner set on a bare table. "We've got company. Want me to put on a tablecloth?"

He expected a flurry of getting a cloth beneath the food on the table. Instead Narcissa snapped, "No cloth today. I don't have one ironed."

"What do you mean?" Marcus raised the lid of the box beneath her dish shelves. "Look. You've got plenty."

Narcissa swung her frying pan away from the fire and out in front of her offended chest. "We don't use bleached tablecloths for everyday in this household, Doctor Whitman."

And then Spalding and Gray were at the door. Narcissa welcomed them but with no warmth.

"Mr. Spalding, you should have brought your wife. Oh, and Mr. Gray. Come in."

The men washed, splashing water over Narcissa's bench and making streaks on her towel. But she went ahead with getting dinner on until Gray lifted their family comb that hung on a string by the wash bench and raked it through his hair.

Narcissa turned on him then. "Mr. Gray!" But, catching herself, she shrugged and said, "Dinner's ready. Marcus, you show them where to sit and I'll bring in Alice Clarissa."

Dewy-eyed from her nap, Alice Clarissa would have charmed a wooden Indian. And it took Marcus only a few seconds to decide that the two childless men didn't appreciate the smartest, most beautiful three-months-old baby in the country. Their toneless compliments might have been suitable for an ordinary child. Before Alice Clarissa's precocious handling of her head, her intelligent blue glances, the strength in her hands when she squeezed her papa's finger, her tiny rosebud mouth—why not a word they uttered was worth one of her "Ga-gas."

Narcissa was aware of their inadequate expressions, too, so it wasn't a mere doting father's fantasy. Narcissa took Alice away, almost at once, and tucked her into the new cradle Marcus had just finished. Then, unsmiling, she attended to feeding her guests.

The men cut into slabs of horse steak, broiled over live coals.

Gray complained, "I expected cow meat here by this time, Doc. Maybe you save it for Sundays."

"Saving my beef herd, Mr. Gray. Take two years to get it established. But, as Joe Meek says, 'when a man works hard enough, meat's meat.' Makes sense."

Narcissa brought a pan of biscuits hot from the tin baker that stood by the fireplace. Marcus smiled up at her and got a toss of her head in return. Spalding and Gray slapped great chunks of home-churned butter on her biscuits and kept her going back for more.

Finally, Spalding had eased his appetite enough to talk. "Har-r-rump. Doctor Whitman, we came to settle matters about Mr. Gray. We must take some action."

"For instance?" Marcus asked, pushing back his chair.

(130)

"Just this," Gray answered. "I demand my rights. I get my own station to run independent, or . . ."

Marcus smiled. "Or else you go home? Is that it, Mr. Gray?"

"Somebody's been gossipin' again," he said. His eyes popped open but still seemed too close together. "If it's you, Mr. Spalding . . ."

Spalding held up a defensive palm. "I haven't seen Doctor Whitman. Truly."

"Whispering winds again, Mr. Gray. The desert has eyes and ears, you know."

With a teeth-edging clatter, Gray pushed back and stood up. Then, looking down on his associates, he waved his arms and ranted. "I never had me a chance here. I, with all my talents, given menial tasks fit for a dirty Indian. I claim you both tried to keep me from my destiny." He walked up and down the room, his angry face eclipsing the glow of the embers. Then he turned and shouted at Marcus. "My mind's made up. I'm starting for the States and on to Boston. The Board will be glad to give me a new appointment—one suited to my ability and not to a common laborer. I've just decided to take a lot of horses back to the frontier. Drive them through and trade for cattle. Coming back, I'll guide out a party of white settlers. You'll hear from me, you will!"

"This news breezed in last week, too, Mr. Gray. But it's hard to believe any grown man could be so stupid."

"What do you mean by your insinuation, Doc Whitman?"

"Just this. You'd never get through."

"Ermatinger of Hudson's Bay says I can."

"Spokane Gary says you can't. Every war party between here and the States would do their best to prove it. Don't be a flap-eared fool, Mr. Gray."

Spalding sat and squirmed. Narcissa moved about the table, gathering up the dishes. Marcus did not miss Henry's frown as he glanced in her direction.

"Doctor Whitman," Spalding mused, "maybe we should let Gray have his way."

"Why? Why let his poor judgment get us all in trouble?"

Spalding countered, "Well, I'm not positive he'd fail. Now I could name some, not too far distant, whose judgment I'd discount. Some who think they're so high and mighty."

A plate slipped from Narcissa's hands and broke. A small china triangle with a curved blue border bounced to Marcus' feet.

He smelled the kind of dust that precedes a prairie tornado. He heaved himself up. "Work won't wait, gentlemen. Irrigation ditch must be finished. Besides, Mr. Gray made up his mind last month. And you, Mr. Spalding, seem to have fallen under the spell of his talk. But if you persist in this fool plan, Gray, you and your trusting Flatheads do it at your own risk. Yet Mr. Spalding and I will have to pay for it—one way or another."

Gray grabbed his hat from the peg, slammed out with no word of good-by, and stalked to the corral for his horse. The others watched him from the doorway. He grabbed his horse's bridle and jerked the animal around to be saddled. His horse pulled back. Gray slapped it across the head with his reins, threw on the saddle, and yanked the cinch. Then he mounted and spurred into a gallop—across the unfenced field and into the sagebrush sea to the north.

"Take a last look, my friends," Marcus said. "A man with what Joe Meek would call 'a hankerin' for trouble.' And just when we need men here."

Narcissa's voice had a bitter edge. "The infallible Mr. Gray!"

Spalding asked, "Think he might stir up trouble with the Board in Boston? Might misrepresent our situation here?"

"Might," Marcus agreed. "Might very likely. If he gets through."

"I suggest writing a letter of explanation to Doctor Greene, then."

"Not a bad idea," Marcus approved. "Always cauterize a snake-bite."

CHAPTER

6

RETURNING from a good day's work a full year after Mr. Gray's foolhardy putting out for the East, Marcus' saddle squeaked under his weight and all was well. With Narcissa riding at his side and Waiilatpu gathered into snug fences before him, he gulped down whiffs of summer-dried sage. Good. All of this.

They'd found an ideal site for a sawmill at the edge of the Blues. They'd picnicked beside a mountain stream. It had been a day to forget William Gray and his flap-eared schemes. A day to forget Umtippe and his attempts to break down fences, to cave in irrigation ditches—"Umtippe's irritation ditches," Narcissa called them now. A day to forget Feathercap's rantings.

Today, Narcissa hadn't even scolded Marcus for eating with his bowie. She'd been dealing in powder and balls a great deal the past year. Her fireworks had been a little hard to take at times but, looking back, Marcus could understand. She hadn't been well and, too, the Indians got on her nerves—always squatting in her kitchen, always watching, always leaving their filth around in her way. But today, she'd been the old ready-for-anything Narcissa. They'd dreamed a brilliant future for Alice Clarissa. They'd decided to start school early this fall. They'd resolved to learn the Indians' language far better than they had so far.

At the corral, Narcissa clung to Marcus a moment after he lifted her down. "I do hope everything's all right. It's been such a heavenly day."

Marcus kissed the end of her nose. "If you've been in a worry about whether your new girl would take good care of your favorite daughter, you've done a fine job of hiding it all day, Mrs. Whitman. I do believe you forgot you had a daughter until sight of the house reminded you."

"Silly, we've talked about her half the day." She sobered. "But Margaret is young and so many things can happen."

Marcus unsaddled Narcissa's horse and gave him a token rub. "Nothing bad ever happens when Umtippe and Feathercap are both off on a hunt and their village left yesterday. As for Margaret McKay, I think she's going to work out so well that you'll be able to ride with me lots of days."

Narcissa said, "You forget that Mr. McKay left Margaret for us to educate. I'm going to have my hands full. Here." She reached for another sack. "Let me help you rub down Old Muddy so we can go in together."

In the house, they found Margaret McKay setting the table for supper and Alice Clarissa riding the knee of a strange Indian.

"Papa. Mama. Look!" Alice made no move to desert her friend.

A chief, Marcus decided. Not so much from the beading on his elkskin tunic but more from the generations of pride in the lift of his head. And this in spite of the obvious fact that the man was sick. His skin hung in crepy festoons from the too sharp bones of his face. His chest, through the rawhide lacings of his tunic, looked plucked and blue like the breast of a new-born bird. The Indian coughed and the hand that he laid on his sunken chest seemed to fascinate Alice Clarissa with its trembling.

Marcus hesitated then took the child and swung her once above his head before standing her on her feet and giving her a little spank. "You're too heavy these days for riding feet." Wondering why no Cayuses squatted around the kitchen wall, he turned back to the Indian and spoke tentatively in Nez Percé. "What is it, my friend? Medicine?"

The cough again, deep down, racked the frail body. The Indian struck his heaving chest with his fist. He answered in Nez Percé, "Pain. Stab like knife here. No more strong man. Weak like squaw. Stickus hear report concerning white *te-wat*."

So here sat the famed Chief Stickus of the Umatillas to the south. Marcus searched the man's face for any telltale sign of treachery.

Had some *te-wat*, despairing of the chief's life, sent Stickus to Waiilatpu? He asked, "Umatilla *te-wat*—he sent you?"

Stickus' cough tore at his lungs. He shook his head. "*Te-wat* make fist when Stickus leave. No like." For a long minute he studied Marcus, seeming to weigh him against Indian medicine men. "*Te-wat* dance. Show medicine bag. Hit sticks together. Paint black on skin. Make trick like take bad spirit from sick one. Stickus feel pain here." The blue-veined hand trembled on his chest. "Tack-en-su-a-tis say white *te-wat* at Waiilatpu work big medicine. Medicine-in-the-mouth. Medicine-in-the-mouth Stickus think good. Go in neck where cough live. Heart much tired from cough."

Narcissa stepped forward. "Chief Stickus, we want to make you not sick," she said in Nez Percé. "But you know the custom. If doctor try but cannot make you not sick, he will be killed."

Stickus' head lifted and fell. Then, without a word, he pushed himself to his feet. "True. Stickus go now." He tottered toward the door.

Marcus had grown fond of many of his Indian neighbors but he'd never before felt such a rush of love toward one as he felt now toward this suffering chief. He caught both Stickus' arms and urged him back. "Chief Stickus will stay here until not sick," he said. "Doctor will do all he know. Chief Stickus stay and most welcome."

Narcissa frowned but did not speak out when Marcus moved Margaret's pallet from the little bedroom into theirs.

Margaret said, "He's nice. He's been here all day."

Marcus helped Stickus remove his tunic. Then he listened to the chief's labored breathing. He thumped his chest and back. The man was weaker than he'd thought at first. Courage alone held his head erect. Another day in the saddle, two at best, and Chief Stickus would have been caught by one of those coughs that tightened like a shrinking rawhide band until it cut off his wind. Even with rest and proper food, a cure looked most unlikely. Not even medicine-in-the-mouth that went in neck where cough lived was apt to save him.

Still, Marcus wanted to try. He spread on the floor in the small bedroom off the north end of the kitchen a buffalo robe, a bear robe, and three blankets. To raise the chief's head, he rolled another buffalo robe and laid across it a remnant of striped ticking that Narcissa had saved from her curtains.

(135)

When he went to his medicine shelves, Stickus reminded him, "Medicine-in-the-mouth."

Marcus frowned at the inadequate supply of medicines on his shelves, frowned at the inadequacy of all medical knowledge. In this case, the best he knew to do for the poor man was to keep him quiet, feed him nourishing food, and pray that God would cure him. But Chief Stickus had come for medicine-in-the-mouth and nothing short of that would prove the white doctor's claim to making big medicine. Marcus reached for his bottle of quinine and poured out a generous helping.

Stickus opened his mouth. Marcus got a cup of water. He raised the chief's chin, tossed the quinine far back on his tongue, and handed him the cup.

But instead of washing the dose down in a hurry, Stickus held the cup in his trembling hands and deliberately tasted the bitter crystals.

Wincing in sympathy, Marcus told him, "Swallow. Drink water fast."

Stickus swallowed and gasped. But instantly he rearranged his face. "Good," he said. "Trapper Joe Meek say trust doctor. Good."

Marcus wanted to laugh and at the same time he felt humble. A man who could call a dose of quinine good was giving more trust than any doctor deserved. Helping Stickus with his tunic, he asked, "When chief see Joe Meek?"

"Trapper on Umatilla time past seven suns. He say he come Waiilatpu."

Marcus was glad to hear that his old friend traveled in the neighborhood. But getting the chief to bed and trying to make him comfortable drove all thought of Joe Meek from his mind. He forgot to tell Narcissa.

The chief submitted to the pallet and Marcus covered him with one of Narcissa's white blankets. Working by candlelight, he inserted a thin scalpel in Stickus' wrist to bleed him. But he soon closed the vein and went into the kitchen to make a pepper poultice.

He sat with the chief through the night in order to keep the poultice on his chest. Stickus was a good patient. Even the hot, itchy poultice made more sense to him than a *te-wat*'s juggling. But Stickus was no better by morning. His cough came just as dry and rending. His color remained as pasty gray. And, having trusted the doctor, his own will had relaxed so that he appeared much weaker.

He lay like a dead man on his pallet, moving only under the attacks of coughing, then settling back with a telltale smear of blood on his chin. By nightfall of the second day, Marcus felt it an imposition on Providence even to pray that Stickus might live until morning.

At midnight, Narcissa came into the room to send Marcus to bed with the reminder that he had done all he could.

He reached for her hand and held it against his cheek. Absently he asked, "Finish dipping candles?"

"Sixteen dozen," she answered. "They're nice, too. Very white."

"Always something that's no part of our main job."

Narcissa bent to lay her cheek on his hair. "You're so tired, my husband. No sleep at all last night. Just go take a nap, at least."

"Always something," Marcus mused. "Then when a job like this comes along, it comes too late."

Startled, Narcissa pulled away to lean over Stickus. "Marcus, how you frightened me. Why, he's only sleeping and breathing a bit easier, I do believe."

"Don't get your hopes up."

"Husband, go to bed for an hour. I'm not sleepy and I want to read for a while—with no Cayuses staring at me."

Feeling sure that Stickus would not reach the crisis within an hour and knowing that they'd need some reserve after the end had come and the news gone out, Marcus kissed Narcissa's forehead and dragged across the kitchen. He collapsed on the bed.

With a guilty start, he became aware of gray light and of the river outside the bedroom window. The river's tone was no longer the dirge of the past two days. Stopping only long enough to bend over Alice Clarissa's cradle and touch his finger to her cheek, he hurried to the other bedroom.

Narcissa, still sitting by Stickus' pallet, her Bible on her lap and the candle at her shoulder spluttering in the last of its own juice, greeted him with a proud nod toward their patient.

Marcus squatted beside the chief and found him sleeping, his respiration regular. His pulse, too, had steadied—seemed almost normal. And Stickus' thin hand, still blue, had now the weight of life about it. Peeling back the blanket, Marcus laid his ear on the Indian's chest. Convinced at last, he twisted on his heels to Narcissa. "You've saved him."

Her fingers brushed his temple. "No, Doctor, it was your medicine-in-the-mouth and on-the-chest. I only asked the Great Physician to bolster your efforts."

Marcus stood up and Narcissa, laying aside her Bible, stood beside him. Together they looked down on one of God's orderly miracles—medicine, prayer, time, and a sick body recovering. The everydayness, the newness of it held them for one long moment.

Then, hardly knowing that he spoke, Marcus whispered, "I love this man."

Narcissa nodded. "He seems truly like a brother."

Stickus' eyes drifted open for a second only and his face lighted even though the smile he attempted didn't mature.

"We've made one friend in Oregon," Marcus said. Then, with the meager sound of it pressing in upon him, he added, "One friend in two years."

For answer, Narcissa shuddered.

He hadn't intended to frighten her nor to sound discouraged. Actually he felt hopeful. One little success gave a man yeast enough to make him sure he could bake a loaf. He hugged Narcissa against him. "Nobody needs more than one friend at a time, my sweet."

CHAPTER

7

GIVING him an occasional dose of medicine-in-the-mouth when he begged for it, they kept Stickus in bed for three weeks. Mostly, they treated him with wholesome food, Narcissa's songs, Alice Clarissa's chatter, and long discussions of Indian customs and Christian teaching. Henry Spalding took a vociferous part in these discussions during a brief visit he made to Waiilatpu.

The Whitmans grew so fond of Chief Stickus that they declared a half-holiday the afternoon he first sat up in a chair for an hour. Exhausted but delighted with himself, Stickus went back to his pallet to celebrate. Narcissa told Margaret McKay that she could try her hand at baking a cake. Then Marcus and Narcissa took Alice between them and skipped off to the river.

"Alice love water. Come Trapper. Come swim with Alice."

"Must we swim with that dog?" Marcus asked, stooping to scratch the head of the cheerful black and white mongrel that had stopped growing well before he got to be a collie.

Narcissa teased, "You know you're as daffy about that dog as she is."

At the water's edge Narcissa skinned off the child's calico dress, leaving her in long ruffled drawers. Then Narcissa sat on a log and pulled off her own shoes and stockings. She tied her skirts into a draped apron that barely covered her knees. Marcus rolled up his leather pantaloons and caught Alice who had already waded in alone to capture a green leaf boat that floated on the lazy current.

"None of that, young lady. Mama and Papa hold Alice's hands in the water."

Taking her between them, they waded her out waist deep. She laughed and splashed, finding it only fun when her bare feet slipped on the smooth stones and she went down to her neck before they pulled her back.

"Alice drink!" she screamed in delight.

Since she was wet all over anyway, Marcus balanced her firm middle on his hand and told her to kick and splash to her heart's content.

"She's too little," Narcissa objected.

But Marcus watched her determined striking out and knew that she would soon learn to swim. A precocious child, every inch Narcissa's daughter.

Then from across the river and upstream, a bit, they heard a long animal wail. Even Trapper froze to listen. Marcus set Alice on her feet and hooked her fingers in his rolled-up buckskins. Then he let out an answering howl.

The response rolled back like an echo.

"Well, come on in, you old beaver. Where you hiding?"

After a long minute a bewhiskered head poked through the willows directly across the river and Joe Meek's eyes grinned out at them.

"Doc," Joe shouted, "can you stake me to a pair of britches? This child's done stripped bare as a jaybird fresh outa the shell."

"You sound crazier than a loon but I'll see what we've got handy."

Joe yelled again. "Sorry, Mrs. Whitman, but this child aren't presentable and that's a fact."

Marcus thought a second and then led Alice to her mother. He waded ashore, got the child's dress, tied a rock in it, and waded out again with a "Sh-h-h-h," to Narcissa. Bursting with his joke, he heaved the dress across the stream.

Alice Clarissa clapped and squealed.

"You women have no modesty," Marcus told Narcissa when she and Alice giggled at the sight of Joe Meek, clutching at shrubs and sidling out for the bundle.

"Shut your eyes, Mr. Meek," Narcissa called. "We can still see you."

"Always hear your wife's a flirt, Doc." Joe ducked under cover.

Then, when he'd had time to get his costume untied, the shrubs that clothed him started shouting mountain man epithets that were music to Marcus. That was all he'd wanted. Now he'd go to the house and get Joe some clothes.

But Joe Meek, having made good use of Marcus' joke, appeared on the bank. He'd managed a fine calico diaper from the dress. And, while the Whitmans laughed, Joe waded and swam the river. When he shook himself in shallow water before them, Narcissa's hilarity failed to disturb old Joe.

He pointed to her high-water drapery and a flush touched Narcissa's cheeks. Sheepishly she untied her skirts and shook them into place around her bare feet.

Marcus wrung Joe's hand. "Well, this sure does beat all. Been without clothes some time, judging from the way you're scratched up."

Joe explained. "Squaw jumped camp. Went off with her people. Took my little Helen Mar. I'm trailin' 'em to get her back."

Marcus shook his head and clucked. "Well, well. Looks like old Joe Meek's losing out all round. Took your daughter and your clothes to boot?"

"Helen Mar were that squaw's idee. Clothes were some Cayuse's idee—smelled mighty like that Feathercap's doin's."

Narcissa flew to the riverbank and caught Alice by the seat of her drawers. "No. No," she scolded and turned. "Mr. Meek, you haven't met our Alice Clarissa. Here's a friend of your papa's, my little mud hen."

"You don't say!" Joe squatted to catch the child under her arms and swing her high.

When he set her down, Narcissa draped her skirt around the little girl. "Say how do you do to our friend, Alice."

Alice pointed and giggled. "He wear Alice' drawers. No . . . Alice' dress." Then, remembering her mother's request, she tucked her chin down and said "How do" to her own stomach.

"Just like an Indian," Marcus said.

"She are the spittin' image of you, ma'am. Purtier'n a picture."

Pleased, Narcissa said, "We'd love to see your Helen Mar, Mr. Meek."

"You will, I'm tellin' you. This old hoss'll get her back. Then, previdin' you're willin', ma'am, I'm bringin' her hyar for you to l'arn her readin' and manners. Old Gabe and me got it all laid out. Jim's got him a sweet little gal, name of Mary Ann and hair the color of October grass. He want me to ask could he send her hyar to l'arn to be like you, ma'am."

Narcissa glowed. "Why, how wonderful, Mr. Meek. She'll be more than welcome and your Helen Mar, too. Marcus, it's an answer to prayer—two playmates for Alice Clarissa. You can't get them here too soon to suit us, Mr. Meek."

As Marcus piloted him through his grain fields, over to the long fence to see the small Cayuse farms, and into the house, Joe Meek kept repeating, "This is some now." He sniffed at the odor of Margaret's cake. He had to talk above the sizzle of horse beef that Narcissa was broiling at the fireplace. "Makes a man sorta hanker to . . ."

"Hanker to try it yourself?" Marcus asked.

"Mebbe so," Joe said, peering into the fire and scratching his woolly face. "Or mebbe it's just a hankerin' to slice off these hyar whiskers so's this old hoss'll fit with all your fofarraw doin's hyar. Borrow your bowie?"

"Sure as shootin'." Marcus reached his knife from its sheath that hung by the door. "Remember how nobody'd ever ride in front of old Shunar?"

They were off then into reminiscences that chained through supper. They interrupted themselves only long enough for Joe Meek to tell Alice a bedtime story while Narcissa took Chief Stickus a bowl of thick soup.

Joe's story about old Hugh Glass and the mother grizzly knotted Marcus' very insides as he leaned in the bedroom doorway listening. But Alice Clarissa, a serene smile on her face, fell asleep at the goriest part. She kept a deathless grip on Joe Meek's trigger finger.

When Joe finally maneuvered an escape and came into the kitchen, Marcus motioned him toward a chair. But Joe crossed his moccasins and eased himself to the floor in front of the fire. Marcus sank down beside him.

They sat in silence for a long time. Marcus listened to the murmur of Narcissa's voice in the little bedroom. She had to talk with Stickus to keep him eating. Margaret's shyness made her move, without intruding, from table to dishwashing bench. The river beyond the house was, gradually, no longer the Walla Walla, but the Green, repeating its invitation to move on west. Marcus said, "Didn't see Gray at Rendezvous last summer, did you?"

"That lousy skunk! Seed him and smelt him. Wouldn't take no advice from me or old Gabe or nobody. 'I can take care of I,' he says." Joe spat into the fire. "Like as not, some other Injuns finished the Sioux's job for 'em."

"Claimed he'd get a better appointment from the Board. Trade the Flatheads' horses for cattle. Then bring out a party of settlers. I was against it at first but we need white helpers."

Joe Meek sighed. "Thar's two sides to that, Doc, but I reckon you know 'em both. Bring a pa'cel of whites in hyar and it'll be good-by beaver."

"But men's souls are important, Meek. And besides, there's more money in Oregon soil than in buffalo runs and beaver streams, if it comes to that."

"It'll come to that and you can go your pile on it, Doc. Has come to that with Hudson's Bay a'ready. They aren't goin' to let no sizable party of Bostons in hyar."

Remembering the letter that he and Spalding had sent to the Board the week before, Marcus winced. That letter had been nagging at him a little ever since he signed it. Still, he wasn't quite ready to give up. "Spalding and I just wrote our Board to send out two hundred helpers and enough plows and other equipment to get something done here."

Narcissa, coming in, asked, "What do you honestly think, Mr. Meek?"

"Two hundred settlers from the States," Joe Meek ruminated.

"Someday they'll come," Marcus asserted. "Come in wagons, by the hundreds."

"But what about Injuns?" Meek asked. "Think they'll stand for bein' pushed around? Like the Cherokees and Creeks and such? Or fight, mebbe?"

"Tete teluit ainees koonapa kapseish."

They all turned to see the Umatilla chief clinging to the door frame. In spite of his threatening "Indians make bad spirit" his eyes looked on them as his friends.

Marcus got to his feet and led Chief Stickus to a chair on the

(143)

hearth. He spoke to him in Nez Percé. "Talk now, my friend. We need wise counsel."

Stickus raised his hand to greet Joe Meek. Then, concern in his voice, he said, "Stickus not feel good when hear many Bostons come. Many white men make much trouble."

Marcus tried to reassure him. "White men come as friends of Indians. Bring many cattle, make big farms, raise much food. Help Indians."

"Buffalo leave when white man come. Indians feel pain in empty stomach."

Truly wanting information, half arguing against himself, Marcus tried to show Stickus how the coming of whites could help the Indians and help the Oregon Country.

"Stickus friend of white *te-wat*. *Te-wat* save life. Singing-white-squaw good. Still, many Cayuses, many Walla Wallas, some Nez Percés say Bostons must not come. First chiefs say, 'No. Will fight. Will kill.' "

Marcus saw Stickus' hands begin to tremble. He led him back to his pallet and tucked him in. "Soon you'll be well," he told him. "Can go home to lodge. Then, have no fear. You and I will keep the peace with a firm hand, no matter how many Bostons come."

When Marcus went back to the kitchen, Narcissa dropped her sewing and caught his hand. "Darling, I'm afraid that letter was hasty."

"I'm sure of it," Marcus admitted, "now that Joe Meek and Chief Stickus both agree. Only hope that letter gets lost on the way East."

"That kind never gets lost," Narcissa replied. "Only letters we want to receive."

"And that's a fact. Recollect onct—"

Marcus dropped to the floor again, prepared for another of Joe's stories.

Narcissa stood up and snuffed the candle on the table. "If you two are going to reminisce again, I'll be excused. Plenty of blankets here on this chest, Mr. Meek. Please make yourself comfortable for the night."

"Thank you, ma'am, and sweet dreams to you."

After Narcissa had gone into the bedroom, Meek rocked back on his borrowed pantaloons and stared at nothing, but what he saw set his jaw forward and pulled his lips into a sneer. Suddenly he turned and fixed Marcus' eyes. "Kin you take a blow, Doc? Seems I just oughta tell you straight."

"Anything, Meek. You know that. Level your hindsights and shoot."

"Know Gray had four Flatheads with him?" Joe paused for Marcus' nod. "Well, I warn't thar but I got it straight from some drunk Sioux braggin' at Laramie. They claim that son-of-a-coyote sold out them Injuns to save his own hair. Traded all four of their lives for his what aren't worth a buffler chip in hell. Now that make him lower'n Shunar hisself and it puts you ag'in' a wall facin' the muzzle of every Injun rifle west of Rendezvous. All that without no more Bostons, too. If he did happen to bring a party of whites through, it'd just add logs to the Injuns' fire. That white-livered posy—" Joe spat and the fire hissed—"he'll be the death of you yet, Doc. Give the word and this old hoss'll get him sent under, clean and proper."

Marcus laughed, but not Joe.

"I'm warnin' you, Doc. I know Injuns and I know how they'll stick together ag'in' whites."

"But what if Gray brings out a real party of settlers? We might be strong enough to take care of ourselves."

"Injuns'll stick together ag'in' two hundred, same as two, Doc, and have all the more reason for stickin'."

"But what can I do?"

"Get word to Boston that you're not nowhar nigh ready for two hundred whites and give me the word to get that skunk, Gray, sent under."

Marcus grinned. "Don't be ridiculous, Meek."

Joe Meek unbent his knees and stood tall against the mantel. "Doc, ever notice how a Injun'll lay a fire with just the ends of his wood on the heap? Injuns got a sayin' that a white man builds his fire so hot he can't get up to it to warm hisself." Joe folded his arms on his chest. "For my pile, Doc, you're burnin' your logs right through the middle. It's your life you're gamblin' with and you'd best go to bed and sleep on it till you come to your senses."

Marcus went to bed but not to sleep. If it were true that William Gray had actually got in a tight place on the way East and bargained for his own life with the lives of his four Indian companions, all of the Board's work in Oregon could be doomed. And, if the tale were true, Joe was right. Their lives were at stake and the lives of any other white families who might come out. Still, what could he do? Perhaps Mr. Gray wouldn't return. But, even while he toyed with this hopeful supposition, Marcus knew that a bad penny could be counted on to come back.

CHAPTER

8

NEWS traveled in the Oregon Country without benefit of post or paper. Tales could shape up in Pawnee or Sioux, speed westward through Shoshone or Spokane, arrive in Nez Percé, and come out in sign or broken English with alarming accuracy. Thus, one evening late in August, a band of Cayuses rode up to the Whitman home and interrupted a front-step visit with the Spaldings. Shaking their fists, they muttered an impossible story.

Marcus turned to Henry and Eliza Spalding, standing in the shade near the door. Maybe they, with their better handling of the language, could make some believable sense from the sputtered Nez Percé sounds. Narcissa came to the doorway. She breathed in the dust raised by the milling ponies and coughed.

"What do you make of this, Mr. Spalding?" Marcus asked. "Must be some mistake."

Chief Tiloukaikt who still sat his heaving pony leaned down. "Braves speak true. Barking-dog-man bring many Bostons." His signs indicated both men and women.

Marcus reached for the chief's halter rope. "Tiloukaikt, how many white men? And are you sure that Mr. Gray comes again?"

"Chief and warriors come from Rendezvous. See many Bostons. Barking-dog-man," he paused to spit, "bring to Waiilatpu. My people not like."

Spalding turned to Marcus. "Do you suppose the Board is answering our request for two hundred helpers? Or has Mr. Parker been busy?"

"Board hasn't had time to get our letter yet," Marcus reminded him. "Maybe Parker raised money and an army of re-enforcements when he got home." Then, at the chief's sour expression, he decided to step inside and bring out a rope of tobacco. Handing it up to Tiloukaikt, he asked, "You say many Bostons come. How many? Two hundred? One hundred? How many?"

The chief lifted the tobacco to his nose. *"Elahne."*

Marcus frowned. "Plenty." Plenty in this country usually meant lots. "But how many?" he persisted.

Tiloukaikt turned his pony and quirted him with the tobacco. His braves followed, kicking up a cloud of dust on the river trail.

Narcissa and Eliza covered their faces with their aprons for protection. Henry Spalding blinked. "Har-r-rump. Preposterous!"

"This must call for a cup of tea," Narcissa said with a wink for Marcus and led the way inside.

The hot liquid soon loosened their tongues. Marcus could not hold back their burst of words—planning, placing re-enforcements at strategic new stations, picturing Christian homes among the scattered tribes, and stocking them with food and seed from his and Henry's storehouses.

While they talked, Marcus watched his light-struck Alice struggle to teach scooting, ten-months-old Eliza Spalding to "stan' up straight and *haum teets.*"

Narcissa stopped sipping tea to correct her. "Alice, no! Stand up straight and go fast." To Eliza she added, "That will be one of the most grateful things to me—to have other white families and other children for Alice. The Indians love to have her learn their words for everything but I prefer an American daughter."

Eliza massaged her still youthful hands. "She will learn both," she said. "It will do her no harm. And maybe some good will come to the Indians."

Marcus broke in, "The Cayuse even claim our daughter."

This talk fascinated Alice more than her unresponsive walking pupil.

"Alice Cayuse *te-mi,*" she boasted. Then, placing her hand on her head, she frowned. "But Alice have very bad *hookoo.* Not like Cayuse."

Marcus lifted her high. "You have beautiful *hookoo.* Just like Mother's."

"Hair, Alice. And you, too, Marcus. Please talk English to her."

Alice giggled and Marcus swung her down between his legs and up again. "Funny little cub," he said, holding her close. Her heart beat against his. Her arms set up a kind of panting happiness within him. "I'll tuck her in," he told Narcissa and tipped Alice down for her mother's good-night kiss.

"*Penemeek, penemeek, penemeek,*" Alice Clarissa chanted.

Narcissa gave her a spank as Marcus turned away. "Sleep, sleep, sleep," she insisted. "And you wake up in the morning talking English or Papa will have to put up a lodge for you in the yard like a real Indian."

When Marcus went back to the kitchen, he added another log to the fire. Mrs. Spalding had settled small Eliza on her pallet and picked up her darning. The fire blazed yellow and talk broke out again.

But Marcus, somehow, couldn't toss in with the others' rosy plans. He kept remembering the anger in Tiloukaikt's eyes when he brought the news, "plenty of Bostons." And, the morning Stickus set out for the Umatilla, a well man, he'd repeated his warning. "You Stickus' friend. Stickus fear for you in this country, if many Bostons come. White men make much trouble."

Still, if they could get the right kind of white men. And get enough whites to break out this great country and show the Indians how to live in the health and peace of plenty— Or, if they got whites in sufficient numbers, would they simply take the land away from the Indians as had happened in other parts of the country? No. By the eternal, no! Not if they selected to live near them white families who'd come to Oregon from unselfish motives. True, whites and Indians hadn't managed well together in New England or Georgia, for example. As Stickus said, white men started Indian wars. But surely the right kind of whites—

While the others planned, a war between hope and history went on within Marcus and came to no decisive battle. Relieved when he could finally bank the fire for the night, he suggested, "Maybe we'd better sleep on it and see what tomorrow brings forth."

Eliza broke off her yarn and leaned near the candle on the table to inspect the darn she'd finished in Henry's sock. Then she rubbed at the needle pricks on her index finger.

When the Spaldings had gone into the north bedroom, Marcus

slipped his arm around Narcissa's waist. And he saw Spalding, in the shadow of his room, watching. On his face, Henry wore again that old tight-lipped disapproval that he'd worn, night after night, across the continent.

Marcus' arm tightened its curve. He said, "Better get a good night's sleep, Mr. Spalding. We'll have plenty to keep us awake when Gray arrives. He'll be bloated with the glory of having led a large party over the mountains."

Early the next Tuesday morning, Mr. Gray—"Doctor Gray," he corrected—and his bride arrived in time for breakfast. They'd ridden on ahead to prepare the way for "Doctor" Gray's large party.

Mary Dix Gray dropped an inert gloved hand into Marcus' palm. Her full lips continued to droop as she spoke. "How do you do."

Narcissa, given her turn, kissed Gray's bride on the cheek. "Let me take your cloak. And do sit down or have you been sitting too much and too hard across the mountains?"

Mrs. Gray ignored Narcissa's knowing humor. She said, "Mrs. Whitman, I wonder if you can show me to my room. Doctor Gray had to ride so fast—well, I'm very tired."

Marcus, expecting almost anything, marveled at Narcissa's answer. "Dear me, let me see, Mrs. Gray," she said too sweetly. "Your husband's return to Oregon catches us with our house only half completed. But make yourself at home in my room for now."

Marcus motioned Gray to a chair and listened, astonished then relieved, when the man translated Tiloukaikt's "plenty" into nine. Nine!

"Yes sir, nine," Gray bragged. "I came through safe—with three other couples besides I and the wife. I brought, like I promised, good workers. Three ministers with their wives, a young man as a laborer, besides a Swiss general, name of Sutter, on his way to California. Also, Ermatinger—a big man in Hudson's Bay. And," he laid his hand on his own flat chest, "another doctor to civilize Oregon."

Marcus longed to let go in a laugh. Yes, of course, nine would seem like a great number to the Indians, especially since that nine included four white women. He still hadn't caught the wilderness news service in error. Nine were "plenty." Instead of laughing, Marcus raised his right hip from the chair to pull a short length of rope from his pocket. "When did you get to be a doctor, Mr. Gray?"

Gray squirmed in Narcissa's favorite chair and propped his dusty boots on the bench by the fireplace. "I went to Fairfield, same as you, Doc."

"When?"

"I went last winter, of course. I'm a good doctor, I'll have you know. More than good enough for Indians."

Marcus knew that the only training Gray could have received while in the States had to come from sitting in on a short course of public lectures on health. He said, as Narcissa came back from the bedroom, "You'll need to help us build some beds around the wall here in the kitchen. Need you more as a carpenter than a doctor."

Gray plunked his feet on the floor and stood up. "I plan to take the wife on to see Walla Walla. Right after I've had breakfast—if you can make out without me."

"We'll struggle along, Mr. Gray." Surely not even Gray could miss the scorn in Narcissa's voice.

Marcus untwisted the end of his rope. "You might enjoy Walla Walla, Mr. Gray. But you'll be healthier if you stay clear of Flathead country."

"Flatheads!" Gray snorted. "I hope never to run into any more cowardly Flatheads. If I told you the treachery of them Indians I took to help drive horses to the States, I'd dumfound you, Doc."

"You might, at that."

Marcus got up, selected a coil of rope from the peg by the door and started splicing. Gray launched into a red-faced tirade about the four Flathead boys. Marcus recognized in Gray's account nothing that resembled the rumors whispered and signed through the country. Here was a tall tale of a white man's bravery and brilliance, a sole surviving hero who surmounted the toughest odds to carve out a noble victory. His Indian companions deserted this hero and suffered the just consequences—arrows in the back and lifted scalps.

"We'll just let this lie," Marcus began, then—realizing the sentence couldn't end there—he added, "until we've settled our little party of re-enforcements." He was thinking that he must take time to ride down and explain to Tiloukaikt that nine white men and women who would be scattered among neighboring tribes were nothing for the Indians to fear.

The next afternoon as Marcus returned from his chores, Alice

Clarissa ran to him, calling and pointing toward the east, *"Shecum, shecum."*

"Horses, Alice." Narcissa, following, lifted the child in her arms. "They are coming, Marcus. This must be our party. Whatever shall we do with them?"

"Feed them first. Then settle the families where they'll help the country most." He reached across to Alice Clarissa's extended arms and grabbed her up to a seat on his shoulder. "Come, my little Cayuse *te-mi*, let's welcome our guests."

"I'll set the table and cut some melons," Narcissa called back on her way to the garden. Marcus knew she'd been baking pumpkin pies all morning. There'd be food a-plenty.

In the meadow a half-mile east of the house, Marcus met two galloping riders. First off his horse, a thickset man with one drooping eyelid that gave him a roguish look, Francis Ermatinger introduced himself and turned to the other.

"This dapper young man," Ermatinger said, "is Captain John Sutter—all the way from Switzerland and bound for California."

"Welcome to Oregon, Captain."

Sutter swung from his saddle and returned Marcus' grip.

"A man with gumption," Marcus approved to himself.

Ermatinger's thick arm waved back over the way they'd come. "Your helpers are bringing up the rear, Doctor. They'll be a couple of hours yet. Mostly they're not folks to go it all in one pull."

Captain Sutter slapped his thigh and guffawed at this. Something told Marcus to change the subject and the same something kept him from getting his hopes too high about the helpers Gray had brought to Oregon.

Narcissa hurried across the yard, the Spaldings behind her. Alice Clarissa still on his shoulder, Marcus made introductions.

Narcissa, always elated by company, said, "Come inside. You're to sample our Oregon melons first thing."

Marcus screwed Alice into her high chair and motioned the others to the table. But before they could be seated, Indians began to flock in. Old Indians in calico and buckskin. Young Indians in beaded tunics and painted faces. Clean Indians. Dirty Indians. Bucks in breechcloths. Squaws bundled into shapeless mounds of all the clothing they owned. Half a hundred Cayuses filed into the kitchen to shake hands with the new Bostons. Narcissa fumed. Marcus hurried the procession as best he could while the feast waited. Finally satisfied, the welcoming party filed out to stand at the windows, peering in. When Marcus got his guests seated and the blessing asked, Narcissa's pleasure in company had all given way to nerves. She squirmed and moved her chair, trying to escape from the eyes at her back.

Not even the babel of compliments on melons and pies restored Narcissa's party mood. But from reminiscences of food and famine along the trail, Marcus disentangled a few basic facts. Francis Ermatinger, Hudson's Bay trader, rather than Mr. Gray, had guided the party through. Gray had obviously not suffered from popularity along any part of the journey. Marcus decided that, before outsiders, they ought to keep off the subject of Mr. Gray. He turned to Ermatinger across the table. "About this financial panic in the East— think it's serious?"

"Sure is painful, anyway. But Hudson's Bay is sound. Can't bother us out here much."

Henry cleared his throat. Their work had already been bothered —expense money drastically cut, supplies limited.

Marcus asked, "How was beaver going at Rendezvous? Holding up pretty well?"

Ermatinger frowned. "Trappers mighty short on plews this year." Then he lowered his voice. "Doc, your man, Gray, had a close shave at Rendezvous. A lot of Bridger's boys got mightily riled up. Almost raised hair. Gray had to hide out. Don't see how you put up with him."

Marcus pulled Captain Sutter into the conversation. "Captain, didn't you come from Washington recently? What's the news from the capital?"

"Big news for Oregon," Sutter said, "if you haven't heard. Your country renewed the Joint Occupation Treaty with Mr. Ermatinger's Great Britain."

Marcus grinned at the Hudson's Bay trader. "Well, Ermatinger, if Hudson's Bay has any trouble clearing a profit in this country, maybe some American company can step in. Friendly competition."

Sutter and the trader both laughed. The Captain slapped the table. "Spoken like a native son, *oui*. You believe in this country."

Narcissa said, "Don't encourage him, Captain. Give him half an opening to talk about Oregon, and you'll grow to that chair before he stops. I'd rather hear the news from the States."

"*Merci,* Madame Whitman." Sutter bowed. "Thank you for the warning. I might not get on to California if the Doc really cut loose on Oregon. He lights up like a hot flint at mention of the name."

Marcus pushed back his chair. "If you won't let me talk Oregon, chores are waiting. Got some sheep last week—imported from the Islands. Have to make them at home. Too, got to cut out animals to butcher tomorrow before the rest of the party arrives."

"Butchering sheep?" Sutter asked. "Sounds better than buffalo."

"Not yet. Take a few years before we're ready for that. Horse meat this time. Can't beat it for steaks anyway."

CHAPTER

9

SPRING in Oregon came as the crest of a harmless flood down a river. Marcus saw it wash before it all traces of winter's ice, and leave behind a gently rippling swell that filled the banks but did not overflow. With spring he watched peace come to Waiilatpu. Indians, cold and hungry through the winter, built fires of the Bostons' fences, raided the Bostons' storehouses. They had lived for generations, shivering and empty through the winters, sick with too much buffalo, too much camas at whatever infrequent times they chanced to find these animals and roots. For generations they'd sought ways to appease the Great Spirit that he might favor them with year-round spring, year-round spawning salmon, year-round plenty.

During the winter want and hunger, sickness from too much plenty—everything, perhaps, could be blamed on the Bostons. They had come, at the Indians' request, to show them how to manage the Great Spirit so he would send them constantly enough food and keep them constantly from eating too much of it. So he would send them springtime through the winter and keep their enemies from feeling so confident during fine weather that they rode out in vermilion and feathers to make war. Night and morning the Cayuses and Nez Percés had faithfully performed the incantations prescribed by the Bostons, and the Great Spirit had not responded by changing the course of things. Obviously, the white men were to blame. Perhaps they had left out some of the incantation. Perhaps they were using a stronger magic on the Great Spirit than the one they showed the

Indians. Perhaps, as some of their number said, the white men wanted Indian lands and horses and were working some "medicine" to get them.

But spring with its swelling bunch grass to fatten horses, its curling buffalo grass to lure food near, its sunny days—who could doubt that the Great Spirit was on his side during spring in Oregon?

The Board's new missionaries were settled far enough away to suit even Tiloukaikt. The Walkers and Eells had gone to Tshamakian, four days' ride to the north of Waiilatpu where they'd work among the Spokane Indians. Mr. and Mrs. Smith had moved into Chief Joseph's country and set up their home at Kamiah. The Grays and Cornelius Rogers were at Lapwai with the Spaldings. With no extras in the adobe house by the river except Compo and the usual squatting, peering Cayuses, Narcissa's voice lost the icy edge that had often slashed at Marcus during the winter. Alice Clarissa, a baby until now, became a person along with spring.

Narcissa wrote to her sister, Jane, "I so want Alice to have an aunt with her. And other white children for companions. She needs them now that she's no longer a baby. Won't you and brother Edward plan to come to Oregon by the very next caravan?"

"We'll get them yet," Marcus promised. "You'll see. Even if I have to go back to the States and drag them out. Your daughter won't grow up a heathen even though she does often talk like one."

Marcus cleared extra land for garden. He glowed with the triumph when he led a few of the Cayuses to break out little ragged clearings for themselves with hoes he gave them. Their clearings nestled close to his like baby chicks, trying to force their way under a sheltering wing. "White te-wat keep safe," they boasted. And refused to listen to Feathercap when he ranted, "White te-wat want fields close. Him take. Him keep."

The irrigation ditches that Marcus helped them contour carried water to their garden patches. They planted the seed potatoes that Narcissa cut. They grinned, showing scraggly gums, as Alice Clarissa tried to help her papa cut potatoes with a dull knife and often sank her sharp teeth into crisp potato eyes.

"Young lady," Marcus said, giving her a pat on her plump spanking place, "you're going to have eyes in your stomach, if you don't stop that." And for days he reveled in the child's imagination.

Narcissa had to force her clothes on her every morning for a week because she didn't want to cover up the eyes in her tummy.

Days grew drowsy warm. The potatoes flourished even for the Indians. Pea pods filled almost overnight. Marcus watched his corn push up green pennants to wave against the earth. Then it was time to cut the wheat that leaned modest heads—the color of Narcissa's hair—away from the breeze that fanned Waiilatpu Valley.

The garden north of the house changed from black to striped green with rows of turnips, beets, and radishes. Marcus, at rest from his weeding, sharpened the edge of a small slab of wood with his bowie and pegged in a peeled willow handle to make a hoe for Alice. He loved to have her insist on doing everything that Mama and Papa did. Even when she'd have been better off in the house with Margaret, he gloried in her wanting to be with him.

The day he decided that something must be done about Boxer, Alice had to be on hand. She cared little for the old blind dog that had wandered in to their place several days before. None of them did—they felt sorry for him but he was too feeble to be any fun. They'd called him Boxer by contrast and kept hoping he'd go someplace else to die. When he didn't, someone had to put him out of his misery. Alice insisted on watching every move when Marcus tied and weighted the half-conscious dog and carried him to the river. She tagged along with a firm hold on Trapper, the dog she really loved. When he let Boxer into the water, Alice watched with matter-of-fact, dry eyes.

But one Friday late in June, the three Whitmans were working in the garden when Marcus accidentally hoed up a radish. He tossed the dirty root to one side and moved on behind Narcissa. Then, missing the string of chatter that usually followed him in the row, he asked Narcissa, "Where'd Alice disappear to?"

"I don't know," she answered carelessly. Then she flung down her hoe and started on a run for the river.

Marcus ran the other way. They met around the house behind a bright-haired ball of dark blue calico, squatting at the edge of the water.

"Alice," Marcus called, trying not to frighten her.

"Just a minute," her sweet voice called back. "Alice is washing the radish for Papa."

Marcus shook his head at Narcissa. Fright fluttered in her hand

(157)

that he took in his. "Come, dear. That's clean enough," he told the child.

She climbed importantly up the slant of grassy bank.

Narcissa stooped and crushed her in a hug. "Baby, don't ever come down here to the river by yourself. We've told you and told you. You must obey."

"But it was all dirty," Alice reasoned. "All clean now. Papa *hipsh*." She screwed the radish free of Narcissa's hug and held it out to Marcus.

"Think I'll eat you instead," he said and took a playful bite of her neck. "Come on, you girls, or those weeds'll grow over our heads."

At bedtime that night, Narcissa tried again to impress on the child the danger of the river. And Alice took up the argument on her mother's side. "Alice mustn't go in river or she will die like Boxer and then Mama won't have any Alice."

Marcus turned away from the sudden death he saw in Narcissa's eyes above the little girl's shoulder. So, they had driven that lesson home.

The next morning all but a handful of the Cayuse rode off on a hunt. Watching them wind away and fade into a curling lift of dust, Narcissa sighed and breathed deep of the morning air. Alice Clarissa wound her arms around Trapper's middle and strained to lift him, murmuring, "*Enip coeta. Enip coeta.*"

Marcus tousled her hair. "You can't carry Trapper, you little prairie dog. Get *coots mēaits* I carved for you."

"Doll," Narcissa corrected absently. Her eyes still followed the departing Indians. She sighed again. "Well, maybe we can talk a little English around here for a change." Catching the child by a handful of the back of her dress, she said, "Come, Alice. Let's scrub the kitchen floor."

Later Alice came tearing down to the corral to fling her arms around Marcus' buckskin legs and cry, "I love you, Papa."

As he swung her to his shoulder, her dress dripped sudsy scrub water on his bare arm. She giggled when he threatened to hang her on the clothesline to dry. "Is that what you came so head-over-heels to tell me? That you love me?"

"Papa *hipsh*. Dinner."

This really relished well, he had to agree with Narcissa, to eat

(158)

their noonday meal with no Indians about. To relax in their own home all by themselves. He looked forward to the next day, Sunday, when he could do some neglected reading and just rest. He'd have a quiet afternoon and evening with his two girls.

At the worship hour the next morning, only eight or nine Cayuses straggled into the kitchen and asked for hymns and prayers. They alone remained at home from the hunt. Miraculously they looked clean. As Marcus read and explained to them the parable of the lost sheep, they actually paid attention. He illustrated, where he was short on Nez Percé words, with sign language and, outside in the sunlight, his own sheep baa-ed an accompaniment to the story. The Indians' faces seemed to relax in understanding. When Marcus asked which hymn they'd like to sing in closing, the Indians actually let themselves smile at Alice Clarissa's quick piping, "Rock of Ages."

They sang the hymn, Narcissa humming so that Alice would be able to hear herself. Marcus pronounced the benediction, "May the God of peace go with you and watch over you. Amen." Surprisingly not one Cayuse lingered to squat against the kitchen wall and look on with hungry eyes while the Whitmans ate.

"Don't hurry dinner," Marcus heard Narcissa tell Margaret. "We'd like to read awhile and just enjoy the peace and quiet. Isn't it wonderful?"

She moved her favorite chair close to the open door and sat with her book on her lap, staring off toward the Blues. Marcus settled himself into the other comfortable chair and scraped it across the floor to the window. He opened a year-old *Missionary Herald* for June, 1838. He'd read only half a page when Alice interrupted.

"Papa, Alice wants a piece of rhubarb and Trapper wants one, too."

Marcus laughed and laid his magazine aside. "Well, it's nearly dinnertime for Alice, but Trapper can have all his tummy will hold."

She giggled. "Alice will carry Trapper's rhubard for him."

Marcus got his bowie, stooped to give Narcissa a quick kiss on the top of her head, and led the child to the garden. Her chubby hand had never felt so alive and loving. He cut her the fattest stalk of rhubarb he could find, sliced off the green leaf. "There you are, my bunny rabbit," he said. Contented, she followed him back to the house.

Narcissa glanced up from her reading and gave them an absent smile. Marcus settled himself in his chair once more and took up his magazine. The sheep's bleating sounded far away. A cowbell clunked across the river now and then. None of the usual throaty monotony that the Indians called "sin'in' " cawed out to mar the quiet. Margaret McKay moved lightly from the dish shelves to the table and to the pantry. Compo dozed against a stump near the river.

"Mama, almost time *hipsh*?" Alice asked finally. Then quickly she corrected herself. "No, almost time for dinner?"

"Yes, dear."

"Let Alice get water."

Marcus and Narcissa both read on.

When Margaret dragged Alice Clarissa's high chair to the table, Narcissa looked up. "Margaret, get Alice and wash her hands for dinner. And did you pull some radishes?"

"Yes, ma'am. I mean, I will."

Narcissa read awhile and looked up. "What's keeping Margaret?"

Compo sauntered to the kitchen door and squatted, sniffing, on the doorstep.

Narcissa asked, "Have you seen Alice?"

"No'm. But she can't be far. Trapper's lyin' here asleep."

"Well, take a look around, will you, please?"

"*Oui*, ma'am."

Narcissa returned to her book. "Marcus, I want to read you a little here when you get to a stopping place."

"Umm. Just a minute."

Before he'd reached the end of a paragraph, Compo eased up outside the window. "Doc Whitman," he said low, "they's two cups a-floatin' on ze river."

Narcissa slapped her book shut. "Cups? How did they get there?"

"We'll get them out—after awhile."

Narcissa stood up. "But how could they get there?" she persisted. Frowning, she stepped outside.

Marcus tossed his magazine onto the trunk and followed her. "I'll get a pole and fish them out," he called as she started around the house. But instead, he walked the other way, calling, "Alice. Oh, Alice. Come hopping, you little bunny."

Margaret sauntered toward the river with an apronful of radishes. Narcissa's voice, higher-pitched than usual, stopped her. "Margaret, I told you to wash Alice Clarissa's hands for dinner."

"Yes, ma'am," Marcus heard her answer, "but you said to get some radishes, too, and when I didn't see her . . ."

The search was on. Frantic frightened running, calling. Around the house, down to the corral, and, in desperation, along the river. The few Indians around, quick to sense trouble, glided from their lodges to join the hunt. Marcus followed Compo and the Indians up and down the river bank.

He fought against believing that it could have happened. He re-assured Narcissa and led her to the house. They'd find Alice in the bedroom or at the barn or in the garden, playing hide-and-seek. He took Narcissa's trembling hand and hurried her through the kitchen door to search in the safety of the house.

Then, they heard the cry, a wailing moan from down river.

Marcus ran out to see an Indian scramble up the slippery bank. To see him straighten. To see on his two extended arms the limp body.

Narcissa jerked from Marcus' grasp and ran. He tore ahead. He caught the child in his arms, clutched at an Indian's blanket to spread on the ground, dropped to his knees and drained water from her mouth. He chafed her wrists, her arms, her legs. Blew his breath into her, willed and prayed the quiet heart to beat.

He felt Narcissa kneel beside him. Dimly he heard her incoherent murmur of prayer.

He jerked off his tunic and wrapped it around the child's wet body. Then, more chafing. More breathing into her mouth. More listening for one faint beat of her heart. But from the first, he had known what he could not admit. The doctor had come too late.

And Narcissa on her knees beside him, her whole lovely living body a prayer, waited with knowing in her eyes.

When wishing could no longer be stretched into motions of try-ing, Marcus wrapped the blanket around the child for the long death march to the house. Narcissa held his arm and steadied him.

That night, Narcissa was the one who sent off Compo to bring Mr. Spalding for the funeral. And a strangely quiet Narcissa bathed and dressed the fragile body. Aloof, even within the circle of Marcus' arm, Narcissa stood beside him above the cradle while he silently denied the truth of what had happened.

And into the blackness of the house, Narcissa—head high, hands clasped and at peace—spoke firmly, "Thy will be done, not mine."

Night, then morning, and another night. All without meaning.

(161)

And Marcus learned that the absence of a child's quick laughter could speak louder than the silence. He learned that a mother's, "Thy will be done," could hold her head erect but freeze her heart within her until her eyes looked at him and saw nothing. He learned that he was not the man he had supposed himself to be.

He was a father, unwillingly alive, whose child was dead. His ears still heard her voice caught in the curtains around the bed. His arms felt hers a hundred times a day, reaching up to him. His knees hungered for her solid body flung against him.

He sawed and split a log.

His eyes saw Alice in never-ending motion. Plump legs curled under her on the bench before the fire. Bright hair falling over her face in concentration while she dressed the doll he'd carved. Tearing through the long rye grass for no reason but that it felt so good to run. Bouncing in exaggerated gallops on some Indian's knee.

He finished a box to set before Narcissa. He watched her rip and tear a dress to line his crude pine coffin.

He was nothing. He was a man whose life had stopped within a body that still moved.

And across from him at the table, behind him as he dug the grave, beside him in his bed, there was a woman. But he could not reach her.

Remembering again her voice, alone, singing her renunciation of home and friends and country at their wedding; awed by the towering strength of her dry-eyed, "Thy will be done," Marcus could not take Narcissa in his arms to give her sympathy. Nor could he turn to her for comfort.

The Spaldings came and the Grays. The funeral was held. Expressions of condolence were given. And Henry Spalding offered a kind of apology for things he'd said and trouble he had caused. Mr. Gray spoke words of kindness like a piece at school. Eliza Spalding, saying nothing, did the work with Margaret.

Marcus and Narcissa moved through it all, side by side but not together. Two people with nothing to say because the only words worth saying were too horrible for shaping. Two people whose glances turned away from a wall between them. Two people who could not meet in understanding because neither knew the other's need. Two people alone.

(162)

Numb, incredulous, they paced through the summer. Both filled their empty hands with chores. The longer into the night work lasted, the better. The earlier they could begin, the better. Until they both were sick and had to spend dreaded, unbusy days in bed, chiding themselves for getting behind in all they had to do.

When the Indians returned in the fall, Marcus and Narcissa both plunged into a frenzy of teaching, of doctoring and nursing, of harvesting and storing crops far into every night. Their talk was all of speeding up the work, of making the three years they'd spent in Oregon begin to show results. Their thoughts were often of giving up, of going back to the States.

"We'll never get anyplace," Marcus would say, "with our work on this basis. We asked the Board for two hundred helpers to settle in white communities and be an example to the Indians. Look what we got. Ask for equipment and they send word for us to cut down on expenses. It's all wrong."

Narcissa's voice would answer dully, "The Board doesn't understand. If they only knew how hopeless it is to work with Indians who are always off on hunts or diggings."

"It takes so long."

One evening late that fall when Marcus ached in every muscle, he took Narcissa's hand and urged her from her sewing. He led her across the meadow and up the winding path to the summit of their knoll. Early winter rains had started up a carpet of young green beneath the trampled brown of last year's grass. Low across the willows that fringed the Walla Walla, a red sun eclipsed and sank into the distant haze. Above the willows a cloud picked up the color and flung it down to coat the surface of the Walla Walla, turning it into a river of blood.

For a moment, Marcus remembered that awful Sunday and then the wind-borne whispers that he'd denied even hearing at the time: "Evil spirits take little Cayuse *te-mi*. Evil spirits punish Bostons." And then Narcissa pressed his hand.

She, too, was looking at the blood-red river. But she said, "It's beautiful. We can't give up. This is our country. We must get Christian families to join us here—those who can love this country with us and make it great."

"Settlers to keep the Indians in line while our doctoring and teaching takes effect." Marcus caught and ran ahead with her mood. "Let's write again to your sister Jane and to your brother Edward, and to my brothers and to the Board. If we can get a settlement of homes and show the Indians the benefits of raising food instead of hunting for it—"

"Father and Mother might even come. What a help Father would be with the building!"

"And if Americans don't hurry and come before Hudson's Bay brings in colonies of English settlers," Marcus added, "we might need to send someone back to the States to wake the people up."

And then they both fell silent, watching the river that had turned from red to gray and now groped slowly, through a darkened valley, but surely to the sea.

PART III

*

CHAPTER

1

THE Cumberland stage clattered along the cobbled avenue and pulled to a panting stop across from the Capitol. Marcus climbed down and swung his saddlebag over his shoulder. A mighty pretty sight, that dome. Narcissa would love to see it. But right now, he was cold. The wind off the Potomac pierced even his buffalo coat. Seemed awful unmanly to feel a March afternoon blow after all he'd gone through. All those freezings on the way made his skin touchy, he reckoned. He turned and padded up the hotel steps.

The desk clerk looked up with a smile that faded and ran like Fourth of July bunting caught in the rain. He spread both palms on the desk and teetered over on them in order to survey Marcus from fur cap to boot moccasins. Then he remembered to say, "Filled up. Haven't got a room for love or money."

Marcus trudged to the next hotel and the next. . . . Always the same look of astonishment, the same answer. "Sorry, filled up."

But finding a room turned out to be simple compared with finding a sympathetic ear in Washington. Then Marcus remembered that an old friend back in New York State had risen in the political world. John Spencer, from near Wheeler, had been appointed Secretary of War in President Tyler's cabinet. Spencer would be the man to see. He'd be able to arrange appointments with Senators Linn and Benton who were known to be interested in Oregon. These senators would get him in to see Secretary of State, Daniel Webster, and possibly, the President himself. Tyler, Marcus knew, was related by marriage

(165)

to Jim Bridger. He'd use talk of old Gabe as an opener to fix the President's mind on Oregon.

But the first day when Marcus called to see Secretary Spencer, a young clerk took one look at his fringed shirt and said curtly, "The Honorable Mr. Spencer is now Secretary of the Treasury and he's not in. Mr. Porter, for your information is Secretary of War and he won't be in either."

At the Treasury office, Marcus got the routine, "In conference," "Unavailable," and "Out of the city indefinitely." After his seventh call, one clerk said, "Look here, Dan'l Boone, you're barking up the wrong tree. Why don't you just stop bothering us?"

Ignoring him, Marcus went to the last vacant chair in the line along the wall. A strident voice stopped him as he bent to sit.

"Didn't we tell you yesterday the Secretary can't see you? He's got no time for whatever you're selling or begging."

Marcus straightened and glanced along the waiting row of men. Some smiled knowingly at the clerk. Others bit their lips to stifle a laugh.

Deliberately, Marcus folded his buffalo coat and laid it on the chair. Then he walked across the room. For once, he wished for hard soles on his boots. He caught the astonished clerk by the lapels and made his voice come soft and slow. "That's a-plenty of your impertinence. Spencer's my friend. Knew him back home in New York State." The clerk tried to shake himself loose but Marcus held on.

"That's what all the crackpots say—knew him back home. Now get out of this office or I'll call an officer."

At that moment the outer door swung open and a large size broadcloth morning suit walked in. It removed its silk topper to shake off a couple of snowflakes. Delicately it tapped its gold-headed cane against newly blackened boots to knock off a rim of slush.

Marcus let go the clerk to allow him to bow in deference to the suit and trappings.

"Good morning, sir. You are right on time. The Honorable Mr. Secretary will see you at once." He bowed again and swung open a low gate.

"They tell me Mr. Spencer's busy," Marcus blurted. "Always too busy to talk about the most important issue of the day."

Unruffled, the big man stopped. "And what is the most important issue of the day, my friend?" The suit's voice sounded almost human.

The clerk snapped his fingers for the officer by the inner door. Then he bowed again. "I'm very sorry, your honor. I'll have this backwoodsman thrown out."

The silk hat interfered. "Hold on. Let the man have his chance. Speak your piece, my friend. This is a democratic country, you know."

Marcus hesitated, wondering now just what it was he wanted to say. The waiting line stood up and closed in to hear. Marcus looked around him at a wall of curled lips, of derisive eyes. Even the dignitary smiled now—that indulgent, derogatory smile that Marcus had met all over Washington. So, they thought he was a freak, a backwoods oaf with some crackpot idea. Well, he'd tell this politician and these grinning hangers-on.

He grabbed the portly man under his broadcloth arm pits and sat him down hard on the clerk's tall desk. The gentleman was too surprised to protest.

"Now you listen to me." Marcus gave his words plenty of time. "I've come four thousand miles by horseback, boat, and stage. Came it with just one companion zigzagging across the Rocky Mountains in winter as any sane man would tell you couldn't be done. But I came anyway to talk about the most vital issue in America. And now young whippersnappers lower than muleskinners stand around with a smirk on their pasty faces and say I can't see secretaries or congressmen or senators. Nobody wants to hear about Oregon."

"Unless my ears deceive me, you said 'Oregon.' Ha! Gentlemen, do you hear that? I need to wake up on the Oregon question!" The big man threw back his head and laughed.

The others joined in. One shouted, "That's a good one on you, Senator."

The man wiped laughter tears from his eyes and turned back to Marcus. "Tell me, my friend, where is this Oregon Country? And is it, by any chance, worth as much as a New England fishery?" He winked at a dandy in the crowd.

Marcus knew that he was being ribbed again. "I'll tell you where Oregon is and what it's worth. I'll put you on a horse and lead you through Pawnee war parties at the risk of your scalp. Over blistering sands, covered with sagebrush that smells like all the spice cupboards in Washington. I'll swim you across a hundred rivers. Then you'll be in Oregon. I'll march you down rows of nine-foot corn. Walk you through virgin forests of pine and fir that reach taller than this Capitol. Take you into orchards and vegetable gardens and melon patches. I'll stake you out in that rich, healthy land till you're ready to fight to make Oregon a part of the States—instead of a squeezed-dry possession of Hudson's Bay Company. That's what I'll do. You —you—"

Out of breath, Marcus stopped. He'd never made such a speech before.

The man on the desk applauded. More ridicule, Marcus knew, but he felt better.

"My friend," his prisoner said then, "that's the speech I've made in the Senate a hundred times. Only not half so well. You must know what you're talking about. Who are you, anyway?"

"Whitman's the name. Live in Oregon. Lived there almost seven years now. Marcus Whitman. Doctor."

"And my name is Benton," the other replied, bowing. "Senator Benton of Missouri, if that means anything to you."

Marcus stretched out his hand and grasped Benton's. Then he burst into a deep belly laugh. "Sorry, Senator Benton, but not for bragging on Oregon. Been busting to tell somebody for a week. Thought my friend, Mr. Spencer, might get me an appointment with you. That's one on me."

"Gentlemen," Benton said to the room, "meet Doctor Whitman of Oregon. Now come with me, compatriot. Any friend of Oregon is a friend of mine." He slipped down from his perch and caught Marcus' arm. "If Spencer and I can't get you in to see anyone in Washington, I'll resign and go to Oregon."

Doors began to swing open. Benton ushered Marcus through gaping rows of office seekers in Senator Linn's anteroom. Linn and Benton rushed him past rows of generals and congressmen, waiting to see Secretary Porter in the War Department. Linn, Benton, and Porter escorted him to the White House to talk with President Tyler.

The chief executive stood behind his desk, iron-gray hair floating over his collar. His direct blue eyes and prominent nose reminded Marcus of mountain men he'd known. The President stepped from behind his desk to shake hands and betrayed no consciousness of the difference between broadcloth and buckskin. His speech had a touch of Kit Carson in its tone. He spoke man to man. "You are a welcome visitor to Washington, Doctor Whitman. Our late President Harrison fought against Indians and campaigned for Oregon. We are interested in whatever you can report, first hand, from that little-known country."

Finally, Marcus got in to see the Secretary of State.

Daniel Webster greeted Benton and Linn and acknowledged their introduction of Doc Whitman with a side-swinging handshake. "Black Dan'l" motioned his visitors to chairs and rared back himself against a map of North America that covered his office wall. He straightened his flowing cravat and set square a signet ring on his middle finger.

"Senators," he began, curling a corner of his mouth in playful cynicism, "your combined presence makes me feel that the Oregon issue is about to spring into life again."

Benton smiled. "Mr. Secretary, the Oregon issue has been a live one ever since Captain Gray harbored in the mouth of the Columbia and commenced a lucrative fur trade."

"That, Mr. Senator, proved only that Captain Gray could outtrade the ignorant natives. Since then, the British company has outwitted all our Yankee traders—from John Jacob Astor to Nathaniel Wyeth."

Senator Linn gestured as if bowing in defeat to the rebuttal of the great Webster. He said, "But our mission here today rises above the past. Doctor Whitman is a living example of the Oregon of today. However, his concern deals with the Pacific country in the years ahead. He proposes to take a caravan of settlers from the States to the Columbia."

Webster turned on Marcus. "A rather ambitious order, isn't it, Doctor?"

Marcus went around to the map. "Mr. Webster, nearly seven years ago my party started here—at Liberty, in western Missouri. We traveled safely by Indian trails to Fort Vancouver—approximately here, within a hundred miles of the Pacific."

Senator Benton stood beside Marcus. "Mr. Secretary, you met my son-in-law, Lieutenant Frémont. He explored generally this section of the Oregon Country. He mapped the eastern slope of the Rocky Mountains from the Missouri to Fort Laramie, down to the headwaters of the Arkansas, and back to the frontier. He proved it safe traveling. Safe enough that I allowed him to take my nine-year-old son along for the experience."

"Yes, yes," Webster fumed, "but Doctor Whitman talks of taking a caravan. A caravan of families. Isn't that unnecessarily foolhardy?"

Benton answered, "Mr. Secretary, you are a man of wide reading. Undoubtedly you have read those same words in similar context. Perhaps said in criticism of our Massachusetts colonists who first pushed beyond gunshot of Plymouth. Or perhaps it was thundered at Roger Bacon and his wilderness settlers. Probably those words were hurled at your own ancestors who pioneered near the New Hampshire line."

The Squire of Marshfield nodded at the deft *touché*, and then frowned. "The Oregon Country which you gentlemen contend for so valiantly—that vast, uncharted section on the map beyond Thomas Jefferson's dream of expansion, that wilderness—is claimed also by Great Britain and is now dominated by the Hudson's Bay Company. Our nation cannot lightly interfere with treaty agreements, gentlemen."

"Seems more like a race to us who live in Oregon," Marcus pressed. "To Hudson's Bay officials and to the Americans in Oregon. The Company brought in British subjects in '41. Last summer one hundred and fourteen emigrants arrived from the States and settled in the Willamette Valley. A fair race, Mr. Webster—even under treaty agreements."

Webster sprang from his chair and swung around to the map. "Our treaty with Great Britain, negotiated through Lord Ashburton, extends roughly from the coast of Maine, along the Great Lakes, to this point—Lake of the Woods here, west of Superior. The President and I held it to be of primary importance to safeguard this northern boundary along our inhabited regions. What lies beyond that—" He shrugged. "Well, yes, in due course of time."

Benton bristled. "Mr. Webster, the rumor circulates that you contend for a western boundary along the Columbia River. Is that correct?"

Webster's smile was tolerant. "Senator, you have heard rumors that 'Black Dan'l' is in league with his Satanic Majesty, too, no doubt. I give you my word as a farmer and a gentleman, I do not advocate a settlement south of the forty-ninth parallel." He paused and then added, "That question, too, will be settled in due time."

"In due time!" Marcus leaned over the polished desk. "When on earth is 'in due time,' Mr. Webster? Our American settlers in the

Willamette Valley are already impatient, seething like the volcanic Mount St. Helens. They're about to blow off and take matters into their own hands. They want laws and protection and the rights of American citizens."

"I must remind you, Doctor Whitman, that this is the United States, governed by law and order, controlled by our Constitution. No little handful of settlers can take matters into their own hands."

"May I respectfully remind you, Mr. Secretary, that the colonists in this country took matters into their own hands—to write that Constitution you contend for. And American patriots in Texas are getting considerable encouragement to take matters into their hands against Mexico."

Senator Benton placed an approving palm on Marcus' shoulder. "The doctor has a point here. Our executives and legislators need to feel the heart throb of their scattered people. Always the fact, sir. Always the fact."

"Isn't it a fact, Senator," Webster rose and paced the floor, "that Hudson's Bay Company will have something to say about all this? They use every means possible to settle Oregon."

"True," Marcus agreed. "The Company is calling for emigrants to populate Oregon. And yet Chief Factor McLoughlin is the best friend an American could wish. All our settlers will swear to this. The British company resents his co-operative attitude. But actually, all of our settlements owe their existence to his gifts and supplies on credit."

Senator Linn jumped into the pause. "The Senate and the House need to fight the eastern vested interests that perennially snow under my bill. Pass this bill, granting six hundred and forty acres to all male emigrants over eighteen, and you'll stampede emigration to Oregon. We can win that Pacific paradise—and soon—if Congress will pass my bill."

Webster sat down and drummed on the desk with his stubby fingers. Finally he asked, "Doctor Whitman, what assurance do you have that a caravan could get through to Oregon—overland with wagons?"

Marcus moved again to the map. "Mr. Secretary, in the summer of '36 I piloted a party of four greenhorns to Vancouver, including two genteel and cultured ladies from New England. We herded twelve horses, six mules, and seventeen head of cattle—two thousand miles from the edge of the States across mountains and deserts. But what is most important," he slowed down to give it its real significance, "we drove two wagons from here at the bend of the Missouri to Fort Laramie—about here on the plains. The light wagon, we rolled on through as far as Boise on the Snake."

"But the wagon couldn't go all the way."

"Not at that time, Mr. Webster. Lack of assistance and of black-smithing equipment prevented. However, four years later several mountain men drove four wagons from Fort Hall to Vancouver. That proves wheels can make it all the way."

"Such proof is all we need to carry my bill through Congress," Senator Linn shouted.

"You gentlemen can be eye witnesses this summer," Marcus asserted. "Just meet the hundreds of frontier settlers gathering right this minute on the Missouri."

Webster stood up. "Gentlemen from Missouri, you will have to show me. Produce this proof you claim, and I promise you that President Tyler and I shall be compelled to respect it. Until then . . ."

Outside, Marcus thanked the senators and hurried to Spencer's office.

"Daniel Webster was fair and square," he told the secretary. "Now we're going to give him proof. Thanks for all your help here."

Spencer grinned. "You did pretty well for yourself, I'm told."

"By the way, can't you keep Porter stirred up on that business of the War Department setting up military posts at intervals along the trail to Oregon? Emigrants need protection from Indians to get through safely."

"Porter wants a written report from you on that proposal," Spencer said. "He'll do something—if you get the caravan through this summer."

"They'll make it. I promise."

"You can count on my interest. And Porter is showing more than mere interest. He tells me he plans to send young Frémont West with the caravan to protect you from Indian raids. I believe in you. It's up to you now."

Confused and elated in turn by his Washington visit, Marcus caught the stage for New York. Next, he must persuade the venerable gentlemen on Beacon Hill to back down on their decision to

(172)

dismiss Henry Spalding and close up both Lapwai and Waiilatpu. A trip to Boston now would leave him less than a month for rounding up settlers for Oregon. Still, emigrants would have to be fed and doctored at his Oregon way station or they'd never make it through to the Pacific. Now, of all times, the Board must not close Waiilatpu.

The northbound stage, slower and rougher than an Indian travois, jolted over the turnpike. Marcus fretted and screwed in his seat, longing for a fleet-footed buffalo pony to cut short the drab miles to New York.

CHAPTER

2

THE ferry from the Jersey stage churned across the Hudson. When, at last, she moored to the Battery dock, Marcus threw his saddlebag over his shoulder and jammed up the gangplank through the crowd.

"No boat to Boston for two days!"

"That's what I said, Dan'l Boone."

Two precious days! Marcus had no time for sitting still. If only he could be talking to farmers and carpenters and teachers who might go to Oregon. But where could he find just plain human beings in a city where folks tore around every which way like a buffalo stampede?

At the hotel he picked up a *Tribune*. Mighty fofarraw doin's for him—having a newspaper and time to read it. Soon, still reading, he came up on his moccasins. This editorial about the West! Here was a human being—this man Greeley. If he could talk to him, get him to write a piece that would stir up settlers—

At Greeley's home a servant gaped. "Mr. Greeley's not in. Good day."

Marcus scuffed down the brownstone steps. Then a voice called from a flung-up window, "Just a minute. Who is it?"

"Whitman's the name. Marcus Whitman from out Oregon way."

"I'm Horace Greeley. My man's mistaken. I'm very much at home."

Climbing the steps again, Marcus found the door opened wide by a thin, clean-cut man in a velvet dressing gown. "Come right in, traveler. Don't mind my clothes," Greeley said, pumping Marcus' hand. "You have the earmarks of flavorful news and news is my job. Peel off your coat."

On board the steamer, *Narragansett*, bound for Boston, another newspaperman pelted Marcus with questions. Before the mail packet dropped anchor in Boston harbor the next morning, this fellow who signed himself "Civis," asked Marcus to approve his story for the New York *Spectator* of April 5, 1843.

Rarely have I seen such a spectacle as he presented [Marcus read]. His dress should be preserved as a curiosity. . . . But stamped on his brow is a great deal of what David Crockett would call "God Almighty's common sense."

Marcus felt warmed by that about common sense but what, by the eternal, was wrong with his clothes? And what did they have to do with anything?

Climbing the stairs to the Board's headquarters off Boston Common, Marcus thought only that, at last, he was here. Down the hall he shoved open the door lettered, THE AMERICAN BOARD OF COMMISSIONERS FOR FOREIGN MISSIONS.

Above the reception desk a jaw dropped. When Marcus gave his name and asked for Dr. Greene, it took the young man at the desk some time to reassemble the equipment for gulping, "Surely you can't be the Doctor Whitman of Oregon! Are you expected?"

"Whitman of Oregon," Marcus assured him.

"Well, I'll be— I'll see whether Doctor Greene is in."

Marcus sat down and twirled his fur cap until a spare man in Prince Albert and sideburns bustled through the swinging gate.

"Doctor Whitman? Not our Doctor Whitman?"

"Marcus Whitman from Oregon. Glad to see you, Doctor Greene."

"Doctor Whitman! You will pardon my astonishment. You are the last person on earth whom I expected to see in Boston today."

Marcus chuckled. "Indians haven't scalped me yet, Doctor Greene. And your Closing Order of last year made me come. Letters are misleading. Had to talk it over with you."

"I see. Come into my office." Dr. Greene ushered him to a chair beside his roll-top desk. "Now then," Greene pursued, "may I ask first why you left your station without authorization from the Board? It's quite irregular, you know."

"Our group in Oregon authorized it, Doctor Greene." Marcus stretched his right leg half across the little office to pull a sealed letter sheet from his pantaloon pocket. "Here's a letter signed by Mr. Spalding and the others. We think the Board should reconsider its action."

"Quite irregular, quite irregular," Greene repeated, keeping time with a pencil he tapped on his desk. Then he dropped the pencil and smiled. "But, here you are. We shall give you every consideration."

Marcus stood up to suck a good breath out of this stuffy office, somehow, and to cut loose with what he'd come to say.

"Must you go?" Greene asked. "I shall be engaged in committee all morning but I should be free by twelve. Can you lunch with me then?"

"Can I! You forget I rode four thousand miles through winter to talk to you."

"Good. I'll expect you at twelve. Now then," Greene's eyes combed the fringes on Marcus' buckskins, "ahem—I shall introduce you to our treasurer. He will take care of an advance so that you may purchase . . ."

Marcus knew, all at once, how naked Adam felt after the Lord pointed out his sin. But President Tyler had received him at the White House in these clothes. Even the Squire of Marshfield had met him man to man. But Boston— Yes, he admitted, his clothes felt out of place in Boston.

Promptly at twelve Marcus stomped back into the office. The hurriedly selected suit of woven black cloth bagged over his stocky frame but still seemed to cramp his movements. The stiff store shoes bound his feet. Even the black felt hat he'd insisted on, in place of the topper that clerk had urged, made his face look caved in.

The youngster at the desk stifled a smile. "Doctor Greene is still in committee, but he'll be out soon."

The treasurer inspected Marcus' store clothes from a cage no bigger than a beaver trap.

But Dr. Greene hurried in and said, "You should not be kept waiting, Doctor. My apologies. We shall lunch at the Parker House."

Along with their chowder, Dr. Greene inquired about Mrs. Whitman and the other workers in Oregon. While they ate codfish,

Greene asked about their farms and provisions. When they got to apple pie, Marcus swung the conversation bluntly to the Board's Closing Order.

"Everything's different at Waiilatpu and at Lapwai now, Doctor Greene. All the—the differences have been ironed out with Mr. Spalding. You were informed of the reconciliation by letter."

Dr. Greene wiped his pince-nez glasses, eyed them, and wiped them again. "Yes, your letter came not long ago but—"

"Then the Board has reconsidered?"

Dr. Greene settled the glasses on his nose and brought out a folded paper. "The Board reconsidered last week and passed this action: 'The statements made by the Oregon group do not seem to be of sufficient importance to justify a change in the Board's original action closing Waiilatpu and Lapwai and ordering Mr. Spalding to return home.' "

Marcus swallowed an underdone lump of apple and overturned his tumbler. "But Dr. Greene! Things are different. Really different. Those complaining letters were mistakes, instigated by the trouble-maker, Gray, and by Smith who never belonged in the West. Smith's gone now and Gray— Well, I left him, for want of anybody else, in charge at Waiilatpu when I started here. But rumor has it that Gray pulled out before my dust had settled. From what I hear, he's looking for work with Hudson's Bay. The situation's wholly different."

"Different? Perhaps. But there have been so-called reconciliations before. I can show you your own letters."

"Admitted. I've made mistakes in judgment a-plenty. But Spalding's a changed man. It's a change I'll remember to my dying day."

The secretary leaned forward. "Suppose you tell me all about it. Then I'll decide."

That rainy, cloud-enveloped afternoon at Waiilatpu came back to Marcus clear as yesterday. The annual meeting of the Board's Oregon missionaries had wrangled since morning. Henry Spalding had opposed every constructive idea. Finally, Mr. Walker drawled, "I can't stomach this spiritual indigestion. I'll just go home to my savages for a little peace of mind."

And the meeting broke up.

"I knew if everyone left then all our years of work out there would fall apart like an adobe house in forty days of rain. And the future of that great country would be, once more, in the hands of savages. I found Henry Spalding at the corral, putting pack saddles on his horses."

" 'Mr. Spalding, could you let that go for thirty minutes or so?' I asked. 'Couple of my calves have strayed. Like you to ride out with me to have a look.' "

"Henry hesitated. Then he said, 'Har-r-rump. Could, I reckon.' " Greene stopped polishing his glasses.

Marcus filled in, telling how he stopped the Walkers and the Eells in the middle of their packing, " 'Wait an hour,' I said. 'Can't promise but I hope then you won't have to leave like this.' I remember I chucked Mary Walker's baby under the chin—the little fellow's named for me, Marcus Whitman Walker. Then I hurried back for my ride with Spalding. As I ran, I prayed."

Marcus and Henry had ridden in silence west along the Walla Walla. Thirty minutes passed and Henry wasn't seeming to think of time. Finally, they saw the calves. Marcus rounded them up and headed them for home.

Then he reined in. "Mr. Spalding," he said, "let's get off and have a drink."

Marcus led Henry around a cottonwood and stooped to scoop a handful of river water. Then, he sat down on a boulder and Henry, shoulders stooped, eyes blank, sat down too.

"Wasn't joking back there in meeting, Mr. Spalding," Marcus began. "About some of us starting over and growing up to be different people. Should have said 'all of us' probably. Fact is, I was wrong back there in New York State when I argued with you and Mrs. Spalding about coming to Oregon."

"I never should have come with Mrs. Whitman," Spalding said. He looked up at Marcus as if startled by an idea. "I've got nothing against you, Doctor. It's just her."

"And just what is it you've got against her?" Marcus asked.

Spalding hesitated.

Marcus helped him out. "Hard to say, isn't it? I know because I've been trying to put my finger on it since I saw you and Narcissa meet in Cincinnati there in the yard by your light wagon. You weren't in love with her—I knew that, then and there." Marcus selected a flat stone from the pebbles at his feet and tossed it in his hand. "That day and ever since, you've been trying to strike back at Narcissa. A man in love doesn't feel the way you do, believe me. But you had loved Narcissa enough to ask her to be your wife. Or had you? All I can figure is that it hurt your pride when she said 'No.' And that's not a man in love either. Pride doesn't have much to do with love. But what is it?" He tossed his stone and waited.

"Judge Prentiss called me in," Henry said. His voice sounded young and frightened. His eyes stared upriver.

The silence was carrying them both back through the years and Marcus was content. It was back, he knew, that they'd find the answer for the future, if they found it. Finally, when Henry didn't speak, Marcus said, "The Judge could be pretty hard on a man, I reckon. Talked about family stock, no doubt. About his grandfather, old Henry, who came from England and settled at Cambridge before 1640."

Henry took up the story then and it poured out of him as if Marcus had poked a leak in a dam and the whole structure was crumbling. He confessed that Judge Prentiss had reminded him of his illegitimate birth, told him that he aspired too high when he asked for Narcissa. When the story got out around the little town, it came in the form of "What do you know! That Henry Spalding had the nerve to think he could marry Narcissa Prentiss, of all people!"

The dam down, Henry talked about his childhood. About the teasing of schoolmates because he had no parents, about the whispers and speculation because no one knew for sure which hired girl had been his mother. About his own torment through the years, his longing to do something worth while with his life, his fear that the sin of his parents, whoever they were, would be visited on him. Jibes. Epithets. Closed doors.

Tears rolled down Henry's cheeks and into his beard but he talked on and Marcus listened.

"I don't suppose I ever loved Narcissa Prentiss," Henry admitted. "I didn't know it then but I'm sure Mrs. Spalding is much better for me. I reckon my wanting Miss Prentiss was a kind of ambition to climb out of the hole I was in. She was the most popular girl in school, the most beautiful—everything. Before God, Doctor, I didn't know it at the time, but I must have thought, someplace inside me, that if I could win Narcissa Prentiss folks would quit using the word 'illegitimate' and that other worse one."

Henry stopped to blow his nose but he wasn't finished. "You're right, Doctor. Since then, I reckon I've been trying to get even with her. I must have blamed her for my whole childhood and for what everybody around town said and for her father. I . . . I ought to apologize to Mrs. Whitman."

"Henry," Marcus said and it was the first time he'd ever spoken to him using his first name, "you're a good man. You've done a fine job here in Oregon. You and Eliza have built up a respectable school. You've set your Indians to farming and raising sheep. Their very children will rise up to bless you for that. You've got down in print the unholy sounds of Nez Percé and soon our people will be able to read some of the Bible in their own language, thanks to you. You've done more good in six years here in Oregon than most men are privileged to do in a long lifetime."

"But those letters everybody's been writing back to Boston about me. I know all about them. Word gets around. It's the same thing all over again—just like when I was a boy in school and everybody was against me."

Marcus skimmed his flat stone downstream. "Henry, you may not like this but I think you've made your own jibes and slights and letters of criticism. Think back. If you'd started out—as soon as you were old enough to find out you had no parents—with your head up and your shoulders back, I think everything would have been different. And why not? You've gone through life expecting other people to hand you the dignity you felt your mother robbed you of. Actually, that dignity was always in you. It's in every man and has nothing to do with his birth. We're all created little lower than the angels, remember. Recognizing that one fact is a kind of salvation, Henry. Don't you think you've lived like a fatherless waif long enough? It's high time you started thinking of yourself as a son of God."

The sun had broken through by the time they rode back to Waiilatpu but they found the others huddled in exclusive little knots around the house.

"Come outside in the sun, everybody," Marcus called from the dining-room door. "You'll get moldy in here. And my friend, Henry, wants to make a statement."

Spalding stood erect. He did not clear his throat. Straight from the shoulder, he took full blame for the trouble he'd made in Oregon.

Marcus had seen deep into the man that day and had known that Henry was buying his birthright at a stiff price. But he'd known beyond all doubt that it had been bought and paid for. And the others had known it, too. They wanted Marcus to ride to Boston and ask the Board for another chance. At last, they were ready to pull together.

Secretary Greene's slow nod broke off the story. "Doctor Whitman," he said, "in view of your deep conviction, I shall break a precedent. I shall call the Prudential Committee to hear your case. I do not venture to predict their action. I warn you not to be too hopeful. These men are not given to reversing decisions."

"A fighting chance is all I ask."

It all took precious time—getting the committee together, making his plea, waiting for them to deliberate. But, at last, Dr. Greene called Marcus in.

"The Committee is not yet convinced that Mr. Spalding has had a complete change of heart," he began. "But, if you are willing to take the risk of staying on at Waiilatpu in the face of dangers from your associates as well as from the Cayuse Indians, the Prudential Committee will reverse its decision of last year."

Preaching Oregon, Marcus crossed Massachusetts and New York State. Encouraged, then disheartened, he saw his Yankee prospects consider and shake their heads.

"My grandpap settled here. It's good enough for me."

What had happened to the descendants of the Mayflower?

By the time Marcus reached his mother's home in Rushville, he sank into his father's old easy chair, baffled but not defeated. Grown men in the East seemed to be bogged down in their plowed furrows. Maybe he needed young blood for Oregon.

When he visited his brother, Marcus and a motherless nephew took a great fancy to each other. Perrin was a lanky, freckled kid of thirteen. He sat until midnight, cross-legged on the hearth, his roan fetlock flapping over his eyes, while he listened to Injun stories and hair-raising mountain man tales.

The next morning Marcus coiled a lasso, twirled, and tossed it over Perrin's wingy shoulders. He pulled him in as he would a maverick. "Perrin, my boy, I reckon you'd better go to Oregon with me."

"I reckon I'd better, Uncle Marcus."

Perrin's father agreed and received a suit of Boston store clothes in appreciation. They drew up adoption papers. And back in his buckskins, Marcus, with Perrin, put out for the frontier. He'd found one settler for Oregon. Not very convincing proof for Daniel Webster and President Tyler. Still, who could tell what might result? None of this trip had looked like any great cheese from its start until now.

And folks were already collecting. Riffraff, a lot of them, but surely he could find in the crowd some men with gumption enough to take wagons through, come Hudson's Bay or high water. He'd better get on out to the Missouri.

CHAPTER

3

AT WESTPORT, Marcus picked up his horses that he'd left there in the winter and they traded until Perrin possessed a black and white pony—wiry, sure-footed, and as excited about going West as Perrin himself.

"What'll you call him?"

"Indian ponies should have Indian names, I think," Perrin answered. "I'll name him for your Indians, Uncle Marcus. Cayuse. That's it. Cayuse."

"Fair enough. Our Indians are rich in horses."

They spurred on to the clearing beyond the Missouri line where the wagon caravan was assembling.

Grass greened late that year. The middle of May, the third week in May, and still the caravan must wait so horses and cattle could graze their way to Oregon. Impatient to hurry toward Narcissa, Marcus scolded himself for not visiting longer with relatives and friends in the States. But he kept busy while he waited.

As the camp grew his spirits rose. There'd be plenty of families to convince Washington that Oregon must be kept in American hands. Maybe folks weren't as dug-in and tethered in the States as he'd thought. And he felt pleased when the settlers kept holding meetings at which they demanded Doc Whitman's advice. Night after night they pumped him for intelligence on getting West.

"Can we really depend on wagons all the way to carry our families and household goods?" big, soft-spoken Jesse Looney asked. "We ain't got horses enough to mount everybody, Doc."

Practical Peter Burnett added, "And if wagons won't go through we'd better sell or trade off the stoves and bureaus we're hauling. Otherwise, we'll have to leave 'em by the way."

Burnett was one of the men Marcus had picked to persuade into settling near Waiilatpu. The trouble was, all the best men seemed to have their noses pointed toward the Willamette.

"Come on, Doc. You been over the Trail. Tell us, straight out. If wagons can't get through, I'm goin' to start tradin' trunks for extra mounts so the woman and kids won't have to walk."

Marcus squirmed under the responsibility they heaped on him but kept his voice sure. "Wagons'll go through. All the way," he said, over and over.

Only at night when the others were snoring, did he start from a sound sleep and sit up on the cold ground to find himself in a sweat. Then he'd pull his blankets around him and try to figure just how he could save the settlers' household goods and, especially, their lives when the "ifs" began to pile up—as they always piled up—to block the trail. If Pawnees stole the horses. If rivers flooded. If wagons broke down. If disease broke out. If Sioux burned the wagons. Still, wagons had to go through. He'd promised the President. He'd promised himself.

He met young Frémont who was to follow the wagon train with a band of picked soldiers. The two men stood eye to eye and Frémont's first words were, "So! The man with more courage than I have." At Marcus' question-lifted eyebrows he went on, "Don't think I haven't heard about your meeting with my father-in-law in Washington. It takes insides to speak up to Thomas Hart Benton. Rather than do it, I married Jessie on the sly."

When the wagon train finally began to wheeze and blow and squeak its way westward, Marcus felt proud and elated out of all proportion to any part he'd played in getting the caravan assembled. But he and Perrin stood by on their mounts, counting aloud. One hundred and twenty-five Conestogas and Pittsburghs lurched past. "Write this date on your memory, son," Marcus told Perrin. "The day the first wagon train to go all the way to Oregon left the settlements."

"I'll never forget it, Uncle Marcus. May 22, 1843." Perrin looped his lariat and twirled it. "Some say the wagons won't get through but I just tell 'em you say they will."

"Keep believing it, son. Might help a bit and they've got to get through. I promised."

Proud high-chested wagons rolled west behind sleek horses. Wheels turned and kept on turning to the west, plowing two endless furrows through June grass. Bows sagging, tilts whiffing off eddys of dust, wagons panted on under the July sun. . . .

But wagons with seven hundred desert miles put on them aged into old-men wagons—gray, stiff-jointed, cautious. And then the Laramie ford ran high. The company bunched and swore and eyed the current, rolling level with its banks. Marcus and Perrin left the cattle and spurred into the commotion.

"What's up?" Marcus called to the scowling captain.

"The blasted river," he answered. "And you're the very man I want to see. You said we could take these danged wagons through to the Columbia."

"Sure did," Marcus agreed. "And do."

The captain flung out a furious arm. "Why you blasted idiot! How you aimin' to ford wagons through that roarin' hell?"

Marcus turned to Perrin. "Son, bring up old Sage."

Marcus changed from the mule he'd been riding to rest his horse and rode his fresh mount into the water and swam him across. From the other side he waved, turned Sage back into the river. "Now then." He looked out over the crowd. "Burnett. Peter Burnett. Drive your wagon up here."

Peter Burnett, a man with a jaw that Marcus had noticed at their first meeting, hawed and geed until his wagon faced the obliterated ford. They tied logs under the wagon box so she'd float. Then Marcus secured the tongue to the end of a man-sized coil of rope. "Perrin, want to come along?"

"Sure, Uncle Marcus."

"Let's go, Sage." Marcus took the end of the rope and plunged once more into the water. The rope looped and twisted off the coil and, from the opposite bank, Marcus and Perrin urged Burnett's horses through. The wagon rolled, then floated, and came on. It slipped and groaned, peeled back mud to a footing, and creaked onto the bank.

"Thanks, Burnett," Marcus called and swam Sage back with the rope to get the next wagon.

That night, travelers turned hopeful once more, met to draft Dr. Marcus Whitman to lead them through to Oregon.

"Don't know about that," Marcus said. "Got my medical duties to see to—baby due any day now and several contagious cases down. Besides, my son and I've been helping the cow column along. Think the cows could get along without us, Perrin?"

"Sure they can, Uncle Marcus. Wagons need you more."

"Guess that's the answer then."

Before the party reached the Continental Divide, Marcus had to motion young John East's wagon out of line and off to the side. He built up a fire and told slowing-down inquirers to keep moving. The job took awhile but at sundown the East wagon rolled into night camp. Mother and child were doing fine. And Marcus, bringing up the rear on Sage, found a cluster of patients willing to trust him now with their breakings-out and diarrhea.

His hands full of doctoring and guiding, Marcus decided at the Divide to follow a short cut newly discovered by Catholic missionaries. The caravan needed to save its wind.

"De Smet claims it cuts off a deal of travel," Marcus told Perrin at the Divide encampment. "Add to that a chance to see Jim Bridger at his place on Black's Fork of the Green and there's no argument."

The wagon train saw Jim Bridger long enough for him to shrink their tires, shoe their horses, weld their rims, repair wagon boxes shrunk unjointed by parching sun, and sell them supplies at his store.

Jim invited Marcus and Perrin to supper that evening. They found old Gabe cross-legged in front of the stone fireplace that formed one wall of his mud-roofed cabin.

"Doc, you old hoss thief. Don't this beat all?" Jim came up on his feet as if hoisted by a string. He took Perrin's hand and turned to Marcus. "Boy looks like ye, Doc, sure as yer born." His eyes fixed Perrin's. "Jest make sartin sure ye'll never turn out to be as big a man as yer uncle yere, though, and ye kin lay to that."

"Yes, sir."

Marcus noticed that the boy had sense enough to stand straight and look him square in the eye when he talked to a real man.

"How's your back?" Marcus asked Jim.

"Aren't a back nowhar kin shine with this child's. Dang blasted Blackfeet!" Jim made the sign to "set and eat" and they crossed their feet to drop to the buffalo robes spread near the fire.

Inhaling blue smoke, Bridger leaned over his red clay pipe, elbows on his knees. "That waar some spree, Doc. That time'll never come ag'in. And it's sartin sure yer part the cause fer it. Ye and yer wagons and yer white women."

Jim's wife, a handsome Shoshone woman this time, served their supper of buffalo stew, filling their tin plates in silence and leaving the pot on the hearth.

"You seem to be doing all right on my wagons and my whites," Marcus said. "Straddling the Trail and waiting for American dollars to roll in—looks easier than trapping to me."

Bridger knifed in a cube of meat and set his jaws to work. "Maybeso tradin' are lookin' easier to ye. But puttin' up with these yere greenhorns traipsin' acrost my mountains aren't no picnic. Ef thar's any quicksand 'thin a mile of a ford, they gotta waller in it. Ef thar's a rattler anywhar, they look till they onkiver him and git therselves bit. They onhitch come night and drop their saddles and harness with invites all over 'em fer the wolves to chew 'em. Doc, hell's full a sich greenhorns."

Marcus drew his face long and made his voice stern. "Full of greenhorns and of old sinners like you who ought to know better."

"Better'n which?"

"Better than to teach that innocent daughter of yours such language."

Relieved, Gabe sank back into his pelvis. "Ye meanin' that 'please' and 'beg pardon, marm' and that?" He shook his head. "Feared ye'd think she waar puttin' on fofarraw doin's. Still, this child figgered Miz Whitman mought take a hankerin' after sich."

Marcus' held-in laugh exploded. "She's the sweetest little antelope you ever saw, Jim. We couldn't get along without that little rascal. She's full of the old Gabe and we love her like our very own—dang blasteds and all. I hate to think what would have happened to Mrs. Whitman these last three years without your Mary Ann and Joe Meek's little punkin, Helen Mar. Those girls have saved Narcissa's reason since Alice died."

Jim's head wagged. "Too bad about the pesky Injuns l'arnin' her bad words. Must fret Miz Whitman a sight."

"My whites, as you call them, fret Mrs. Whitman a sight more." Marcus leaned over to set his emptied plate on the hearth. "But there's one good reason for them. Get enough settlers in here and I've got the promise of the President himself that whites'll be protected from Indian savages by the American government. You'd like that yourself, Gabe, and you can't deny it."

Jim turned to Perrin. "Thar's what I mean, boy. Yer uncle are a leetle mite crazy. Wagh! Thinkin' he kin beat out Hudson's Bay and all them Britishers wot's had everthin' ther own way all these y'ar. But ye kin lay yer pile on it, ef this old hoss don't say this yere Oregon Country are goin' to come under the stars and stripes. And yer uncle will be mostly to blame."

Perrin raked the flap of hair off his forehead. "Not 'blame,' Mr. Bridger. It'll be grand. It's what Uncle Marcus wants more than anything."

Jim's grin skimmed over the boy's head at Marcus. "Like a boy that'll git his dander up! Yer right, Perrin. Country aren't goin' to be same as the old days ag'in nohow. Better be American, then."

Reveling in the slow pour of Jim's voice, Marcus waited but Perrin spoke up.

"Settlers'll learn how to live in this country. Uncle Marcus has taught them lots already."

"They'll l'arn, I reckon. Ef prehaps they don't go under fust." Jim wiped his mouth on the back of his hand and filled his pipe. "Ther aren't much to l'arn, Perrin. When in Injun country, do as the Injuns do—and do it better. And be ready to fight at the drop of a hat or the cussed Injuns got no use fer ye—unless to sculp ye." He pulled a taper from the fire and drew on his pipe. "I rayther calculate yer uncle's settlers'll manage to git along, son. 'Cept fer gittin' past Cap'n Johnny."

Marcus sat up. "Gabe, how much truth is there in talk of Johnny Grant sending folks to California on Hudson's Bay orders?"

"Settlers play hob with trappin', Doc, sartin sure. Ye kin figger it yerself."

Perrin said, "And Hudson's Bay depends on trapping."

Jim's grin met Marcus' over the boy's head again. "Doggone my skin ef them Britishers are goin' to give up 'thout tryin' to hang onta that thar big business. Cap'n Johnny's got his orders and ye kin lay to that."

Marcus' jaw set. "My settlers are going through."

Jim nodded. "That thar mought be considdible of a skrimmage. Doggone my skin ef it moughtn't."

4

NEXT morning Marcus' early cry of "Travel, travel, travel," rang through camp and soon wagons rolled to the northwest—brassy sun to their backs, gently peaked mountains to their right, and everywhere sage.

Sage waded in watery mirages ahead and to the left. Sage edged the patches of summer dried grass in the distance. Sage, near at hand, scraped the horses' bellies and clutched with bearlike claws at passing wagons. The smell of sage filled the wilderness.

Travel, travel, travel. Marcus never let the caravan stop two nights in the same encampment. "Travel," he insisted. "Nothing else will take you to the end of your journey. Nothing is wise that doesn't help you along."

In less than two weeks, Marcus and Perrin—scouting ahead of the train—caught a glimpse of peeled log walls varnished by the noonday sun. "Next stop," Marcus said. "Let's go back and hurry them along."

"This is where Mr. Bridger said Captain Johnny would stop us, isn't it? Will we stay here, Uncle Marcus?"

"Not for long. Got to fix up some of the wagons a mite before we start trailing the Snake. Then we'll move on." He hoped against all he knew of Hudson's Bay policy that he could make good on that promise.

The wagon train ringed up to the east of Fort Hall beyond the cornfield. Marcus made a hurried check, demanding strict observance of the rules. Fort or no fort, this was Blackfoot country and they'd take no chances with their scalps.

Inside the cluttered store, Captain Johnny grabbed Marcus' hand across the counter. "Doc Whitman, old thing!" His English accent starched his mountain man jargon stiffly out of shape for some reason today. "So, you actually made it East last winter! Come inside and gratify your dry."

Grant's English background had come sharply to the fore. Something was afoot. But the factor had seen Narcissa. Refusing his offer of a drink, Marcus pressed him, instead, for intelligence about his family.

Captain Johnny's full-moon expression sobered at mention of Narcissa. "Been ill, Doc. Your spouse got a real scare at Waiilatpu right after you left. That chap, Gray, appears mighty untrustworthy although Mrs. Whitman said nothing of the kind. Doctor Barclay at Vancouver's been taking care of her." He brightened and slapped Marcus' buckskin shoulder. "Say, those little girls of yours are some punkins. That Mary Ann does beat all!"

"What about Mrs. Whitman?" Marcus pumped. "And what about Waiilatpu? All I've heard is hints."

Captain Johnny didn't know. Mrs. Whitman hadn't wanted to discuss it. "She was back at Waiilatpu once that I know of. Went with that so-called Indian agent, White, who claims he's authorized by the United States government. He took Mrs. Whitman with him to Waiilatpu when he called the Injuns into council to make them ratify his so-called laws."

"Heard hints about those laws, too," Marcus said. "You got a copy?"

"Righto," Captain Johnny said, offhand, and started fingering through the pigeonholes back of the counter. "Say, I've got a letter for you. From your spouse, as a matter of fact. Plumb forgot it." He pulled out a folded and crumpled sheet of paper. "And that reminds me. Injuns came in here the other day with flour for you from Waiilatpu. Sent by that new chap they put in charge there after Gray skedaddled. Guess maybeso some of your settlers could use extra provisions before they get to California."

Marcus heard but he was breaking the seal on Narcissa's letter. He'd attend to that California business after awhile. He backed away from the counter and sank onto a bench to scan the letter. Later, he'd take time to fondle every word. For now, it was good merely to feel the letter in his hands and know that Narcissa had held it not so long before.

Good to have her say the Indians missed him and needed him because they had no one else they trusted.

The principal cause of the excitement is the Cayuses did not wish to be forced to adopt the laws recommended by the agent. They say the laws in themselves are good—but do not wish to be compelled to enforce them. This arises from what was said at the meeting to this effect: We advise you to adopt these laws but if you do not we will put you in a way to do it.

They took exception to such language as this. Call it threatening them. . . . Various remarks carelessly made by unwise Americans and taken to be facts have caused a very great commotion. Some of the Indians say you have gone to the States to bring troops to fight them. Poor creatures. They know not what they do. They are like sheep without a shepherd. None misses you more than the one who pulled your ears.

Marcus grinned and scanned on. Joe Meek converted at a Methodist revival! Imagine that. Perhaps it was even better not to read Narcissa's letter word for word at first. Cull out the good news and skip the other.

For instance, talk that he'd gone to the States to get troops could have unpleasant, even dangerous, repercussions. Would have, unless it was stopped.

On the other hand, a Mr. Geiger had been hired to keep things in hand at Waiilatpu. He was sending packs of supplies to meet the wagon train at Fort Hall and at Grande Ronde, Narcissa said.

Do hurry home, my husband [she finished]. I'll wait at The Dalles for you. Mary Ann and Helen Mar are a great comfort to me but your society is my life and while I had you I never knew that I was lonely. Now I am restless and uneasy, numbering the past, anxiously looking forward, struggling between hope and fear.

Marcus could not put the letter from his mind during the sick calls that took most of his night. After an hour's sleep, he rolled from his blankets and made the rounds of the wagons, inspecting wheels and axles, pointing out the ones to be drawn inside the log compound for blacksmithing and grease. But his mind was on Narcissa. And then more sick calls and he didn't have time to read Narcissa's letter word for word. Perhaps, if he had not been so preoccupied, worrying

(191)

about her health, enjoying her eagerness to see him, he would have noticed what was going on in camp. As it was, Perrin burst into a tent where he was splinting a broken arm. The boy waved toward a dust-raising commotion among the wagons.

"Uncle Marcus, come. It's Captain Grant. He's—he's— Come quick, Uncle Marcus. They need you."

Marcus followed Perrin at a trot between two rows of corn to the camp.

He found an uproar of cursing voices and women's wails in a welter of dumped household effects and baggage. In the middle of this fracas, Factor Johnny Grant stood wide-legged.

As Marcus came up, Grant broke in on a volley of curses pouring from a burly Missourian who tugged at, without budging, an iron cookstove. "Sorry as can be, old fellow, but I'm not responsible for mountains or rivers between here and the Columbia. All I'm telling you is that wagons can't go through. If you want to start out from here and leave them where they turn over, I won't stop you. But if you want to leave them here, I'll pay you every shilling they're worth to me."

Marcus shoved backs aside and stepped high over trunks and bundles into the noise and litter. "What's this, Captain? You're not buying these wagons."

Men straightened from hauling their belongings over the tail-boards of their wagons and turned their curses out into the open. Stepping over saddles and stacks of iron pots, they strode in to form an angry circle around Marcus and Captain Johnny. Sunbonnets askew, women followed their men, a favorite possession clutched in their arms, their tears unchecked. Excited children dug in discard piles, demanding, "Ma, where's my doll?" . . . "Ma, my wagon. You can't leave that!"

Captain Johnny locked his hands behind his back, tilted his round face up to Marcus, and smiled.

Marcus insisted, "What's going on here?"

Several men shouted answers with furious wavings of their arms— first at Captain Johnny and then at Marcus. "He says the wagons can't go through. Nor the cattle neither."

A big farmer from Virginia thrust his nose in Marcus' face. "You dang blasted idiot. You said we could take 'em all the way. By golly, you-all will pay for this!"

(192)

Another big emigrant—this one a stockman from Illinois—chimed in. "You liar, you, with your highfalutin' talk about takin' wagons all the way to the Willamette. What in tarnation wuz you tryin' to pull? Think you'd get all our stuff we couldn't pack and take it for your own?"

A little fellow from Kentucky grabbed Marcus' arm and pulled him around. "You know we ain't even got hosses enough for everybody to ride. And you let us get way out here in this fix."

Marcus waited for a lull. Curses closed in on him. Women's sobs sucked at any moment of near quiet. Marcus stepped up on a wagon tongue and the crowd closed in. He waved his arm for order. Accusations and oaths peppered him from every side. He hooked his elbow over the high frontboard of the wagon. "Quiet. It's my time to talk!"

"Ain't you talked enough?" someone yelled. "You talked us into startin' out with these infernal wagons and all our cattle."

Captain Johnny stepped forward. "Gentlemen and ladies, let's not have an argument. The Doc's a fine fellow—friend of mine. Let's just say he made a mistake when he advised you back at the frontier." He grinned out over the crowd and then, in an instant, lifted his chins off his chest and laid back his ears. "We all make mistakes. But let's not go on making them. It's nothing to me, if you don't mind losing your trappings and shooting your cattle out there on the Trail. But, if you'd rather get what you can out of them, I'm trying to keep you from making another mistake."

Half a dozen big men stepped up to the factor. Applegate said, "I've got two hundred head of cattle. What'll you give me for the lot, Captain?"

Jesse Looney fumed, "Captain, I've got five kids and a wife and only four horses. Where'll I get enough horses to go round?"

The factor's wide smile promised to take care of everything and everybody.

Helpless, Marcus stood on the wagon and looked over the crowd. These families planned to make a living in Oregon by farming and they were dooming themselves to failure. How could they break out farms, build homes, raise their families if they arrived without household goods, without work horses, without cattle, without wagons? Half of them would die off the first winter. No more than a handful would be able to buy from Hudson's Bay Company enough equipment to get started. Word would fly back to the States and new settlers would stop in their tracks. Hudson's Bay would claim Oregon for Great Britain.

"Stop it," he cried. "Stop!"

The most influential men in the body clustered around Captain Johnny, asking what he would pay, too desperate to haggle over the pitiful prices he named.

"Come inside, gentlemen," the factor invited, "and let me write this in the books. You'll all get a square deal and you can lay to that. Besides, you'll have the satisfaction of knowing you made the right decision." He turned and led the big men zigzagging through the piles of unpacked goods toward the fort.

Marcus watched them swing away and saw Daniel Webster's broad back twitch in righteous laughter. So, he'd heaved and tugged and wet himself in icy rivers and sweat and doctored and promised, all for nothing!

Many of these women and children and some of the men wouldn't even make it through to Oregon without their wagons. They were low on food and sick. They couldn't set a horse the rest of the way, even if they had horses to set and many of them hadn't. Still, a man could supply other men with their guts just so far and no farther. Marcus wouldn't, if he could, force them to go on through with their wagons. They had to go through of their own choice or not at all. And they'd made their choice. He let go the wagon and flexed his knees to jump down.

"Doctor." The small voice came from below him.

He looked down on young John East and his wife. To her skirt clung three children. In her arms lay the baby delivered on the Trail a few weeks back. "How's the baby?" Marcus asked.

"Doctor, we're going to drive our wagon through, if you'll lead us." John East's voice, insignificant, without weight until now, suddenly had power to dry up tears, to blot up curses.

A few other families moved in near the Easts.

Marcus heard a little eddy of hope whir over the crowd like a breeze running through sage. "Say that again," he told East.

John East took a deep breath. "We're driving our wagon through." He dragged in another breath and went on. "We never coulda come this far without you, Doctor, and if you say wagons can go through, ours'll try it." He turned toward the others. "We got nothing to lose," he said. "How could I get my wife and little baby through without the wagon?"

A strapping young giant from Kentucky whose first baby was due within the week, stepped up and waved his arms. "Listen, all of you. East's right. Get them other fellas back here. We gotta take our wagons or rot in our tracks."

Desperate whispers, "That's right," and "Let's give it a try," encircled Marcus. Stragglers and those on the verge of trailing off through the corn with Captain Johnny turned and came back. Marcus saw his chance. He yanked his pistol from his belt and fired into the air.

The men with the factor stopped, turned, and started on. But three ran back to see what was up.

Marcus gave those who would listen time to wonder a minute and then, keeping his voice low, he spoke. "These wagons are going through to the Columbia! I've been over the Trail five times. Took a wagon through myself as far as Boise seven years ago. Since then, wagons have gone all the way. You can take yours through, if you've got the gumption."

From beyond the circle, Captain Johnny interrupted. "But Doc Whitman, think of the suffering and hard labor."

"Any who are afraid of hard labor can turn south to California, the way Hudson's Bay Company hopes you will. The rest can come with me—in wagons. Straight through to Oregon!"

Women dried their eyes and tugged at their husbands' homespun sleeves. Men who had been cursing a moment before asked quick hopeful questions.

Marcus stood tall on the wagon. "Folks, it's up to you. We've been across flooded rivers, down mountainsides, through scorching prairie together. Ahead of us there'll be rivers and prairies and the steepest mountains we've crossed yet. It won't be easy. But people all over the States have got their eyes on us. Thousands of men and women just like you are waiting to follow along the wagon road we'll flatten through the sage. People in Great Britain are watching, too. Hoping we can't get through because they know their companies can't hold Oregon against a tide of American settlers. I promised President Tyler, promised Secretary Webster I'd get you through. I'll get you through. You and your wagons and your cattle. Get you through in shape to break out farms and set up homes."

Cries of "Let's go," "Lead the way, Doc," and "On to Oregon," blew off the lid of despondency that had covered the crowd. Men fired pistols into the air. Women wept now for joy and started sorting their belongings for repacking. Children whooped and turned somersaults on the trampled grass.

Marcus looked down into the surprised moon of Captain Johnny's face. "No hard feelings, Captain?"

The factor hesitated for an instant only. "Righto!" he cried and reached up his hand. "I'll be doggoned if I don't half hope you make it."

Marcus jumped down. He ran his fingers into Perrin's hair and gave the boy's scalp a loosening.

Perrin's eyes, dark now, threatened to overflow. "Uncle Marcus," he said, reverence in his voice, "you were like a statue."

Wheels rolled beyond Fort Hall. Wheels waddled like fat old women over stiff unyielding sagebrush. Wheels eclipsed in desert sand but kept on rolling. Wheels rumbled through stony creek beds, tossing sparkles of water into the sun. Wheels lumbered on a slant through hillside forests. Wheels treaded water to cross swollen rivers. Wheels locked to slide down shaly slopes. Wheels creased the tasseled green carpet of Grande Ronde Valley. And on and on they turned, tracking across the continent.

But days moved beneath the wheels and meant to Marcus only that the train still rolled three weeks, then two, then one away from the Blues and September was running out. Winter must not catch them in the Blues.

"Travel, travel, travel! . . . Pick it up a little, Mr. Looney. . . . Can't camp yet. We've made only twelve miles today. . . . Try your horses today, Burnett. They'll move a little faster than those oxen and the going's not heavy now for a spell. . . . You'll have to speed up the cow column, men, or else fall back and join Frémont. Wagons have got to move on."

Travel, travel, travel . . .

PART IV

*

CHAPTER

1

STEALING a moment to stop and admire the few pumpkins ripening in the field beyond Alice Clarissa's grave, Marcus straightened and took a slow turn around the place—to the knoll where he and Narcissa had said good-by just a year and a week ago, then on to the dozen battered Conestogas squatting in the meadow. He must get on to those wagons and make his sick calls. It seemed nobody in the caravan had stopped except the sick and destitute. And after all his plans for luring to Waiilatpu a colony of stable, industrious settlers! As it was, the main body of the train had cleaned him out of grain and rolled on down the Columbia.

Now the meadow, and their large adobe house which he'd managed to complete only a short time before his trip East, and the old house, too, were filled with needy families who would be a care through the winter and would then move on, come spring. His early fall grass, cropped short by the caravan, would have to hump itself to put on new tips ahead of winter. And the Indians, instead of welcoming their doctor home, were filled with angry questions about the wagons and about the land these many Bostons would take away from the Cayuse.

When Marcus tried to answer their questions, they covered their ears and would not hear. "White *te-wat* not friend toward Cayuse. Bring Bostons. Take Cayuse land."

Impatient to get things in order so he could hurry to The Dalles for Narcissa, Marcus didn't have time to wheedle the Indians into understanding.

Perrin had fallen back with Frémont and his soldiers to help herd their horses. He should be along any day now.

As soon as he'd welcomed Perrin, Marcus made up his mind, he'd go to Narcissa whether the houses and farm were in apple-pie order or not. All at once, being this near to Narcissa became too much to bear. While he'd been so far away that seeing her was out of the question, he'd managed to put up with the separation. But now . . . He grabbed up his medicine case and hurried on to the wagons.

When Kit Carson arrived in advance of Frémont, Perrin still didn't show up.

Kit lounged off his mount and over to the corral where Marcus was mending fence. "Howdy, Doc. Mind if my party lays over hyar a mite?"

"Carson, by the eternal, it's good to see you!"

Kit hitched up his buckskins. "Joe Meek come yet?"

"Haven't seen him."

"He'll be hyar."

"Fine." Marcus turned back to his fence—had to get it mended before anybody came with horses. "That boy of mine with Frémont?"

"Is so. Kid's good with hosses." Kit wiped his hands on his britches and picked up a rail to help with the fence. "Got any flour, Doc?"

"Got what was burned when the Indians set fire to my mill," Marcus answered. "Wagon train about cleaned me out of everything else. Got potatoes. You and Frémont are welcome to whatever we can scare up. We'll see that you don't leave here hungry."

"Injuns actin' up?"

"Some."

"Hyar some 'bout Mrs. Whitman havin' trouble. Feathercap, the way this child hyar it."

Marcus nodded. "I'm waiting to get her version of it before I go after that Indian's filthy hide!"

"A skeared Injun are the only good Injun, Doc."

The corral was almost finished when Frémont and his men appeared across the Walla Walla. Perrin was the last one in. Dusty from herding horses, his body looked hard and even taller than when Marcus had left him at Grande Ronde.

"Knew you wouldn't mind if I helped Captain Frémont all the way, Uncle Marcus," Perrin said.

"Glad you could be of help to the United States Army, son."

Joe Meek trotted in at noon. The men were just sitting down in the kitchen to a meal of potatoes and mud-colored bread baked from grain burned in the mill fire. But Joe Meek was too excited to care about food.

"Whatcha know, Doc, them hosses at Champoeg clean outvoted the Britishers. Provisional govermint in the name of the United States, we got, sure as shootin'."

He socked Marcus a blow on the back that knocked a quarter of potato down his throat in one piece. "Just look what you done, Doc. You and your purty wagons and all your hollerin' about white settlers from the States. Hudson's Bay are even downin' their sights on McLoughlin for ever lettin' you camp hyar. Ruint fur business and that's a fact. But scalp my old head, if I aren't glad. Thar's somethin' mighty purty about that United States flag them settlers histed over Champoeg."

"Religion's done you good, Meek," Marcus told him.

"The real thing'll do anybody good, Doc, and that's a fact."

Frémont said, "Meek, you talk like a senator instead of a trapper. And I found Jim Bridger sitting smack in the middle of his own fort out there on Black's Fork, talking the same way. What's got into you mountain men?"

"Reckon us old hosses are just got around to figgerin' out the only way to keep on bein' our own boss—like when we were trappin'. The only way are to hitch onto that free and equal business. No bellyin' around under any king for us!"

Kit Carson thumbed tobacco into his pipe and pulled a light from the fire. "Country hyar's civilizin' mighty fast and mostly thanks to you, Doc." He took a long draw on his pipe. " 'Course, Injuns don't like it. Gettin' sorta rambunctious all over."

Meek said, "This old beaver's glad to see the captain hyar account of that. Can't you skear the Doc's Cayuses a mite with your howitzer, Captain?"

Marcus laid back his head and laughed.

"Your laughin' aren't goin' to shine when these Cayuses see fresh sign of whites settlin' on their land."

"Sorry, gentlemen," Frémont said, "but I'm here for map-making purposes only—at least, that's the story and they gave me orders in Washington to keep it looking that way." He stood up. "Doc Whitman, I'll be getting on down to my camp. You mind if we cache some howitzer balls with you? I'm tired of carrying them."

"Not shooting your way across the country, I take it then, Captain," Marcus answered.

"Haven't so far and I don't expect to. They tell me California's going to be mighty tame after a man has passed through Blackfoot country. Where shall I have the men stack those balls?"

"Down by the corral, I reckon. Make a sort of monument for us to remember you by."

"Got a big mule I'm going to leave you, too. Help pay for those fine potatoes you let us have."

"You paid for those."

"Well, this is a good mule. Help pay for what you've done for the country, then. And for that bulldogging lecture you gave my father-in-law in Washington."

Perrin spoke up, "And what a mule, Uncle Marcus! He's as big as a house. Come on down to the corral and see him."

Frémont scraped back his chair. "We'd better all get moving. Carson, you see to getting those cannon balls unloaded first thing."

His eyes dancing with pride, Perrin led Marcus down to meet his new mule. "See, didn't I tell you? Big as a house."

"Almost," Marcus agreed, stroking down a drab, thick-muscled foreleg.

"What'll we call him?"

Still musing on the conversation in the kitchen, Marcus said the first name that came into his mind. "How about Uncle Sam?"

"Sure," Perrin approved. "Uncle Sam."

As they turned back toward the house they both stopped, their eyes fixed on a procession worming along the Walla Walla.

"Your Indians?" Perrin asked.

Marcus dropped his hand to the boy's shoulder instead of answering. Yes, they were Cayuses, all right. Returning from fall Hunt. But returning too early and moving, now, too slowly. And, instead of heading for their lodges across the river, they curved to the right and were coming through his meadow. Something strange here. They rode in a weird quiet—not even their dogs were barking. And then,

(200)

as they came closer, Marcus saw slung across the black pony at the head of the procession, the body of Chief Umtippe. Umtippe dead.

Feathercap, wrapped in the dignity of his new position, reined in and leered down on Marcus. "Funeral," he commanded. "Like for Cayuse *te-mi*. Chief Umtippe sleep in box. Box in ground—" he pointed beyond the house to the grave of Alice Clarissa, "there."

No. Not beside Alice. Narcissa would hate the thought of the obstreperous old chief lying, even in death, near their daughter. And for Feathercap, the very one who had tried to attack Narcissa the minute Marcus turned his back and started East, to make this demand! By rights he should be sent packing. Still, perhaps this was a time for turning the other cheek. And actually, Marcus told himself, it could do no harm. Might even draw the Indians closer to Waiilatpu, make them feel more kindly toward their white neighbors just now when settlers seemed to upset them so. He said, "Hold fine funeral for Chief Umtippe. Sorry Umtippe die in hunt. Chief Feathercap send braves to dig in ground tomorrow."

"Braves dig now," Feathercap answered. "Already ride three day. Too hot for keep Umtippe long time."

At once, more Indians than Marcus could supply with shovels slumped off their horses. Nothing to do but lead them to Alice Clarissa's grave. He would have to mark off the rectangle to guide the diggers.

But then he felt rather than heard the Indians stop and draw back. Turning, he saw the mounted Cayuses in a pulled-up wall. Horses, yanked in, pawed at the air. Eyes stretched with fright, nostrils flaring, the Indians stared into the black mouth of Frémont's howitzer. Frémont's men, busy unloading cannon balls, bustled about their job with a purpose that the lazy Indians could, Marcus knew, mistake for warlike.

Grinning, he held up his hand to get their attention and explain.

At that, the Cayuses stampeded. They jerked their horses around and slammed into each other, yelping in fear in their desperate rush to escape. The pony carrying Umtippe's body lunged into the river. Dogs, trampled underfoot, shrieked and wailed.

Feathercap stood his ground long enough to grasp that Marcus' upraised arm was not a signal for firing the cannon. Nevertheless he jerked his pony beyond range of the pointing howitzer. Then, having seen that his blood brothers were making their escape, he waited.

(201)

Marcus watched the play of guilt in his shifty eyes, in the working of his mouth before he spoke. Then he called down, "A trick!" His ruff of hair bristled. "White *te-wat* no let Chief Umtippe lay on Cayuse land. White *te-wat* bring soldiers to shoot." One suspicious eye still on the cannon, he pulled his rearing pony close. His fist beat the air. "White *te-wat* drive Umtippe far off. Now Cayuse make trick. Drive Bostons far off. White *te-wat* find this so." And he splashed into the river.

Marcus discovered his still upraised arm and consciously hauled it down. Slowly he shook his head. Filthy, flea-bearing Umtippe! Having found it hard to hate them enough in life, Umtippe had, in death, managed to go on hating.

Strange how little death affected the flow of a man's life. As if dying were no more than a sudden drop in a stream bed—a waterfall and then the same river flowing on in the same direction, its water sweet or bitter as it had been before. A reassuring thought in the case of a man whose life flowed toward good. In the case of Umtippe . . . This afternoon had clearly shown that Umtippe had not finished with Waiilatpu.

CHAPTER

2

YES, Narcissa had received his message. She stood on the embankment above the river where Marcus could watch her growing from doll- to life-size against the sunset as his boat approached The Dalles. And then they docked and Narcissa stood above him, steady in spite of winds that whipped the flounces of her black merino dress and loosened gay pennants of hair around her face.

Marcus leaped from the boat and up the bank.

"Oh Marcus, Marcus. I thought you'd never come."

His arms folded her close. His cheek lay quiet against her hair. At last, he was home.

Hours later, walking arm in arm through their hosts' moonlit orchard, the wonder of being near her still caught at his throat. Terror at the thought that he might have lost her pressed hard against his heart.

"You'll have to tell me what happened at Waiilatpu," he said. "I've heard so little."

Her shudder shook him. "Not tonight, my darling. Not this perfect night." She hid her face against his chest. "Marcus, Marcus!"

"I shouldn't have gone."

Instantly she straightened. "Don't think that. How could you, after all the wonderful things you accomplished? Changing the Board's decision about Mr. Spalding. And getting President Tyler and Mr. Webster worked up over Oregon! Why, that alone was worth it all. And the wagon train! To think that you finally got to bring wagons all the way through. Oh Marcus, it's going to be a great country, our Oregon. And thanks to you, it's going to belong to the States. There's talk of it everywhere. I'm so proud of you, my husband."

Marcus caught her mood. "Be lots of excitement around Waiilatpu now," he said. "Next year more wagons will come and more and more each year until the country's crowded. We've got to raise a lot of food so we'll have supplies for emigrants. And fix up the blacksmith shop, get new equipment. Out of all those people, we're sure to find the ones we want to settle near us at Waiilatpu. Make it a hand-picked community where the Cayuse can see how civilized people live in peace and comfort."

"Marcus," Narcissa's voice came small, "must we go back to Waiilatpu?"

"Narcissa!"

"It's been so wonderful here and in Vancouver," she explained. "Doctor McLoughlin is a wonderful man. I've had such nice people to visit and meetings to attend. And the Indians around here are so much easier to get along with than the Cayuse. Haven't we stayed long enough under those eternally peering eyes?"

In a flash of understanding, Marcus knew how she felt. She'd gone through a nightmare at Waiilatpu. Several nightmares, climaxed by one worse that the others when Feathercap tried to break into her bedroom. But, back of that, Narcissa was a social creature. And Waiilatpu had given her little but loneliness.

"We'll have to think about it," he said. "See what we can figure out. Hadn't counted on leaving this soon but I always intended we'd get us a farm in the Willamette someday. Might work it sooner, if you're ready."

"Oh Marcus, could we?" Narcissa's arm tightened around his waist and then fell limp. "No. We can't do that. You've counted so on helping travelers. And you've worked so hard to open the trail to wagons. No. Forget I said it. I'll go back to that dark spot."

Marcus squeezed her hand. "Not so fast, young lady. Wagon trains have to come through The Dalles, too. This is the logical halfway station along the Columbia."

"But—?"

"Talked with Mr. Perkins right after dinner. He says the Methodists are drawing in their forces. They're going to concentrate in the Valley. They wondered whether we might want their buildings and equipment here at The Dalles."

"The answer is yes, of course!" Narcissa cried. "Oh, I do wish—" Then she interrupted herself. "No. No, we can't, naturally. We've put our hands to the plow."

Marcus linked her arm into his. "Afraid we'll have to go to Waiilatpu this year but maybe later . . . You're shivering. Let's go in. Got to have a peek at Helen Mar."

"It wasn't easy, putting her to sleep before you came, I can tell you. But she has grown into a sweet child. Mr. Meek seems very pleased at the way we're bringing her up."

"Old Joe Meek has changed some himself."

"You've seen him?"

"He came to Waiilatpu while Captain Frémont and Kit Carson were there."

"I should have been there to cook for you."

"How good are you with burned grain?" Marcus asked. "Emigrants pretty well cleaned us out. They didn't want what was burned, of course."

"I'm sure of that."

"Mr. Spalding will spare us something," Marcus told her. "There's another changed man."

"Thank heaven—and you—for that." Narcissa turned on the step as they started into the house. "You're a big man, Doctor Whitman, and I'm proud. I want to go to Waiilatpu with you for as long as you think we should."

When they arrived, they found the houses at Waiilatpu still crowded with needy families. And Narcissa had developed distressing abdominal pains. Since her bed was occupied by an emigrant woman who'd given birth to a son that afternoon, she insisted that Marcus spread her a pallet in the dining room. Later he could build her a bed.

That night, even to Marcus, Waiilatpu looked a "dark spot," as Narcissa had called it. And when he went to unhitch the horses he found a ring of silent Indians around Frémont's cannon balls.

He remembered Rendezvous and its shooting, shouting clusters of whites and Indians. He heard distinctly in Kit Carson's drawl, "The only good Injuns, Doc, are noisy as all hell broke loose."

At his approach the Indians slid away without a sound. The voice of the river came muted this evening. Marcus glanced back at the house. He felt almost glad that Narcissa had arrived too sick to come down to the corral. This way, he could tend to all the worrying himself.

INDIANS were back in greater numbers at choretime the next morning. Frémont's monument of cannon balls drew Cayuses like a magnet. Chief Feathercap lent the gathering this morning a kind of official sanction and an air of real trouble.

When Marcus got near enough to speak, he called out in their language, "Good day." He stepped into their circle and turned to Feathercap. "What is it, Chief? Why do Cayuse come here?"

Feathercap's eyes shifted away from Marcus' gaze. He blurted, "Powder. Balls."

Marcus nodded. "Of course. Balls for gun."

Several Cayuses got into the argument then. Pointing to the balls, their arms accused him. Their eyes bored in as if to read his mind.

"Why gun balls here?" . . . "Bostons bring balls. Bostons kill Cayuse." . . . "White *te-wat* ride far off. Bring Bostons. Take Cayuse land."

Marcus quieted them with his fingers over his mouth in the sign for silence. "No understand. White *te-wat* ride far off to bring Cayuse good, not bad."

"Bostons," the Indians screamed. "Plenty Bostons."

"Sure," Marcus agreed. "Plenty Bostons. Plenty more follow in land canoes. But no take Cayuse land. Bostons go to Willamette."

The Indians pointed to the adobe houses. Their voices furious, they accused, "Plenty Bostons. Bostons stop. Stay on Cayuse land."

Marcus sighed and tried once more to explain. "Bostons stop

here small while. Not stay here. Bostons sick. White *te-wat* make well. Then, they go."

Feathercap sneered. "Go way like barking-dog-man. Leave poison behind. Kill off Cayuse. Take Cayuse land."

"What do you mean?"

In his fury, Feathercap's hair stood out like porcupine quills. "White *te-wat* understand. Him make trick."

This accusation seemed to lend Feathercap the defiance that his guilt had robbed him of before. Through brown snaggled teeth he seethed. "That right. White *te-wat* go way off. Leave barking-dog-man put poison in melons. Kill off Cayuse. But—" He raised himself to chief stature and swirled his blanket around him. "But Cayuse great people. No die from poison. Puke some. That all. Barking-dog-man scared. Go way off. So white *te-wat* must come back. Bring plenty Bostons help kill great Cayuse people."

Horrified by this astonishing version of their movements, Marcus could see how it might make sense to the Indians. He could guess about the melons. Gray had threatened that he could put a stop to the Cayuses' stealing. "I'd stick a good dose of calomel in them melons. I'd learn them thiefs a lesson. I can understand why you can't handle the savages, Doc. You're too easy."

It would be like Gray to rush to the melon patch with calomel the minute Marcus' back was out of sight. And, naturally the Indians would think they'd been poisoned. But Gray had left at once—as if he believed that the Cayuse would all die off. And Feathercap, furious about the melons, had tried to get even by breaking in on Narcissa that night. So Gray was responsible for that, too—not Feathercap. But the Cayuse must not be allowed to believe that Marcus had brought Bostons to kill them off because the first plot had failed.

Busy as he was, he took time to explain, over and over—in English and in Nez Percé to be sure they understood. Finally, all but Feathercap loosened. One or two even gave Marcus a foolish smile to admit their error. But Feathercap, his black face fixed on the cannon balls, had stood through all this without changing expression.

Marcus stepped up to him. "Talk now, Chief Feathercap. Not wait till dark, talk to blood brothers over lodge fire. Talk now. I hear."

Feathercap backed away from Marcus' direct gaze and continued to scowl at the cannon balls.

Marcus moved into range and caught his eye. "White *te-wat* know what happen while he great way off," he said. "Feathercap have guilt in heart so he fear white *te-wat*. But white *te-wat* decide, let live but watch. Feathercap best send bad spirit far off. Understand?"

Glowering, Feathercap answered, "Understand," and turned on his heel to stride toward the river. The others followed.

Marcus knew that he must go to their lodges and smoke with them, take hours to explain. But for now, he thought of Narcissa too miserable to get out of bed, of the children to be dressed and fed, of the sick calls he had to make on the emigrant families in order to get them on their way, of repairs calling him to every corner of Waiilatpu. . . . He went on about his chores.

Narcissa asked when he went in, "What was the commotion by the corral?"

Marcus glanced through the west window of the dining room and saw that she could watch the corral from where she lay. "Welcoming party," he answered. "Uncle Sam's the biggest mule these Indians ever saw. We've got them all jealous."

Helen Mar, walking on her flannel nightgown and bending herself more nearly double with each step, somehow made it to the window. "Helen see Uncle Sam *hooshus*."

"No, no," Narcissa corrected from her pallet. "What is it?"

Helen Mar's eyes sparkled just like Joe Meek's while her mouth tried out several words and her forehead wrinkled in concentration. When the word came, it was a squeal. "Ears!" And, throwing the hobbling nightgown over her head, she dashed across the room and flung herself upon Narcissa.

No one was sober enough to scold her except Mary Ann who had astonished Marcus several times, since his return, with her properness. "Helen Mar," she said firmly now, "Mother's sick. Come let me help you get dressed." But when Helen continued to roll on the pallet, Mary Ann's civilized veneer wore through. "Helen," she bawled, "dang blast it, you git off thar and come hyar!"

Narcissa was able to reprimand the child for this but Marcus felt a kind of unholy relief to find that his friend, old Gabe, hadn't completely deserted him. The meeting around the cannon balls had left him in need of friends.

Narcissa lay in her dining-room bed for more than a month before he could finish a room above the cellar for the families who occupied their bedroom. He wished he could clear the emigrants from the big room they'd built on the south wing of the new house for the Indians. But he couldn't turn out the Looney family.

Narcissa was sick all winter. And emigrants stayed on at Waiilatpu —people thick in the old house by the river, twenty-six people in the big house, people in the meadow. They all needed food and medicine and shelter. They were all too poor to pay, too defeated to work.

Marcus made many sick calls among the Indians that winter but found no room at the house and little time for conducting worship and sings or for teaching school. It was all he could do to keep his family clothed and fed on the meager rations they had left—potatoes, milk, and flour-and-water cakes made from burned wheat. He felt guilty about not being able to carry on all the Indian work but he also felt trapped. When he sat beside Narcissa to rub her head and soothe her to sleep, he could not hide his worry from her.

"We've got to have more emigrants," he blurted. "That's the only way I can see. Got to have enough God-fearing white men to stand up against these Indians when need be."

Narcissa sighed. "Personally, I've had enough emigrants to last me all my life."

Marcus tweaked her nose. "I mean the kind who are well and strong and willing to work."

"Oh, that kind," she said. "Show them to me when they get here."

Marcus sobered. "They'll get here, my sweet. They've got to. Otherwise, there's nothing left. We've got to have a real government in this country with authority to keep order."

Narcissa came up in bed. "Marcus, you mean it. You're frightened."

He took her face in his hands. "Not frightened. Desperate." He put his arms around her. "It's just that we can't give up now and lose all we've gained. We've got to have settlers—enough to make Washington sit up and take notice. Quick."

Narcissa raised her head and kissed him. "Marcus. Marcus, my love, you're a driven man."

CHAPTER

4

THROUGH early spring plowing, planting, and on through summer harvests, Marcus lived for the coming of white settlers. He wrote to Dr. Greene in Boston:

I see the emigration of white settlers as one of the onward movements of the world and it is quite in vain for us to wish it to stand still. The Indians have made great progress in tilling the soil and in raising cattle, but the Indians are few in number and not of a character to stand before the influx of whites. For where has it been known that an ignorant, indolent man has stood against money, intelligence, and enterprise? The command is to multiply and replenish the earth, neither of which the Indians obey. Their indolence, violence, and bloodshed prevent the first and indolence and improvidence, the second. How can they stand in the way of others who will do both? I beg you to send us Christian laymen.

Narcissa read the letter and asked, "But Marcus, won't Doctor Greene object to these ideas on the ground that you were sent here to work with the Indians? He doesn't understand our situation."

"Telling him the situation," Marcus answered and let the matter stand. "The Cayuse will soon leave for the Hunt. And then the wagon train will come. Maybe, if things go well, we can see about that move to The Dalles after the fall work is done."

Narcissa felt better that summer than she had for a year and a half. With the Indians away, she had time to spend with her children, taking them for swims in the river and for long walks along the creek. But toward fall she grew nervous and depressed. Several

(211)

times Marcus found her weeping as she sewed or as she stirred the soap on the fire or as she read.

"What is it, my wife?" he asked finally.

Narcissa laid aside her book and moved with a sigh to the bench beneath their bedroom window. Gazing out at the river, she spoke while tears rolled unnoticed down her cheeks. "It's the emigrants, I suppose. It's getting late for them to come. I keep thinking of them in snow in the Blue Mountains. I don't feel as if I could bear to see them again. They arrive in such destitute circumstances. Sick. Hungry. Dirty."

Marcus stood above her and looked beyond the river. "But they've got to come. We need them. Oregon needs them."

Narcissa reached for his hand. "But you wear yourself out, feeding them and doctoring their sick and you get nothing in return."

He stooped to kiss the top of her head. "It'll be different this time," he promised and it was.

It was much, much worse. Winter had caught the wagon train on the other side of the Blues. Because of delays, food rations had given out. Game could not be had. Measles had gone through the wagons like a prairie wind.

As little bands of hungry, desperate travelers began to straggle into Waiilatpu and camp in the Whitman meadow east of the house, the Cayuse who had returned from Hunt long before, watched and squatted around the houses with stolid faces in which burned angry eyes. Marcus doctored white sick day and night. Narcissa cooked and nursed and mended, her face drawn with worry, her tears near the surface. They had to neglect their children. They had to neglect the Indians.

"Won't last long," Marcus kept saying. "Best ones are all headed for the Lower Columbia. These'll move on and our settlers are bound to come next."

With some of the first half-starved, half-frozen families came word of the Sagers. Marcus and Narcissa listened with aching hearts to the captain of that band.

Their wagon had dropped out of line, one day late in May, long enough for Mrs. Sager to give birth to their seventh child—a baby girl. Mrs. Sager had made a slow recovery but they must move on with the wagon train or be left among warring Indians.

Near the Continental Divide, Mr. Sager took sick. Just before he died, he said, "Captain, I want my family to stop at the station of Doc Whitman."

In less than a month the mother, too, was dead. Now a German doctor was driving through with the six older children in an ox cart. Women of the caravan were caring for the baby.

"I hope you can take them in when they get here," the captain said. "That's what their father wanted."

"Seven children added to those we have already?" Marcus was sorry but it was out of the question. "Mrs. Whitman isn't well enough for that and we haven't room. But we'll help make arrangements for them."

Only a few days later, the captain of the first band came to the kitchen door and called, "Doc Whitman, come outside and meet your new family."

In the meadow beyond Alice Clarissa's grave, the German doctor had unyoked the oxen from his wobbly cart and his team had sprawled in their tracks. Narcissa ran from the house and linked her arm in Marcus'. Before the pathetic little outfit, the captain introduced the children.

On the far side of the cart a black-haired boy, his arms on the wheel and his head on his arms, sobbed aloud.

"That's Francis," the captain explained. "He's ten."

In the cart at the front, sat a brown-haired boy, taller, more reserved but with tears flowing down his cheeks and dropping off his chin onto his ragged jeans.

"That's John in front. He's fourteen."

"Perrin's age," Narcissa whispered.

On the near side of the cart, the frightened girls huddled together, bare heads bleached by the sun, bare feet caked with dirt, hunger the one fact bare on their faces.

"Can't keep the girls straight," the captain said. "Catherine's the one that broke her leg, jumping on the wheel. Then there's Matilda Jane and Elizabeth and Hannah Louise. An old woman's got the baby."

As Marcus and Narcissa approached, Narcissa pushed her plaid sunbonnet back and let it hang on her neck by the strings. Marcus saw the little girls' eyes open wide at sight of her hair gleaming in the sun above her blue calico dress. Transfixed, they all backed to the other side of the cart and Francis raised his tear-stained face.

(213)

Narcissa stepped around the cart and held out her hand to the tallest girl. "I think you're Catherine," she said. "And how perfectly your broken leg has healed. You don't even limp, do you?"

"No'm," Catherine answered and let Narcissa help her down.

"Come in the house," Marcus invited. "Think we've got enough milk on hand to wet your whistles."

The boys smeared tears across their faces with the backs of their hands. John climbed out on the tongue of the cart and hopped to the ground.

Marcus said, "We've got a boy just your age, John. He's out with the cattle right now but you'll see him soon."

Then Marcus reached his arms over the side of the cart to the smallest girl. Her pinched face was as weathered as a mountain man's. "Now, let's see whether I can guess your name," he said.

The next girl in the stair steps of assorted sizes had managed to stay round and chubby in spite of hardships. Her teeth showed milk-blue against her coffee-colored skin. "She's Hannah Louise and she's three. And I'm Matilda Jane and I'm five. Will you take me next?"

"You bet I will." Marcus caught her under her arms and swung her down beside her sister.

"I'll climb over myself," Elizabeth said when he turned back to the cart.

"Come on then. All of you."

When they reached the house, an old woman waited by the kitchen door. Saying nothing, she got rid of the Sager baby by dumping it into Narcissa's arms.

Marcus pulled down the soiled rags in which the baby was wrapped. Figuring back to May, the child must be five months old and yet she looked about three weeks and too poor to live through the day. Tears ran down Narcissa's cheeks and wet Marcus' hand.

Mary Ann and Helen Mar came from their play in the dining room and stood on tiptoe for a peek. The Sager children huddled in a knot, backed up to the cookstove.

"What'll we do?" Marcus asked Narcissa. "You're not able to take them all on, especially not that baby."

"Could we divide them?" Narcissa asked. "Maybe send the boys on to the Willamette?"

Marcus saw the sudden hurt in John's eyes. "The boys should be with their sisters." He looked again at the starved baby and shook his head. "You just can't take that on yourself. The others, yes, if you want."

Narcissa held the baby, filthy rags and all, to her breast. "But I'd want the baby for a charm to bind the others to me."

Mary Ann's blue eyes widened to take in all this. "Father, are we going to get all these new sisters and brothers? Are they for us?"

Marcus asked, "Would you like that? You and Helen Mar?"

Mary Ann blurted, "That'd be some now, wagh! Doggone my skin ef it wouldn't!"

This brought all the Sager children to attention. But Mary Ann was disgraced. She hadn't been that excited for a long, long time and, to hide her shame, she covered her face with her pinafore and flew into the pantry.

Marcus swallowed his grin and turned to Narcissa. "Well, what do you say?"

"I can't give up the baby."

"All or none," Marcus decreed.

"All, then," Narcissa answered with a radiant smile.

Helen Mar, choosing her favorite by size and likeness, marched across the room and offered Matilda Jane her clothespin doll. "Let's play," she said.

"Milk first," Marcus told them.

"Milk for everyone," Narcissa added. "Will you get it, Marcus? I'll take a bit for my baby and then I want to give her a bath. Her poor stomach will be weak. Maybe we'd better put a little water in the milk for her."

Marcus, never sure just how Narcissa had managed, soon found their large family organized with places to sleep and duties to perform and bath schedules arranged. Somehow they even maneuvered so as not to run into each other very often at the backhouse. And Narcissa thrived under the added responsibility. Marcus caught her far less often in one of those shudders when Feathercap was mentioned. And she never asked, these days, about moving to the Willamette.

Twelve families, in addition to the orphans, wintered at Waiilatpu. Narcissa said that sometimes she felt she was going crazy but her health was better than usual and she managed her many children without scolding. When Marcus asked, one day, how she felt she answered, "My poor husband, I'm the one who should worry about you. If you had a hundred strings tied to you, pulling in every direction, you could be no worse off." And her understanding gave him the strength he needed to keep going.

The Indians made little trouble that winter. But they also made little effort to worship or to attend school at the Whitman house. When convenient a few showed up—different ones from day to day so that teaching became eternally starting over. Some days, none came. Then winter weakened and finally succumbed to the gentle caresses of April. Marcus and Narcissa expected mild weather to bring the Indians around again. But, instead, the Cayuse slept through the days and, at night, held noisy gambling parties at their lodges.

At three o'clock one morning when Narcissa got up to change the baby, loud Cayuse voices still pestered the night and the reflection from a council fire across the river wigwagged against the bedroom window. Marcus hadn't been able to get to sleep.

When Narcissa came back to bed she whispered, "Still awake?"

Marcus wrapped his arms around her and laid his head on her breast.

"My husband, you mustn't worry so."

"I shouldn't have brought you back here."

"You're tired, that's all. Tomorrow let's forget everything else and take our children to the mountains for a picnic. Stay all night, maybe."

Marcus tightened his arm around her but did not have the energy to move his head. "And what about the cattle and Tiloukaikt's daughter who's sick and that baby I'm expecting any minute at the other house?"

"Well, then," Narcissa countered, "we'll have a picnic at home. The children can have a longer swim than usual and we'll eat our dinner around a campfire on the river bank. And you, my husband, will cook a stew to show the children what a clever father they've adopted."

Marcus chuckled but when he started to move away she held her hand against his cheek. "I'm going to sing you to sleep now. You listen to me instead of those Indians."

Day came picnic-perfect and the new baby was considerate enough to arrive at eight o'clock that morning. At noon, Marcus lugged a basket of food to the river and Perrin followed him with another heaped-up basket. Narcissa wrapped baby Henrietta in a white blanket and carried her. The other children joined the procession with towels and underclothes to put on after their swim because Narcissa said, "Today, we're going to forget we have a house. And," she added, "the first one who mentions the house or anything that sounds like work is a rotten egg."

They took turns on the bank, playing with the gurgling Henrietta who was plump and rosy now—thanks to Narcissa's careful feeding, her daily tepid baths, and her rigid schedule of sleep and milk. The children stayed in the river longer than they had ever been allowed before. Marcus gave swimming lessons for an hour and Perrin interspersed instruction with the story of how Uncle Marcus and old Sage swam the flooded Laramie. And then Narcissa told how Marcus, without Sage, swam the Platte and how they raced to catch the caravan with Pawnees on their heels.

Leaving the children still shouting and trying to swim, Marcus climbed out, wriggled into a change of underdrawers and his faithful buckskins while half-hiding behind a skimpy cottonwood. Then he hiked downstream a ways and built his fire to cook dinner.

Soon the smell of boiling beef and potatoes filled Waiilatpu Valley with an odor such as it hadn't known all winter. This was meat that Narcissa had salted down and hoarded for a special spree.

Marcus fed the fire and went back to sit beside Narcissa where they could watch the others. Whenever a child sputtered water from his throat and nose, Marcus knew that Narcissa's memory of Alice Clarissa must stab as his did, but neither called out a reprimand or warning. The children must not be frightened. Especially not this day.

Marcus took Narcissa's hand. "Wonderful idea you had, Mrs. Whitman. I feel like two new men already. And just wait till you taste my stew. Too bad I don't have a fat dog to toss in the pot."

Narcissa sniffed. "Ummm." Her head tipped to the side. "You forgot the onions, Marcus. We have some at the house."

The children heard her and began a chant. "Mother's a rotten e-egg. Mother's a rotten e-egg."

Narcissa laughed herself to tears.

"Sorry," Marcus told her, "not allowed to go to that place you said. This stew will have no onions nor any dogs. And unless I get it on the fire, the dinner will have no coffee."

"I knew there was something more than onions missing from that fragrance," Narcissa said. "Almost time to get out of the water, children. Finish playing in a hurry."

They were only half through their picnic dinner when Indians began to come. They came by twos and threes, gliding up on stealthy moccasins, to stand nearby and watch.

Marcus saw laughter drain from Narcissa's face and leave it frightened. He saw Perrin make a conscious effort to keep the children amused by turning somersaults between bites of dinner and laughing loudly at the others when they tried it. All at once, Marcus felt tired again. When ten or twelve Cayuses had gathered round, he forced his voice to quietness and smiled before he spoke. "Good day, friends. What you want?"

Grunts from unchanged faces answered his greeting but Marcus had learned to read anger when it came into stolid, staring eyes.

"Might have small food left when finish," he said. "Cayuse wait. Welcome."

Chief Tamahas stepped forward. No doubt of him, his eyes were angry and his square face was made for anger. "White *te-wat* rich," he snapped. He pointed to the pot of stew and then to each child's heaping plate of food. "Great feast. Come out Cayuse land. Cayuse no eat. No find buffalo. White man drive buffalo far off. Cayuse hungry."

Marcus stood up. He, too, pointed to the stew. "Not buffalo. Cow meat. Cayuse can raise cow same as white man. Cayuse no hungry, if raise cow, not go on Hunt."

But Tamahas had grown tired of this subject. Now he stooped and, between his blunt thumb and forefinger, felt Narcissa's calico sleeve. And then, Elizabeth's new dress of hickory shirting that Narcissa had made that spring. And Helen Mar's pink gingham. "Woven cloth. White *te-wat* rich. Cayuse no got woven cloth." And then Tamahas made the mistake of touching the round collar that Narcissa had made on Mary Ann's soft blue chambray. That collar was Mary Ann's great love of the moment.

Tamahas had to back away from kicking feet and clawing fingernails. "Take your dang blasted hands off my new dress, you stinkin' old coon or, by gor, you'll find yourself layin' wolf's meat, you cussed devil!"

Marcus caught Mary Ann's flailing arms and made a quick apology.

(218)

That reminder was all Mary Ann needed and she threw herself down in the rye grass to cry out her shame.

The Indians listened to Marcus' words with rigid jaws and did not return his gaze. They slunk away as they had come, by twos and threes.

But the picnic fun was over. Mary Ann could not be comforted and finally, at Narcissa's suggestion, Perrin took her to the house and put her to bed. She was still crying when Marcus went in to kiss her good night and to assure her that even grownups forget and make mistakes at times.

Late that night, Narcissa slid from bed and came to Marcus on the bench beneath their window. "Marcus, you must get some sleep," she whispered. Touching his buckskin knee, she forgot to whisper. "Darling, you're not even ready for bed. You'll catch your death of cold. What have you been doing?"

"Just sitting." He pulled her to his lap. "Listening to the river."

"But darling—"

"I'm all right. The river rests me more than sleep. Tonight I can still hear in it our children's laughter."

Narcissa kissed his forehead.

"I'll get you away from this 'dark spot,' my wife. I promise. Someday we'll follow that laughing river." But, even saying the words, he wasn't thinking of the river nor of Narcissa. Before him in the darkness glared the resentful eyes of Chief Tamahas and in his ears the spiteful silence of the Cayuse sounded louder than the rush of water to the sea.

CHAPTER

5

THE Walla Walla ran slower when November's crisp mornings skimmed the water along its banks with ice. But Marcus failed to find its quiet reassuring. He couldn't close his ears to the chilly whispers borne on the winds that frisked across Waiilatpu.

A few friendly Indians helped around the farm these days— pulled and stored pumpkins, shucked corn, hoed weeds, and herded cattle. But Tiloukaikt kept his three children away from school. And Feathercap seldom showed up on the Whitmans' ground. When he did, he refused to talk.

Bit by bit through the winter, Marcus pieced together the rumors as he might collect the jagged cuttings of a picture puzzle after a twister. Many of the village chiefs were saying, "Bostons not keep word. Make big talk with mouth, keep not many promises with heart." Word came by way of Lapwai's north wind in late winter that some of the most influential Nez Percé chiefs turned their ears to Tom Hill's talk against the Bostons. They had sent a delegation, on advice from the white *te-wat*, to Indian Agent White. They had asked redress for the murder of Elijah Hedding, son of the Walla Walla war chief, Yellow Serpent. The agent had listened to their delegation. Had made wide smile. Had promised many things. . . . Indians turned their backs. Agent White packed up his horse, rode off to States.

Word burned through the tribes that the white men's laws wore two faces. "One face smokes the pipe of peace and blows out prom-

(220)

ises," they said. "The other face howls with the voice of the medicine wolf." The tribes would find their own justice as they had before they listened to big talk from Bostons, to soft easy words from white *te-wat.*

Marcus doctored the Cayuse into spring. He gave them seed and helped them plow and plant. He talked to them whenever he could gather a few blanket-wrapped men beside his house on warm spring evenings. Narcissa sang to them as usual. But only a few of the Indians entered into the singing themselves. Favorite hymns had lost their hold. Folk songs no longer lured them. With the coming of hot weather, the Cayuse stayed on their side of the river. Even medical calls dwindled to a mere two or three a day.

One warm night late in August, Marcus slipped a rope halter on Uncle Sam and sprang, with a boost from the corral fence, to the mule's bare back. Along the river trail he noticed the litter sign of recent departures. The lodge villages of Tiloukaikt, Tamahas, and Feathercap had gone off on Hunt. Didn't seem right, he admitted, to feel so relieved. And yet, just now, he and Narcissa both needed a few weeks for letting their sense of humor catch up.

Marcus patted the mule's neck. "Come on, Uncle Sam. Got to find the cows." But Uncle Sam, nearing a clump of willow shrubs, flicked his ears forward and stopped. When the mule refused to move in spite of pleas and threats, Marcus investigated the spot pointed out by the ears. He saw that some of the upright willow fronds bent to the north before the warm evening breeze. But others leaned to the south.

He slid off Uncle Sam's far side and now the mule moved forward without urging. Marcus eased his pistol from his belt. He leaned his ear against Uncle Sam's swaying ribs and they felt their way toward the willows. "Wish you had a window in you," Marcus whispered to the mule. Then, for an instant, he was afraid his wish had come true. A shot exploded in his ear.

Before he could return fire, a voice from the willows called, "Friend."

Diving around Uncle Sam, gun ready, Marcus found—instead of the trick he expected, Chief Stickus with three of his Umatillas.

Stickus motioned him into the shrubs. *"Cóme."*

"What's wrong?" Marcus asked. What could require this secrecy? Stickus' voice evoked an ugly picture. Marcus had to translate rapidly to keep up. "War party ride over mountains. Meet Bostons at Grande Ronde. Burn land canoes. Kill white men. Capture white women. Feathercap say, 'Kill Bostons. This Indian country.' Chief Yellow Serpent say, 'Redress son murdered at Sutter's Fort in California.' Stickus say this make trouble."

So this was the trick that Feathercap had threatened. The trick that was to pay for Gray's poisoned melons, for the pile of cannon balls at the corral, for the scare that had broken up Umtippe's funeral, for Agent White's unkept promises. Marcus covered his eyes but he could still see the smoldering, flesh-scented embers of the wagon train from the States, hear the cries of desecrated white women, doomed to life. He could feel the snatching away of Washington's pulse-taking fingers.

"How many?" he asked Stickus and tried to make the chief's, "*Peelep pooetap tit*," mean some number less than four hundred. But it was no use. Four hundred angry braves under Feathercap! And an unsuspecting wagon train of emigrants, moving into that!

Stickus spoke again, calmly now, giving Marcus ample time to understand. "Chief Stickus have called friends of Bostons. They wait. Ready to ride where white doctor lead."

Marcus grasped the chief's hand. "*Ai*." He did not trust himself to try expressing his gratitude.

With Narcissa's worry tears still damp on his cheek, Marcus joined Stickus and a score of friendly Indians on the river trail east of the house. By silent consent, they chose a cutoff to the southeast and rode through the night, hoping to outdistance the war party.

They snatched guarded quarter-hours of rest by day. Then, under cover of the forest, spurred their mounts on—over the Blue Mountain barrier and down the long slope into sight of the open, marshy valley. At noon the third day, they circled within the protection of trees along the north rim of the valley bowl. At dusk their scouts panted in with news.

Marcus urged his horse up a cliff and turned to look between two shaggy junipers. There, in the distance, wearing a plume of amber dust, the long queue of the caravan squirmed out of Powder River canyon. Motioning his friends to wait and watch for trouble, he spurred down into the bowl, keeping to the scrubby pines until they gave out. Then, with a glance over his right shoulder toward the western slope of the valley where a hundred natural blinds of rocks and trees might now be alive with four hundred angry warriors, he tore into the grassy clearing and across the floor of Grande Ronde Valley.

Coming within dangerous rifle range of the caravan scouts, he fired his pistol into the air. He saw the scouts fall back to wait for their captain. Rifles ready, three men rode up to meet him.

Marcus moved in and jabbed out his hand to the caravan captain. He nodded to the scouts. "Name's Whitman," he said. "From Waiilatpu. Came to tell you you're going to be attacked. War party of Cayuses and Walla Wallas."

They thought he was joking at first and, for a time, the captain—a black bear of a man—refused to call the wagons into the open. Instead he was letting them stop helter-skelter near low timber and water in the kind of encampment that would make warring Indians lick their chops.

Struggling to stay patient, Marcus went into details. He pointed out the boulders and shrubs that might, that very minute, conceal painted warriors with loaded rifles.

Finally, with the air of a man humoring a child, the captain called for the wagons to turn into the valley floor and circle up.

Marcus sent a rider to bring in Stickus and his friends. He called a hurried council, told his story.

The hotheads of the wagon train spoiled for a fight. Indians had dogged their trail the whole journey from Pawnee country, they claimed. War parties, never big enough to attack, had nevertheless kept the caravan on edge day after day and on guard each night against their thieving. Now to pay off every Sioux and Blackfoot from there back to the States, they'd just turn their new two-shoot guns on the Cayuses and Walla Wallas. They'd show them!

But Marcus had no intention of getting this issue settled at the expense of even one white man's blood. Word of such a fate must never go back to Washington. Somehow, he must avert a battle. He asked Stickus to describe for the Americans how the war party could be expected to operate.

The Cayuses and Walla Wallas would, undoubtedly, plan a dawn attack, the chief outlined with Marcus interpreting. They'd tear in just as the wagons skirted the north rim of Grande Ronde near small timber suited to their kind of warfare.

Marcus proposed that he and his Indian friends ride out to meet the warriors and try to negotiate a truce. He could not guarantee success. But, if he failed, the caravan had at least been warned. If he failed, they could use their own judgment about fighting the large war party. In any case now, they wouldn't be mowed down from the back.

"No!" someone shouted. "Let's go hunt 'em down and give 'em hell."

Marcus pinned this bushy-headed chap at the end of his gaze. He made his voice as soft and slow as Kit Carson's. "Young man, I've seen greenhorns give Indians hell before and they've mostly gone to heaven in the attempt. If you're ready, all right. But I figured these men and women were planning to settle down in Oregon instead."

"Go ahead, Doc," a skinny Iowan sang out. "But what's to keep you from gittin' picked off before nobody rides in from that war party to talk?"

"Worth that risk to get you through. Oregon needs you—all of you. Give me three good scouts, double your guard here, and the rest of you get your sleep. No fires after dark."

When dusk settled into the bowl of the valley, Marcus led his twenty mounted Indians and three wagon train scouts in single file across Grande Ronde to the north and west, toward the fringe of trees on the hills beyond. They reined in a mile and a half from the first sizable boulders and large huckleberry bushes. They picketed their ponies to lariats tied to their wrists, allowing them good grazing in the knee-deep grass. Marcus posted a guard of Umatillas. He doubled its line toward the mountains. The others bedded down on their saddles.

Lying awake, drinking in the sweat and leather bouquet of his saddle under his head, Marcus knew in his bones that painted Indians peopled the woodland and the sheltering ravines nearby. He felt Indian sign this night.

He wakened from a nap when the first beacon of dawn flared from the south to touch the jagged granite peaks of Chief Joseph's country to the northeast. He smelled the horses and the fragrant odor of cropped swamp grass and sweet clover. He sat up to strain his eyes into the blue bowl of Grande Ronde. Toward the west and north the Blue Mountains showed black-green triangles of timber, notching down their sides. Two miles beyond their camp a low ridge formed a natural rampart for a war party. Marcus felt certain that the Cayuses and Walla Wallas were waiting there—waiting and working themselves into a frenzy of hate, ready to attack the encroaching Bostons when they dared pass.

He tugged at the fringed sleeve of the nearest Indian. The signal passed along. They all sheathed their bowie knives, chucked pistols into their belts, examined their rifles, checking flints and powder. Then they stood up, stretched, and coiled in their lariat pickets. Marcus and the scouts saddled their horses. The Indians tested their halters.

Slowly Marcus counted to one hundred. Then he swung into his saddle, motioning the others to follow. He turned toward the grassy slopes and the rolling rampart ridge, and sent his horse forward at a lope.

He searched the trail ahead for signs of movement, reined in to ask Chief Stickus his advice. Together they rode ahead, at a slow walk now. And then, near at hand, Marcus saw a fresh-peeled tree trunk. Stickus pointed but said nothing. They rode ahead. Soon the pines developed bloated trunks. At Marcus' quick glance, Stickus nodded.

"War party, moving this way," Marcus called back softly. "Just as we figured. You know what to do." He repeated it in Nez Percé for the Indians. They moved out onto an elevated clearing.

Indian ponies burst from the woods and raced at them from right and left. Too soon to see them but Marcus knew that an Indian warrior clung to each pony—body flattened, head low on the neck of his mount. He remembered the generally accepted figures—that any one of these Indians was worth three Blackfeet in a battle. Their war cry wailed up as they came. Down the boulder-strewn slope they poured now like water overflowing a pass.

Marcus speared his white handkerchief on the end of his long rifle. He took Stickus on with him and waved the others back.

The war party split into two flanking lines. Then it swerved and slowed. Bonneted, painted war chiefs stared in amazement. They yanked at their ponies' rope halters, making them rear. Finally, they wheeled and pawed to a stop not twenty paces away. Amazement on the chiefs' faces gave way to fury. So, their plan for surprise attack had sprung a leak. In place of scouts and hunters from the wagon caravan, they confronted their own white *te-wat* and men from neighboring tribes.

Marcus fired his gun into the air. He dismounted and walked forward under his flag of parley.

Chiefs Tamahas and Tiloukaikt and Yellow Serpent of the Walla Wallas slid from their ponies and stood waiting. Chief Feathercap sat his horse, his hair bristling forward under his feather bonnet, his face a mask.

The war party kept on coming over the rolling ridge and their horses milled in confusion at the broken pace of attack.

Marcus kept his eyes fixed on the chiefs, watching for any sign of trickery. He raised his hand in salute, first to one and then to another of the chiefs. "Chiefs of Cayuse and Walla Wallas, listen to friend and to blood brothers. You do foolish thing. You blacken your hearts with hate like paint on faces. You listen to lies. You open your ears to Tom Hill. He say, 'Easy to raise hair, to send under Bostons on trail.' Then he stay home. You come. Tom Hill lies."

Feathercap growled and spat at Marcus' feet.

Chief Tamahas scowled. "Cayuse listen to own tongue. When snow cover mountains, Cayuse and Walla Wallas listen to white man's agent. Trust white laws. Believe white promises. No good. No keep promise. Cayuse make own law now."

Without explaining, Marcus mounted. "Four chiefs come with Chief Stickus and white *te-wat*."

Curious, they mounted.

Marcus led the way, knowing that Stickus was on guard. He guided them to the high clearing at the northwest rim of Grande Ronde Valley. There he swept his arm toward the valley floor where the caravan showed now in many forted clusters. "Look, chiefs of Cayuse and Walla Wallas. Many men in caravan—like wild horses of the plains. Many guns. Kill war party like coyotes if *te-wat* give signal. Listen to white brother who make your sick ones well. Listen to Nez Percé brothers. To Umatillas. We see caravan. See guns. Come to save you before you do foolish thing. Before you die like buffalo in hunt."

Yellow Serpent stiffened. "Son, Elijah Hedding, die like buffalo. Agent White no redress."

Feathercap sneered. "You Boston—like barking-dog-man. Try

scare Indian braves. War chiefs not squaws. Not run from barking dog."

Marcus said, "Chiefs come with me. Hold council with Bostons. You see many guns. Hold talk. Then, can smoke or fight. Chiefs decide when talk finished. *Te-wat* say no more words. Chiefs say then, peace or war. Come."

Feathercap dissenting, the chiefs made their decision. They wheeled back and counted out five braves of each tribe to go with them to the council. The remaining warriors grumbled and waited, trying to hold their nervous ponies.

Marcus and his friends pulled their horses around to follow the chiefs and their party. Down they jolted. Down the trail that might by now have been the seared and bloody deathbed of a hundred Americans. A trail that might by now have been splattered with the dashed-out brains of the caravan's children. A trail on which girls and women would have gladly chosen to die.

Approaching the caravan, Marcus signaled, shouted orders, saw guns pull back into fortress circles. Ten picked men came out from the encampment, unarmed except for sheathed bowie knives at their belts.

A council fire, as Stickus had suggested, had been laid a hundred paces from the nearest circle of wagons. Dozens of curious, frightened eyes peered out from beneath the Conestogas but no rifles poked their noses through the barricade. Marcus gave orders for the Indians and the whites to take seats on the ground. He caught up a handful of dry grass, struck into it a spark from his flint, poked it among the fire logs. Standing, he made a slow turn—along the row of nearly naked savages, along the stiff façade of homespun emigrants, and on to the four thwarted and stern-faced chiefs. To the chiefs he said, "Tell council why Cayuses and Walla Wallas come with arrow and gun."

Tamahas stood. Bronzed, rugged, sinister, he smote his square chest. "Chief Tamahas, Cayuse war chief, come against sneaking wolves. Cayuse councils say no more Bostons cross mountains. This land of Cayuse, of Walla Walla, of Nez Percé. Bostons steal land of fathers."

Feathercap spat into the fire to emphasize this point.

Marcus planted his feet. "Chief listen with heart to evil spirit. Hear now true. Bostons not want Cayuse land." He paused to gesture to the west, the north, the east. "Much land. Land for Cayuse and for all blood brothers. Also land for Bostons—make farms, grow good food, help Indian brothers learn way to live. Go home now. Welcome white men to help Indians make fine country. Our people promise to keep peace."

Defiant and sullen, Tamahas shook his head. Feathercap beat on the ground with his fists.

Yellow Serpent rose to speak. "Bostons strike down my son. Steal my horses. Make sick my braves. Yellow Serpent kill Bostons and leave on desert—wolf meat. Walla Walla braves not squaws."

Impatient with this same old argument, Marcus nevertheless recognized that the chief had a point. And he himself would make every effort to see to it that the murderer of Yellow Serpent's son was punished. But right now, these Indians must prove themselves ready for law and order. He searched for words that would be as convincing as rifles. As he paused, Tiloukaikt stood and pointed toward the mountains to the northwest.

"Bostons no cross mountains," he boomed. "Cayuse burn land canoes. Take cattle to eat. Let talking squaws turn and go home toward rising sun. Then my people let go in peace. Bostons not cross mountains. Go home or die. Chief of Cayuse have spoken."

Marcus made his voice so quiet that the council had to lean forward to hear. He had tried reason and persuasion with no results. Perhaps fear—"Chiefs of Cayuse and Chief of Walla Wallas, you listen. Great father of Bostons will send warriors to watch over settlers. Great White Father will send ships with cannons. Send soldiers like Frémont with guns and balls—shoot down Indians. Burn villages of Indian warriors. Leave bones for wolves. If you want to live, go home. Live in peace with white men." Then, coming as an inspiration, he remembered the new rifles that the men of the caravan had spoken of the evening before.

He whispered to a rawboned Kentuckian, chief hunter for the caravan.

The fellow loped off to his wagon. Soon he returned with his two-shoot gun.

Marcus turned to the sullen chiefs. He said, "Watch." He threw his felt hat high into the air.

The Kentuckian lifted the rifle to his shoulder, pulled the trigger

(228)

once, then again. The hat fell outside the council circle. In it were two holes.

The fourteen Indians gasped as one.

Matter-of-factly, Marcus spoke. "Bostons' new guns shoot two times while Indians' shoot once. Cayuses and Walla Wallas ride in circle around caravan, braves die like grasshoppers. Each white man carry gun. Take word of white *te-wat*. Indians' guns old and rusty. You have seen with own eyes shining gun of Bostons. If war party go in peace, *te-wat* promise Bostons not kill with two-shoot guns. Promise."

Among themselves the Indians spoke behind their hands.

Marcus watched their covert glances at the Kentuckian who methodically cleaned the barrels, reloaded, and leaned himself against his shiny gun. He watched Feathercap spew out invectives into the long ear of Yellow Serpent and then subside with a veil of cunning drawn over his beady eyes.

At last, Tamahas rose to speak. "Chiefs say Cayuse, Walla Wallas go home in peace. Let Bostons pass through Cayuse country. But Bostons must not stop on Cayuse land. First chiefs have spoken. Why Bostons not make dog feast? Then chiefs smoke with white men."

Marcus wanted to accept this truce with a general shaking of hands and nothing more. But he knew Cayuse trickery and he knew Chief Feathercap. He knew that the truce he'd won must still be fought for with his wits. He held out his hand to each chief in turn. "White *te-wat* say chiefs show wisdom. Make heart glad to see red brothers smoke in peace with white man. Chiefs have promise of white *te-wat*. Let Chief Tamahas come to lodge of Stickus. Chief eat there."

Watching Feathercap's eyes, Marcus was afraid that his ruse had been detected. But perhaps the chief burned with greed for food. Revealing no suspicion, Chief Tiloukaikt produced a pipe and kinnikinnick bark for smoking. Tamahas and Marcus mounted and followed Stickus to the lodge they'd raised in a wooded hiding place on the northeast rim of Grande Ronde. Marcus hoped he'd find some remains of food at the lodge to make good on his promise of a feast for his hostage. He hoped, too, that the twenty emigrants appointed to guard the lodge were at their stations.

Inside the skin cone, he found a slab of ribs from the mule his

Indians had butchered and cooked the night before. Tamahas ate and seemed not to suspect that he was being held prisoner.

Leaving him with Stickus, Marcus stepped outside. He waved toward the fallen tree where the nearest guard was supposed to be stationed. A wagging rifle barrel answered his greeting.

Back at the council circle Marcus stated, "Tamahas stay tonight with white *te-wat*. Eat feasts with Bostons. White brother promise safe journey to Waiilatpu. If Cayuses and Walla Wallas keep promise of peace, no harm come to Chief Tamahas. If war party attack wagon train, Tamahas pay with life for evil scheme."

Feathercap stormed.

"Tamahas safe in circle of twenty two-shoot guns," Marcus pointed out. "Think Feathercap best not act crazy. Go in peace."

Caught, the Indians mounted and filed away to collect their war party and retreat.

Marcus led his horse across the valley floor toward his lodge. On his spirit lay a depression strange for a man who had just won a total victory. The caravan was safe. Seeking the lift he should feel, he looked up to the granite peaks of the Wallowas. Their heaviness bore down upon him.

Coldly he faced the truth. His victory had raised a mountain barrier between him and the Indians he had come to serve. He'd taken his stand for the whites. And that stand had to be, by its very nature, against the Indians. His Indians would not forget this day.

PART V

*

CHAPTER

1

THE emerald arrowhead that had been Waiilatpu in the summer of '37 no longer kept within the bounds of the Walla Walla and Mill Creek. Ten years' irrigated crops had bulged the fertile farm lands into an irregular tomahawk. The road, gouged now by emigrant Conestogas, formed the tomahawk's handle, running along the base of the knoll on which Marcus had first met Umtippe. Cooling themselves at the close of a hot day, Marcus and Narcissa stood on the top of their lookout, gazing toward the slate-blue mesas of the Columbia Valley.

"See that big thunderhead?" Marcus pointed to the west. "There above the rise of land overlooking Tamahas' village?"

Narcissa laughed—her old up-scale laugh. "Yes, let's do overlook the surly chief's village."

Marcus took her hand. "Where rolls the Oregon," he mused.

"Rolls past The Dalles," Narcissa added, "and our grown-up Perrin. It's hard to believe that Perrin is seventeen and really teaching Indians. I'll never cease to be amazed at the ease with which he picked up the language when he first came. I miss Perrin. He helped so much with the other children."

"But things change for us all. Think of McLoughlin, for instance —his whole life turned upside down."

"I do hope he got to take his lovely furniture and dishes with him to Oregon City. Do you really think Hudson's Bay Company dismissed him as a reprimand for helping white people settle here? Seems awfully little of them after all his years of service."

(231)

"Not so little," Marcus told her. "The Company stands to lose millions of pounds along with the Oregon Country. Hope Congress remembers to set up a territorial government before our Indians return from Hunt this fall."

"Marcus, I heard today that a war party of Walla Wallas—two hundred, the story went—had ridden off to California to avenge the murder of Elijah Hedding. Why don't you write to Colonel Frémont about that affair? Now that he's been appointed governor of California, I think he'd take a real interest. With him and Captain Sutter both working on it, you might get some action."

Marcus nodded. "Might and, by the eternal, something ought to be done. Strange about young Frémont," he went on. "Did you know he started out just like Henry Spalding? Illegitimate child, poor, no opportunities. And I reckon old Thomas Hart Benton used about the same words to him that your father did to Henry. Now, Frémont's governor of California."

"And Mr. Spalding has done great things at Lapwai these last few years," Narcissa said. "The Spaldings have a wonderful school and Mr. Spalding has translated parts of the Bible into Nez Percé and they always seem to raise more grain than we do."

"It's the way a man thinks of himself that makes the difference, I'm convinced."

"That," Narcissa agreed, "and the way his wife thinks of him. And I think you're a big man, Doctor Whitman."

"I think you're a flirt," he told her and pulled her to him for a kiss.

Irrigating, hoeing, reaping bumper crops—the summer of '47. In the house, Narcissa filled the summer with scrubbing, washing, bleaching, sewing. But, more significant, Narcissa sang again at her work. And she stopped to play with the children as she moved through her endless tasks. "Do you know, my little Matilda dumpling, that our Auntie Jane may come with the wagons soon? . . . Mary Ann, my big girl, you'll simply adore your Aunt Jane."

"Marcus," Narcissa called one sweaty afternoon when he passed with Helen Mar riding piggyback to the corral, "don't you think Edward will come with Jane? You know, they nearly made the caravan last summer."

"Hope so. Could use a good college man here. But don't get your

(232)

heart too set on it." He bounced Helen Mar higher on his back. "There'll be other wagon trains and other years, you know."

And then on a sweltering August afternoon, Mary Ann burst into the kitchen. "Mother! Father! They're rolling in. The dangedest lot of land canoes you ever seed."

Marcus and Narcissa ran to the window, then out the kitchen door. A cluster of children met them. They'd dropped their hoes in the garden. Marcus saw them shiver with excitement. They were still primitive enough to be nosy and civilized enough to quake a little at the coming of strangers.

He said, "A twist of peppermint taffy to the first one who finds Aunt Jane or Uncle Edward."

The children scampered off, then slowed to a walk, awed again by the yelling and shooting from the first group of wagons.

Narcissa fumbled with her apron strings. "Oh Marcus, I'll have to change my dress."

He watched her scurry into the house. "Society girl," he said to himself. "Needs people like a cornfield needs sun and rain."

He hustled John and Francis to the east meadow where they could help the emigrants unhitch. Then he ran to the corral and sprang onto the nearest horse.

He rode along the line of wagons and shouted welcomes. Drivers waved arms and hats and bonnets. Children poked tousled heads from canvas flaps and stared. Men on horseback rode up and asked where they should circle. Marcus told them to break routine at last. They'd be safe at Waiilatpu. Just round up the stock at night in his fenced field near the river. Set a light guard to keep out prowlers and see that hungry cattle didn't steal his corn.

Twenty-five of the sturdier wagons arrived at Waiilatpu during the afternoon. Sure, more would be along. As soon as they could climb the blasted mountains and keep the wagons from tumbling end over end down the shaly slope this side. Four or five thousand folks had started from Missouri in May. A few peeled off from the line at Fort Hall and went down California way. Some cut off by the Umatilla to The Dalles. But there'd be a pa'cel of emigrants through Waiilatpu, maybe fifteen hundred, off and on during the next month or so.

As Conestogas pulled up in the meadow and unhitched, Marcus led their men to his granary to weigh out sacks of grain and flour.

He sent them to the smokehouse for meat, to the storehouse for potatoes and late vegetables. Little campfires began to smoke and then burst into flame under strung-up kettles of soup and stew and coffee. The smell of coffee and simmering beef and roasting ears drifted over Waiilatpu and to the Indian lodges. Marcus caught glimpses, now and then, of Cayuse men and squaws and naked children creeping slowly from cover to cover to stare at the Bostons' encampment. Once when he crossed with an emigrant from the mill to the smokehouse, he found Feathercap and Tamahas leaning against a tree at the edge of his clearing. They did not return his wave.

Marcus told his customer, "Cayuse chiefs—bad hearts, these two. Many Cayuses are friendly. How much meat do you want?"

"I'll take as much as you'll let me have on credit," the emigrant replied. "Too, my woman's ailin' and she thought she ought to have a doctor since one was handy." The man's tone excused her foolishness. "Had a baby back near Fort Bridger somewhere. Neither one's been right perky since."

Marcus hurried to the house for his saddlebag.

It was near dark before he could think of winding up his doctoring for the day. Just one last wagon down the meadow trail. But moving from behind the ragged tilt to enter the wagon, he saw two Indians dash off, trailing stolen blankets. He shouted but they kept running and disappeared in the willows. Turning to the patients in the wagon, he found a mother and three skinny boys—all low with measles.

As he worked, his mind followed those thieving Indians. They'd run to their lodges with the blankets jerked off the sick boys. In a few days, the Indians would feel dull, begin to burn with fever, break out in splotches. Then, they'd call in their native *te-wat* to work his magic. Marcus had seen this happen in other years. It always ended by the Cayuse pointing at the white *te-wat* who welcomed Bostons, who let loose evil spirits to kill off Indians—who wanted them to die so he could take their land and horses.

At the house, Marcus saw glistening, unshed tears in his wife's eyes. "Maybe Jane will come tomorrow," he said. "These are only the first of the wagons. They tell me many more are on the way."

"But I've waited so long."

More wagons came into the meadow the next morning. Most of those that had arrived the day before hitched up again and creaked on west. Many such tomorrows came and went, many hopes came on the morning breeze off the mountains and perished in the searing heat of afternoon. Always the children searched from wagon to ox cart and dragged home again to report, "No Aunt Jane or Uncle Edward anywhere. Won't they ever come?"

Marcus walked from party to party to welcome the emigrants to Oregon. He weighed out flour and chunks of meat. He felt their burning heads and gave them medicine or dressed their festering wounds. Then he sent them on their way to the Columbia.

"Mind now," he'd say when they got ready to leave, "stick together. You'll still meet up with scattered tribes. Not vicious like Blackfeet or Sioux—but pestiferous. They really believe they have a right to take anything they can outwit Bostons for. So hang together and keep a strict guard. Godspeed, my friends."

"Thanks, Doc," the driver of a rickety wagon might call back. "I'll send you money for the potatoes and for the team you loaned me. Thanks."

Back at the house, Marcus would feel in his pocket and dig out a handful of notes scribbled and signed. He'd smile at Narcissa and toss them on the fire. "If they're going to pay, they'll do it without these. Seems like they've paid back all they owe, just coming."

When the caravan had come and the healthy settlers gone, Marcus watched Narcissa doctor the sick and tend her family and noticed that she stopped mentioning Aunt Jane and that was all.

Knowing she couldn't, he begged her to rest.

"Oh, I'm all right," she protested. "I have to go see about the Osborn children. They're the worst right now—Salvijane, particularly. She's a fragile little thing. But our school for white children will soon open with the new teacher you hired from the caravan and then I'll have more time. It's you I'm worried about."

"Measles and dysentery are spreading among the villages. I can't stop them."

"Never did I see such speedy retribution," Narcissa said. "And yet the Indians still don't seem to understand that they caught their sicknesses from the things they stole of emigrants. Poor things, will they ever learn?"

A knock on the kitchen door startled them. Marcus answered.

A white man stood there. He gasped news of emigrants in trouble. Marcus turned back to Narcissa. "Hurry call, dear," he said. "Party of emigrants have had a run-in with Indians toward Walla Walla. Pushed on alone, in spite of our warnings."

He turned to the fireplace for his long rifle and kissed her good-by. He bent for the little girls' hugs and waved to John and Francis on his way to the corral.

When his guide led Marcus into a tight ravine running back from the south bank of the Walla Walla some twenty miles from home, they intercepted a dozen braves from Tiloukaikt's village. With their dirty blankets hugged around them, they walked hobble-legged, heads down, toward their mounts. Marcus spurred his horse and reined in between the Indians and their ponies.

Beyond, he saw three Conestogas, canvas ripped to shreds, naked men and nearly naked women trying to hide their stripped bodies behind the wagons. Marcus pulled his rifle from its sling and, cocking the gun, he spoke in Nez Percé. "Stop where you are. Let's look into this."

The Indians halted and pulled their blankets closer. Marcus swung his leg over the saddle horn and slid to the ground. He walked toward the line of Indians.

A man from the wagons came running, a strip of canvas clutched around his mid-section. "Stop them varmints," he screamed. "They're thieves and robbers. Shoot 'em down in their tracks, mister."

"Calm down, man, and state your case."

"Them thievin' coyotes took our horses and our clothes and everything. Now, they been hangin' round for hours, pesterin' us and eatin' up our provisions and goin' through our wagons, pickin' up everything they could lay their sticky hands on. Go ahead. Shoot 'em down!"

Marcus turned to the Indians. He knew most of them by name, others by sight. He'd doctored many of them, at one time or another. "You make mistake, my friends, to take what white settlers bring over mountains. Might scare small white rabbits, all right. Not scare white *te-wat*."

The canvas-draped emigrant shouted, "That son-of-a-rattlesnake, he took my woman's dress and petticoats. He scairt her nigh to death, the heathen savage."

Their eyes unblinking, the Indians stared at Marcus. He began to talk. He tried to shame them for rewarding, in this way, all his efforts to help them grow food, to make them well. He reminded them of beads and tobacco and scalping knives he'd paid them through the years. He spoke of Narcissa's songs, the school, and worship at Waiilatpu. He pointed out that Oregon now belonged to the United States in name at least and that they must obey the laws of the States or else soldiers would come with cannons.

"Eagle Claw, drop what you took and go in peace. *Te-wat* command it."

A skillet and two forks clattered to the ground from beneath Eagle Claw's blanket.

Marcus said, "More," and moved on. "And now, No-Horns. . . . Red Mountain. . . . And you, Broken Shoulder, let fall what you steal. Indian who steal have evil spirit."

Spoons, tin plates, folding knives, iron pots, women's dresses, button boxes, and ribbons fell from beneath the blankets onto the shale around the Indians' scuffing moccasins.

When the Indians' blankets fit, once more, the shape of rugged bodies, Marcus told them, "My friends, you do right. White *te-wat* thank you."

The band of crestfallen Cayuses walked on in single file to their ponies. They flicked off their horses' rawhide hobbles and mounted. At a sedate walk, they headed toward Waiilatpu.

Riding home, Marcus made up his mind to write again to the Secretary of War, urging the government to delay no longer the establishment of that chain of forts along the Oregon Trail. If forts were set up with government officers in charge, emigrants would come in hordes. They'd demand a governor and law enforcement agencies. These petty raiding parties could be wiped out and both Indians and whites would be far better off. If only he could speed them up in Washington.

CHAPTER

2

DISEASE burned across Waiilatpu like a prairie fire. The two Indians who first stole blankets from the wagon of sick emigrants had become walking torches. They'd thrown off sparks that burst into flame at the river's edge in Tiloukaikt's village, burned to the right across the lodges of Tamahas and Feathercap, jumped the river and reached the people of Chief Yellow Serpent.

Marcus rode and ran and limped from one conflagration to the next. Day and night he stamped at new outbursts of fever and crimson rash. Days stretched into a week, and into two and then three weeks.

Some Indians still came to squat in the Whitmans' kitchen, to sing at the Sunday services. But the fire roared and spread—from the main house where Salvijane Osborn, just recovering from dysentery, came down with measles, to the other house where the Saunders' four girls were stricken, and the Hall's five girls, and the Kimball's two boys. It swept to the blacksmith shop and the sawmill cabin and even to the skin lodge beside the corral where the half-breed hired men, Finley and Joe Lewis slept.

Lewis had been sick when he arrived with the caravan and Marcus hadn't liked his spirit. But he was in need of help and got it along with the rest.

Seventy-four, in all, at Waiilatpu but the population of the Indian villages was dwindling at an alarming rate. The Indians had no resistance to these diseases. Marcus lost cases that he'd put down as mild. He lost others that he'd checked off as past all danger. Becoming suspicious, he added watching to his doctoring.

In one lodge his powders and pills and bleeding and isolation appeared to be getting results. His patient, a middle-aged Indian, had begun to respond. Then a medicine man stole into the lodge and Marcus eavesdropped.

The painted *te-wat* reminded the burning, itching sufferer of the sweat baths that their tribe had used since long before this man could remember. Stooping to enter the stinking lodge, Marcus was pushed aside.

"White *te-wat* no good. Make fire burn here, here, and here."

"Make well soon with big medicine. Lie down and rest," Marcus pleaded.

From the shadows of the lodge the Cayuse *te-wat* emerged to shake his rattles in Marcus' face and spit out accusations.

"No, you bungling charletan. White *te-wat* not evil spirit. No make fire. Not kill Indians."

But Marcus' patient staggered outside to the mud-plastered oven where he would steam himself with wet grass piled on heated rocks.

Marcus waited with the chanting medicine man and two of the Indian's squaws. He argued. They shook their heads. After a long time the patient's feet poked from the small opening in the sweat bath and his naked sweat-soaked body wriggled out. He ran and plunged into the cold October river. He splashed and spluttered and, quaking, came out.

His eyes, like holes in leather stiff from improper tanning, shot a gloating look at Marcus. "No more itching fire," he crowed.

Marcus pleaded with the squaws to cover the poor man with blankets and robes.

The squaws shook their heads. They would tell their warrior nothing. Cayuse *te-wat* would tell him how to drive out evil spirit.

As Marcus passed that way toward evening, he heard the chanting wail of the widowed squaws. When he stooped at the lodge opening to offer sympathy, the squaws spat at him and called their dogs to drive him off. He did not see the painted *te-wat* alive again.

Day after day Marcus spent in doctoring and holding funerals. And gradually the allotments of time for each of these duties exchanged places. John and Francis took over all the chores and added to them digging graves in the Indian burying ground on the

(239)

Whitman farm. And after Narcissa had sung a hymn, Marcus would commit the body to the earth with a few verses of scripture and a simple prayer. Then he'd turn away only to be called back for another funeral. At night the wolves, made bold by easy conquests among the Indians who refused a deep-dug grave and Christian burial, howled near at hand. One night the eery dirge of the medicine wolf wakened Marcus, but the Indians were too sick to move in an effort to escape whatever evil he might be foreboding.

Tiloukaikt came to the kitchen door at dawn that morning. "Small girl child need medicine-in-the-mouth. *Te-wat* try but not take out fire spirit. Girl child say white *te-wat,* singing-white-squaw good to her at school. Beg and cry for medicine of white *te-wat*. So, Tiloukaikt come."

Marcus hurried with the chief to his lodge. He doctored the little girl and lost the hope that had flared with Tiloukaikt's call. This would not change the chief's heart. His daughter would die.

And Marcus put both of Tiloukaikt's sons to bed with sore throats and burning foreheads. Depressed, he hurried home to make the round of patients among the emigrants.

Chief Tiloukaikt knocked before daylight the next morning. When Marcus left his patient and padded to the kitchen door, he found the chief overflowing with words and in no hurry for medicine. Tiloukaikt's daughter burned with fire, worse than before. "Medicine-in-the-mouth make worse. Strong sons worse, likewise. Sons not sick till white *te-wat* come," he accused.

All night Tiloukaikt had walked among the lodges of his village. He'd listened to the moaning for their dead ones. He'd ridden to the villages of Feathercap and Tamahas. He'd found the same sickness, same moans, same cold breath of *koonapa kapseish*. He'd come across Joe Lewis who said, "White *te-wat* evil spirit. Bring Bostons to squat on Cayuse land. Try get barking-dog-man-Gray to poison Cayuse. Now white *te-wat* let evil spirit out from bottle on his shelf." Tiloukaikt shook his fist. "White *te-wat* not come back to lodge. Keep evil spirit medicine. Strong sons not die." And he slapped onto the kitchen floor the papers of calomel that Marcus had left for his children the day before.

Marcus retrieved the calomel—his supplies were running too low. Quietly he said, "Chief Tiloukaikt, make people stop sweat bath. Get too hot. Then get too cold in river. Die every time. Sweat bath bad medicine. Take medicine-in-the-mouth that white *te-wat* give. Much better."

Narcissa came in from the dining room, tears bright in her eyes but not spilling over. "It's Salvijane, Doctor," she whispered and turned to the glowering Tiloukaikt. "Chief Tiloukaikt," she said, "I hear your words. You come now with me. See white daughter also die. Perhaps you know then how wrong are words of poison and evil spirits."

Fascinated, Tiloukaikt followed her across the kitchen and into the dining room. Narcissa led him to the bed beneath the stairway.

There lay the body of six-year-old Salvijane Osborn—her blanched face specked with measly eruptions, her hair still showing furrows plowed with a wet comb back from her brows, her hands like milk glass folded on her sunken chest.

"Look and see what your heart not believe in words," Narcissa ordered. "Whites die, too. Die from same sickness as your people. Sorrow presses on our hearts the same as yours."

Expressionless, the chief stared. He leaned forward to listen and be sure that the child did not breathe. Straightening he folded his arms on his chest and raised his face to the ceiling. Then he opened his mouth and let out an animal wail of triumph, "Ow-oo-oo-oo-ahhh!" Pouring forth a torrent of bloodcurdling laughter, he stamped from the house.

Marcus knew that Tiloukaikt would go now to spread news of the evil spirit who had made a mistake and killed a white child.

Yet, by the light of the next dawn, with sickness and death and hate on every hand, Marcus and Narcissa decided that he must ride at once for medicines. He had on hand barely enough to tide them over at Waiilatpu while he made the trip. At Oregon City he could buy what he needed. In addition, he could see McLoughlin and get his advice on what to do with the half-crazed Indians.

"And Mr. Gray," Narcissa reminded him, "Don't fail to get our infallible Mr. Gray's advice while you're in his part of the country." She wrinkled her nose and Marcus kissed it.

"The lady shows her claws," he teased.

"Well, then, just give my warmest greetings to Doctor McLoughlin. And tell Joe Meek that his little Helen Mar shows no sign of measles."

On the way to Walla Walla, Marcus—taking a short cut—rode

through the village of young Bloody Chief. The big savage hailed him from the shadow of his lodge. By rights Marcus should have refused to enter, he told himself. But, as a doctor, he couldn't pass by on the other side when, within, Bloody Chief's fat squaw suffered from dysentery and his five sons scratched and whined with measles.

Marcus swung off his horse and stooped to enter the lodge, turning his back on the Indian's outstretched hand.

Bloody Chief grabbed his shoulder. "Why you not shake hand?" he demanded.

Marcus looked him in the eye. "Perrin send word that Bloody Chief help murder Sheppard at The Dalles. White *te-wat* not shake the hand that murder white man. Will doctor sick. No more."

The Indian sprang to the lodge pole to grasp his tomahawk. But when he turned, Marcus held him under the black eye of a cocked pistol. The savage dropped his weapon. His face knotted in anger. Then he spun on his heel and, muttering threats, strode off toward his campfire.

Marcus eased the pain of the squaw and the naked children as he could with the meager supplies he'd dared take from Waiilatpu. Then he rode on to Walla Walla to spend the night.

Before sunup word breezed into the fort that Bloody Chief had choked to death the night before on a piece of dried buffalo meat. Word spread like cholera. The Indian population around the Hudson's Bay post raised an uproar that echoed along the canyon walls of the great river.

Friendly Indians got to Marcus first. They boiled over with excitement too great to cool down into English. Their Nez Percé steamed and spewed. But Marcus made out that Bloody Chief had stalked from the lodge where the white *te-wat* refused to shake his hand and had told everyone in his village that the doctor insulted him— him, first chief! When Bloody Chief died so soon afterward, his people said the white *te-wat* had worked some evil magic with his not shaking hands. Bloody Chief's friends and relatives had painted themselves and gone on the war path. They would put an end to this Boston sorcery. And that was not all.

Joe Lewis had ridden into Bloody Chief's village that night like a wolf, scenting the blood of a wounded man on the desert. He sat before a blazing lodge fire and smoked kinnikinnick while spreading word that the hearts of the people welcomed—word that Dr.

and Mrs. Whitman scattered poison into the air. They brought Boston poison in bottles and boxes, Joe Lewis said, to kill off all Cayuse and Walla Wallas. The doctor knew that the Indians would all die soon. Then he would take their horses and land and leave their bones for the wolves.

Marcus calmed his chattering Indian friends and gave them twists of tobacco. In case there was any truth in these rumors, he needed to hurry on—to get medicines and some sound advice and rush them back to Waiilatpu.

CHAPTER

3

THE Columbia gorge in early November had power to soothe. Marcus rode under a turquoise pasture on which frisked lamb-like clouds. He listened to the song of the Columbia and refused to hear discordant savage notes in the melody. Stirrup high, empty sprays of wild oats were silver in the sun. He gave himself up to the rhythmic rub and squeak of leather on leather beneath him.

This gorge did not seem wild or savage. The life-giving water of the river, the fertile silt washed down from the plant life of millenniums, the thousand-foot lava cliffs and their laughing water-falls—they all spoke to him of purposeful creation.

Cutting off to the southwest for Oregon City, he picked up the Willamette Valley. Here beat the legendary heart of the Indian world—falls set up by the gods to hold back spawn-crazed salmon so the hungry god, Lo, would always have plenty to fill his belly. Marcus saw power going to waste—power to turn sawmills and grist-mills, power to house and feed settlers from the States.

He prodded his buckskin into a trot and clattered down the gravelly street of the settlement on the river's east bank. No missing Mc-Loughlin's two-story house. Its freshly painted siding beamed a wel-come from the end of the street. And the big man himself swung the front door wide before Marcus stomped up the steps.

"Doctor Whitman! Come right in. Welcome to the heart of Oregon."

Then, as Marcus took his hand, McLoughlin peered up and down the street. "Mrs. Whitman?" he inquired. "Don't tell me you failed to bring her with you. When we received word you were coming, we all hoped the lovely lady would come, too. For a long, long visit."

"Thank you. Mrs. Whitman would have given her . . . her highest note to come. But children, sickness, responsibility— She takes them seriously."

"I'll let you in on a secret, Doctor Whitman. Mrs. McLoughlin and I had hatched up a scheme against you both. We planned to impress Mrs. Whitman and you into staying through the winter. Do you both good. I'm disappointed."

"Mighty good of you. Narcissa still dreams of that first fall in your home. I'd like to take an option on that invitation. Maybe next winter. Or the next."

"Our home is always open to you both, you know that." McLoughlin caught Marcus by the arm and led him toward the stairway. "Let me show you to your room. You'll want to get rid of the dust from your Upper Columbia. I'll have a boy take your horse to the barn."

McLoughlin would have talked right through that night. He wanted to know about Mrs. Whitman and about each child. About the work at Waiilatpu, among Indians and emigrants. He frowned at Marcus' account of their epidemics. He promised to give the situation some thought, do what he could to help. Now, he had to tell Marcus about developments in the valley. About new business enterprises taking shape, about organizations bringing the people together for mutual protection and cultural pursuits—churches, a school, and the first newspaper west of the Missouri River. They had the first Masonic Lodge in the West and the Multnomah Circulating Library. And Oregon City was the only seat of organized government west of the Rocky Mountains.

"A government without power," Marcus commented.

"Well, not much," McLoughlin admitted, "but power will come, in time."

"Time! Wish I had a little of the time that Congress seems to have so much of."

"Something will make Congress sit up and take notice soon now," McLoughlin said. "Joe Meek has turned into quite a patriot. He's been picked Oregon's High Sheriff. By the way, Meek's coming in tomorrow. I sent him word you were coming."

(245)

"Fine. It'll be good to see old Joe Meek."

McLoughlin finally stared in disbelief at his big gold watch. "I say, man, it's late. Up to bed with you, quick."

Marcus slept like a hibernating grizzly and wakened on the prowl for food and sights. McLoughlin fed him and walked him over his grounds. Then they hiked down Oregon City's one business street— between Waller's Christian Store and McLoughlin's "heathen store."

"Got any heathen medicines in stock?" Marcus asked. Inside, he bought up all his saddlebags would pack. "Better hitch up your prices, Doctor," he told McLoughlin, "if you're to live up to your name against Waller's."

"He picked his name and I pick off my share of the business." McLoughlin pulled out his watch. "We'll be having company at the house."

Sure enough, from the board walk in front of the store they could spot Joe Meek, squatted on his heels at McLoughlin's hitching post.

Meek cupped his hands and let out a low howl. "Ow-oo-oo, wagh!"

Marcus ran forward to pump his hand. "Well, by the eternal, you old prairie wolf."

"Danged if you aren't good for the eyes, Doc."

"And you, too," Marcus said. "We're all proud of you, Joe. You should listen in sometime and hear Narcissa talking up her father to that Helen Mar of yours. Your little gal is plump as butter and always laughing."

"Come inside, gentlemen," McLoughlin invited. "We'll talk in my office."

He led them through the dining room with its gleaming furniture and Irish crystal and into his office.

Marcus had always enjoyed leafing through the doctor's books. While the others lit their pipes and slumped into easy chairs, he turned through Hargrave's *Operative Surgery.*

Meek glanced up. "Doc, you old carver, you don't need that. McLoughlin, you oughta holed in at Rendezvous in '35. Some doin's, seein' Doc hyar cut fancy and deep into Old Gabe and him just married to Big Star what Feathercap was honin' after. Some spree, that were."

Marcus slapped the book shut. "Since you're interested in surgery, how's a man going to cut an evil heart out of a savage? And grow a decent, civilized one in its place?"

McLoughlin turned from his desk. "You remember, Doctor Whitman, what Parker wrote and how I begged you to stay clear of the Cayuse tribe? A bad lot, those Indians. Treacherous."

Marcus nodded. "The kind who need a doctor and Christian teaching."

"A lot of good your teaching or doctoring will come to, if an Indian raises your hair with a tomahawk," McLoughlin pointed out.

"Well, if a man keeps his eyes peeled—" Marcus sat down. "Had to pull a gun on Bloody Chief on the way down here. Hated to do it. Sort of an emergency."

Meek bristled. "You meanin' that murderin' varmint raised his hand ag'in' you, Doc? Why, I'll carve his white-livered heart out myself."

"Won't be necessary, Joe. He dropped dead an hour later."

McLoughlin's white brows met and lifted. "Better accept my long-standing invitation, Doctor. Worries me to think of Mrs. Whitman up there among those heathen Cayuse. Emigrants tell me Indians are dying fast—measles, dysentery, and other white men's diseases."

"Tiloukaikt claims about half the tribe has gone under," Marcus said. "But as long as there's a chance to break up the epidemic, I'm needed at Waiilatpu."

"Need a good doc down this way, too. This hoss has got a hankerin' to see his Helen Mar, anyhow. And to hyar that purty voice of Mrs. Whitman's a-singin' sweet."

"Next spring, maybe," Marcus said. "Thought for a while we'd move to The Dalles this fall but that looks most unlikely now. Keep hoping the Board can send out some new doctors and teachers and farmers to make a fresh start with the Cayuse."

An insistent knock sounded through the house. The men stopped talking and waited for Dr. McLoughlin to answer the door. They heard him exclaim, his voice too loud for mere surprise, "Why, Mr. Gray. To what are we indebted for your call?"

"I and the wife come to town for a spell." Gray whined more than Marcus had remembered. "Heard as how my old colleague, Doc Whitman, is visiting you, on business I hear. I thought I'd be generous and forgiving and offer my experience and advice. Oregon needs sound counsel these days, I always say."

Gray led McLoughlin back to the office. His eyes seemed even closer set than Marcus had kept in mind. But then, he'd found little time in the last five years for keeping green his memory of Mr. Gray. Now, as he shook hands and listened to Gray's account of his singlehanded discovery of the Oregon coast below Fort George, he merely wondered why the Cayuse had not named him whining-dog-man.

"And how are you gettin' along without me, up at your little settlement, Doc?" he tossed out, all hooked and baited.

Marcus hesitated, thought of several answers—all apt, all too caustic. He said, "Just limping along, Mr. Gray."

"Waiilatpu, now that's a big mistake, like I always say. Walla Walla's the place—or more likely, The Dalles. Wagon trains bound to hit The Dalles. Our Board made a A-1 mistake, lettin' the Methodists get that spot."

McLoughlin sat down. "Mr. Gray, you apparently haven't heard that Doctor Whitman has taken over The Dalles."

Gray hung by his thumbs to his lapels and teetered on his heels. "I always knew the American Board would get around to capitulizing on my advice sometime."

To break up the empty silence, Marcus fumbled in his pocket. He pulled out a wrinkled sheet of paper. "Here's the business I sent word about. Need your help on a memorial. I sent Secretary of War, Porter, a letter about it when I got back in '43. But nothing's been done. This time, I've got to make it more impressive. Need your help."

Gray said, "I'll be glad to help. It's fortunate I heard you was here, Doc. Let's have a look at your plan."

Marcus explained his scribbled notes and roughly sketched-in map. "Both Porter and Senator Linn liked the idea of a string of forts across the country—starting at Fort Leavenworth, then up along Platte, and out over the Trail. Figured you, Joe, could spot the best locations with your eyes shut."

"Talkin' right up my crick, Doc." Joe reached for the map. "Let's begin, well, say with Jim Bridger's dilapidated fort and work both ways."

The two men bent above the paper while McLoughlin stood at a wall map hung over his desk. They checked, discussed, argued, and settled on likely places. From each location they picked, a garrison of troops could patrol a section of the trail to prevent Indian attacks. Marcus scribbled more notes—descriptions of the countryside around each site, the suitability for raising crops, for getting supplies hauled out from the frontier. Basically, the three men agreed. Satisfied, they reached for chairs.

Marcus was folding his papers when Gray put in the first full sentence they'd allowed him for an hour. "If you'd ask me, I'd map out a entirely different trail. I, personal, think this old one's all wrong."

Marcus glanced toward McLoughlin's rearing shock of white hair and spoke up fast ahead of Joe Meek. "Mr. Gray, if you don't mind, another time. Rode here, for one thing, to ask Doctor McLoughlin to write a letter to Congress. Doctor, your name carries weight in Washington. A letter from you, asking for forts to protect emigrant trains—well, even Mr. Webster will respect your judgment."

"Seems to me he respected yours," McLoughlin said, dropping his hand on Marcus' shoulder. "He and President Tyler did just about what you asked. Now don't protest. Those of us in this room know it—and many others know it, too. Whether additional forces helped bring about a fair settlement of the Oregon boundary is beside the point. Your ride East helped in a hundred ways."

Meek picked up the argument. "The doc's always sayin' emigration to Oregon couldn't of been stopped—had to come, he says. But this old hoss knows how us mountain men fought settlement out this way. And you, McLoughlin, know Hudson's Bay bucked it with all they had."

Marcus held up his hand to get in a word. "You're my friends, that I know. What I say is, this emigration that has barely begun as yet, is one of the onward movements of the world. Can't be stopped. But it needs to be guided. To guarantee a just and peaceful Oregon." He reached into the case and slid out a volume of Robertson's *Historical Works*. "Read this sometime. Take a look at other great world movements. Been writing to the Board in Boston, trying to get them to see it. Doctor Greene's afraid we'll turn Waiilatpu into a restauran: and an overnight stage station—instead of a mission for Indians. But both are needed for the good of the country."

Joe Meek chuckled. "Say, Doc, you got no need to argufy with us. We're back of you—tooth and claw."

Marcus said, "My friends, I'd like to count on that. Want to know

I can bank on you to follow through— Well, just in case something should happen to go wrong at Waiilatpu."

Gray blurted, "Don't talk rubbish, Doc. You're not in no danger."

McLoughlin frowned, hesitated, and got to his feet. "Doctor Whitman, Joe Meek and I have spoken about you many times in recent months. We've known the danger from the beginning. Those superstitious savages have always considered you a *te-wat*. You're liable to their traditional treatment of *te-wats* when a patient dies."

Meek said, "Doc, if that's what you mean, we'd raise hair on the last cussed Cayuse that so much as laid a hand on you. You can go your pile on it."

"It's not just that, Joe. They're half out of their heads right now with all the deaths from measles and such. But we've been through worse times than this—eleven years of threats—and we've come through all right. But, in case anything slipped— Well, I'd like to know that my friends would finish my work. See to it that a territorial government's set up—one that'll give Indians a square deal as well as whites. Help along this great onward movement that's started. See that this country's riches are developed, its beauties kept."

Joe Meek said, "You can count on us to fight to clawin' for a Oregon that'll be fit to house her mountains and her waterfalls and rivers, Doc. Sure as shootin'."

"Doctor, you need a rest," McLoughlin said. "Let me send for Mrs. Whitman. Heaven knows she has no business in that Upper Columbia country now. You're welcome to bring all the children and spend the winter here as my guests. Help us campaign for our new government. We need you."

Marcus sighed and pushed himself up. "Thank you, Doctor. And you, too, Meek. Just wanted to know you'd follow through. I feel like a new man already."

"But Doc, my old eyes fairly burn for a good long look at Mrs. Whitman."

"Meek, that's nice, and I'll tell her what you've said. But her answer would be, 'Sorry. Not now. Maybe later.' That's my answer, too. You see, Waiilatpu is in the midst of an epidemic. I had to come down for medicines or I wouldn't be here now. Besides the Indians, we're crowded with sick emigrants who dropped off there, too weak to travel farther. We've got seventy-two whites and two half-breeds living in Waiilatpu buildings right now. We can't leave

(250)

them. They can't come. And what kind of doctor would run out on an epidemic?"

Gray yawned. "Aw, Doc, I'm sure nobody would blame you, if you let a few dirty savages go under."

Waiting for control, Marcus stared at the man who had antagonized Umtippe that first day. The man who, according to rumor, had led four Flatheads to their death at the hands of Sioux. Who had worked his clever trick of calomel in melons. Who had left Narcissa unprotected at Waiilatpu to receive a fright from which she'd never recover. Forcibly, Marcus stopped this train of accusations. "Mr. Gray, heaven help me to be charitable," he said quietly, "but how many people might have lived in Oregon, if you had not!"

Undisturbed, Gray blinked. No gleam of comprehension touched his face.

"Why," Marcus thought, "must weak men be given the protection of blindness?"

McLoughlin said, "I'll be glad to write that letter to Congress, Doctor, for whatever good it may do. Our combined efforts may bear fruit."

Brightly Gray spoke up. "Yes, of course, co-operation is bitterly needed. A letter to President Polk from I and my colleagues will have repercussions."

"Undoubtedly," Meek snorted. "Repercussions, without a doubt."

Apparently feeling that he'd been complimented, Gray nodded. "Think nothing of it, gentlemen. My patriotic instinct led me to practically lay the foundations of this country. I set on the seat and held the reins of the first wagon to come west of the Rocky Mountains. And I'm thinkin' of settin' down a history of this country —so even admirin' children in our schools can appreciate what I done to extend the boundaries of our fair land. Not that I crave glory and honor—but just so proper credit can be accorded to I and others."

"Putrified buffler chips!" Joe Meek clamped his teeth down so hard he splintered his pipe stem.

McLoughlin coughed and stood his full six-four. "Mr. Gray," he said, "would you mind stepping into the hall with me, please?"

A door slammed almost as soon as they left the room. The office windows still rattled when McLoughlin came back. "Your pardon, gentlemen. I apologize for having to be rude. Let's proceed."

He stepped to his desk and flicked up the lid of his bronze inkstand. He laid out paper and a quill. They worked out together a strong memorial to Congress on the Oregon situation and on the need for a chain of garrisons along the Oregon Trail.

When they'd finished a rough draft, Marcus folded the copy and deposited it deep in his pocket. "Must say good-by, my friends. Everything has been attended to here. I have my medicines. And your promise, awhile ago, I consider a covenant between us. Just in case—"

No need to complete the sentence. Each man's handshake signed the pact.

And then, ahead of him at the barn, Marcus found Joe Meek, his horse saddled and ready to travel. "Figgered I'd ride along a spell, Doc. Danged if this child aren't goin' to cook a fish with you this night like that fust day we met up back in New York State. Toast my feet at your campfire tonight—thinkin' up messages for you to tote home to the missus and my little Helen Mar."

"Never gladder for company, Joe Meek. Let's ride."

Alone the next morning, Marcus started up the Columbia in brilliant sunshine. The country smelled clean and new. Waterfalls glistened. Small breakers patterned white sprigs on the calico blue of the river.

But at the house, he barely had time to kiss Narcissa before a horse pounded up. Reluctantly, he went to the kitchen door.

A young man, clean-shaven, stood with his foot on the low step and looked back along the trail over which he'd come. His buckskin jacket was covered with dust, his long hair disheveled.

"Welcome to Waiilatpu again, Mr. Kane," Narcissa greeted him. "Doctor, this is Paul Kane, an artist, all the way from Canada. He's been painting some of our Cayuse braves."

Kane acknowledged the introduction with a handshake but his eyes searched the kitchen.

Narcissa asked, "What is it, Mr. Kane? Are you in trouble?"

Kane whispered, "You're to come to the fort with me at once. There's no time to spare."

"Sit down," Marcus ordered. "Take a good breath and then tell us."

"Doctor, Factor McBean sent me to fetch you and Mrs. Whitman.

Indians at Walla Walla are dreadfully stirred up. You're to pack and come with me to the fort at once."

"Relax. You're all wrought up. Mrs. Whitman, I prescribe tea."

"Mrs. Whitman, I appeal to you. You must listen," Kane insisted. "You must lose no time in getting to Fort Walla Walla for your protection!"

"I don't understand," Narcissa said. "Do start at the beginning."

Kane reached for Marcus' long rifle and sighted down its barrel. Then he looked out the window and turned back. "It's this way," he began, keeping his voice down. "Late last night a commotion broke out among the Walla Walla lodges. The factor and I went to investigate. The youngest son of Chief Yellow Serpent arrived— ragged, weak, blood draining from his mouth. He'd ridden ahead of what's left from that war party of two hundred that went to California this spring. When this poor fellow arrived and told the waiting mothers and fathers and sweethearts what had happened you could have heard the wails all the way here."

"What of the war party?" Marcus asked.

"Wiped out. Almost to a man by whites, Indian raids, measles. The chief's son blamed everything on Bostons."

Marcus drew Narcissa onto the settle beside him and kept her hand in his. "Sounds like an old story, doesn't it, wife? They blame everything on Bostons. But they'll forget."

"But, Doctor," Kane persisted, mopping sweat from his face with a paint-smeared handkerchief, "they mean trouble this time. I heard the death chants all night outside the fort. I tell you, you're not safe here."

Narcissa said, "Mr. Kane, we appreciate your kindness, but we've lived at the edge of this volcano for eleven years."

"Yes, Kane," Marcus extended his hand, "thanks to you and to McBean. But what you suggest is impossible as well as inexpedient."

Kane looked from Marcus to Narcissa and back again. "You don't mean to tell me you aren't afraid!"

"Afraid?" Marcus gazed into the fire beneath the tea kettle. "If you mean do my knees ever knock together when I see the natives cast savage looks toward my wife and children, the answer is yes. But we expected that when we came to Oregon. A man is always at the mercy of the savage heart—unless Providence has more work for him to do. The same is true in the States—in any city from St.

Louis to Boston. If you mean afraid of death, the answer is no. Mrs. Whitman and I have been through this many times. We believe we still have a job to do in Oregon."

"Doctor Whitman," Kane said, "I wish I could understand you two."

Marcus grinned. "Then look at it this way. Mrs. Whitman and I have ten children here dependent on us. And some sixty emigrants. If we should stampede toward the fort, we'd draw war parties by the score to hunt us down. We can't leave. That's all there is to it."

"Please tell Factor McBean that we thank him," Narcissa said. "He's a Catholic—a staunch Catholic—and certainly not responsible for Protestants in this country. We'd be an embarrassment to him, hiding behind his gates—even if we could get away which we can't. But do tell him we're grateful."

Kane shook his head. "For the life of me, you two are beyond my comprehension. I can't decide whether it's faith or courage or stupidity."

"Time will decide, not you, Mr. Kane."

CHAPTER

4

DISEASE gripped Waiilatpu and the surrounding countryside through that gray November. Marcus made the rounds of Indian lodges—diagnosing, advising, doctoring. He argued with Indians at the steamy entrance holes to their sweat baths. He examined Indians who stopped him beside the trail, urged them to hurry to their lodges and keep warm. Glum, silent Indians came to his kitchen-office, holding out bony hands for pills and powders.

Within the circle of his own houses and meadow, Marcus had sufficient patients for any one doctor. Measles swept through the tents and wagons and houses. Children and adults alike succumbed. And Marcus could do nothing to relieve their crowded quarters and the inevitable mingling of sick and well.

Henry Spalding came down from Lapwai, bringing a pack of seventeen animals loaded with grain to help feed Waiilatpu. He also brought his daughter, Eliza, as round-eyed and sober at ten as she had been at nine months when Alice Clarissa had tried to each her to "Stand up straight and *haum teets*." Eliza would attend the Waiilatpu school for white children this year.

Marcus was delighted to see them. The emigrants had eaten too far into his food supply. And so many of the Indians were sick and dying that few of them, if any, could go off on Hunt this fall. They, too, would have to be fed throughout the winter.

Henry Spalding went to Walla Walla for two days while Marcus tended his old patients and a dozen new ones among the Indians.

Measles seemed to be dying out a bit but now dysentery in an extreme form increased its toll and brought Indian spirits low.

The evening Henry Spalding returned from Walla Walla, Marcus was just saddling up. Stickus had sent word that the Umatillas must have medicine-in-the-mouth.

"You're not going tonight," Spalding protested. "It looks like rain."

"Ride with me," Marcus invited. "The trail will be shorter with company."

"But why go at night?"

"Best time to get away. A few patients, at least, are asleep at night. Go and come at night and I'll only be away from here one day."

"I'll go with you."

Narcissa clung to Marcus when he told her good-by. "I wish you didn't have to go." She wore her blue chambray dress and, thrown around her shoulders, the old gray shawl that always made Marcus think of Shunar. The work of caring for her large family had left Narcissa thin but her face no longer tightened in worry lines. At last, Narcissa had enough children to satisfy her tremendous need to mother. Not even epidemics could depress her for long these days. Marcus had never seen her more beautiful than she was right now, standing beside their horses, her hair reflecting flame from the autumn sunset, her eyes contented.

She extended her hand to Henry Spalding and Marcus saw him return her smile without restraint.

As Henry mounted, Marcus took Narcissa in his arms again. "Back tomorrow night—late."

"You have your India-rubber coat?"

"Right here." He slapped his saddlebag.

She slipped the gray shawl from her shoulders. "You'd better have this, too, my darling. Be careful."

They had ridden not more than five miles when a cloud blacker than the night appeared before them and soon rain pattered on their rubber coats. Marcus wrapped the gray shawl over his hat and tucked its ends into his collar. The horses found it rough going over slippery stones, through gummy mud, but Marcus dared not stop and thus delay his return to Waiilatpu.

So, as they rode, the two men talked against the drum of rain.

They talked of their first trip along that trail. Of their dreams at the time, of their accomplishments since.

"I hated you every step of that trip out here, Doctor," Spalding confessed. "Felt all the way that you and Mrs. Whitman were laughing at me."

"You're a better man than most, Henry. Few in your shoes would have aspired so high," Marcus told him. "You've come a long way and you've still got big things ahead of you at Lapwai."

"We appreciate what you did, Doctor—going to Boston and all the rest."

"Eleven years."

"We've come a long way," Spalding said, breaking off memories. "Let's rest a bit when we get across this river."

They were just wading into the Umatilla ford. "Sure. Not far now." Marcus urged his horse into the water with his moccasined heel. "Think of all the rivers we've crossed in eleven years!"

The Umatilla was up. But this trip was child's play compared with swimming back and forth across the Snake, back and forth across the Platte. Back and forth, back and forth—riding, wading, swimming. Pulling mules tangled in harness, bearing the weight of a loaded wagon at the end of a rope, floating spread thin on an elk-skin—Indian squaws swimming with its corners.

Marcus' buckskin pawed for footing and they pulled up on the bank to wait for Spalding. But, as Marcus turned in his saddle, he heard a thud and a splash. Spalding called out.

He found both Spalding and his horse in a heap. By luck, the horse could get up. Spalding could get up, but he was in pain.

Marcus searched in the dark for wood dry enough to start a fire. When he had a flicker going, he examined Henry by its light. Bruises only, but the man was uncomfortable.

"We'll rest awhile," he said. "Stickus won't have to wake up quite so early to greet us."

Marcus searched and found more wood to build up his fire. He pulled up logs for them to sit on, out of the mud. They tried to dry their clothes but the rain, passing slowly, left behind a raw wind, making it more uncomfortable to take off clothes for drying than to wear them wet.

Abruptly Henry said, "Sit down, Doctor Whitman. There's something on my mind. I've got to tell you."

Marcus tossed on another log and sat. "Shoot."

"The other night I was in the lodge of Peupeumoxmox at Walla Walla and a . . . a . . . ." he stalled and, as if he had changed the subject, went on, "a niece of the chief's died. I held the funeral the next day."

"Too bad." Marcus thought of all the nieces and nephews and sons and daughters who had died near Waiilatpu. "Look, the rain's over."

Spalding shifted his position on the log and groaned. His voice, when he spoke, came barely above a whisper. "A Nez Percé came in. Several of us were sitting around the lodge fire. This fellow came in, panting like a dog that's been after a rabbit. Blinded, he must have been—by the fire. Didn't look to see who was there."

Marcus waited but Spalding had stopped. He must have decided not to tell the rest. Marcus started gathering up their things. He pulled on his steaming hat. Already he was thinking about getting the trip over and hurrying back to Narcissa and the children. They needed him. He tramped out the edge of the fire. Offhand, because Spalding still sat on his log, seeming to expect something, he asked, "Well?"

Spalding got to his feet and backed away from the light. His voice came out of the night. "That Nez Percé rushed in and said, 'Is Doctor Whitman killed yet?' "

Stunned for an instant, Marcus then remembered to lift his moccasin from the fire. He stared into the dark from which Spalding's voice had come. One moment and he was himself again. He tramped out the remaining embers. "I'll help you mount, Henry. Dirty spill you had. Examine you better by daylight. More plainsmen die of falls from horses than from bullets, you know."

The rain quickened and soon they rode through another downpour. The trail forced them into single file—impossible to talk.

Gray smudged the blackness to their left before Marcus pulled up to rest again.

"Feel worse or better?" he asked Spalding, helping him dismount.

"Worse," Henry answered and picked up their conversation where they'd dropped it. "You're not afraid?"

Marcus helped Henry to sit down on the dry side of a cottonwood. "Afraid?" He took off his hat and beat the water off against his leg. "No, I'm not afraid."

Spalding's brow furrowed and his long middle finger jabbed out to emphasize his words. "But I tell you it was serious. That Nez Percé expected an affirmative answer."

"I know, Henry," Marcus answered. "I know. But I'm the only one they want. I'm the *te-wat*. The others will be safe. And, the way I figure, my death will probably do more for Oregon than my life can."

The trail widened as they went on. Bare slopes of the foothills through which they rode changed from gray to pink to white as the sun lifted in a sky that had rained away its clouds.

"Your Indians still wanting pay for the land you're on?" Marcus asked.

"Land? Our Indians want pay for the water that flows from our spring. They want pay for the timber on our hillside. For the air we breathe. Some of them are devils. Why, Indians come naked right into the schoolroom and do obscene dances before Mrs. Spalding!"

Marcus said, "Indians will never hold this country, Spalding. Mark my words."

But there were Indians and Indians in Oregon. There were those who listened to the malcontent half-breeds, Tom Hill and Finley and Joe Lewis. There were those who plotted murder. And then, there was Stickus.

When Whitman and Spalding reached Stickus' lodge, the kindly chief greeted them in Nez Percé and asked them to breakfast. He had been expecting them for some time and everything was ready. His lodge village stood quiet and friendly on its clean meadow.

They breakfasted on buck steaks and coffee and then Chief Stickus took Marcus to call on all the sick among his people. At each lodge, the chief introduced the doctor and cautioned the family to do exactly as he said.

"Because," Stickus explained each time in melodious Nez Percé, "Stickus have come to know medicine-in-the-mouth is good. Save Chief Stickus' life."

As Marcus examined, diagnosed, prescribed and administered medicine-in-the-mouth he thought how different his life at Waiilatpu might have been, if some respected chief had lent him this kind of authority.

That morning, Henry Spalding conducted worship and the Indians

(259)

gave him rapt attention. Marcus felt he'd never known such serenity as prevailed here in Chief Stickus' village.

His medical calls finished, he mounted a gray mule the chief insisted on lending him and rode across the Umatilla to call on the new Catholic missionaries who were guests at the house of Chief Tawatowe.

Bishop Blanchet was a plump man with a wealth of white hair and a childlike face. He offered Marcus tea and they chatted about the country and the weather until Marcus abruptly brought up the purpose of his visit.

"I understand you gentlemen have got your eye on Waiilatpu."

Bishop Blanchet's English sounded more like French but Marcus could make out his meaning. "Ah, Doctor, you know thees country well. *Oui?* Ees country of wide space weeth no obstructions to interfeer with rumor. You see, we are heer. We are not at Waiilatpu."

Marcus leaned forward. "I'll make you a proposition," he said. "The first minute a majority of the Cayuse come to me and say they want you instead of me, Waiilatpu is yours for a fair price."

The Bishop smiled. "Your proposition ees fair. I am sure your price would be also fair."

Marcus did not get back to Stickus' camp until sundown. He'd hoped for an earlier start toward home.

Stickus pleaded, *"Tàx collo kene, sextua."*

"That buckskin of yours is in no shape to make that ride back tonight," Spalding reminded him. "Stay over until tomorrow like Chief Stickus says. I may feel up to riding back with you by then."

"Promised Mrs. Whitman. Besides, I'm needed at home."

Stickus insisted then that Marcus ride his mule and let the buckskin rest.

"Thank you, Chief Stickus. Your mule and I get along fine and I'll be home in time to sleep a couple of hours." He turned to Spalding. "We'll look for you back in a day or two, as soon as you're better."

But Stickus followed Marcus from the lodge. And when he mounted the gray mule, Stickus stood in his path. The voweled tones of his Nez Percé gave the words the somber sound of medicine drums. "My people hear of trouble at place of rye grass. People tell Stickus of one, Joe Lewis. This half-breed tell Cayuse white *te-wat* poison Indians."

Marcus laughed and stood in his stirrups to arrange his coat beneath him. "True, Chief Stickus. Your people hear true. But you know white *te-wat* long time. You know white *te-wat* do not poison. Cayuse know this, too."

But Stickus would not be put off. "Cayuse listen when half-breed talk. Cayuse not listen to sign how white *te-wat* act." The chief came around and took Marcus' hand. "You go way till my people have better hearts."

Touched, Marcus said, "Thank you, Chief Stickus. You are a faithful friend. But my people are sick. They need me."

"Stickus like you go far off till good spirit enter people," the chief said once more but he backed away. "Still, white *te-wat* not one to go hide when black bear come."

Spalding's and Chief Stickus' warnings rode with Marcus through the night. Thinking back over the years—the busy, driving, threat-filled years since he left New York State—he could see mistakes he'd made. Perhaps, if he could go back, he might avoid the end of this road he traveled. On the other hand, he wasn't sure that he'd choose, even now, to take another way.

He'd made a beginning with the Indians. Someone else could take over now and go ahead. Emigrants were flocking West. Soon they'd show the Indians how to settle down and live in peace off the land. And his work for Oregon he'd given into better hands than his. McLoughlin and Joe Meek would carry on. True, it would be pleasant to lean back on the plow a few years and help things along in comfort from The Dalles. It would be nice to see Perrin take hold and become a big man in this great country, to see all the children grown up and settling Oregon. •

But, actually, all he really wanted, more than he now had, was to know that Narcissa would be happy. He so hoped she would be but— He'd wondered at first whether Narcissa really loved him or whether she'd been willing to put up with him in order to come to Oregon. He'd been awed by her ability to stand alone, even when Alice Clarissa died. But since then, somewhere along the way, they'd ceased to be two individuals. Narcissa loved him now, he knew, and they were one. If anything should happen to him . . .

Deliberately he put the thought away and spurred Stickus' mule ahead. He was almost home. Probably nothing would happen. If the Indians should be plotting against him, they'd plotted before and he'd always avoided serious trouble. He could handle them again, if need be. "Must be tired," he told himself.

In the house he found Narcissa bending over Helen Mar. She turned at his step and flung herself against him almost as Alice Clarissa used to do.

"Marcus, my darling, you've been gone a year."

Marcus held her close. "Worth it for such a greeting." He kissed her hair, her eyes, her mouth. "You ought to be in bed."

"I couldn't sleep without you."

"How're the children?"

She tipped her head toward Helen Mar's pallet. "I'm frightened," she whispered. "I've been singing 'Rock of Ages' to her for hours. She wouldn't let me stop."

Marcus examined Helen Mar and reached for a stimulant.

"John and Francis are sitting up with Catherine and Hannah Louise. John isn't strong enough for that yet but he felt he ought to take your place."

Marcus smiled. "They're boys to be proud of, those two." He measured out the dose for Helen. "You get ready for bed, my sweet," he told Narcissa. "I don't believe you've had that dress off since I left here."

"Will Helen live?"

He nodded and roused the child. Seeing him, she reached up hot arms.

"Father!"

Marcus squeezed her tight.

Narcissa said, "She needs that more than medicine. I guess we all do."

When Helen Mar had gone to sleep, Marcus scuffed into the dining room and sent John and Francis off to bed. "Put on an extra blanket," he told John. "You're chilled."

"Good night, Father," they both called, and hurried into the school room where they slept these crowded nights.

Feeling foreheads, checking covers, Marcus made the round of the other children. Then he found Narcissa in her blue dressing gown, sitting on the bench beneath their bedroom window. "Not in bed?" he asked.

"Marcus, do you know what Eliza told me today? She said that Chief Timothy always closes his prayers, '. . . in the name of Jesus

Christ and Mrs. Spalding.' I wonder why the Spaldings don't tell Chief Timothy he shouldn't pray that way. Those Indians practically worship her."

"Love and reverence aren't far from worship." Marcus sat on the bench and put his arm around her.

"There's something about Mrs. Spalding that's just plain good," Narcissa went on. "Marcus, our Indians don't love me. They never have."

Marcus tightened his arm around her shoulders. "I must tell you something, my wife."

Quietly he told her what Henry had heard in the lodge of Peupeumoxmox at Walla Walla and then of Stickus' warning. He finished, "There may be truth in these rumors. If so, the Indians will rise against me alone. No one else. And I can probably handle them. We've done it before."

"Marcus, Marcus," Narcissa whispered and pressed her head against his chest.

"If something happens, I want you to take the children and go to The Dalles. I've been saving that for a surprise but things are ready there now. You'll be happy and the children can grow up to be fine men and women—the kind this country needs. Perrin will see that you're taken care of."

Narcissa's nails dug into his palm. "Marcus, my husband. Don't you understand? We're one. Whatever happens to you must, inevitably, happen to me, my darling."

CHAPTER

5

MARCUS started from a haunting dream. He stirred in his chair before the kitchen fire, glad to fix his eyes on gray windows instead of enshrouded black ones. He stood and stretched out the cramps of his long night's vigil. He padded across to the small bedroom, hoping to confirm his predawn opinion that Helen Mar had passed the crisis.

The child barely made a mole ridge under the white blanket. Seven years under Narcissa's care had trimmed down her baby plumpness and slimmed her out to look much like her father. As Marcus touched her forehead, Helen opened one sleepy eye and then the other. She reached up and gave Marcus a feeble hug.

"Sleep now, my little bunny," he whispered. "Story time after awhile."

As she flattened out again under the covers, Marcus tiptoed back to the kitchen. Without a sound, he opened the door of the cookstove and found embers of the fire Narcissa had banked. He added wood from the box, fanned the coals into flame with a pie tin, and eased the door shut.

Stepping to the window beside the pantry, he looked at his watch. Almost seven-thirty. Should be lighter by now. He'd better get at his chores. So much to do and so little time.

Pulling into his buckskin jacket, he slid back the bolt and ventured outside. A cold fog pressed in around him. It wore the moldy odor of rotting straw. An unnatural silence blanketed the valley of Waiilatpu.

Marcus cocked his head, listened for familiar sounds. What had happened to Narcissa's rooster? And to old Uncle Sam? The seesaw greeting of Frémont's big mule never failed to usher in a new day at the place of the rye grass. Never, until now.

The sheep and cows in the pasture this side of Mill Creek stood silent, dripping wet. No stomping of restless horses thumped through the rails of the corral. No coyotes yapped at the dawn. No sound of squaws chopping wood for breakfast fires hacked at the morning from the lodges across the river. Even the Walla Walla itself seemed to have sung away all its song in the night.

Marcus found himself straining for these absent sounds more intently than he'd ever listened to their usual presence. He scuffed to the corral with consciously softer tread. This was a morning, he felt, that should be left sleeping for as long as possible.

Beside the path he avoided the pyramid of Frémont's cannon balls. He must bury these useless missiles since they still made the Indians frown. Someday he'd do it—when he could get around to it. He forced his eyes to pierce the fog hanging over the river. But he could make out only a few of the nearer lodge cones, pointing to the bare white branches of cottonwoods webbed and bound by streamers of fog. He told himself that the Cayuse lodges stirred with activity as usual. That nothing was changed. That the low moans filtering through the gray curtain were not, as they sounded, from mothers grieving over their dead. And that the sun, shining just above the trees, would soon win its argument with the fog. Then Waiilatpu would be itself again.

He began to whistle but cut short the effort and milked and fed the stock in silence.

Back in the kitchen, he clattered the milk pails onto the bench and picked up his whistle. He'd change the mood of this day. He might build up the open fire and broil a steak for breakfast. The men had butchered one beef a few days ago. He'd cut out from the herd another fat yearling to kill today. No need to skimp on fresh meat now. At least half of the seventy-two members of his household had been sick. They needed solid nourishment. And today he'd take some fresh meat to the Indians, too.

He'd arouse his family with the fragrance of broiling steak. Then they'd laugh and chatter and celebrate—because Helen Mar would recover and Catherine, perhaps, could get out of bed today.

(265)

Soon this siege of sickness would lift, the same as fog burned out by a November sun. Indian rumors would sound foolish then. He'd take Narcissa's hand and they'd stroll along the river, scoffing at the night they'd talked of dying. Soon he'd move Narcissa to The Dalles and comfort. From there, she could visit the McLoughlins and Joe Meek in the Willamette Valley.

Marcus hurried into the bedroom. Narcissa frowned in her sleep. She mustn't frown. He bent and pressed his lips to hers. Her arms clung to him. But when he spoke playfully and rubbed his bristles on her cheek, she turned to the gray window and shuddered. He sat on the edge of the bed and drew her to him.

"What an odd silent morning," she whispered.

"Never mind, my darling. I'm broiling steak for breakfast. Better put on your blue dress for the occasion. We'll fix this foggy morning."

Narcissa raised her head and kissed him. "Then wake the children. I'll hurry."

Marcus poked his fire down into coals and began rousting children from their pallets.

Francis reached for his buckskin pantaloons.

Raising himself on one elbow, John asked, "Father, can I help butcher today?"

Marcus looked at the boy's thin face, at his eyes still dull from his long bout with measles. "Sorry, son. You're not quite up to butchering. And Mother needs help making brooms. This looks like a dandy day to stay inside."

When Marcus shook Mary Ann, she flopped over on her stomach and looked out the window. "But, Father, what makes it so dark?"

"Fog, my little antelope." Marcus spanked the bulge under the blanket. "Out you come."

Mary Ann, at twelve, seldom slipped into her mountain man jargon—only when her feelings counted coup on her Narcissa-like reserve. Now, she rared up on her knees and locked her arms around Marcus' neck. He patted her sturdy back and gave her a squeeze. But she kept hanging on.

"What is it, sugar?" he asked finally.

When she raised her head, tears welled up in her eyes. "I don't know, Father. I just feel like crying."

"Not sick, are you?"

She shook her blond braids. "No, it's not that." One tear over-flowed.

Marcus tried to lure her into a more cheerful mood. "Helen Mar is much better this morning. Another week and she'll be out to play."

Mary Ann's arms gripped his neck. "Then I'll cry because I'm glad she's better. I've just got to cry about something."

"All right, but hurry. Steak for breakfast."

Marcus found Narcissa in her blue chambray, dipping water with a tin cup into the big coffee pot.

"Elizabeth," she said and pointed to the table.

Elizabeth, up several days from measles, showed signs of filling out again. "Yes, Mother," she called and rattled knives and forks in the silver box on the shelf beneath the dishes. "Come help me set the table, Matilda Jane. Father's broiling steak for breakfast. And I'm going to have a bath today. Mother said so."

Marcus cut steaks from the quarter of beef in the pantry and stopped on his way to the fire to rub his cheek against Narcissa's hair. "Sleep well?" he asked.

She closed her eyes to answer. "Such muddled dreams—sickness and Feathercap and scalping knives." She shuddered.

Marcus laughed. "And you're using your bowie for peeling potatoes."

She tossed her head. "Uh-huh. Comes in handy. But I wish you'd give it a stroke or two on your whetstone."

"Now?"

"No, later. Get on with the steak. Come, children. Hurry."

But when the family sat down to eat, Narcissa asked them to go ahead without her. She went to her room.

Marcus tried to joke with the children but he got only sober responses. Finally, he served a plate with steak and potatoes and asked Matilda Jane to take it to her mother.

"Mother's crying," Matilda reported when she came back.

"She's just tired," Marcus assured the child. "Maybe a bit lonely. No mail from her mother or sisters for a long time."

"Father, why is everything so still this morning?" Francis asked. "I'm kinda lonesome for our Cayuse friends. Nobody's squatting in the kitchen."

Marcus glanced around the wall. "Many are sick, son. They'll come when we butcher today. Tiloukaikt can smell meat as far as a prairie wolf. They'll be back."

Then, without knocking, in barged a messenger from Chief Tiloukaikt. He panted that the last of the chief's three children, his favorite son, had died in the night. Tiloukaikt wished a white man's funeral. He commanded that the white squaw sing "Rock of Ages." Same as for funeral of little Cayuse *te-mi*.

"Of course," Marcus answered. "Go tell chief. Funeral soon."

Tiloukaikt had been a devil at times. But at other times, he'd been a real friend. This made three children the chief had lost to the white man's measles. The messenger's words, "The child the chief loved," touched Marcus. David had been not merely the father's favorite but the one he'd counted on to become second chief of his village. Poor Tiloukaikt.

Marcus left the table and hurried to the carpenter shop to nail together a pine box. Narcissa came later with half a blanket to line the coffin. They walked, hand in hand, to the burial ground where Francis had finished digging the grave. Fog blew in filmy veils across the valley.

Then, out of the gloom, four Cayuse braves appeared. As they approached, their moccasins making no sound, Marcus saw that black streaked the upper half of their bodies. On a travois they carried the corpse of Tiloukaikt's loved son, wrapped in a blanket.

Then, face expressionless, arms crossed on his chest, Chief Tiloukaikt loomed out of the fog. After him came Tamahas, then Feathercap, their eyes cold and unseeing. No more. No Indians squatted near the open grave.

And yet everywhere Marcus saw blanketed forms—lurking, slinking, all at a distance. They were alone or in silent, watching groups —at the blacksmith shop, among the trees by the river, by the back-house, leaning against the gristmill, squatting beside the pile of cannon balls.

Narcissa stepped to Tiloukaikt's side. "Very sorry," she said softly. "Your last son. And your favorite." She laid her hand on her heart. "His death makes my heart heavy for you."

The stolid face did not change. The chief did not look at Narcissa to thank her for her kindness.

Marcus opened the Bible and read briefly, translating into Nez Percé:

Lord, thou hast been our dwelling place in all generations. Before the mountains were brought forth, or ever thou hadst formed the earth and the world, even from everlasting to everlasting, thou art God. . . . So teach us to number our days, that we may apply our hearts unto wisdom. . . . And let the beauty of the Lord our God be upon us; and establish thou the work of our hands upon us; yea, the work of our hands establish thou it.

Head high, shoulders squared, Narcissa sang "Rock of Ages." Marcus knew her heart was bleeding. He himself heard, not Narcissa, but the baby voice of Alice Clarissa. He ended the funeral with a prayer.

Then, glad to be busy, he lifted the blanket-wrapped body and laid it in the coffin. He nailed on the lid. He helped lower the box into the grave and shovel in the fresh-turned clods. He heard them drum on the crude pine box.

No sound came from Tiloukaikt nor from his friends.

The watching Indians out in the fog continued to stand and stare—silent, unmoving, unmoved, like propped-up dead men in blanket shrouds.

Tiloukaikt marched away without a word. Tamahas and Feather-cap followed.

Marcus took Narcissa's hand. Cold fingers of fog pointed in on them. They left the path and turned aside to Alice Clarissa's grave for a moment.

A thunderbolt exploded the quietness. Narcissa shuddered. She clutched Marcus' arm.

He looked toward the corral. Yes, of course. "Don't be frightened, my sweet. That was just Francis, shooting the beef at the butchering rack."

Narcissa hurried inside. She had a thousand things to do, she said—the house to clean, beef tallow to render for candles, and a hot meal to prepare for the children when they came in from school at noon.

Marcus collected his medicines and soap and made the round of his patients among the emigrant families. Then, back at the corral, he decided to hop on Uncle Sam's bare back to cross the river and look in on the Indians.

The Cayuse dogs stopped their fuss as soon as he spoke to them. But the Indians poked their noses through their hanging skin doors when he asked whether they had any sick and "No" was the answer at each lodge. He knew that many suffered from both measles and dysentery. But he wouldn't force his way in. He nudged Uncle Sam back into the river. The Indians would be in a different mood tomorrow, he reckoned. Maybe he should have said he'd bring them meat as soon as they got it cut up.

At the house, he met Francis. Importantly, the boy carried the rifle he'd used to shoot the beef. He stood the long gun in the fireplace corner, saying, "Just leave it here, Father. I'll clean it right after school this afternoon."

Francis was growing up. A boy to trust. He ought to be encouraged, Marcus decided, and pulled his pistol from his belt. "Mind giving this piece a cleaning at the same time, son? It needs it."

"Sure, Father. I'll unload them now. Then, they'll be ready."

The fog did not lift through the morning. At noon the family gathered for a subdued meal. Nothing Marcus found to talk about seemed to lighten the heavy atmosphere. Mary Ann mentioned again the empty places along the squatting wall.

"For once there'll be no lice to sweep out, Mother," she said.

"Eat your dinner, Mary Ann," Narcissa replied. "You'll need your strength."

Elizabeth asked, "Mother, when do I get my bath?"

"Dishes first. You next."

"I'll be late for school."

"Not much."

Marcus pushed back his chair when the meal was finished and went to his desk in the corner. He thumbed through Macintosh's *Practice of Physic*. If only he could find something more on measles! Something strong enough or magic enough to bring around the Cayuse. Finding no help in the medical book, he picked up his Bible. It fell open to the page from which he'd read at the burial of Tiloukaikt's David.

"Father," Helen Mar called from her bunk in the corner, "read me something."

Narcissa was sudsing Elizabeth in the big wooden tub. John had gone to the kitchen to work on his brooms. It would be quiet enough in here for reading.

"Well, my little bunny, how about the Ninety-first Psalm?" He began, " 'Thou shalt not be afraid for the terror by night; nor for the arrow that flieth by day; nor for the pestilence that walketh in darkness; nor for the destruction that wasteth at noonday. . . .' "

A loud pounding shattered the quiet.

Leaving Elizabeth in the tub, Narcissa hurried to the kitchen door.

At once, she came back to Marcus. "Doctor, you're wanted. Medicine for dysentery."

Marcus laid the open Bible on the foot of Helen Mar's bunk and stepped to the cabinet under the stairway. He selected papers of calomel and ipecac. "Bolt this door," he whispered to Narcissa and went through to the kitchen.

Three chiefs, arms folded in their blankets, stood near the doorway. How long it had been since Feathercap had come demanding medicine for old Umtippe! Now Chief Tiloukaikt, clutching his blanket in one fist, held out his free hand for medicine-in-the-mouth.

Starting to question him about symptoms, Marcus glanced toward Tamahas and Feathercap. They had moved over near John. The boy sat by the window, examining the empty pistol that Francis was to clean after school. Around him on the floor was piled the litter of broommaking. Mary Ann, Marcus saw, was wringing out the dishrag. He remembered her outburst at the picnic they'd had on the river. He winked to let her know he trusted her now not to roil the Cayuses. He turned back to Tiloukaikt. "*Etu ke,* Tiloukaikt? Where sick, my friend?"

Tiloukaikt backed toward the cookstove. He placed his hand on his forehead. His hair sprawled onto his shoulders from a snaky center part. His eyes stared. His heavy jaws corded. He spoke hoarsely, "*Comitsa.* Very sick." He touched his belly, and held out his hand. "White *te-wat* give Tiloukaikt medicine-in-the-mouth."

Marcus said, "Of course, but let me feel head. Maybe ipecac cure."

Tiloukaikt continued to back away. Tamahas and Feathercap stood motionless.

"Don't be afraid, Tiloukaikt. White *te-wat* cure you many times. Sorry loved son of chief die. Doctor cannot always cure sick ones. Can only try."

Marcus held two white papers of ipecac toward the chief.

Tiloukaikt backed away farther.

Before Marcus could turn, he heard John draw in a sharp breath, heard him scream.

And then Marcus felt a dull pain—numbing pain at the back of his head. Then came a sharp blow from behind. His knees buckled. He crumpled onto the kitchen floor.

Hot searing pain now, then numbness. Marcus opened his eyes. He caught a glimpse of Mary Ann's blue dress drop beyond the window. He heard a pistol shot near at hand. Fighting the pain, he tried to get to his feet but blackness closed in. When he forced his eyes open again, John lay on the floor, empty pistol beside him.

From far off, Marcus heard human screams. Doors banged. Rifles barked. He could cull out the wolflike howls of bloodthirsty Indians. Then silence. Blackness. . . .

Marcus stirred and fought for consciousness. Pain surged up in his head—hotter now and more insistent. He recognized the dining room. Someone had moved him to the settle there. Narcissa kneeled beside him. She bathed his face, his head. The children stood above him—wild-eyed, quivering like cornered animals. Then Narcissa was speaking. She must have been speaking for some time. He strained to make out the words, to give them meaning.

"The blood . . . my darling. Try to hear. . . . How can I stop it? What can I do?"

Marcus tried to wet his lips to answer but his tongue had no moisture in it. His head throbbed, seemed detached and then aflame. Finally, he heard his own voice as if it rolled in from far away. "Do? Nothing. . . . Physician, heal thyself."

He watched Narcissa rise and blur out in the distance. Then she came back. Through a veil of fog, but slowly she came nearer. Her face went deathly pale. He must remember to give her a tonic. But she hummed. Faintly he heard it and then it came clear. He could make out the melody. A hymn. The hymn she sang at their wedding. Still humming, she bent above him. She pressed a towel with a compress of wood ashes to the back of his head. He could smell the ashes, like all the campfires he had known. Narcissa hummed on— that song of resignation and dedication to whatever might befall in a savage land.

And then the sound of a gun crashed through the music. The melody stopped.

Marcus fought the black silence. He got his eyes open. Narcissa stood now by the door, peering out through the glass. Marcus wanted to smile, remembering old Chief Umtippe and his "No like door."

Then, without Umtippe's slam, a rifle cracked. The door glass shattered.

Narcissa staggered. She turned, clutching her breast. She came to Marcus and slumped on the floor beside him. His hand found hers.

Someone screamed. Elizabeth, half dressed, stood weeping at the foot of the settle.

Mary Ann's deep voice then sounded like a prayer. "Them cussed Injuns! They killed Father and now Mother, too. Godamighty, can't somebody stop 'em?"

Horrified, Elizabeth asked, "Mother, aren't you going to scold Mary Ann for those naughty words?"

Blackness threatened Marcus again. But he must see Narcissa's face, her hair once more. Blood stained the blue bodice of her dress. She raised herself until his cheek rested against her bosom. The pain felt less hot now. Grayness drifted in, cool and inviting. A trickle of blood caressed Marcus' temple.

He tried to speak but he could hear only screams, far off. And then Narcissa's voice, faint but near—very near.

"It's all right . . . my darling. Our last river . . . we cross . . . together."

Then he heard the sound of the river—the threat of the Platte delaying their caravan, the roll of the Laramie in flood, the ripple of the Green at Rendezvous, the drumbeat of the Snake, the moaning of the Walla Walla, mourning over the life it had taken. And then, he heard the Columbia and its open sweep to the sea, touching with life-giving fingers the land of Oregon.

EPILOGUE

Oregon City
Oregon Territory
June 3, 1850

Miss Jane Prentiss
West Almond—Allegany County
New York

My dear Miss Jane Prentiss:

It has been on my conscience for some months to write you concerning your sister and brother-in-law. But allow me to introduce myself. I am John McLoughlin—chief factor of Hudson's Bay Company situated at Fort Vancouver at the time Dr. and Mrs. Marcus Whitman arrived in Old Oregon.

I know something of how you have suffered. In my own grief over events at Waiilatpu, I have felt drawn to you. Mrs. Whitman spoke of you so often that I feel, in a way, acquainted with you and impelled to write for whatever peace of mind I may be able to afford you.

On May 22, last, here in Oregon City began the trial of five Cayuse Indians who gave themselves up in order to save their tribe from wandering—always pursued by the Volunteers who organized soon after the massacre at Waiilatpu. Among those brought to trial were Chiefs Tiloukaikt and Tamahas whom your sister may have mentioned in letters home. I asked Tiloukaikt during the trial why he had given himself up. He answered, "Our missionaries teach us that Christ die to save his people. So we die to save our people."

This morning at sunrise these five Indians were hanged. Joe Meek, our U. S. Marshal, served as executioner.

I realize, Miss Jane, that these bare facts may be of little comfort to you. How much better, if you and I could sit before the fire here in my home, among my effects in which your sister so delighted. We should exchange many reminiscences of the Whitmans. We would speak of your sister's charm, of her delightful and often witty conversation, of her glorious voice. And of the doctor's skill, of his drive, and of the prodigious amount of work he did.

The Whitmans made many friends in this country—even among the Indians. Chief Stickus of the Umatillas never tires of talking about them and when he speaks of their tragic death, tears roll down his cheeks.

I, too, shall always remember them with love, Miss Jane. But, if we could say what lies deep within us, I should be compelled to tell you more. You see, that 29th of November had to be. Your sister and the doctor were in no way suited by temperament to the position they chose to occupy. The Indians always thought and spoke of Mrs. Whitman as haughty. The very lift of her head could give a thread-bare apron the air of a royal garment. The Cayuse never got close to her. She was, by nature, unable to approach them. The Indians could not love her, nor could she love them.

As for the doctor, he was my dearly esteemed friend and I admired him greatly. But he was always at work. Carefree Indians could not be expected to understand this. It was always "Yes" or "No" with him. He never had time to parley.

Still, who can say that God's purpose was not working out from the first? Marcus Whitman came to Oregon with a sincere desire to serve the natives. He never lost that desire nor swerved from it. He was murdered because he refused to leave during an epidemic. But, as he saw it, the Indians could never be civilized or Christianized until they ceased to roam and make war for their food. His plan for settling the Cayuse called for a white community to provide both example and leaven. And then, Marcus Whitman fell in love with Oregon.

Just what place history will accord to Dr. Whitman, it is too soon to say. However, the massacre at Waiilatpu did bring the Oregon question—so long dallied over in Congress—to a head. Mr. Meek, a good friend of your brother and sister, rode to Washington in the spring of 1848, seeking U. S. protection for emigrants and laws for this land—both long advocated by Dr. Whitman. The day after Meek arrived, President Polk sent an urgent message to Congress. Senator Benton made a powerful plea for Oregon. On August 13 of that year, Old Oregon became Oregon Territory with a governor sent out under the stars and stripes.

I am enclosing a lock of your dear sister's hair, secured at Waiilatpu by Joe Meek at the time he helped bury her body and that of his daughter, Helen Mar. I asked an Indian the other day, "What color was Mrs. Whitman's hair?" He stared through my office window a long time and then answered, "Color of gold in sunset."

We shall miss them always and so will you. But Mr. Spalding tells me that when he warned him of danger, Dr. Whitman was convinced that the stroke, if it should come, would fall on him alone—not on your sister nor on any of the others. For myself, I shall remember them with love and gratitude whenever I ride a trail or sail a river or lift my eyes to the snowy peak of Mount Hood. Truly, their life and their death did much for Oregon. I am,

Your obedient servant,

John McLoughlin